I Left My Heart In Harlem

He Made It Big In Hollywood

By
Margaret Clark

HOLON
PUBLISHING

Holon Publishing & Collective Press
4001 East 3rd Street Ste. 9
Bloomington, Indiana 47408

www.HolonPublishing.com
Twitter: @HolonPublishing

Printed in the United States of America

ISBN-10: 0615597025
ISBN-13: 978-0-615-59702-7

Contents

Chapter 1

Harlem Becomes Home

My life took an unexpected turn the winter that I was thirteen years old. It was on a cold day in February of 1971 that we moved to 124th Street, to the projects in Harlem. The day we arrived at the apartment seemed like the coldest day so far that year. I looked around and shivered, as much from fear as cold. I was filled with a feeling of foreboding like I had never felt before.

Maybe it was a premonition of what was to come. I looked around at the drug dealers on the corners, and the hoodlums lurking in the doorways. There were seven of us moving into Harlem. I wondered how many of us would make it out of Harlem alive. Looking back now, I know why I had that feeling of foreboding. Six children were going into Harlem and six grandchildren would one day come out. What happened to us and our mother as we fought to survive in the streets, the hallways, the apartments of Harlem, is my story.

Mama didn't prepare us for our move to Harlem from the Flatbush area of New York where we lived with Grandma. Right out of the blue, the day after my Grandma's funeral, Mama announced we were moving. When we asked why, Mama said, "Since your grandma died we can't afford to live here no more. We got to make it on our own now. I guess that will have to be in Harlem."

There were seven of us—my older brother Roland, seventeen, my older sister Lynne, fifteen, my younger brother

John, nine, my younger sisters Sharon and Becky, ten and seven, and me. I'm Liz, the one Mama always said was a special child.

When my brother Roland asked her why Harlem, she just said, "I can't find a cheaper apartment here in Flatbush than we already got and Harlem got some that is cheaper." There were people everywhere I looked. I didn't know how many then, but I would learn later in school that more than 200,000 people, almost all either Blacks or Mexicans or Latinos, lived in the 70,000 apartments in Harlem. Since most of them didn't have jobs, they made their living on the streets either selling something to or stealing something from the other people who lived here.

Even just walking up to that fourth floor apartment, I could see there were problems with this place. The hallways and the doors to the other apartments were filthy! We waded through the trash in the hallways and on the stairs and dodged people coming and going. When we opened the door to the apartment, a horrible, sickening smell washed over us. I almost vomited.

I wished we could move somewhere else but I knew it wasn't going to happen. I knew we could not go back to Grandma's house now that she was gone. Just thinking of staying here in Harlem made my heart start to race as fast as a car's engine. I knew I would never like the apartment or the neighborhood. Mama just kept saying, "Where else could I find an apartment for this price?" like that was all that mattered.

We started to clean the apartment and put things in order the best we could. I stopped cleaning every once in awhile to look out the window. The fear got worse. Seemed like everybody in the street was either selling or buying drugs. I didn't know it then, but almost everyone in all the apartments were also either selling or buying drugs also, and everybody seemed to be high on something. I guessed that was the only way they could stand to live here.

We had been cleaning for a couple of hours when Becky started to cry. "I'm cold and hungry," she said.

Mama told Lynne to go to the corner store to buy some lunchmeat and a big bottle of soda and I told her that I would go with her. On our way, we passed another apartment building where they were playing music as loud as they could. Lynne stopped to listen, then started to dance to the melody.

"I like this," she said.

"Lynne, I don't like this place. Let's go to the store."

"Shut up, Liz! The problem with you is you think too much of yourself."

I got quiet because I could see the expression on her face. She started to yell at me and looked at me with a mad expression, so I busted out and said, "Okay Lynne! I hear you."

When we got back home, she said, "Liz, I don't want you to go to the store with me anymore."

Roland jumped out of bed. "What happened?"

I started to tell him, but Mama said with a sigh of relief, "As long as you two got home safely."

"Lynne, I won't be going to the store with you either," I said.

Two months after moving to Harlem, Lynne met Gary one day when she went past loud apartment building on her way to the store and. She ran home to tell me about him.

"He's cute Liz, and he's talking to me!" she said.

"Girls are always running after him."

"There you go picking with perfect!"

"Don't let him make a fool out of you, Lynne. You don't really know him at all. We just moved here two months ago."

"So? It don't take ten years to get to know a guy." She slammed the bedroom door so hard, the pictures on the wall shook. I went into the kitchen and started to cook some dinner, but we were out of bread. Mama had left me some bread money on the kitchen table, so John and I went to the store. On the way, Gary saw me and asked me if I had a sister named Lynne.

"Why?" I asked in a low voice.

He said, "She's going to be my new girlfriend."

3

"So? What are you telling me that for?"

Gary started to laugh.

John and I found what we needed and walked out of the store. As we were leaving, this girl kept looking at me. I'd seen her around Gary before and was pretty sure she was his girlfriend. She stepped in front of me.

"Hey. You tell your sister she comes around here, she better be watching herself."

I looked down and John and I started to walk fast. When we got home, I yelled for Lynne. "So Gary don't have a girlfriend?"

She opened the bedroom door. "So what, Liz?"

"Lynne, you are just asking for trouble, and you are in the right place for it."

"Oh yes, Miss Perfect. You're not going to tell Mama, now are you?"

She started to call me names and I started calling her names back. My voice began to quiver, I was shaking and the tears started to fall. John rushed over to hold me. "Lynne! Leave her alone," he said.

I didn't respond. Instead, I just sat in the chair in the kitchen until the food started burning and our apartment started to smoke. Even then I didn't move. It wasn't just what Lynne said, I realized. I was depressed because I hated this apartment. I hated the neighborhood and all the people around us.

Suddenly, the door opened and Mama asked, "Is the apartment on fire, or is your food on fire?"

"No, the food got burnt," I mumbled.

John started telling Mama what Lynne had said and how she was acting.

"Lynne, what are you going to do with yourself? You're just sixteen years old. Sixteen! Now who picked up John from daycare?"

"Me," I said flatly.

"Where are Becky and Sharon?" she pressed.

"In our room looking at TV."

"Where is your brother Roland?

"Who knows?"

Gary came upstairs, knocked on the door, and asked for Lynne. "Where's your sister?"

I replied sarcastically, "I don't know, but I bet you can find her."

Chapter 2

Life in Harlem

When we had been in Harlem six months, Mama transferred us from the Flatbush area school to a Harlem school. As I walked slowly down the hall on my first day there, I met a girl in the hallway named Sissy who asked me for an ink pen. I gave her a pen and told her, "You can keep it."

She said, "You know, I live in the same apartment building as you."

"Oh? I live on the fourth floor," I replied.

"I live on the second," she said.

On my way home that day, I saw Sissy and she introduced me to her friends Wendy, Shane and Carol, and her brother Charles.

I asked her in a soft voice, "Is he gay?"

He heard me and turned around. "Ugly as your mama looking, she best be gay!" Everybody started to laugh, and I laughed with them.

Soon after I got home that day, Gary came upstairs, knocked on the door, and asked for Lynne. "Where's your sister?"

"I don't know, but I bet you can find her."

John told Mama that Gary came by our apartment looking for Lynne.

"Is that right!" Mama demanded.

"That's right!" Becky hollered out.

"Did Lynne go to school today, Liz?" Mama asked. Even though Lynne was two years older than me, we were both in eighth grade because she had flunked—twice.

"Well, I don't know. She didn't go with me."

"Did you see Roland?"

"Roland's in his bedroom asleep."

Mama immediately opened Roland's door and said loudly, "So Mister, are you going to school?"

"NO!"

"Why?"

Sharon hollered out, "Because he has a girlfriend, and he's always over her house."

Roland sat up. "Sharon, you need to stay out of my business before I slap you!"

Mommy was standing inside his room now. "Listen, if you don't go to school, you won't be staying here."

"Lady, I don't need that, and why am I going to school anyway?"

"To get your own job and apartment!"

Roland jumped up, put his clothes on and slammed the apartment door on his way out.

Mother hollered, saying, "If you don't go to school, and you don't have a job, don't come back here."

He hollered back and said, "I won't be back!"

"That boy is asking for nothing but trouble for himself!" Mama said, shaking her head sadly.

The apartment was a mess, the dinner uncooked. "What time did Lynne get in this evening?" Mama asked.

Becky said, "You mean what time tonight?"

I could see the tears brimming in Mama's eyes. "Mama, I will finish cooking dinner. Becky and Sharon can clean the apartment and John can take out the trash," I said.

Mama wiped her eyes as she told me how hard it was raising children and how they brought a lot of problems.

"Mama, I love you for just trying to be a mama."

She smiled, but I could see the hurt on her face. She walked to the couch and sat down while I fixed her a big plate of food. Then, seeing her in so much pain, I took off her hose and rubbed her feet. They were red with blisters and calluses and her toes had corns on them. I put her feet in some warm soapy water. When her feet touched the warmth, Mama she put her hands in her face and started to cry. I got a napkin and wiped her tears.

She started to reflect on what her own Mama once said. "My mama told me my love for my children and the joy of being a mama was all I needed, so I just worked hard to take care of my children. Looks like she was wrong." Then she sat up. "Liz, get the children ready for school tomorrow."

Mother remained sitting in the chair in the dark apartment. Suddenly the door opened up, and Lynne walked in.

"Oh Mama, I thought you were asleep."

"Do you go to school at all anymore?"

"Yes, I go to school. I'm fifteen years old."

"So, that doesn't make you an adult," Mama said. "You haven't even made it to high school yet—fifteen years old and in the eighth grade! Girl, cut my kitchen light out. I don't want to hear that nonsense from you."

"I'm looking for something to eat!" Lynne snapped.

They started to argue. Mommy got up and pushed her, saying, "Put my food back! I'm going to tell you the same thing I told your brother Roland—no school, no job, then you won't be living here and eating my food! At 7:30 tomorrow morning, you better be out of my apartment, going to school, and if I find out you're not going to school but going out with Gary and cause my social service check to get cut off, girl, you ain't seen no trouble yet! Anyway, what is so wrong with going to school with your sister Liz?"

"I don't like her friends, and I don't like Sissy and Charles. They are so boring."

"Least they get to school before 8:30!"

Lynne got up the next morning and said to me, "Oh Liz, did you tell Mama about Gary and school too?"

"No, but I could!"

She bumped up against me. "Yeah, but you could. Miss Perfect, you make me sick. I can't find nothing to tell on you."

"Yes, you could, but at least I go to school."

"Whatever," Lynne said.

"You going to school!" I said.

She looked so mad that I left, slammed our door, and ran out to meet Charles downstairs.

"Is Sissy coming?" I asked Charles.

"No, she just hanging around with her boyfriend today. Girl, if my father finds out and if he's drinking, there'll be BIG trouble! Oh, and he better not lose his check; he and Sissy will get into it. That is another chapter in her life. Once they start back and forth, I just run to my room and shut my bedroom door."

"How can you sleep?" I asked.

"Believe it or not, I do it all the time. I guess I just shut them out."

"Lynne and Roland talk bad to me and my younger brothers and sisters. I know, I hear it all the time, and with these apartment buildings you smell food and hear bad language—even though you don't know how to spell the words." I said.

"I hear you and Lynne all of the time, yelling at each other," Charles said.

I slapped him on his back and started to laugh. "I feel like running away all the time to anywhere."

"Girl, stop that talking. They're just jealous of you. Now for some important stuff. Harlem school is getting some extra money from some basketball players and singers for our scholarship fund."

"So, what does that have to do with me?"

"Stupid, that means a job or college grant for some students. Girl, just talk to your counselor. Go right after school, okay?"

"Yeah, Charles, I'll go to her right after school. Wait a sec— Charles, you didn't come to school yesterday morning."

"Yes, I did. I went to gym to play some basketball. By the way, what are you doing after school today?"

"Nothing."

"Did you ever see me play ball before?"

"Uh-uh. Nope."

"Just meet me at the gym today."

"Okay, I will." When I got to the gym after school that day, Wendy was already there.

"Hey girl, you going to the gym to see Charles play some ball? Girl, I never forgot when you asked Sissy about Charles, asking if he was gay!" We both started laughing, and then Charles came over with Mike.

"Liz," Charles said, "this is Mike. He's in that program I was telling you about."

"Boy, he's going to be a professional basketball player. He lives with his grandmother at the end of our street." Wendy started to say he was cute, but stopped.

Mike made all of the points in the game. "Charles is a loser," Wendy giggled. Wendy started to tease him some more, so Charles bumped her up against the gym door, knocking her coat out of her hands, and they started to call each other names.

He said, "You need a new weave."

Wendy replied, "So, it's mine, and your mama needs a new wig!"

I started walking away slowly and laughing inside. Wendy hurried to catch up with me. "Girl, I won't walk with a loser," she said.

Charles said, "That's the nastiest girl I ever met, and she's skanky too. Her and her stinky hair."

Sissy came running and got on the bus with us. "She only came down with us so my father won't think that she missed school," Charles said.

Sissy said, "Charles, that's none of your business!"

"That's right, I'm not going to lie for you or Liz," Charles replied.

Sissy said, "Yeah that's okay if you don't lie for me." She walked behind us.

"If my father asks you if Sissy went to school today, say nothing or tell him the truth," Charles said.

When we got off at our street, we saw some movers bringing furniture upstairs. "Who's moving in?" I wondered.

"Who knows," Sissy replied. "But look, the nasty dope selling bums got put out. Girl, look at all their nasty broken down furniture thrown in front of our apartment."

Charles nudged me. "Liz, they moved next door to YOUR apartment!"

"My God, that's right, they're in that vacant apartment next to me." I stopped in my tracks. "Oh, I forgot my little sister and brother at day-care!"

I got back on the bus, and when I got to daycare, they were standing in the rain, soaking wet and cold. Becky ran up to me. "Liz, you forgot us!" John started to cry.

I said to them, "Come on now. This is the first time I did this to you."

Sharon said, "I'm going to tell Mama!"

"No. No, you are not. Listen, I'm only fourteen years old, and I have all the responsibilities on me. Remember, I don't have any children but I always feel like I do."

Sharon refused to be silenced. "Mama always said you must pick us up on time!"

"Yeah I know that, but what about Roland and Lynne? Why can't they pick you all up? I mean they don't go to work or school!"

Their faces dropped down and looked sad. "Well, are we going on the bus?" Sharon asked.

"No."

"But we're cold and wet," John said.

"I know, but I don't have any more money."

Sharon started to complain. She was angry with me.

"Girl, if you don't shut up, I'll leave you right here!"

"But, Liz, I called home, and there was no one there. Where did you go?" Sharon whined.

"None of your business."

Becky finally piped up and said, "I bet you were with Sissy and Charles."

"Look, I said none of your business. Just let's get home. Hold my hands." I got quiet and then they started to get. Silently, we walked down to our apartment.

As we were going up, we saw drug addicts and drunks falling out in the hallways and on the stairs. "You sure are pretty children," one of them said. We started running upstairs faster. I said to the kids, "Never answer them. Just run home, okay?" We got to our apartment, finally, and saw the new neighbor that was moving in. Her back was to us and we didn't speak.

We ran inside and Becky, John and Sharon started to change their clothes. I got a napkin to wipe their wet faces. "This won't happen again, me being late to pick you all up, if you don't tell Mommy. She will be sad and hurt. Roland and Lynne hurt her all of the time as it is."

"Okay, Liz, we won't say anything, if you don't let it happen again." Becky opened our front door. She said to one of our neighbors, "Did you see our new nosey neighbor?"

One of our other neighbors said, "Girl, they sure are filthy people! They complain about rats that run in their apartments, but they are human rats! Rats complaining about rats!"

I chimed in, "They're nothin' but some drug selling mommies that live there!" We all start to laugh at what I was saying. "I'm going to cook some dinner. Y'all go and get ready for dinner and clean up your room and get your homework out."

Just as I was finishing dinner, Mama pushed open the door. "Umm, that smells good."

"You want a plate, Mama?"

"Yes I do, I am so hungry."

Sharon said, "We have some new neighbors—they just moved next door."

"Don't let them in MY apartment," Mama replied, "and stay away from them."

The next day, Sharon yelled, "Liz, someone is at the door."

I howled, "Who is it, Sharon?"

"The lady next door."

The new neighbor told me that the men who moved her in forgot her chair, and asked if she could use our phone to call them at their office. I told her she could. I knew Mama wouldn't like me doing that at all, but she seemed nice. She made her call and thanked me. A few minutes later, the phone rang and I answered it. Mama said she would have to work late tonight.

"Aww Mommy, why do you have to work late?"

"I need to pay these bills for us. They're never on time, but they get paid. Plus, I need this job."

"But Mommy, we never see you anymore."

"I know, I know."

"Oh, by the way, the lady next door used our phone."

"Liz, you really don't know her! Make that your last time letting her use our phone. That is one of my bills I am working so hard to pay. You never know who or where she called! Are the children washed up for school, and did they do their homework?"

"Yes, they are sleep." As I hung up the phone, Lynne asked where Mama was. I rolled my eyes. "Why do you really care?"

"Liz, you don't need to tell me about my feelings!"

"The only person you seem to care about is Gary and his friends. You don't even go to school anymore."

"Liz, you're not my mama! At least Gary loves me!"

"So, he loves some other girl too!"

She said, "So?" Then she swished her hand at me and turned off the light. I started thinking about my mother, how she worked so hard, where she worked, and the area where we lived. The tears started falling as I tried to remember what she always said, that I was a "special child."

That was hard to remember right now, however. What I remembered was that at fourteen, I was a mama to my younger brothers and sisters. I also started to worry about what my future was going to be like. Was I going to get a good job, or was I going to have to work all the time like my mother and still not have enough money to feed my children? I wiped my eyes and started to pray for God to keep my family and me together even though we lived in Harlem.

Chapter 3

Becky Gets Sick

Overnight, my tears dried up. The next morning, I got up slowly and got dressed for school. Becky woke up sick. Mama had told me to make sure that the children got ready for school, so I said, "Lynne, Becky is sick."

"So, what are you telling me that for Liz?"

"Because now you have to get the other kids to school."

"Liz, I want you to know, you aren't my mother, and girl, I'm glad I am not your mother!" Becky yelled.

In the middle of our argument, Becky suddenly fell onto the floor, hitting her head, and then she started to shake and vomit. Lynne just stood there with her mouth hanging open.

I started screaming. Lynne finally shut her mouth and ran out to take the other children to school. I ran next door and started banging on it until the lady came to the door. I told her that my little sister was sick and vomiting all over the place.

She gasped. "Call an ambulance. I'll be right over to help you." I ran back to Becky's side and tried to shake her. She was breathing but she was still out cold. When my neighbor came in I told her that I had called an ambulance but it wasn't here yet.

"Let me call my boyfriend and see if he will come over," she said.

"You run out there and call a cab." Suddenly Becky's eyes fell back in her head. I was so scared I started to cry.

"Come on, honey," my neighbor said, putting a hand on my shoulder. "Go out and see if you can get a cab, okay?" I did, but as I stepped outside, a man in a red car started honking his horn.

"Hey little girl, go upstairs and tell the lady in 4-B that Paul is waiting for her."

I ran back upstairs to tell the neighbor that her boyfriend was outside. She yelled out the window, "Hurry Paul, it's a little girl that's sick and laying on the floor." He said okay, then he went around the corner to park his car just as the ambulance pulled up outside.

Disgusted with him, the lady said to me, "Just lock your front door and go with them to the hospital." I could tell the lady was thinking that Paul was stupid to worry about his car and a parking space so much. "If that were my child, he wouldn't be my boyfriend anymore!" she said.

I got to the hospital, sat, and waited. Becky had regained consciousness but she was still shaking and vomiting when they brought her in. Once they had wheeled her away, I tried to call Mama on her job, but I couldn't get through. About thirty minutes later, the lady next door and Paul came in the waiting room. I realized I still didn't know her name.

"Did you call your Mother?"

"Yes, but the line was busy."

"Try it again." They went outside to smoke a cigarette. The nurse finally came in after what seemed like an eternity. She asked me what was wrong with my daughter.

"That isn't my daughter, she's my sister."

"Where is her mother?"

"She's at work."

"So, you don't know what type medicine she takes?"

"No."

Paul and the lady came back in and the nurse looked up. "Are you the mother?"

"No, Miss."

"Will you please call her mother?" The nurse asked.

The lady said, "Give her your mother's job number and let her call.

Don't keep calling on that pay phone—you might not get your money back, and you don't have that kind of money."

I thanked her and her boyfriend for helping me. He went over to find a chair and watch television.

The lady said, "Girl, he's cute but stupid and lazy. He's just a man. Child, oh my goodness, I do have a name, and my name is Terry."

I started to giggle.

"See, he's just got to turn that TV onto the news so these sick and nasty people can curse us out. But I'm just going to pretend I don't even know him. You want to get something to eat while you wait for your mother to come from work? I know you're hungry too. And, another thing, if these people call Paul some bad name, I won't be here to hear it."

In the cafeteria, we got some ham and cheese sandwiches and two sodas. She said, "I'll pay for it." I was grateful but my stomach had a such a knot in it that I couldn't eat. I ate a few bites of the sandwich and I was going to save the rest for lunch. She said, "Girl, you better enjoy this food. Some of this money is my bill money!" I smiled and started to eat the rest of my sandwich. I was scared. I hoped Becky would be all right, and I hoped Mama would be there soon. I finished eating and we went back to the emergency waiting room. As we were coming down the hall, we saw Mama running toward us.

"What happened to Becky?" She demanded breathlessly.

"She started to complain about her stomach and started vomiting," I replied.

"Did Lynne take the other children to school?"

"Yes, and I locked the door."

Terry put out her hand. "Oh, my name is Terry."

"Oh, Mama, this is our next door neighbor. She helped to get Becky to the hospital."

"Thank you, and my name is Tracy," Mama said.

Paul took that opportunity to interject.

"My name is Paul. You can see they forgot about me."

"No, we didn't forget you," I said, and started to smile.

"No, you didn't, but Terry did."

Terry said, "Did I say that to you?"

"You didn't have to," he replied, as they left the hospital to go back to her apartment.

Chapter 4

More Drama

Mama and I finally left the hospital. Unfortunately, Becky was still real sick and had to stay for a couple more days—at least that's what the doctor said. They still didn't know what was wrong with her, though. They said she had something called a seizure. What that was, I didn't know, but I guessed it wasn't good or else she wouldn't have had to stay. I hoped she'd be home soon. Even though she got on my nerves sometimes, I still missed her.

When we got home, we found our door standing open. Mama stopped dead.

"Liz, did you lock the door before you left?" she demanded.

"Yes, Mama, I did," I assured her. Closer inspection revealed that someone had kicked the door to our apartment in.

"I can't believe this. They took everything! Everything of a little value, that is." Mama went to check in her secret hiding place, the place where she kept her money for bills, the place she thought no one knew about.

"They stole the rent money, too!" She started crying. "Where in the world are we going to get the rent for this month from NOW?"

Tears started rolling down everyone's faces. Mama told me to go out to the playground. I guess she wanted to be by herself. I went outside with Sharon and John, only to find out that earlier that day, Lynne had left them in front of school by themselves and didn't give them any money for their lunch tickets.

When we got back upstairs, Mama asked me, "Where is Lynne?"

"I don't know, Mama."

"Sharon," Mama asked, "Did Lynne go to school today?"

"No, she turned around and went back home, and she didn't even give us any money for lunch!"

"What about Roland?" Mama demanded.

"I don't know. He was still asleep when we left."

"So Sharon, what did you have for lunch then?"

"Well, my teacher offered me a sandwich, but it looked real old and smelled funny, so I didn't take it." Sharon said as she sat in the chair and shook her head. "I didn't have nothin'." Tears started rolling down her cheeks, and then she looked up. "Mommy, where's Becky?"

Mama explained that Becky got sick, that she had to take her to the hospital, and that she wasn't doing too well right now. "I have to go back to the hospital this evening or tonight. Liz, I don't have any money for you to take the bus to school tomorrow. I'm sorry."

"But Mama, it's too dangerous for me to walk to school."

"I know that child, but it's bad enough I don't have any rent money for this month, or any money for food, either."

I started towards my room thinking maybe I just wouldn't go to school tomorrow when I noticed that the TV was gone, and so was the new winter coat that Mama had just got me for school.

"Liz, call the police," Mama said, slightly calmer now.

Sharon came running in from her room. "Mommy, my Barbie doll-house is gone too! John's new suit is gone also! That was the only suit he had!"

As I was trying to call the police, for some reason, I couldn't get a dial tone. Then I realized that the phone cord had been cut. After I told Mama, she told me to see if I could find a cop outside. While I was on my way out, Mama told John to clean up his room and told Sharon to clean up the kitchen while she tried to fix the front door. "I don't know how I'm going to fix this door. I don't even have a screwdriver! Sharon, go next door and ask Terry if we could use her hammer and some screws."

"But Mama, I thought you told us not to bother with her."

"Child, go next door and ask her for what I just asked you to get before I pop you in your mouth!" Pouting, Sharon slammed the door behind her.

After I found a cop and told him we needed him because we had been robbed, I came back upstairs. Mama asked where the cop was. I told her he said he would be up here soon. She said, "Maybe if I killed somebody, they would come faster!"

I asked her how long she thought Becky was going to be in the hospital.

"Liz, I really don't know. I need you to stay home from school tomorrow so you can let the repair man in, okay?"

"But, Mama, I have a big math test tomorrow!"

"I know Liz, but I'm not going to work tomorrow either. I'm going up to the hospital to be with Becky."

Just then, Terry pushed what was left of our front door open. "Girl, what in the world happened here?"

"Some fool kicked in our door and robbed us."

"Well, this is Harlem." she said. She then went back to her apartment to call her boyfriend Paul again. Mama and I followed her.

I asked Terry how she could live in Harlem for so long, seeing how bad it was here. "I'm just used to it, I guess." She dialed the phone and waited. "While I'm calling Paul to help us with this door, I should ask him when he's going to buy me my dream house."

Paul must have heard her, because a few seconds later, Terry snorted. "Oh, that's right—your wife already left you."

21

Mama took the phone from Terry. "Paul, I really need you to help me with this door. I know if you fix this, it will look like a brand new door. The only thing is, I don't have any money to give you for this. Somebody stole my rent money so now I don't have ANY money! They stole some if the kids' clothes too."

Whatever Paul said next made Mama smile.

"Thank you...No, our phone line was cut, but I sent Liz outside for a cop and he should be here soon." Mama hung up, sounding slightly relieved. "He says he'll be right over with some tools."

We went back to our apartment and Mama and Ms. Terry sat on the couch to wait.

Terry said, "By the way Tracy, if you don't mind me asking, where is the kids' father?"

That was my cue to leave. I didn't want to hear this again. I went to my room, but something made me stand just inside my door, listening to my Mama's story, our story.

"That stupid man is in jail and he's been in jail for years, right where he belongs! Girl, that husband of mine is nothing but a sick junkie that stays in jail. I hope that your dream house won't become your worst nightmare. When Paul finishes fixing this door, I'll show you my wedding pictures. Girl, the ring he put on my finger was hotter than July! I found that out later. I thought I could change him, though. He was my first and last love.

"Girl, here's the story. I got pregnant with my first child Roland with this guy named James. He said that he wanted to marry me, but he hooked up with the girl next door to my cousin's apartment named Marie. When I heard about it, I thought I would DIE. Then I ran into Ray working at a local department store. He worked with me. He was cute and a cool guy, and boy could he dress!...But that's all he had going for him. I thought he was all that, but he came out to be a bum. And the thing is, I knew that, but I still married him that next summer. See, I thought I could change him just by being his wife."

I heard her sigh. "We used to fight like every day! When I used to have to call the cops, they already knew who I was. He went to jail for four to six years when Becky was a baby, then he went back in for ten. He's barely been in my children's lives. I think he got sick in jail years ago, 'cause he asked his mother to send pictures of the children. She called me one day asking for them. I asked her if he was going to send the children any child support, and she just got mad with me."

Mama said our grandma told her, "My son only has three children by you!"

Mama told her, "No, that's not true; my last child is his too, believe me!" So then, Mama asked her, "Well, why don't you come and see me and the children? We don't even have enough money to eat or pay the rent. So why would I waste my time to go see him in jail, or you for that matter? He never came to see them or spend time with them, or anything! Ray always wants to have someone in his life. But it won't ever be me again. You also can rest assured that he won't be able to see his children again!"

Finally, Mama cut to the chase and asked her why she was calling.

Grandmother told Mama, "Well, Ray isn't doing too good."

"That might be true, but that's not what I want to talk about, or what I want to hear," Mama said.

"Okay, but please give the children my phone number and the picture of their father that he took last week. I'll send it to you."

"Okay, I might let them see it," Mama answered.

I cracked my door and peered out as Mama, her back to me, shook her head. "That was eight years ago. Since then, I haven't seen or heard from her. I saw her niece a few months ago. She said that she was in a nursing home. She had a stroke and can't walk anymore. I know that sometime soon, I have to go visit her and make peace with her before she dies."

Finally, I couldn't stand it anymore, and I ran into the room.

"My daddy has a mama that's alive?" I asked, astonished.

"Yes, Liz."

"Why didn't you tell us before?"

"Because she never asked about you all or cared. She always believed everything her son, your father, said."

"Mommy, what nursing home is she in?"

"I think its Long Grey, or Long Green. Child, it's been eight years. I don't know exactly where she is now, Liz."

Puzzled, I rubbed my head. It was pounding. She had never talked about my father's people before. I couldn't stop thinking that if Ms. Terry had not come over to the house, she never would have said anything about it. I tucked the information away in a secret place in my mind. I started thinking of the picture album I'd once found. Mama had tucked it away, but for some reason she'd kept it. I wondered if maybe the kids in those pictures were my father's brothers and sisters. They looked like Spanish people, and I knew my father had Spanish blood. That was why Mother said that we had nice hair and skin. But, Roland had dark skin and bad hair.

Finally, Mr. Paul got the door in but it was bent in a little. Mama thanked Ms. Terry and her boyfriend. "Thank you for trying to help me. You did a way better job than I would have, that's for sure!"

After Paul and Ms. Terry left, we got ready for bed. It was so cold in my room that I couldn't sleep. Believe it or not, Lynne was in bed before 6 PM. She never came home, let alone went to bed, before 11 PM. She was always over at Gary's. That was strange to me but I kept quiet about it and let things be. Lynne looked so peaceful as she slept that I decided to keep all the things that I had learned about our father to myself and let it be my secret. I couldn't sleep though, not only because of the cold but because I knew that the front door still wasn't really fixed and would be easy to break into again. Finally, I turned out the light and tried to sleep.

It seemed I had just closed my eyes when I heard banging. It was still night, but someone was knocking on the front door so hard that at first I thought they were going to break it down. It was the police. I could hear Mama talking to them, but I couldn't make out what they were saying. They told Mama that we needed to get a new door and to get one tomorrow. They gave her a police report and told her to take it to her rental office.

The next day, Mama took the police report to the office but couldn't take the rent money. They at least said they would put a new door on as soon as possible. That made me feel better. Mama's mind was on Becky in the hospital. At 9 AM she went up to the hospital. Lynne had to stay and wait for the maintenance man to put on the door. I knew that just killed her to wait like that. She was so impatient.

I took the rest of the kids to school. I knew that Mama depended on me to get the kids to school and pick them up. After I dropped them off, I got to thinking about my life and I started to cry. I wondered, "Who is going to love me?" The tears began to fall and I wiped my face with my sleeve.

I started towards my school with no money in my pockets. If I didn't get there early, I wouldn't be able to get a lunch ticket. Still, I made my way down the street slowly, counting the cracks in the concrete. Living here had become too much. We had no one to help us, not even my mama's sister Rose. My aunt had two sick sons and she wasn't able to work. Mama wasn't working today because of Becky, so her paycheck was going to be very short. Boy, I started to think, if Mama were to die, there would be no one to take care of me and my little brothers and sisters! Don't get me wrong, I really loved taking care of them, but I knew there would be no one for us! Lynne was always off trying to find her man, and we never saw Roland anymore.

Well, I was late. Maybe I'd just stay in the library while everyone was having lunch. I hoped I didn't see Wendy, Shane, Charles or Sissy. I just wanted to be alone. I tried to keep my mind on seeing Becky in the hospital later that day. I couldn't wait to find out how she was, so I called the hospital and talked to Mama. After I hung up, I thought about getting Mrs. Jones, my guidance counselor, to help me get lunch money. But if that didn't work, I'd just sit around in the library as I planned in the first place and hope my stomach didn't growl.

I stepped into Mrs. Jones' office.

She said, "Elizabeth, I want to talk to you. You look so sad this morning."

"Mrs. Jones, I have to get a job to help Mother. My sister is in the hospital."

"Oh, is it Lynne?" she asked.

"No, it's my younger sister, Becky."

"Oh, I'm so sorry to hear that."

"So that's why I need a job, and I need one right now!" I said.

"How old are you?"

"Fourteen," I replied.

"Okay, let me see what I can do. You have to bring in proof of your family's income."

"What income? Mama took off because my sister is very sick. I don't think she can keep her job and still take care of Becky. No job, no money!"

"Does your Mama get welfare?"

"Yes, but I don't know how much."

"Did you fill out a lunch ticket form?"

"No," I said.

"Well, we can start there. Now in order for me to help you, I need to see proof of your mama's income and a list of how many people are in your house. I need it in writing, understand?"

"Yes."

"Also, Liz, all of the teachers need to see your mother."

"But, how? She's going to be at the hospital all of the time. Is it about me?"

"No, it's about your sister Lynne and brother Roland. If they are going to remain in school, we need to see your mother right away! Tell her to give me a call, so all of the teachers can talk to her after school."

"I'll tell her as soon as I get to the hospital. Thank you, Mrs. Jones." Homeroom was over by then so I went to my first-period English class.

Chapter 5

Mike

I was on my way to English class but the noise in the hall was, as usual, so deafening I could hardly hear myself think. It reminded me of where I lived, what type of school I went to, and that nothing but thugs and crooks were here in Harlem. The pain in my heart made me sick and, as the day went on, it traveled through every part of my body. I went from class to class, hearing little that the teachers said and saying nothing.

Finally, school was over. I darted out of my last class to my locker, hoping no one would see me or want to talk to me. However, my locker was broken and it made a creaking noise every time I tried to open it. It sounded like it needed some oil. Finally, I got it open, grabbed my jacket and turned to go. That was when I spotted Sissy down the hall. I didn't say anything and pretended not to see her, but Sissy ran towards me.

"Hey girl," she said.

I just looked at her.

"No, I'm not Charles, but you can at least speak," Sissy said.

"I know, okay," I said in a sassy voice.

Sissy hollered out, "What is wrong with you, Liz?" I could see she had an angry expression on her face.

"I just have some problems I need to think about, that's all."

"Girl, don't think too long, before someone puts you in the hospital with your sister!"

"How did you know about that? Did Charles tell you about her?"

"No," Sissy said looking at me with a puzzled look. "Don't we live in the same apartment building with you?"

"Yes!" I hollered back, slamming my locker door.

"Girl, you better be careful where you slam that door, you better not get my hand in here! Girl, you're just asking for a fight!"

The crowd in the hallway started to gather around and move toward me. I pushed through the crowd and went down the hallway. Sissy hollered out, "Liz, you better not speak to me anymore! If you do, I'm going to punch you in your face!"

Wendy put her foot out as I was passing her. I stepped over it. Wendy said, "Liz, you better not step on my foot either!" I still just kept on walking.

Mike saw the crowd, saw me walking away and ran up to me. "Liz, what's going on?"

I kept walking, then he said, "Liz, I'd like to walk home with you." Just then, Charles ran up behind us.

"Girl, what happened to you and Sissy?" I didn't want to talk to Charles either. Charles was Sissy's brother, and I didn't need any more problems. Fortunately, even though I didn't speak, Charles stopped the rest of the crowd from coming. Wendy started calling me names and waving her fist at me.

Mike said, "Girl, that Wendy has a nasty mouth, and she thinks I want to go with her, ha! She'll never be my girlfriend, and I mean *never*. Do you hear me Liz?"

I just looked at him and didn't say anything. I already knew that Wendy liked Mike. Just then, Mike said, "Liz, I would like for you to be my girl."

For a second my heart stopped beating! I stood there and looked at him, then back to where the crowd had been. They were gone and Charles was gone too. The only person left was

Wendy, who was pointing her finger at me. Mike said, "Girl, don't pay Wendy any mind."

I had never told Mike how I felt about him because I wasn't sure if he liked me. I asked him if Charles knew all along how he felt, and he just laughed.

"Yes, he knew. I'm the one who asked him to introduce me to you."

My mouth dropped wide open! The only thing I could say was, "WHAT?" Mike responded by asking me if I was still walking home.

"Yes Mike, I don't have any money to take the bus to the hospital."

"Girl, just get on the bus. I have enough to get you home at least." When we got near my stop, I thanked him for the bus fare and for helping me get away from Wendy and Sissy and that crowd. I told him that I needed a good friend right now, and then I got off.

"Hey Liz, this is where I get off too."

I'd forgotten that Mike lived nearby and I started to giggle.

"I'm going to pick you up for school tomorrow morning," he said.

"Okay Mike, see ya tomorrow."

"See ya tomorrow, Liz."

When I reached the front of my apartment building, Roland was standing there. "What do you want?" he asked.

"Why do you talk to me like that?" I pushed past him and put the key into the front door.

Roland just sat on the stoop. "Here Liz, give this to Mama." He gave me a little brown bag. "Make sure you give it to her. And oh—I seen Lynne today."

"Where?" I asked.

"With Gary down the street. One of these days that boy is either going to get her killed, or he's going to kill her himself. Liz, I heard that Becky is in the hospital. Which one?" he asked.

"Children's Hospital, the one downtown," I said.

"Okay. Maybe I'll get a chance to see her. Are you going upstairs?" he asked.

"No," I said.

"Why? Don't you have a key?"

"No, I lost my key," I told him. "Someone broke into the apartment and stole Mama's rent money. They took our clothes and Becky and John's toys too. They even took the TV and the radio."

"Tell Mama to get a peep hole, and don't let nobody in," Roland said.

"Hey Roland, where ya living now?"

"With Lisa and her family."

"Are you going to try to go back to school?"

He hollered back, "NO!"

"So, what are you doing all day?"

"Liz, I'm 18 years old now. I don't need you or anyone else asking me all these questions. I really don't want to talk about it, okay?"

"Okay, Roland."

"Lisa's family lives next to that boy you were just talking to, oh, what's his name, Mike. Yeah, that's it. He's a nice guy Liz."

"Yeah, he is, I guess. All of the girls want to go with him."

"Oh. Does he like you, Liz?"

"I don't know, Roland. He says he does, but I'm not sure about my feelings for him. Anyway, he's going to my school, and he's on the basketball team."

"Well, that's nice," Roland said. "Let me tell you something important now! Don't get a guy like Gary. Gary is a bum, and now Lynne is too. That guy sells drugs and gets high. So now Lynne thinks she can handle a guy like Gary, but he's just using her up like all the rest of the girls he's been through. Gary looks at me like he'll kill me for just being her brother, and Lynne looks like a fool and acts crazy when she sees me. She's something else; she acts like she don't want to speak. Lisa always asks me if that's really my sister. I tell her I guess she's my sister sometimes, and I start to laugh when she asks that dumb question. Well, Liz, I'm going home now. Tell Mama I love her and I'll call her later."

"The person who broke in cut the telephone cord. For now, we don't have a phone." I told him I didn't know when the phone would be fixed.

"Girl, your life is just falling apart! Mama better not stay here too long, or she won't have anything left!"

"Oh yeah, Roland, I'm looking for a job. Can you help me?"

"Lisa's sister Jackie is a manager at a department store downtown. I know she can get you a job. When I go home, I'll ask Lisa to call her sister tonight. They talk every day anyway. Call me or stop past and I'll let you know. Girl, it's cold out here, go on upstairs and just wait in the hallway where it's warmer. I'll come back one day this week." Then he left.

I had reached the door of our apartment when Charles hollered up, "LIZ!" I had been wondering what he was going to say in school tomorrow. Now here he was, in my face.

"I hope you and Sissy don't fight! Wendy said that she didn't like you from the first time she met you."

"Well, I didn't like her either."

"Stop past this evening and make up with Sissy. She's really mad with you. I know 'cause she cursed me out in front of everybody!"

"Charles, I'm sorry. Me and Sissy had words and maybe I was wrong, but lately it seems like nobody cares about me or what they say to me. It's like I don't have feelings or something."

"I understand how you feel, but y'all fought about nothing. So, keep talking to Sissy and come downstairs, or call her."

"Okay, well, let me know when she gets in."

"Okay. She's at the library this evening. Please, please, make up. Okay? Sissy is wild when she fights and has a dirty mouth!

So please apologize to her. Tell her you are sorry that you used that tone with her."

"Okay, I want Sissy to be my friend, but I don't like Wendy, and she doesn't like me. When she sees Mike and me walking home together, that's really going to make her mad."

"That's not your problem. That's hers, Liz! Mike likes you and not her. Me and Mike been talking about Wendy and how nasty she is. She's nasty looking and has a nasty mouth. No guy wants to her as his girlfriend. I know me and Mike sure don't!"

"Charles, did Mike really tell you that he likes me?"

"Yes, he did. He told me three months ago, and he said that he really liked your family too." I started to giggle again.

Charles said, "Girl, why in the world are you giggling?"

"'Cause I don't know what to say!"

"Girl, I'm telling you the truth, he really cares about you."

"Tomorrow, me and him are supposed to go to school together."

"Dag, Liz. So you don't need me anymore, huh?"

"Charles, I'll always need you!" I answered, smiling at him.

"Oh, you need me now, 'cause Sissy is going to beat you up, and you need me to keep Sissy off of you!" Then he just started cracking up laughing. "Girl, you're still my number one buddy!"

"Well Charles, I'm glad to hear that! Just thinking about it, I really don't have any other friends that really care about me, you know."

"Liz, sometimes I think people don't really care about me at all either." Then, Charles started telling me about his friend and how he lost him, how he used to be in a gang, and was always in trouble. He was killed one day.

I began thinking about needing a job again. I needed one more than anything. It was for everybody, but especially to help Mommy out. As it started to rain hard, I ran back up the steps and Charles went outside. I sat in the hallway for a few minutes but I didn't have to wait long. Ms. Terry opened her door and let me in our apartment with the key my mother had given her earlier.

About an hour later, somebody knocked on my door. At first, I thought it was Charles, so I hollered out as loud as I could, "WHO IS IT?" The voice on the other side of the door sounded sleepy. "It's Terry. Is Tracy home?"

I said no. Mama had just left, and I had started to warm up some food for dinner. As it was warming up, it smelled funny, so I just threw it all out in the garbage. Just then the door opened and Mama, Sharon, and John came in.

"Mommy, is Becky better yet?"

"Well, I'll be seeing her doctor tomorrow, so I'll know then. Is any food fixed?"

"No."

"There's no dinner cooked at all?!"

"No."

"Liz, what happened to the food I fixed last night?"

"It smelled funny, so I had to throw it away."

"Well, is there anything else to cook?"

"No. No bread or meat in the freezer to fix either."

"Man, I forgot to go to the market anyway, but it doesn't matter, 'cause I don't have any money."

"Oh yeah. Roland stopped past."

Mama replied, "What did he want or need?"

"He left that brown bag on the kitchen table for you."

"Sharon, go see what's in that bag." Sharon went into the kitchen to get the bag. I had not looked into it when he gave it to me. I just sat it on the table.

"Mommy, it's money!!" Sharon exclaimed.

"Well, how much is it?"

Sharon said, "I don't know. I can't count it."

"Well, bring the bag in here."

Mommy looked into the bag and her eyes got big. It was obvious that it was a lot of money. She took it all out and started counting. "Oh my goodness!! Now we have money for the rent!! Well, I don't know what he's doing or how he got this money, but this much is going for rent and this much for my paycheck. Now we have enough for next month's rent too." Mama sighed with relief. For once we were going to be okay.

Chapter 6

Roland's Surprise

All of my life, I've been in the same routine. Get up early, wait for Lynne and Mama to get out of the bathroom. Mama is going to see Becky. It seems like I just went to bed and it's already 5:30 in the morning. I am so tired I can hardly move but I have to get up to get my brothers and sisters ready for school.

Mama slept a little bit later since she is going to the hospital to see Becky and speak to her doctor. Unfortunately, Becky is still in a coma. Her doctor told Mama that she might get worse and maybe even die. That really scares me. Even though I had all of that on my mind, I still had to get the kids to school.

After I took them, I ran home to see if Charles was going to school but he had already left. When I came out of the apartment, Roland was on the sidewalk.

"Is Mama still home or did she already leave?"

"No, Roland. Mommy left about a half-hour ago."

"Did you see Jackie about that job yet?" I asked Roland.

"No, not yet." I said.

"Well, here's my address. Come around and ask for Lisa."

I took the address and tucked it in my wallet, and then I went upstairs, got the garbage and put it in front of the sidewalk. I took my time, because I was already late for school. I figured I might as well go talk to Lisa about this job thing.

I went to the address that Roland gave me. It was an apartment building on a little alley. The piece of paper Roland gave me did not give the apartment number, so I was relieved to see her name and number on the mail box. I started to go up but the door was locked. Suddenly, it opened and someone hollered out, "What you want, and who you want?"

I yelled "Roland live here?"

"We don't know no Roland!"

"You know Lisa, his girlfriend?"

"Yeah, Lisa live here. Push 3-C's bell."

There was a drunken man on the stairs and the hall had a filthy smell. I finally reached the third floor. I knocked on 3-C, and the door was so dirty that dirt came off on my knuckles. I could also smell stale cigarettes smoke. An older woman opened the door and I asked for Lisa. She told me to go to the back room. It was hard for me to see because there was so much cigarette smoke around. The apartment also smelled like straight alcohol. I was surprised that Roland lived here. It was worse than our apartment building.

I couldn't see the woman's face who told me to go to the back room, because it was so smoky. I walked down the hall and almost fell over a toy on the floor. There were dirty clothes everywhere in the hallway that lead to the back room.

I stood in the door to the back room and asked, "Is Lisa here?"

"I'm Lisa."

"I'm Roland's sister."

"Oh, come in and sit down on the bed." There were clothes all over her bed so I just moved them and sat down. I didn't say anything.

Suddenly, I heard a baby crying. I was so surprised, I knew she could see it on my face.

"This is Devon." She put the baby in my arms. I just held him for a moment. I finally looked closely at him, and to my surprise, the baby looked just like Roland!

I asked "Lisa, is this my nephew?"

"Yes, honey. Who does he look like?"

"Roland" I said.

"Yes, that's his." I said, "He's got bad hair and dark skin just like Roland!"

We both started laughing. "Does your Mother know?" she asked.

"Well, if she does know, she never told us."

"I know that stupid boy never told her! Maybe she'll send some baby clothes now that she'll know."

"Well, that I don't know," I said.

"Well, you at least seen him and you can tell her."

It was a small room, all closed in. I told her that I would see Mama late tonight and to tell Roland that I came past. On the way out there were people getting high in the hallway and on the steps. I hurried out of there. As I got to the front door of the apartment building, someone called out "Liz, wait!"

It was Roland and Ricky. "Hey, did you meet Jackie?"

"No, I just met Lisa."

"Oh, okay." He rang another bell and asked for Jackie. The person who came to the window, went to get her.

"Who wants me?" Jackie asked.

Roland hollered up, "Jackie, this is my sister Liz. She needs a job."

She asked if I was fifteen yet. "Yeah, she is."

"Okay, come downtown to the department store where I work, and ask for me, Jackie Groon."

"Okay, thanks."

"Roland, don't send no worthless girl to my job, this is only for your sister, okay?"

"Okay, thanks Jackie. This is Liz, not Lynne, the names sound the same but, they're really different."

Tell her to be there at 6 o'clock tomorrow.

I answered happily, "Okay, I'll be there."

Roland said, "Here's some money." I thanked him. "Also tell Mama that I need to be in court on Wednesday morning at 10:15, and ask her if she can come too."

"I'll tell her that."

The bus that I needed to was coming up the street. I also wanted to see Becky at the hospital today. I had two hours to play with before I picked the children up so I decided to go see Becky first.

When I got to her floor, I saw that her door was closed. I ran down the hall and opened it as fast as I could.

Mama jumped up and said, "What in the world is going on Liz?"

I said, "Nothing, Mama. I'm just here to see Becky, and I got scared 'cause her door was closed. I was already late for school, so I didn't go, and I had two hours to kill before I picked the children up, so I decided to come here first."

Becky lay in bed. She looked like she was asleep but she was actually in a coma. Today, however, she raised her eyebrow at me when I said "Hey, honey." I thought I saw her wave her finger while I was talking to her.

"Liz, what job did you get?" Mama asked me.

"Roland's girlfriend's sister works downtown at a Department store as a manager. She told me to come tomorrow at 6 PM for a job. So Mama, please come home before 5 o'clock."

"I will because I only have a 10-day sick slip. I really hope you can get a job, but you're only fifteen years old. Honey, don't make no friends there either. They won't be nothing but trouble, and besides, where does Roland live? Around the corner, up the street?"

"Mommy, Roland's got a baby!"

"A baby?"

"Yes Mama. He looks just like him, too. Bad hair and dark skin."

"Oh lord, I've got to see this! Liz, how did the girl look?"

"Well, not too good, and the apartment is filthy! Clothes are all over the place, and there are lots of bums that run in and out of that apartment. It stinks, and the people stink too. A lot of them are drunk and they have that liquor smell on them."

"Don't go over there too much. Jackie is Lisa's sister, that's okay. You can go to the job, not her house." I said okay.

Becky's doctor came in and told us that Becky's condition was the same but it could get worse. That's a problem we don't need, I thought, but I didn't say much and left to go pick the children up.

I told the kids, "Ya'll, I might be getting a job." They were so excited when I said that!

"Where at?"

"Downtown, at a department store."

Sharon said, "Liz, does that mean we can get better clothes?"

"No, nothing like that."

John asked, "Why are you going to work there if we can't get better clothes?"

"This job can give us one-half price on everything, but we don't get it for free. Let's go home."

Lynne, who was down the hall, yelled to me. "Liz! Wait up. Are you going home?"

I asked, "Are you going home? Are you?"

"Don't be smart."

"I'm not being smart. I just never see you anymore. Besides, where is Gary?"

"That's none of your business."

"Liz I saw you over Roland's girlfriend's house."

"So Lynne, that's none of your business."

Lynne asked, "Did you meet Lisa?"

"Yeah, sure did. She's ugly, and she's got a big nose and big lips. Lynne, you know Roland's got a baby. He's dark skin, and has bad hair just like him. Now, put a big nose and lips on him, that's how the baby looks. That little boy is going to be a sad looking child when he grows up."

We were falling over laughing when someone knocked on the door.

"Lynne, who is it? Don't say nothing, so they won't come in," I said.

"It's Terry from next door."

"Lynne, it's okay, open it."

Ms. Terry said, "Where's Tracy?"

"My Mama's down at the hospital."

"Well, Liz, I would like it if you could pick up my kid from the same daycare John goes to. I transferred them over there. I hope you don't mind picking up the twins."

"No, I don't mind."

"I can pay you $3 a day for bus fare. I can't rely on Paul to pick them up. The last time I did, they waited a long time. Is 6 o'clock okay?"

She left and I finished telling Lynne about the job. When Mama came home she was happy to see that dinner was cooked, the dishes washed and everybody was home. It put a big smile on her face seeing Lynne at home on time. All of the kids were washed and they had finished their homework.

"This is just the best peace that I've had all day," she sighed.

"Mommy, Ms. Terry stopped past and asked if I could pick up the twins at John's daycare."

"Girl, Terry leaves her house at 6 o'clock in the morning."

"That's no problem. Mr. Paul takes them in the morning."

"Now, suppose you get this job tomorrow. Sit down, we have to figure this thing out. I'm going to need everyone's help. Get Sharon and Lynne out here. Lynne came out.

"Ma, Liz's job only pays $4 an hour."

"That can help me put food on the table and pay part on the rent. Sharon, you could help get the twins."

Sharon said, "But Mama, they're hard headed, bad, and don't listen to me. Why burden me with them?"

"Girl, you're my burden!" Sharon started to pout. "Did you hear me?"

"Yes."

"Lynne, you pick up all the children. They get out at 2:45 and you should be at daycare no later than 4 o'clock, get the bus and come home no later than 4:30, 5 o'clock. I can go with Terry in the morning at 6 o'clock and get to work at 7, then get out at 2 o'clock to make it a half-hour day. That's good enough. No one is there that early in the morning shift. I'll call Mrs. Corte tomorrow to ask if I can cut back on the morning shift.

"They're cutting back anyway, they might even ask me for a four or five-hour day anyway. Any money can help. I'll call Terry tonight to see if Paul can take all of the children to school. We can actually save some money now. The kids are going to get reduced lunch money. Liz, be all ready to go to the job tomorrow. Oh yeah, Lynne, your teacher will see me tomorrow."

"Oh, Ma!"

"I need to check up on you. Roland doesn't live here anymore, and now you have to decide what you're going to do. Are you going to school or get a job?"

Just then, I remembered, "Oh, by the way, Roland told me to tell you Wednesday at 10 AM."

Mama said, "Well, you tell Roland that I can't promise him that. Okay?"

"Okay, Mama." Another sigh of relief came from her. I started thinking about the phone. I hoped that it would be back soon, but, I didn't know how because the bill was so high. Someone made an expensive long distance call. We don't have any proof who did it though, so now they won't turn it back on until we pay.

The next day had a nice calmness to it. Mr. Paul picked up the children at 7 AM like planned. The children were dropped off at our house at 6:30 AM with a bag of clothes. After Mama let them in, she started washing them up. Mama asked Lynne to finish the job.

Lynne said, "For $6 a day, we're doing a lot!"

"That's right. When you're on welfare, what can you do? They only pay you scraps for daycare. They don't even include the washing up part. Man, I would love to see you girls with your first child!"

I hollered, "That child would be sad the day it was born! Lynne, you just lazy, you're not responsible, and you can't even clean someone up! You'll be on welfare too!"

"You don't know that, Liz!"

I continued "Look at you now Lynne!"

Sharon hollered out, "Look at Roland's baby's ma! She's dirty, has a filthy apartment, and the baby has bad hair. That ugly little black child is already cursed!"

Mama said, "Don't say that. That's your nephew! Don't let me hear none of you talking about Roland's baby like that, and while we're at it, change the conversation!"

Lynne started to shake her head. "Mama, that's why he didn't tell you about the baby boy in the first place."

Mama said "Girl, just get them ready for school."

After about a half an hour we heard Mr. Paul honk. Lynne hollered out the window that the kids would be right down.

"That man of Terry's is so impatient!" I said.

"I know that's right," Lynne said.

"Liz, put your coat on. The kids can eat at daycare."

Sharon says, "Ma, I don't eat at daycare."

"Well, take a peanut butter and jelly sandwich with you, with that day-old bread. That's all I have, okay?"

"Okay, Ma."

Mama told her, "Run and help Liz put the kids in the car."

By now, Sharon's was at the door. "Liz, Charles is calling you, and he has another guy with him." Smiling, Mama said, "It takes two guys to walk you to school now?"

"No, but I like it." I ran down the hall to meet them. "Morning boring Charles and handsome Mike! I would like Mike to walk me to school this morning."

Charles said, "Stop right now. What happened to you yesterday?"

"Well, I was running late."

Charles said, "Hey, did you make up with Sissy yet?"

"No, Charles." Just then ran out of the apartment building.

Sissy was locking the door to her apartment. "Liz, do you have something to say to me?"

"Yeah, Sissy, I'm really sorry about what happened on Friday. When you said something about Becky, it just set me off. See, Becky is in a coma, she might not wake up and she just might die. I thought you were making fun of her, so I got mad. I'm sorry that I talked to you in that tone."

Mike was lying back on the banister, looking at Sissy and me and shaking his head.

Sissy asked, "Are you begging me, Liz?"

"No, I'm just saying that I'm wrong and that I'm sorry, that's all!"

Sissy started fussing. "There you go, all in my business again!"

Charles said, "Girl, don't beg Sissy for nothing!"

"Just keep quiet Charles!" Sissy said. We all stopped talking and headed for school.

"Liz, Sissy said she accepts your being sorry. Wendy still wants to fight you though," Charles reminded me bluntly.

Charles and Mike both said, "That's her dumb business." Mike said, "I told you before that I never liked that nasty girl! Her and her nasty mouth!"

Charles said, "The feeling is the same here bro!"

Sissy said, "Liz, I accept you're being sorry this time, but, don't it happen again. Next time there won't be no excuse."

Mike leaned over to me and said "Liz, did you forget? We were supposed to go to school together yesterday too."

"I didn't forget, like I told Charles, I was just running late, that's all. Besides, I went to look for a job, and today I go for my interview," I said.

"Where?"

"At the department store downtown." Just then, the bell rang for first period.

Mike said, "Liz, I'll see you this afternoon."

As I got to first period class, "Elizabeth Rosemere, please report to the office and see Mrs. Jones," was blaring over the loudspeaker. So, put all of my books in my crazy cracked locker. Oh man, I forgot about my gym clothes, I thought. Oh well.

When I got to Mrs. Jones office, Mama was talking to her. She told her that everything was all right, and that I could get reduced lunch. She also said she could help me with my job interview.

"I'll help you, but you must keep your grades up over 75 percent in every class." I told Mrs. Jones my interview was today at 6 PM.

"Okay, you can leave at 2:30, go home, get changed, that will leave you plenty of time to go. Do you need a note for your next class? Before I could answer, the bell rang. I saw Wendy in the hallway. She shot me a crazy look. At 2:30, I left school to get ready for my interview.

I actually started feeling good about this whole job thing. I knew it would help Mama out a lot. As I was getting off the bus on the way back home, after the interview, Jackie was getting on.

"Hey girl, did you get that job I was talking about?" I said yes and hurried to get off the bus. Stumbling and cursing, she said, "You can start next week."

I said thank you, but she was stumbling again. I started thinking, how could she go to work while she was drunk? Oh well, I just hope and pray that she isn't my manager, I thought.

As I was walking down the street, I saw Charles. "Liz, where were you after school?"

"I got a job Charles. I start next week."

"Hey, that's great. How did you get it?"

"Roland's girlfriend's sister Jackie. You need a job too, Charles."

"No I don't."

"I know you don't. Your girlfriend's niece gives you her money after she gets off from working at McDonalds!"

"That's right, but I hope you don't think I'm going to give you any of my money!"

I replied, "Charles, you never gave or lent me any money until you heard I was getting a job. Besides, I don't know how much I'm going to get each week. But, that check belongs to me, for me working, not you."

"I know you're not going to get mad over my money," Charles said.

I looked at him as if he was crazy, pushed him aside and went upstairs. As I was going up the stairs, Charles yelled out, "I wish Sissy and Wendy would have beat you up!"

I was surprised and hurt by what he said. I yelled back, "I'm not Niecy!" Then I ran in the house. Lynne was there and heard the whole thing.

"So, Charles is your friend?"

"Not anymore!"

"Girl, I just hope that stupid girl Sissy doesn't try to come up here and fight you."

"I'm not scared of her!"

"Yeah, that's what you say now!" Just then, the phone rang. Charles said, "Liz, I don't want you to walk with me to school anymore."

"That's fine with me. I'm glad I see what kind of friend you are before I got paid!" Then I slammed down the phone.

Lynne started shaking her head again. "Like we need this!"

"Lynne, this is my problem," I said.

"Yeah, but you're still my sister."

Mama came into the room. "Liz, what are your hours on your job now? My job cut my hours to 4-6 hours a day, so your job can really help us."

"I start next Monday at 4 o'clock and get off at 8 o'clock. I can get the children ready for school. Mr. Paul takes the children to school in the morning with Sharon." I said.

"He makes me late for school," Lynne said.

Mama continued, "Lynne, you've got to come straight home from school and start dinner."

"But Ma, we never have any food to cook."

"Whatever we have to cook, cook it!"

"By the way," Mama continued, "now that you're back in school, if you don't continue to go, I'll put you out with the drug dealers and the drunks. Then you can sell drugs with your boyfriend Gary. Okay?"

Lynne poked her lip out but she said, "I'll have the dinner cooked. Now that I have to go to the market to get food, we'll be up early tomorrow and all the children will help carry the food home."

I started thinking of Becky. "Mama, how is Becky doing?"

"She'll be home next week. The hospital is sending a nurse for her. Liz, you need to wash all the sheets and blankets and get her clothes clean. I'll send you to the laundry. I'll bring some change home. Becky doesn't speak too well. The speech therapist is helping her to speak now."

"Mama, who's going to watch her?"

"Well, I've got to be here. I'm going to work at night from 11:30 to 3:30 in the morning. I'll be here to see everybody go to school. Lynne, your job is to bring the children home from day care and watch them while I go back to sleep and keep them quiet and help them with their homework, and also have Ms. Terry's children ready to go home."

I said, "Mama, I'm going to work straight from school. Please make sure you leave me some money."

Mama said, "We're going to need everybody's help.

Lynne said, "Mama, you sure that nurse and therapist are going to want to come to Harlem?"

"Well, that's what the hospital and her doctors said. Whether they want to or not."

Chapter 7

Even More Drama

Just as Lynne started to argue with Mama, the phone rang. Lynne broke her neck to get across the room to answer it. It was Gary. The conversation started out normally, but then they started to argue. He was talking so loud I could hear him through the receiver. He was saying he was going to beat Lynne up.

She yelled back, "No, you go beat up on your new girlfriend Denise. And, don't forget, I don't go with you no more anyway!" Then she slammed the phone down. "Liz, if you see that dumb Gary in the street, don't even talk to him. He'll just start trouble with you just to get back at me."

"Look Lynne, I never liked him anyway, and I never talked to him anyway. So, nothing will change about that situation."

"That's cool. Let's talk about something else. This conversation is doing nothing but making me mad. Girl, how do you like that job of yours?"

"It looks like I'll be there for a while."

Mama yelled out, "She hasn't even started yet!"

"Well, what do you do there?"

"I tag the clothes and then put out."

The phone rang. It was Gary again.

Mama yelled to Lynne, "Tell Gary not to call here anymore, and to leave my daughter alone."

Gary didn't say anything but I knew he was still there because I could hear him breathing on the phone. Lynne grabbed the phone from me and yelled, "GARY, STOP CALLING ME! I don't want to see you anymore!" and slammed the phone down again.

As we started to get ready for bed, I said to Lynne, "So, you and Gary don't go together anymore?"

"That stupid boy wants that ugly girl Denise that lives next to that apartment building he's always hanging around. Me and her were about to fight!"

I couldn't believe my ears. "Girl, I *know* you ain't going to fight over GARY! You will look like a fool, Lynne! You know you already act like one!"

Lynne said, "Acting like one doesn't mean that I am one."

I tried to change the subject. "Well, I actually work tomorrow, so I need to pick out some comfortable clothes and shoes."

Mama was in the kitchen cleaning. Just then she yelled down the hallway to me, "Liz, go with your brother to take the trash out."

I yelled back, "Ma, I'm trying to get my stuff together for tomorrow." So then, she asked Lynne to go with John. Lynne started yelling that Mama was always making her do stuff that Liz was suppose to do.

Mama got mad. "Girl, don't tell me what you will and will not do. Not in my house you're not!" Lynne continued fussing.

"Liz, I know you're going to lose that stupid job!"

I yelled back, "Well, it doesn't matter if I do or not, the point is that I went out there and found a job. Just then, Mama came in.

"You both stop that fussing. Lynne, go get one of those garbage bags from John, and tell him that you were supposed to help him. He's just a little boy." John looked at Lynne and started to whine.

The phone rang again. It was Gary. He asked for Lynne again. I told him she wasn't here. "Tell your sister that I'm going to hurt her!"

I said, "You tell her yourself, and slammed the phone down again. As I was hanging up, I could hear him saying something but I couldn't make it out. I still told Lynne how he threatened to hurt you.

Lynne said, "Man, that boy really makes me sick!"

I looked at her. "Boy, this is a big difference from a few weeks ago. You were so in *love* with Gary! Now, he just a bum. Him *and* his friend!"

"Girl, you don't have to tell me that. I found out the hard way what kind of boy he is. Mama came out and told me that all I need to do is see my father and I'm looking at Gary. They're just alike. Both workless, sellout bums, who never want to work, or never want to just try! Mama said she didn't need Daddy, and I don't need Gary either." Then, Lynne and I finally went to bed.

I didn't get a good night's sleep anyway, so the next morning I got up early. Mr. Paul was supposed to be taking Terry's kids to daycare but he came up to the apartment and told Mama that he couldn't, so Mama had to throw her clothes on in a hurry and take the kids to school.

Mama was angry. She called a cab and rushed out of the house. Lynne and I just looked at each other. I started to wonder what it would be like when Becky got home! Lynne and I left for school.

Charles came out of his apartment. Lynne didn't even speak. Charles said, "Oh, now Lynne's not speaking to me?" I looked at him sadly because I knew that he didn't like me anymore either. Lynne said to him, "Charles, you've never been my friend, but I never stopped speaking to you. So, the question is, why now? Why now all of a sudden are you pulling this stuff? Liz and I don't have to speak to you or your stupid sister! We're not sad though, should we be sad, are we Liz?"

I just looked at him and didn't say a word. Lynne slapped my leg. I said, "That's right," in a sad voice, and started walking away.

Mike heard everything. "So Liz, now you need your sister to talk up for you?" I grabbed Lynne's hand as her mouth was dropping open. We walked out of the building as the bus was coming up the street. After we got on and sat down, Lynne looked at me with a strange expression.

"Are you scared of Charles?" I asked her.

"No, I just don't want any problems from him, that's all."

"Well, I just wanted to know, 'cause if I have to fight him, I want to know if you got my back or not. I hope that you don't get me beat up."

"Lynne, I know you would fight for me."

"Liz, you need to learn to fight for yourself. I'll help out and all, but I'm not going to get my tail beat up for you, or anybody. When I was out in the streets, I didn't depend on nobody to defend me or help me. Me and my girls always took care of everything. There are a lot of gangs in Harlem High, so you better remember that I'm your sister, and I'll be there for you, just as long as you're there for me!"

We got off at school. As we were walking, I wondered what happened to Mike. I was still nervous about dealing with Charles, because I knew he would tell Sissy, Wendy, and Mike what happened. I knew that Lynne and I could take on all three if we had to—Sissy, Charles and Wendy. I knew Mike would have a different view than everyone else.

I was on my way to Mrs. Jones', the counselor's office, when I heard loud laughter down the hall. Charles was making fun of Lynne. I ran out of the office toward them. When Mrs. Jones heard what was going on, she ran up the hall toward them. She took both Lynne and Charles to the office with her.

She asked Lynne what happened, and she started telling her about Charles bothering me, and how she was trying to speak up for me, and then Charles chimed in, "I hope I beat both you and Liz up, 'cause y'all are no good."

I was so mad I shot an evil look at Charles. Mrs. Jones said, "Charles, you just have two months left in the school year. Don't pick a fight her any more, and we shouldn't have a problem. Liz, you never had a problem before, you are a good student and I know your sister wouldn't let anyone bother you."

Lynne yelled out, "That's right. I'm not going to let any little punk beat up on my sister."

Charles started to mumble under his breath, "That's okay, I'll just get Sissy to get Lynne, and get Wendy to beat up on you Liz!"

"Well, you do that," I said, "I'm not afraid of either one of them, and neither is Lynne."

"Okay, QUIET GIRLS!" Mrs. Jones yelled out. "Liz, you can call me anytime you need to okay? Remind your sister of that too, from time to time." She continued, "I just okayed her to go back to school, and I want her to do good, and not to have too many distractions around so you can do well in your grades, so you can graduate with good marks, so you can both go to college. Now Charles, if you and your sister lay a hand on these girls, I will personally make sure you *never* finish school, you *or* your sister. Is that understood?"

Charles had a strange look on his face. "Yes," he mumbled.

"You're nothing but a coward, and you need to take this stuff out on the street where it belongs! Now, Liz and Lynne, you girls tell me if he or his sister bothers either one of you, and I will personally escort him out of the school." I was happy that she took our side. I knew we didn't really do anything wrong, we were just defending ourselves. Then, she told us to go back to our classes.

"Oh, Mrs. Jones I finally got a job!"

"Oh, really? Where do you work at?"

"At the department store downtown."

"That's convenient. What hours do you work?"

"From 4 PM to 8 PM Monday thru Friday."

"That's a great way to help your mother out." By this time, Lynne and Charles had gone back to their classes, and the bell rang. She just closed the door to her office so we could have some privacy. We started talking about Charles and his attitude and how we got in this mess in the first place.

"You see Mrs. Jones, we were great friends but he found out I got a job and he had planned on getting most of my money for himself. He already spends his girlfriend Niecy's money that she gets from McDonalds!"

"Boy," Mrs. Jones said, "she's just making more problems for herself. As teachers, we see these types of problems all the time. You two just stay away from him and his type."

"You don't need to tell me twice!"

"You be careful of Charles knows a lot of gangs around here. If you have any more problems, don't forget, my door is always open, and you can always call me. Well let me write you a pass for your second period class." I got the pass, thanked her and headed upstairs to second period. As I was going up the stairs, I saw Mike.

"Hey Liz."

"Hey Mike." I said it low and sad because I really like him, but I know he is Charles' friend.

"Is Wendy messing with you or something?"

"No," I said.

"Well, what's wrong now? You and Charles just had a falling out, right?"

"No, it's not that simple, but I'll tell you all about it later, after school. Oh, by the way, I got a job downtown."

"Hey, that's great! That's a good start for you now so you won't be lazy later." I looked at him, wondering what he meant. All of a sudden, he pushed me up against a wall and kissed me. I was so shocked, I just let it happen. I kind of wanted it to happen anyway.

Just then Mary, who was in my second period class, came out of the classroom and saw us. She started to giggle. Unfortunately, Janice is friends with Sissy and Wendy, so I'm sure she'll open her big mouth and tell them what she saw.

Mike looked at me and said, "So, are you my girl?"

I said, "I don't know."

All of a sudden Janice was back. She got in Mike's face. "Boy, if Wendy finds out, you and Liz are dead meat."

"Girl, if you don't get out of my face with your hot nasty stinky breath…I'm not kissing you or Wendy now am I?! So stay out of my face and my life."

She started laughing and giggling in his face again, so he pushed her away and said, "Next time, I'm going to hit you right in your face." He grabbed my arm and we headed downstairs.

"Those girls make me sick!" Mike said. "Well, here's my phone number, you can call me anytime after 9:30 at night. I still have to ask my family if you can come over and see me sometimes."

I said okay and I started running to my third period class, not believing what just happened. When I sat down, my heart was beating fast and I felt good for a change.

After school that day, I started wondering about Lynne. I had to leave early so I could go home to pick up my badge I had to take to work. I forgot to take it with me that morning. As I was walking toward my building, I saw Charles looking at me. I could see that Mike was talking to him.

"Hey Liz, come here for a minute." I thought to myself, *Oh, here we go.* I went anyway.

"Why aren't you and Charles speaking to each other?" Mike asked.

I started to tell him all the crazy details in quick form, then Mike said, "Charles, you better not lay a hand on Liz or Lynne, you hear me? You'll have to deal with ME if you do."

Charles didn't say anything and I just walked away. As I was waiting for the bus to go to work, all I could think of was Mike kissing me and how I wanted him to do that for a while. I hoped that he would call me tonight after I got off work. I hoped and prayed that Mama liked him!!

It was my first day on the job and I was hoping I could get along with everybody I worked with. The first person I saw in the locker room was Jackie looking for her keys so she could go home. I said hi to her.

"Well, well, little girl, you're not only on time, but you're a little early. That's good, now. I just hope that you're a good worker." I laughed and put my coat in my locker.

"Girl, make sure you don't put no pocketbook in there, ya' hear?"

I said okay, and thanked her for telling me that. I was glad that Jackie wasn't my manager. I liked her, but she was weird and hard to get along with. Jackie yelled out, "See you tomorrow. But, I'll only see you if you are on time, or come early."

I said okay and went out of the locker room to find my manager, Mrs. Carol. I would be working with her in the back of the store. I saw all of those beautiful clothes in all the right sizes, and I thought, *I just hope I don't spend my paycheck buying all of them.*

I started by putting the tags on all of the women's clothes. As I was working, I still had my mind on Mike. Just then, someone bumped into my clothes bag and knocked it over. I couldn't see who it was but someone said, "Oh, I'm so sorry." I looked around the bag and saw a really nice looking guy. I smiled at him, and said, "That's okay."

"You must be the new girl. I'm Steven."

"Yeah, my name is Elizabeth, but, everybody calls me Liz."

"What school do you go to?" Mrs. Carol was coming so I never got a chance to answer him.

When 8 o'clock came I caught the 8:45 PM bus home. This was a really hard day for me, going to school, and working afterwards. I was so tired I fell asleep on the bus. Somebody woke me up and asked me if this was my stop. It was the bus driver. I opened my eyes, looked around, and all I saw was trees and water. I missed my stop!!

The driver said, "Young lady, you're in uptown New York."

"Oh, my goodness!!"

He put my mind at ease. He told me I could just stay on the bus until he came around again. It was already late and dark and I wasn't about to get off the bus in a strange place.

After awhile we got to my stop again. As I was going up the dark street, I saw Roland with his hoodlum friends, Ricky, Nick and Lament, standing on the corner. "So Roland, where in the world have you been lately?"

Roland gave me a funny look. "With Lisa."

Ricky yelled out, "You know Lisa's pregnant again!"

"Man, stop telling my business," Roland yells back. "I know who you like anyway, my stupid sister Lynne! But, she don't like you anyway."

"So, man, that's okay with me," Ricky glared back. Nick started laughing out loud, but all I could do was look at them in disbelief. Now, it's all coming back to me. That's why Lynne broke up with Gary, and that's why Gary's so mad! I was too tired and shocked to say anything more to Roland, so I just went upstairs and figured I'd deal with him later.

As I was walking in the door, I saw that Lynne was asleep. The phone started ringing. I answered it quickly so it wouldn't wake anybody up. Ricky asked for Lynne.

"She's asleep," I said, and hung up the phone. I was so tired that I swore I heard my bed calling me! I went in my room and went to bed, and didn't even put my nightclothes on I just climbed under the covers and went to sleep. There were some events that happened this day that I wanted to forget, but Mike kissing me? I definitely wanted to remember that. I fell asleep thinking about Mike again, and before I knew it, it was Saturday morning.

Lynne got up before I did that morning. "Lynne, I saw Roland last night."

"So!"

"Lynne, do you go with Ricky? You know, one of those boys that Roland hangs with."

"Yeah, so what."

"So that's why you and Gary broke up?"

"Why are you so worried about that? That's none of your business."

"I know," I said, "but Roland's friend is just like Gary. A bum."

"Girl, the truth with you is you're just jealous of me!"

"That's not true and you know it. Look at your lifestyle, why would I be jealous of that?"

"Then why are you asking me about Ricky?"

"Those are 3-R boys: Roland, Ricky and Randy. And the others, Lament, and Curtis. And, I was just asking a question. Why are you jumping on defense all of a sudden?"

She looked at me with a quick glance and said, "Well, whatever," and we dropped. "Oh by the way, Mike called for you last night."

"Oh, he did? Man, I missed it!" I didn't mean to say that out loud, especially in front of Lynne. I didn't want her asking too many questions about me either.

"Tracy, are you going to the market?" Terry asked as she walked in our front door. "Yes."

"Well, I got us a ride there. His name is Roy."

"Oh, you got one of the 3-R boys. Now Terry, those boys are no good. Roland is friends with them too. He's just asking for trouble hanging around them. What about your boyfriend?"

"Girl, we're just friends, my goodness. You're making this nothing into a big deal."

"Ha, that's what me and Ricky said." Lynne chimed in.

Mama and Ms. Terry were still bickering as they walked out the door. I looked at the phone, and tried to get up but too nervous to call Mike. I picked up the receiver and dialed. His grandmother answered. She asked me who was calling. I told her who I was and asked for Mike.

"Mike's not home right now. He's at basketball practice." I thanked her and hung up the phone. I said "Hmm, she seems to be a nice lady, huh Lynne? But, if Mike becomes a professional basketball player, her greediness will come out."

Lynne said, "Liz, Mike's a nice guy, but money can change a guy."

"That's funny, when they're poor they can change too!" We both start to laugh! I looked at her kind of puzzled. Usually Lynne and I never got to talk like this anymore, so I was glad of this little time to talk.

All of a sudden, the doorbell rang. It was Mike. I went out in the hallway and yelled down the steps, "I'll be down!"

A green car was parking outside. It was Mama and Ms. Terry back from the market already! I ran downstairs to help them. Mike and I opened the car door and grabbed some bags to take upstairs.

Mama said, "Tell the rest of the kids to help me with the rest of these bags." I went upstairs and told everybody to go down and help. I put my bags on the kitchen table.

All of a sudden Lynne yelled out, "Go back downstairs, I'm in the bathroom." I went back downstairs to get her share.

"Where's Lynne?" Mama asked.

"She's in the bathroom."

"That's just like that lazy girl!" Mama said.

We all unloaded the rest of the bags out of the car and brought them up the stairs. Lynne met us at the door. Mama told her, "Girl, you sure pick a fine time to go to the bathroom!"

"But Ma!"

"Shut up, and take this money next door."

I stepped up. "Mama, this is my friend Mike. Mike, this is my mother, Tracy." I was hoping with all my heart that she would like him.

"Hi Mrs. Tracy. I'm a friend of Liz. We go to the same school."

Lynne yelled out, "Bad ol' Harlem school. There are some bad kids that go there."

Mike started to laugh under his breath. "Sit down young man. You did your job today," Mama said. I took a seat next to him. I asked him how was practice today.

"I could have been better," He said, then was quiet. He didn't say much the whole time. The only thing he really asked me was if I saw Charles today.

"No, I don't see him much anymore."

"I don't know what's going with him, he hardly shows up for practice anymore. I hope he isn't in any trouble."

"I do know he used to be in some kind of gang," I said.

Mike looked at me. "That's what he told you?"

"Well, yeah."

"Girl, you better watch what you say around Charles. I like the guy and all, but I watch what I do around him too." He was making me so nervous, my words wouldn't come out straight.

Lynne came into the living room. "So, I want to be impressed," she said.

For some reason, I started to shake inside. "Oh, I called you this morning. Your grandmother answered the phone. She seemed very nice."

"Um hmm," Lynne interrupted.

"Ma, tell Lynne this is not her friend," I yelled. "Man, Lynne, now you're all in my conversation!"

Mama came in. "Well Lynne, at least Liz's friend introduced himself to me and came in to help me! Your friend doesn't do anything, and plus him and his friends are nothing but bad news!"

"That's okay, Mama, that you feel that way about my friend. See how long Mike stays around!" Lynne said.

"I'm not that worried about that. Liz is in good hands," Mama said. Mike chuckled to himself.

Mama said, "Liz, help me put this food away and clean this apartment up. I need you to stay in today. I want to get the apartment ready for Becky when she comes home. I'm going to paint this ugly apartment and this nasty kitchen. I need to go to the hardware store. Can you and Mike go downtown and get a few things I need?"

"Sure, Mrs. Tracy."

"I wasn't doing anything, but I am a little hungry. I haven't eaten anything for breakfast yet."

"Liz, fix him some lunch."

"Okay, Mama." I fixed him a sandwich, he ate it and thanked me for fixing it. We put on our coats and he thanked Mama for everything.

"No, young man, thank *you*. Thanks for helping me today. You're a really nice young man."

We got on the bus to go to the store. I stood up to get off at the store where I worked. "Girl, this isn't a hardware store," Mike said.

"I know, but I want you to see where I work. I know we have to walk back aways, and I know it's cold, so we won't be long."

I showed him where I worked, then we walked back to the hardware store.

"Liz, do you know your father?"

61

"Yeah, but, he's in jail."

"Oh. I never knew my parents. My grandmother raised me from a baby. I think about my father a lot though. I wonder what he looks like, if I look like him. She hates telling me anything that will hurt me though. She wants me to have a better future than she did."

At the hardware store we get all of the things Mama asked for and hopped back on the bus, but instead of getting off on my stop, we get off on his. I went with him into his apartment building. He didn't have his key so he had to knock on the door.

His grandmother answered. "Granny, this is my friend Liz."

I said, "Hi."

"Hello, honey," she said. "My name is Mrs. Maxine. Boy, did you get something to eat?"

"Yes, at Liz's house." He went in his room to change clothes. I looked around, I was nervous just being in his house. I could see that they kept the apartment very clean and the food that his grandmother was cooking smelled good. I felt at home at his house.

Mike came back out of his room. "Granny, I'm going over to Liz's house for awhile. Here's the phone number just in case." She said okay, and that it was nice meeting me.

"It was nice meeting you too, Mrs. Maxine." We went back downstairs and over to my house.

"Liz, I want to help your mother paint the house. I want to start in the bedrooms."

As we were talking, we ran into Sissy and Wendy. Surprisingly, she said hi to us. Wendy sucked her teeth and walked past us. I ignored her, went upstairs to my apartment and put everything on the floor. Mama was moving the furniture.

"Mrs. Tracy, I want to help you paint if you don't mind." Mike told Mama.

"Sure, that would be great Mike."

"Okay, we need to take everything off the walls and wash them down to get some of this dirt off of them first. We will put the dishes in a box to protect them." Mama went next door to Mrs. Terry's and came back with six medium boxes. We put everything in the boxes and started washing out the cabinets.

Mike stirred the paint and put paper down on the floor. Then he put his music on and we all started clowning around in the kitchen. Mike started laughing at Mama, and then we all started to laugh at her. He turned the music up louder, and we all started clowning around and making noise. I felt good because I hadn't seen my family like this in a while.

Mike started spreading the bright, white paint on the ugly, grey walls with a roller while I used a brush to paint the dirty door facings. As soon as we started putting the paint on, the room starting getting brighter. No matter how much we washed those walls, they just didn't look clean. Now they were looking clean for the first time.

All of a sudden, the door came flew open and Ms. Terry came in. "What is going on in here? I can hear y'all all the way down the hall!

Suddenly she stopped talking and looked around. "Oh, y'all are painting? Well, we need some cold beer in here!" She ran over to her apartment and came over with a handful of stuff. Cold beer for her and Mama, and cold sodas for us. She took a few sips and started to giggle. Lynne, John and Sharon started dancing too. It was like a party. "Girl," Ms. Terry said, "This is now officially a painting party!"

Mama and Mrs. Terry started telling stories about growing up and all the problems Mama caused grandma. She told how she and her sisters Rose and Rebecca got into trouble all of the time. My little sister was named after Aunt Rebecca, who died when she was still a baby. Just seeing my mother laughing and happy and enjoying herself brought tears to my eyes. I sure was enjoying myself too. Just being here with Mike at my house made me happy. Lynne was trying to swing Sharon and John. It was so funny watching them. I wished that this day would never be over.

Finally, Mike was done. He cleaned up his roller and the brushes and put the leftover paint away. I looked around. The house was so bright and clean and felt so good. It also felt like Mike and I were family. I was smiling just thinking about that when Lament knocked on the door. He came over to tell us that Roland was in jail for getting into a fight with Lisa's brother, Neil. He said his arraignment was at 8:30 Monday morning, and he needed a bail bond.

Mama thanked him for telling us, closed the door behind him, and we continued to have a good time. Mama said, "That's his business, and if it doesn't get paid, I guess he's going to stay in jail."

Mike said he had to leave so Mama told me to walk him part way up the street. She told Mike he would have to run the other part. "Miss Tracy, I'm a big boy," Mike said.

Mama said, "Boy, there are guns out there, and you're never too big to get shot."

I looked over at Ms. Terry and she was feeling pretty good. Mama asked her, "Girl, where are your children?"

"They're over my brother's house, and my niece is going to keep them this weekend. Girl, you know something, that boy Mike is really handsome. I could look at his smile all day." I looked at her and figured that was our cue to leave. As we were leaving we could still hear Mrs. Terry talking about Mike.

"Girl, please let this girl get this man," she said. Talking to Mama, she continued, "That boy got a beautiful future if he makes it to the pros and she'll be sitting pretty for the rest of her life! Everyone will be trying to get him then."

After I walked Mike home, I saw Lament and his cousin Anthony, Roland's friend again. "Hey Liz, let me tell you what happened to Roland and why he went to jail. Him and Lisa's brother Neil got drunk, and he started to argue with Lisa about his girlfriend Lee-Lee. Lisa wound up punching Lee-Lee in the mouth, and Lisa knocked over her stereo.

"Roland jumped in to break up the fight, but Neil pushed him and knocked him down the stairs. Then, Neil tried to stab Roland, Roland picked up a bottle and hit Neil so hard with the bottle that it broke over his head and blood went everywhere, then he started cutting Neil with the bottle in his face. Neil stabbed Roland in the chest, but, I guess he didn't feel anything, cause he kept fighting.

"We had to call the police. When they got there everyone started running. Roland just collapsed, they took both of them to the hospital and then to jail. I don't know what happened to Neil though, but I do know that Neil's face is messed up! Glass was all over his face!"

Lynne was with me, and she said, "Where is Lisa now?"

"I guess she's at her apartment."

"Where is Ricky?"

"At the corner store."

I looked at Lynne and thought, "He's your problem," but I stayed quiet. I turned my back to her because I knew she would try to find Ricky. She went with Lament and Anthony to see Ricky. I didn't want any part of Lynne's business.

Deep down, I really knew that this wasn't over. I started up the stairs. Sissy was near Charles. She yelled out, "LIZ!"

I yelled back "WHAT?"

She replied, "That boy Roland cut up, you and your family better watch your backs! That was the roughest boy in the neighborhood."

"Okay, thanks," I said. "Charles, I don't know what happened or who was at fault."

Sissy said, "Well, put it this way, Roland lives with Lisa, not here, but he went to jail twice when he was here. I'm just telling you this cause I want you to know he's not in a gang anymore.

That street Lisa lives on used to be his territory. And two streets over is Gary's territory. I know Lynne better watch herself when she's walking around. You know she doesn't go with Gary anymore."

"I know she goes with that boy that Roland hangs around. That's just plain bad! So, who does she go with?"

"I think some guy named Keith, Neil's best friend."

"Listen, like I said, just watch yourself. This is probably the last time we'll be able to talk, for a while. These boys around here don't mind hurting you or your family."

I started to feel sad, thinking about Mama being worried and my little brothers and sisters. I thanked them and went home. Mama asked where Lynne was. I told her she was with Roland's friend. I started telling Mama what happened.

She just shook her head. Mama said, "They never listen to me, and now everybody might get hurt because of her stupidness. Lynne will probably be the first one! She goes with Ricky doesn't she? That's nothing. That girl just likes bum guys until they hurt her. Now, they want to hurt us. That's it. Roland is staying in jail. I'm not going to court for him. He's not going to get me or my children hurt! That's his life, I'm not going to get into it! I don't sell drugs, and don't get high with my life. Girl, please don't go back to Lisa's house!"

"Mama, you'll never have to worry about me going over there again! Even if I lose my job."

Mama said, "Let me pay Lynne and Roland's life insurance. I know we don't have any money, but that's one bill that I want paid! I also think I'm going to get a screen door for this place so in the summer we don't have to smell this stinky apartment. Listen, I don't want you or the kids talking to Roland, and if Lynne goes over there, then don't talk to her either, okay?"

"Okay," I said.

Chapter 8

Getting to Know Mike

I put my clothes in the laundry basket as I took them off. The dirty clothes were piling up and I was going to take them to the Laundromat tomorrow. My heart was still pounding, thinking about what had just happened. I put my pajamas on and went to bed. Suddenly, the bedroom door flew open. Lynne came in but did not say anything. She went right to sleep and so did I.

The next day, Sunday, was a sunny morning. I heard Mama get up and go to the bathroom to wash up. She called Lynne to get all of her dirty clothes together so she could take them to the Laundromat. Lynne yelled out that she was too tired. Mama yelled back, "Girl, get up. Liz works and you are not going to sit home and do nothing all day!" She also got John and Sharon up. She started to divide the clothes into different bags. Sharon came in my room and asked me for some change. I told her to leave me alone.

"Mama needs some change Liz!" she said.

"Look in my pants pocket," I said in a loud voice. "No Sharon, not those pants, these pants over here."

"Liz, there's only two dollars in here."

"Just give that to Mama then." I was fully awake now and I couldn't go back to sleep, especially with everyone moving all around me, so I got up. As I was in the bathroom washing up, the phone rang. It sounded like Lisa.

"Liz, is your Mother home?"

"Yeah, she's home."

"Can you put her on, please?"

Mama took the phone. I heard her say, "Well, that's Roland's business. I'm not going to get Roland out, even if I do have the money. That's Roland's life," Mama continued. "That's his business if he's in jail period. No, but, he should be in jail for fighting somebody anyway. All I can say is you will have to find someone else to get him out, 'cause I'm not going to do it." She hung up the phone and shook her head. "I'm not going to court for him either." She headed back to her room.

"Liz, take some change out of the can and make sure the clothes are dry." I went downstairs, mad that I got stuck with the chore. As I passed Charles' apartment, his father came out and started pulling on me. I tried to push him off.

Mama must have heard me scream because she came running down the steps and hit him over the head with the broom she had in her hand. "If you EVER go near my children again, I am going to call the police on you, and they will lock you up. Guaranteed!"

"Liz, go right where I told you to go. And, you stinky old drunk man, stay away from my children!" I ran downstairs as fast as I could go. When I think back now, even sunny days in Harlem were bad days.

Downstairs, liquor bottles and trash were all over the sidewalk. I stepped over the bottles and waded through the trash until I finally got to the Laundromat. I wondered where Lynne was. I looked around and spotted her at the store next to the laundry. I put the clothes in the machines and sat down with Sharon and John. An old lady we didn't recognize spoke to us and we spoke back. As I started to put the clothes in the dryer, I noticed that the old lady, who was washing her rug, was Mike's grandmother. I went over to her again.

"Hi, Mrs. Mike's grandmother," I said and laughed. I was embarrassed because I had forgotten her name.

"It's Mrs. Maxine, honey."

"Where is Mike, is he up yet?"

"No, he was asleep when I left this morning," she said.

While I was putting the clothes in the dryer, I noticed she was trying to put her big rug in her bag. As she was doing it, the bag broke and the rug fell out. I went over to help her.

"Thank you," she said. "Now, let me see if I can get a cab."

"No, I can help you with my Mama's cart," I told her. I put more money in the dryers, put her rug in the cart and went down the street to walk her back to her apartment. I started to take the cart up the steps. The cart went bump, bump, bump, on each step. It sounded like the wheels were going to fall off but I finally made it up to her floor.

She said, "Thank you," and put money in my hand.

"Oh, no thanks, I can't take that. You just have a good day."

"You too, honey," she said.

I hurried back to the laundry. Immediately, Lynne started in on me. "Great, we had to wait for Mama's cart to be able to load the clothes and we had to wait all day for you!"

"That's right Lynne, you did have to wait. I was doing something nice for somebody else, something you know nothing about! You're just a selfish, uncaring person!"

"No, Liz, you were just showing off for Mike's grandmother!" Lynn said.

"Whatever, Lynne! Just take the cart!" We loaded the cart, but the wheels sounded like they were going to come off. "Take some of the clothes off to make the load lighter." I took a big bag off and tried to cram the rest of the clothes in it. We were still arguing when I put the bag on my back and started walking away.

When we got home, Lynne told Mama what happened. "Liz, that was very nice what you did for her," Mama said.

Lynne yelled out, "Next time she goes to the laundry, she should find people to help on her time!"

"Lynne, just shut up!" Mama said.

"Mama, you never say nothing bad to your 'special child'!" Lynne said.

Sharon looked at me sternly. I went into the bedroom, put my clothes away and pulled out a book I had to read for school tomorrow. I fell asleep before I knew it. Suddenly, someone was shaking me. "Liz, the phone."

I got up and answered. Mike said, "Liz, I just wanted to thank you for helping Grandmother like that."

"It was nothing."

"So, what are you doing now?"

"Just reading a book for a report in school tomorrow."

"Oh, I'm just cleaning up my room. Hey, do you think I can come by tonight?"

"Well, let me ask my mother first."

I called out, "Mama, can Mike come by for a little bit?"

"Well, I don't see why not, yeah, I guess it's okay. Me and Lynne are going to the hospital to see Becky tonight." I told Mike yes, and started cleaning my room up.

My mother handed me some money. "Liz, this is for tomorrow, for work. Now remember, that's all I have for you right now." I looked in my pants pocket and I found $5. Mrs. Maxine must have slipped it in. I told Mama about the money though, because we never have enough money for the week.

I started cleaning up the kitchen and started making some fried chicken for dinner then, I went downstairs to the store for some soda for dinner. I felt someone staring at me so I turned my head and saw Charles and his father. I pretended that I didn't see them and kept walking. I bought the soda and put it in my room so Mike and I could drink it later.

Mike told Lynne to tell me that he would be over around 3 o'clock. Well, it was already 2:40, so I started making tuna fish sandwiches for us. Mama asked if I used the money that she gave me for bus fare to work. "No Mama, don't forget, Mrs. Maxine gave me some money this morning."

"Okay. Now, you both behave. I don't want any playing in my apartment and nothing better not be broken when I get back. We should be back around six. I really need to talk to Becky's doctor today." Then they were gone.

About five minutes later, the bell rang. I got butterflies in my stomach. I had never been alone with Mike before and I was nervous! I ran downstairs to open the door. We said hello quickly and went upstairs. I fixed us a sandwich as Mike watched, then we took the sandwiches and the soda and went into my room where we ate.

When we finished eating, we played cards for a while. Sharon started laughing at Mike when he hit her hand with the fun card. Mike showed us some card tricks he knew. John sat next to Mike so he could watch Mike do some card tricks and learn to do them too. I went into the kitchen to finish fixing the chicken dinner for everybody. Mike came in the kitchen to talk to me about school. We really didn't know what to say to each other.

"You seen Charles lately?" Mike asked.

"Not really," I said. "I really don't talk to him that much anymore."

Mike said, "Lynne and I don't talk to him either. Girl, that boy stays in trouble. He was doing good for awhile, but, now he's back out in the streets again."

As we were talking in the kitchen, the front door opened and Mama and Lynne came in. "Hi Mama, I was just finishing up the dinner for tonight," I said.

Mike looked up. "Oh, hi Miss Tracy, hi Lynne."

"Hi Mike, good to see you." Mama said.

Mike asked, "So Liz, what time do you want me to pick you up for school tomorrow?"

"Oh, around 7:30-7:40."

I walked him downstairs and up the block. Once we got up the block, he leaned over and kissed me. "Liz, I really had a nice time at your house. Thanks for inviting me. Now, I'm gonna go home and eat some fried chicken that Grandma made. She's cooking dinner for the whole week. She cooked a lot of food just for me and her. Some of her church members are supposed to be coming over today, but I don't really know if they're coming. She stays on the phone talking to them. That's why the line stays busy. It's not me on the phone. Not too many people call me. You can call me anytime you want. If you can get through, that is. The only other time people call me is to let me know what time practice is."

"Hey, Mike. I know you were talking about getting a job. Is that what you're going to do?" I asked him.

"Naw, Grandma said for me to concentrate on school and just finish that first. I get a check every month since my mother died. Man, without her, my life would have been a lot worse, I know it. Wow, it's getting late Liz, you better head back before it gets dark."

I said goodbye to him and headed home. As I got to the corner of the block, I had to pass Charles' dad. Just as I was going past him, he slammed a wine bottle on the side of the apartment building and it shattered. I looked down and grabbed the wine bottle's neck, ready for him just in case he tried anything!

He saw that I had the glass in my hand. I wanted him to know that I was ready for his mess just in case he decided to try anything on me again. I ran upstairs when I got home.

Mama asked, "Liz, did you walk Mike home?"

"Yeah Mama, I did."

"Girl, what is wrong with you? You don't walk out there by yourself! Next time take one of your sisters or your brother, okay? Just not Lynne."

"Okay, Ma."

Lynne yelled out, "That's right, not me. I don't ask you to walk with my friends and I'm not walking with yours!"

"Lynne, that's fine with me!" I yelled back.

In my bedroom, I looked at the mess on my bed. Lynne walked in. I yelled at her, "Girl, why do you always have to put your stupid papers on my bed?"

"Girl, just shut up, I'll clean it up, give me a minute."

She was getting on my last nerve! We went to bed angry at each other again. I thought that Lynne was jealous of me and Mike. She turned on the light and asked me if Mike and I were going together.

I replied, "Girl, I don't know. You don't need to ask me nothing about what me and Mike are doing!"

She said, "Okay, crazy girl, Mike's little fool!"

I was getting mad. "Well, look at you and Ricky, you're a fool for him! Ricky's little nasty girl!"

"Whatever!"

"Liz, Mike is graduating this spring."

"Lynne, I know that."

"Is he taking you to his prom?" Lynne asked.

"I really don't know."

"Well, you need to ask him so you'll know, so you can get your prom dress."

"I might have to work that day, so I don't know if will go at all," I said.

"Girl, that's just an excuse not to go, unless he just doesn't ask you!"

I replied, "Well, I'm not even worried about that stupid prom."

"Liz. Don't even tell me that lie."

"Lynne, just cut the light out and go to sleep please."

"Liz, you know I'm telling you the truth!"

"Lynne, like I said, were just friends!"

73

"Well, you be a little fool, and let somebody else go to the prom with him, and see how you feel!"

"Lynne, I'm not going to tell you whether I do or if I don't go to the prom with him!"

"Stupid, I'm gonna see you if you do, so I'll know if you do go with him!"

"That's just what you'll be doing too, watching!"

"Liz, I'm not going to go around telling everybody! You really should ask him if he's going to take you soon."

"Why?" I asked.

"So you won't get your feelings hurt and you can laugh and have a good time."

I sighed and said, "Okay, I will. Now, turn the light out and go to sleep!"

Next morning, Monday, everyone was moving around me. Ms. Terry's kids were my biggest problem. All of the yelling and crying was making me sick, especially first thing in the morning. As I left the apartment, I ran into Mike. "Liz, I told you I was going to come pick you up this morning."

"I know, but, I just needed to get out of that apartment. It's driving me crazy. I work today, but, I'm still tired from the weekend."

"Yeah, I know what you mean. Me too." We stood there talking so long that before we realized it, we had missed the bus for school.

"Girl, see what you did! Now, we've missed the bus."

I said "Well, we can walk or catch a cab."

"Walk, girl? That's a long way. We can call for a cab, but, then again this is New York and I don't think were going to catch a cab in Harlem." As we were discussing it, I heard a honk. I looked over and saw Mr. Paul.

"Mr. Paul, can we get a ride with you?"

"Come on." Mr. Paul continued, "Usually, I don't let other guys in my car but you're alright."

"Thanks," Mike said.

"I know what school you go to" Mr. Paul said, "but I'm gonna let you off two blocks from it. That's a bad school, and I need my car and my life!" He pulled up to the curb and we got out. Mike gave him three dollars and he said, "Thanks, see y'all later."

We arrived at school early, so I got up the nerve up to ask Mike about the prom. "Mike, who are you taking to the prom?"

"You, Liz."

"Oh, me?"

"Yeah, aren't you my girl?"

"Oh, I didn't know. So, when is the prom?"

"Later in June. Graduation is the first of June."

I looked at him. "Well, we need to get things together. I need to look for a prom dress. I'll look at the store where I work this evening. They have a lot of pretty dresses to choose from. I will get thirty percent off of the dress too. I can't wait to see what Mama says about my dress."

"Okay, Liz, that sounds good."

Later on that day at work, as I was tagging all of the clothes, I was still thinking about what Mike said about me being his girl.

"Hi, Elizabeth." I quickly turned around.

"Hi Steven," I said. We began to put all of the clothes on the rack. Meanwhile Mrs. Elaine, the salesperson, came in. "Hi everybody. What are you all doing this weekend?"

"Nothing I know of." I said.

"James is having a party this weekend," she said.

"Who's James?"

"The guy that cleans up in the evening."

"Oh no, I can't go," I said. "I have to work this Saturday."

"No, it's next Saturday. Some of us here are going."

"No, I still don't think I'll be able to go," I insisted.

Steven came up. "I'll take you and I'll pick you up, okay?"

"No Steven! Thanks, but I'm not going."

"Okay, but you can't tell me that I didn't try!"

Elaine said, "Boy, you have to watch that fool. But, he is nice." The rest of the afternoon, I concentrated on my job. It was time to go before I realized it. I said goodbye to everybody, got my jacket, and waited for my bus in front of the store. On the bus ride, all of my thoughts were about the prom. As soon as I got home, I asked Mama what she thought about it.

"Well Liz, I don't have any money for a dress."

Lynne chimed in, "So Liz, you asked Mike about the prom?"

"So what, Lynne? That's none of your business anyway."

"That's right Liz, you'll see."

Mama said, "Liz, you need to get a new hairdo for the prom too. I think it would look nice."

"Oh, I forgot to tell you! Guess who's taking Sissy to the prom? Gary's brother, Dave. Man, that is one nasty girl. I know one thing, she better look out and watch her back cause I don't see nothing but trouble coming from her, and I don't want no mess that night. I'm just excited that I'm going to the prom."

"Liz," Mama said, "Go to the drug store and get a magazine so we can see the latest dresses and hairstyles."

"I will pick it up on my way home tomorrow," I said.

Mama continued, "When I get home, we can pick out a nice dress and a hairstyle that you would like."

Lynne surprised me. "Liz, I'll get it if Ms. Terry pays me today."

We talked all night about my perfect day. I went to sleep feeling good.

Chapter 9

The Argument Starts

I got up the next morning feeling great because I knew I was going to the prom. As Lynne and I were going out of the door, I said "Lynne, don't forget what we talked about yesterday. I don't work on Saturday and I get paid tonight.

Mama came in and said, "Liz, don't get crazy now. This will only be two paychecks that you got. You still need to save for work and school. You and Lynne both. You only work part-time."

"But Mama, you DID say I could buy a dress, right? Besides, I'm going to put it on layaway." Lynne and I were still talking as we were going down the steps. Even though she gets on my nerves a lot, I feel glad we are sisters.

During second period class, Mrs. Jones paged me. "Oh Mrs. Jones, I forgot to bring you my job slip."

"Liz, don't worry about that right now, your sister is sick. She's in the back."

I slowly walked to the back room. "Lynne, what wrong with you?"

"I don't know, I just got sick and started vomiting and I have a horrible headache."

Mrs. Jones said, "I'm going to run you to the hospital. If I call an ambulance, it won't get here before school gets out." I started to get in her car with Lynne but Mrs. Jones told me to stay there and to contact my mother and tell her to meet her at the hospital.

Mama talked to the doctor for a few minutes, then turned to Lynne and asked her who the father was. Lynne looked sad.

Mama yelled at her, "Tell me who it is. Tell me, Lynne, who is going to take care of this baby? First Roland with his baby, and now you too. A bum mother, and probably a drug selling father! So what? Do you think him selling drugs will support this baby?"

She tried to hold it in as long as she could but I could see the tears starting to roll down her face. I felt sorry for her. I rubbed her back, hoping that would make her feel better, but she started to sob. The doctor came in, told us about a doctor she should see, and said she could go home. I wanted to help her with her clothes but I was too nervous to ask about the father of the baby.

I knew deep in my heart that she probably didn't know either, but she didn't want to admit it. Right now, she was sad and I knew she needed me, so I just kept quiet. I started talking to her in a soft voice. I helped her with her clothes while Mama left to go upstairs to see Becky. The doctor kept telling us she could go home but when Mama went to pick her up, they always changed their minds. I was hoping they didn't this time. Mama's mind wasn't on Roland or Lynne at the time, I was sure.

We were waiting for Mama in the hospital emergency room. Lynne was still hurt over what Mama said to her. Lynne started saying over and over that it was Ricky's baby, that it wasn't Gary's baby. "Me and Gary broke up four months ago," she said.

"Lynne, you're just in eleventh grade. What are you going to do for your last year?" Lynn just stared at Mama.

Mama finally came back. "Call a cab," she said. The weight of all of her problems showed on her face. She had so many that I knew she didn't need any new ones, especially something this big. I knew she was now trying to figure out how to cope with this one.

When we got home, Ms. Terry had the kids at her place. They ran over to us. "What happened?" everyone asked at once.

I tried to explain. "Well, Lynne was sick, and we had to take her to the hospital and Mama picked us up there. That's why Mama didn't pick you up."

"Is Becky coming home tomorrow?"

"Yes," I said.

Mama said, "We have to get this house in order for her and I have to arrange a cab to pick her up."

John went to Lynne. "What's wrong with you, Lynne? Why were you sick?"

"Just leave me alone, and don't talk to me!"

Mama yelled out, "Girl, this apartment may be small, but it's still my house Lynne!" Lynne didn't answer her back.

Ms. Terry called again. "So Tracy, what's wrong with Lynne? Is she okay?"

"No, she's going to have a baby!"

"A BABY? Who's the father?"

"Who knows? I know one thing girl. I'm not going to raise this baby too. I have too many children of my own to be raising someone else's!"

"Girl, you're right! That is a big problem! Only thing is, you can't separate the baby and its mother." Ms. Terry said.

"Girl," my mother continued, "We never have enough money for rent or electric or any of the other bills as it is. Liz wants to go to the prom with Mike, so that means a dress and other things. Then we still have to live."

I listened to their conversation but I didn't respond. *So, I guess after work, I'll look for a new dress,* I thought. */ think I will also give her some money to pay a bill or something.* I went to bed with a pain in my heart, knowing that I was going to have to give some of my prom money to Mama for a bill. *I still want to get my prom dress and be with Mike though,* I thought. I went to sleep facing the wall. I knew tomorrow would be another day with its own problems.

The next day, I hurried and got ready for work and left. Walking down the hallway, I noticed that it looked like someone had been in a fight in Charles' apartment. I ignored it and kept walking. Someone yelled out, "Liz, where are you going?"

I turned around. "Charles, what happened?"

"My sister and father were fighting. He was drunk and cursing at me and he put us out of his stupid stinky apartment. That's okay, because this apartment was nasty and smelly anyway. At least I got somewhere else to live. My father never paid the bills on time or bought food anyway. I'm going to live with my aunt up the street. Wait, this is Saturday. You never used to work on a Saturday. What happened?"

"That's right, but I need the money. I need to get my stuff for the prom. I'm going with Mike."

"Have you heard from him this week?" he asked.

"No," I said, "But, I have to run. I have to go to work. I'll talk to him this week and I'll tell him you said hi."

"Okay, thanks," Charles said.

Fooling around with Charles caused me to miss the early bus. Suddenly I spotted Mike's grandmother. She honked her horn and asked if I needed a ride.

"Yes, thank you. I'm going downtown to work." I jumped in quickly, glad to get a ride. Otherwise, I would have been late. "Thank you so much, I really appreciate this."

"My grandson, I think, has found a nice young lady who likes to work."

"I like to work, but I'm trying to help my mother out with the rent."

"Liz, let me ask you. Are you going to college?"

"Yes, I would like to but I'm not sure if I'm going to make it or not."

"Keep trying to get student loans or scholarships. If they look at where you live now, they can see that you need a student loan or scholarship."

"But, I'm just in eleventh grade."

"You need to try now Liz, by the time you're in twelfth grade, you should have something. Who's your counselor now?"

"Mrs. Jones," I replied.

"She's a nice person. She will gladly help you fill out the applications you need and she will work with you to help you anyway she can. That's what she is there for."

"I know, and that sounds good, but I don't know when to go see about it. We have so many problems in the house right now."

"Well, we all have problems, but if you have a goal, then you can do it. It's not going to come to you. You have to go after it yourself. Believe me! I'm right. Look at Mike. He's been going after his goal of being a professional basketball player ever since he was a little boy. Every time a recreational center opened up, he was there to play ball. You need to do the same thing. Fight for your goals in life. Being black doesn't mean that you can't get something for yourself or be successful in life. Mike can help you now too. Don't forget that."

We pulled up to the store where I worked. I got out and thanked her for her pep talk. I really needed it. I knew Mike and his grandmother would be talking about this conversation. I felt sad as I started in to work.

The first person I saw was Steve. "Hey, Liz. What's wrong? It's Saturday, why are you down?" I felt deep down I didn't want to be here.

"I'm okay, Steve," I said.

"Who was that woman who dropped you off today?"

"That was my friend's grandmother," I explained.

"Oh, that was nice of her," Steve said and started laughing. "I'm serious Liz, thought. Can I have your number?"

"No, not my number Steve. I don't like you that way."

"Oh, okay. Thanks for hurting my feelings like that," Steve said.

"Boy, don't put those stupid move on me like that."

"Okay, Liz, treat me like that!"

"Steve, I keep telling you, I like another boy in my school."

"So, what school is that?"

"Harlem Senior High, and he's a senior this year and I'm going to the prom with him next month."

"Excuse me Miss Liz, so already you're getting married to him!"

"No, but I do want to be his girlfriend."

As we were talking, Janice came in. "Hey Liz."

"Hey Janice." She heard everything.

"Girl, don't pay him any attention and kiss that fool goodbye. He's already got a girlfriend, you know. Her name is Joyce. She lives around the corner from me. So, don't pay him any mind."

"Thanks. I like this boy named Mike. He goes to my school, and he's a senior, and we're going to the prom next month."

"Hey, did you find your gown yet?"

"No," I said.

"Do you know what color and type of style you want?"

"No, not yet."

"Go look in the back. You might find something nice. What size do you wear?"

"A size eight."

"I think you might get in a size six. We can try some on when we come to work on Monday. So, you get here at 3:30 and we'll start looking."

"Okay, Janice, that sounds good," I said.

"Don't forget, you have to be here an hour before you go to work. Then we'll see what we can do with your hair. We can look in some magazines and circle the styles you like."

"Okay, Janice, that sounds good. Thanks for helping me."

"You still didn't tell me what color you wanted."

"Janice, it doesn't matter. Any color will do. As long as you help me dress and tell me the truth about how those gowns look on me."

"Well, that's what I'm going to do. That's what friends do. And, I hope that we can be good friends too. We're going to make you into a beautiful lady! I hope you find your dress soon, so that will be out of the way."

"Me too. I hope Mike thinks I look pretty that day."

"Oh, you must be in love," she said with a smile.

"No, I like him and I have a lot of respect for him, too."

"How do his parents feel about you?"

"Well, he lives with his grandmother down the street from me."

"Oh, so you can keep an eye on all of his girls, huh?"

"No, I don't see his girls and I hope I never meet them. I don't think there is anyone else besides me."

"Girl, you don't live in the real world. Nobody can be true or be in love forever. There will be problems, you will see."

I didn't want to respond to that. "Well, Janice, I have to start my shift now. I'll see you on Monday, okay? And thanks for everything." As we were talking, Steve came back over.

"Steve, you need to stop telling these lies to Liz and tell her the truth about yourself! We know you have a girlfriend already."

"We're just friends, okay? You don't know anything about me!"

"Wait, we've been working together in this department for thirteen months and three days so, I don't know you?" Steve starting laughing. Yeah, you know OF me, that's all."

"Boy, I'm not trying to know you at all. Stop playing games. Keep in your mind you lied about yourself and your relationship with your new girlfriend." Steve smirked. I shook my head and headed downstairs.

"Man, that stupid boy is a player! You don't pay him any mind. You don't need that kind of liar in you life. Plus, he's crazy anyway," Janice said.

"Don't worry about it, I came here to work, not look for a man, especially not Steve."

Steve shook his head. "Y'all jumping all over me!" He was still shaking his head on the way downstairs to get James.

"Like I said, don't pay any attention to him, James is nothing but a liar too," Janice said. "He's a two-lie man. He's never been true to his first wife, and can't really talk about that. He also has four kids and never pays child support. Girl, one day the police came over for him because he didn't pay his back child support. So again, he really can't talk and back you up. He's just a sick old man who acts crazy 'cause he's a bum. Don't talk to James either."

Then she started laughing. "These people here are a sick and foolish group. Look at Jackie. She's a drunk, her sister Lisa is a tramp. Girl, who knows what happened to Jackie."

"I gotta go back to my shift, I'm late."

Steve said, "Y'all all are crazy," and left, and James didn't say anything, period. As I was walking to my department, I was still laughing at everything Janice said. Both of those guys are dogs. I knew that. I was glad that someone was able to make me laugh and feel good with all of the problems I was having at home.

I started thinking about Lisa. I wondered what my brother saw in her. Everyone knew she was trashy and had problems. A trashy baby's mama! That somehow sounded funny to me. Mrs. Joan, the old lady, helped me put tags on the clothes.

Mrs. Joan started saying, "Girl, if you live long enough, you will see a lot of bad things happening, especially in Harlem. They live like animals here, and they act like one too. When I was young, I used to live in Harlem with my kids. They would get in fights everyday. I had to go to work while my kids were in school making trouble. I know how it is living around there. So when you go home, say a prayer that you can get there safely."

"Thanks a lot for caring about me, Mrs. Joan."

"Well, you're a nice young lady and I like you." We talked until our shift was up and it was time to go home.

"What bus do you get?" she asked me.

"I get the number eight bus home," I said.

"Honey, first before you go, can you help me with this rack and put it in the corner for Monday?"

"No problem, Mrs. Joan. I can help you clean up and put stuff away, and then we can go.

Chapter 10

Mike and Charles' Senior Year

I had a lot to think about. There was Mike, who I liked very much. I was also thinking about what Mama said and thinking about how sad Lynne was. It was a sad weekend for all of us. Lynne is now pregnant and it is making all of us sad and sick to think about it. I think about her bringing a baby into this world, in Harlem, in this little apartment. I think about her drug-selling boyfriend. I wonder if he is the baby's father anyway. I get ready for school but my thoughts are on Lynne and her problem.

Aw, man, I forgot! This is Mike and Charles' last week in school. I quickly got ready and headed for school. Down the hall, I saw Charles. "Hey, did you pass?" I asked him.

"No, I have to go to summer school for math and, get this, I have to pay to go! $40! This is Harlem. Nobody has any money to pay for any summer school!"

"If someone pays the $40 for you, would you go? You really need to graduate. You'll regret it for the rest of your life. All for just $40!" I said.

"Well, I guess so, Liz."

"Well, let me see what I can do. But first, I have to get my dress for the prom."

"Okay, Liz, thanks."

I kept thinking about the irony. This is Charles' last year here, and he needs someone to help him out. I guess the least I can do is give him $40 to contribute to his future. Maybe he can get a good job and just maybe get out of this rat stinky Harlem apartment building. I thought, *maybe Charles is an okay guy.*

I'm still deep in thought, and changing classes, when I hear someone calling my name. "Liz, Liz!"

"Hey Mike. Did you pass?" I asked.

"Yep, I did. I also have good news. I've been invited to go to a summer basketball league. The best and brightest basketball students in the New York are."

"That's great Mike!"

"Well, you don't look too happy about it."

"Well, I keep thinking about Charles. He really needs our help. He needs $40 for summer school so that he can graduate."

"Well, Liz, I have $22 on me now."

"I have $18 that I can give him when I get paid today too," I add.

"Hey, did you get your dress yet?"

"No, but I go tonight before I go to work to pick one out at the store where I work.

"Don't forget, you're supposed to help me with this prom," he reminded me.

"I didn't forget, it's just that the prom is only one night, and Charles might not graduate. That will affect his whole future."

"I know Liz, I know. Well, gotta go, I have to talk to my English teacher about my grade. I'll talk to you soon, okay?"

"Okay," he said, and off he went, leaving me looking like a lost little puppy. I kept walking, shaking my head.

All of a sudden, I heard a voice. "Liz! Are you sick?" It was Sheron.

"No, I just got finished talking to Mike."

"Well, where is he?"

"He just went up the hall to talk to his English teacher."

Inside I knew she was thinking that I was crazy, but I didn't care. I walked with her to our next class. I sat quietly in my seat, hoping that no one would ask me any question today or talk to me.

My first period class set the tone for my whole day. The bell finally rang and I headed down the hall. Sheron and Rondell came up behind me and started giggling. I was hoping that they didn't laugh at me when I was with Mike. I tried to ignore them as I passed them. I ran out the door so I could catch the bus.

As I was waiting on the bus, I saw Mike talking to a girl. They were laughing so loud, it seemed like they were doing it on purpose. I tried to ignore them. It was just one of those days. I caught the bus going downtown and Sheron and Rondell got on with me.

"Hey Liz, are you and Mike going together?" Sheron asked.

"No, we are just friends."

Rondell said, "Hey, that girl that you saw with Mike was my cousin Leah. She's a good friend of his, you know." I tried to ignore her, but she continued. "He talks to her everyday too. Hey, how did you get into this picture, you being Mike's friend and all?" I tried to move over, but she just kept moving with me. I guess she was trying to prove a point.

"Girl, you just better not get any ideas about you and Mike being together. You just got to Harlem school this year. You really don't know about his history and about some friendships around here. Mike might make you his nasty girl, like Sissy's friend. I don't know what Mike told you, but he used to mess with Leah. Charles is your friend, ask him about Sissy's friend Wendy, and what really happened to their friendship. There's a reason why Wendy don't like you."

By this time, I had really gotten tired of hearing her mouth. I jumped up. "Well, I'll just go to the horse's mouth and ask Mike himself and we'll see about this."

Sheron stepped in. "Liz, don't get mad. We're just telling you about this so you won't get hurt. Everybody's saying that you both are a couple and that you two go together. We also know you two are going to the prom together. Everyone's thinking, well, why didn't he take Leah or even Wendy? We're only telling you what everyone's saying behind your back. Especially since this will be Leah's prom too. We're not trying to start trouble with you or anything either. We're just telling you what's going on in Mike's life right now. He's known to be a guy that doesn't stay faithful to his girlfriends. You know us girls need to stick together, so these guys don't take advantage of us, and make a fool out of us too.

"Well, I have a job to go to, so I better not be late." I told them, as I stomped off of the bus feeling angry and hurt. I started thinking about it. *Man, I'm spending all of this money, and getting ready for this prom, just for him to make me his nasty girl!* I walked slowly into the back of the department, still angry and hurt.

Ms. Elaine saw me first. "Liz, here are some of the gowns you wanted to see. The salesgirl left them out for you."

I began to try them on one by one. I tried on a nice red and white gown. Steve came by and saw me in it. "Wow, that gown looks great on you."

"Okay Steve, be for real. Tell me the truth about these stupid gowns. Do they really look all that nice on me?"

"Girl, I'm real all the time, especially how somebody looks. I like ladies looking like ladies, and you look like a lady. You really look nice in that. All you need now is a corsage to go on your arm and the look is complete."

"Thanks Steve. I really do like this red and white gown the best." I looked in the floor length mirror at myself. I liked what I saw. I also liked how it made me feel. I pranced around the room, prancing, prancing and twirling.

Steve yelled, "Girl, you think you're a model with that gown on, don't you?" We looked at each other and laughed.

Just then, the door suddenly burst open. My supervisor Mrs. Keller, said, "Excuse me, do the both of you still work here?"

"Oh, oh, yes, Mrs. Keller."

She continued. "Steve, hurry up in the back and put the racks on the floor so the sales girls can put their clothes in their departments."

I said, "Ms. Keller, I will be paying for this gown today after work."

"Right now you are supposed to be working and you're not off yet. So please put all of these gowns back and tag them. Other young girls need to be a model for a day too."

I fumed, *Ohh, she really gets under my skin!* I hurried to put my regular clothes back on, grabbed the other gowns and started tagging them. The price of the dress that I wanted was so high, I hoped I got a good discount to help me pay for it. I continued my work for Ms. Mean Lady.

Steve passed by, leaned over and whispered to me, "I hope she doesn't write us up!" I didn't say anything.

The afternoon came and I finally got paid. I opened the envelope and looked inside. "This is it?" I said disappointingly.

My supervisor overheard me. "Child, don't forget. You only work part time."

"But, I worked overtime on Saturday!"

"You'll get that on next week's paycheck. If you want more money, we are open on Sunday's too."

"No thanks. Thank you anyway," I said. I slowly started down the hall toward the formal gowns department to pay for my prom dress.

I started thinking to myself, *Man, its two weeks before the prom and I told Mike I would help him pay for some things for the prom. I also told Charles that I would help him with summer school. What am I going to do? I better call my supervisor and tell her that I will work Saturday, AND Sunday.*

Unfortunately, I was going to have to forget about Mama's bill that I said I would try to help her with. I was still lost in thought as I left work for the day and got on the bus. My mind was a million miles away. As we approached my apartment I noticed a rather large crowd in front of it. As soon as I got off, Sharon and John plowed into me.

"Liz! Roland just got shot and he's dead!"

"NO, this can't be!" I screamed. It felt like I was dreaming but my eyes were open. As I got closer, I saw Lisa and Sissy arguing. Ricky, Lament and Randy were also there cursing at Charles, and hitting him. There was blood all over the place!

I tried to push my way through the crowd with Sharon and John beside me. As I was coming into the building, I heard somebody screaming "MY SON, MY SON!" I knew right away that it was Mama! Upstairs I saw Ms. Terry and her boyfriend taking Mama into the apartment. The crowd started following.

Mr. Roy yelled, "If you don't get away from this apartment and this woman, I am going to shoot all of you!"

I picked up a bottle from the ground and threw it at them. "Leave us alone." All of a sudden, I heard police sirens. I didn't even stop to think of how I felt. All I wanted to do was comfort Mama and the rest of the kids. Even though I was angry, the tears started rolling slowly down my face. I didn't want anybody to see me cry, though. When the police came, the crowd began leaving. Suddenly, Lisa popped Sissy right in her mouth!

"Do you two ladies want to spend the next few nights in jail?" the police officer asked.

"No officer," Lisa said. "My two children are upstairs."

"Miss, I think you need to be with your children right now." She agreed and went upstairs. Lisa pushed Sissy again, and then Sissy pushed Lynne in the chest as they were going up the stairs.

"STOP IT!" I yelled. I couldn't take all of this fighting. I went back downstairs to see how Charles was doing. He was cut pretty badly and bleeding. Someone was getting ready to take him to the hospital. "Charles, I'll be coming to the hospital to see how you're doing, okay?"

He looked at me but did not say anything. I knew he heard me though and understood. As I headed upstairs to the apartment, still in shock, I heard Sissy continue to curse at Lisa. I couldn't believe that they were still at it!

"Come in here, and sit down, BOTH OF YOU!" Mama said. They looked at her in surprise, but listened and sat down. Later I found out what really happened.

Roland was outside hanging out with his friends on the stoop when some guy started shooting at him. One of the bullets hit him in the stomach. Roland tried to get up but instead, he fell over on the stoop without making a sound. Lament ran over, pulled Roland towards him and yelled, *"SOMEBODY CALL AN AMBULANCE!"*

The tears started to roll down his face. "Roland! Please don't die! Talk to me man! Please talk to me, PLEASE!" He pleaded. Roland's head was in Lament's lap. Blood was running out of his head onto Lament's hands and onto the ground. Lament kept rocking back and forward. "Please don't die! Talk to me! Can you hear me? Please, you're my best friend, and my main man!"

Finally, the police and the ambulance showed up. "Is that Roland?" Lisa yelled as she was running up the street.

"Yes, Lisa, it is," Lament responded.

She looked at Roland in Lament's arms, and started crying. "Where is Randy and Ricky at?"

"They ran up the street to their house to get their pieces."

"This trouble ain't over yet! Where is your brother Anthony?" she asked.

"I don't know."

"Do you think that he had something to do with all of this?"

"Yeah, I think he had plenty to do with this."

"Boy, you just better call that funeral home, 'cause that's just where your brother is going to be at if Roland dies!" Lisa said.

"Girl, you better stay away from me, 'cause I don't know what I might do to you or your family," Lament said. He was talking crazy because he was so upset.

Lisa continued between her tears, "I love Roland and I have two kids from him. Why would you try to kill me and Roland's kids, if he is your best friend! He is dying right in front of you!"

The ambulance drove away with Roland. Lament said, "Lisa, this isn't about you or Roland. It's about what happened, how it happened and who started it." When he got up, he was covered with blood. I don't know if he realized it. He was still in shock. "I have to get to the hospital. Lisa. You can come with me."

"Okay," Lisa said.

By the time I got home, everyone had already returned from the hospital. From what I heard, Roland was dead when he got there. A *fatal wound to the head* is how the doctors put it. Whoever did this knew exactly what they were doing.

As Sissy, Lisa, Lynne and I were entering the building, Sissy mumbled under her breath, "That's what the stupid boy deserved!" I couldn't believe Sissy would say something like that to us. Lynne heard her and started punching her. The police came in and broke it up. I couldn't believe we were actually friends at one time. I hated her now for saying that! I held my tears back and concentrated on helping my family out with their pain, especially my mother.

"Did anyone call Aunt Rose yet?" my Mother yelled. "What about Uncle Jerry, and my youngest sister Helen, and James? I don't know where Roland's father, James, is now. Maybe he's still in jail. I'll just have to see. Liz, look in my pocketbook. It's in the closet where the hats are."

"Mama, we don't know where Uncle Jerry and Aunt Helen's telephone number's are."

"Look in the same bag, and you should see my personal telephone book in there, near the insurance policy. Lynne, call Ricky, Lament, Randy, Shawn and Calvin. I want this mess over with! I want this problem to rest in peace, just like Roland is. They are pals, and I want them to be pals when they bury my son."

I couldn't believe it but my mother was not crying. It was like she was on autopilot. "I want to know the truth about what happened today," she said.

As she was talking, Mike knocked on the door. I was so happy to see him, I didn't know what to do. I ran over to him, hugged him and started crying.

"Liz, I heard about what happened. I'm so sorry! I ran over as soon as I heard because I wanted to see if there was anything I could do for your family."

"Thank you so much," I said between tears. "I appreciate it, and we all do."

"Yes we do, Mike!" my Mother said.

Becky, who had finally come home from the hospital a few days earlier, got up from her chair and attempted to talk to Mike but she was talking so slowly that no one could understand what she was saying. When the tears started rolling down her face though, we knew just how she felt.

Now that Mike was here, I felt a little better. Lisa went in the back to clean up her two kids. Now, I guessed that now that they didn't have a father, we were going to have to help her and the kids out as much as we could. *Boy, as if this house wasn't crowed enough already!* I thought. Mama said to Lynne, "Go see if we have any clothes to fit Lisa." I suddenly threw the can of beer. There was beer still in the can and it sprayed all over everybody.

Mama came in again, "Liz, you and Mike go down to the supermarket and get some baby food and some food for us to eat."

"Mama, do we have the money for that?" I asked.

"Just use your pay that you got today." I was upset because I knew I would only have a little left after getting the gown and accessories.

As we walked out of the apartment, Lynne said to Ricky, "Okay, that's fine but, my Mother wants to speak to you." Ricky looked scared.

"Does she want to talk to me about the baby?"

"No, she already knows about that."

"Oh, okay." He looked relieved.

Lament was coming up the steps. "Here's some money for some food if you need it."

"Thanks, that's just where we were going. We definitely need it. We're going to need a lot of help."

"I'll try to do whatever I can for you and your family," Lament said.

"Thanks. Mama wants to try to keep all of us together, especially the little ones. That's important to her," I replied.

Lament continued, "I saw Lynne crying when she went into the house. Is she still mad at Sissy?"

"No, she's not, but you know why she's still crying. She and Lisa are in the bedroom crying their eyes out, I'm sure."

"Are you mad with Lisa?" Ricky asked.

"No, why would we be mad with her? She didn't do anything. Lisa's a good girl. She and Roland had a good relationship. Lisa loved him and he was crazy about her and those kids, especially his son. It tears me up to know that those two kids don't have a father now."

"I'm hoping that Lynne has a boy too."

"Let me tell you something, if you don't get your life together quick, that baby won't have a father either!"

"Please don't talk like that about my baby."

Mike chimed in. "Man, I don't know why Roland got shot, but she's right. If you don't get yourself together, then you can kiss your life goodbye!"

"Man, I know what you are saying but I'm okay. I don't have time for this right now. I'll talk to you both later."

Mike looked angry.

"Mike, don't worry about him. That boy don't want to prepare for his future," I said.

"Liz, you know what he's into. Selling drugs, getting high, and messing with girls all day. They both don't have a future with the way things are going now." He just started shaking his head.

I started thinking about that girl Sheron and what she said about Mike but I just kept quiet. After a while, my emotions started to get the best of me and I started crying on his arm.

"Liz, I am so sorry that you have to go through this!" Mike said.

The tears started rolling down my cheeks and I couldn't stop them this time. Maybe that's what I needed. "Lisa doesn't have her baby's father either!" Suddenly, I said something I would always regret. "Mike, are you planning on getting married? Or should I ask what age are you looking to get married?"

"Liz, don't talk about that right now. You're upset right now. What about the prom? Did you get what you needed yet?"

"Yes, I did, I just have to get it off of layaway."

"You're still working there, right?"

"Yeah, and the gown came from there. It's red and white with white roses in front of the dress."

"Oh good. I'm glad you finally picked one you liked." We finally reached the store with my broken down cart. Mike started laughing at the sound it was making. "Mike, you can tell we're poor just by the sound and condition of this cart!"

"Yeah, you're right, so you really need to get another one at your store where you work. See if they have a good one. It's worth the money to get it." We started laughing. We finally got up the stairs with the cart full of food before it finally broke from all of the weight.

Mama said the police called and that they found the person that killed Roland. The funeral home was going to pick up Roland's body at the hospital and we needed to get one of his suits to them. "What would be nice for him to wear?" Mama asked.

Lynne said, "Mama, can me and Lisa pick out a suit for him?"

"Yeah, that would be fine. I'm going to the funeral home to make the arrangements."

"Who's going with you, Mama? You can't go by yourself." I said.

"Mrs. Terry is. Liz. Would you and Mike like to go with me also?"

"No, Mama, I know my stomach wouldn't be able to take that"

"Okay, that's fine honey. Ms. Terry and her boyfriend will be with me, so, I'll be okay. Mike, are you hungry?"

"No, not really, mam."

"Boy, you better tell Liz to make you a sandwich. I know you'll be hungry soon. Liz, get my sweater out of the closet over there, please."

Lynne came out of the room. "Here Mama, here's a suit that Roland can use."

Mama started crying again. "Let's go, Tracy."

She turned to me and said, "Tell Lisa not to forget to feed the baby" She started to cry again. I went in the kitchen to make Mike a sandwich. I stared at Lisa. She seemed like a really nice girl, I thought, but she has two children now and both look like their father. I know that is going to be hard on her.

We were all in the kitchen eating quietly when Mama came back from the funeral home. "The viewing for Roland will be on Monday and the funeral will be on Wednesday at 11 o'clock," she informed us. The phone wouldn't stop ringing and people from Mama's job stopped by. They wanted to see if they could help her. They also left us money and cards.

Mrs. Terry took the cards and gave them to me. She whispered in my ear, "Keep this money close to you at all times. You need to pay the rent, and you all have to live too."

"Okay." I said.

Mike suddenly gave me a funny look. "Liz, are we still going to the prom?"

Mama said, "Liz, Roland is already dead. No need to miss out on something like this. He wouldn't want that. You know that. You're still going."

Mike said thank you to Mama, gave me a big hug, and went home. I went to bed.

The next day, I got up, called my supervisor and told her that I just lost my brother so I wouldn't be coming in to work today. She asked me when I thought I would be back. I told her probably next Friday, and she said okay. She also told me that Mr. James just lost his son too, so that was two people that were out for the week. I told her to tell him how sorry I was and I would see him soon. She said she would tell him, and that she was sorry for my loss. I told her thank you, and hung up.

Then I started cleaning up Becky's mess. Becky was moving slowly and when she talks now it is hard to understand her. It hurts me to see her like this. She was such an active kid, I thought. Because Becky was now disabled, Mama was now getting a check from the government every month to help with her care. She was also going to a special school. The bus came to pick her up every morning.

"Mama, is she going to school today?" I asked.

"Yeah, let her go. She'll just get in our way today if she stays."

I got Becky dressed then I fixed Mama some breakfast, hoping she would eat it. Lynne was in the other room with Lisa and the kids. "Lisa, are you going home?"

"No, if you don't mind, I'll stay here until the funeral."

"Okay, that's fine." I said. Lynne put Lisa and the children in Becky's room and brought Becky in my room with me and Lynne.

"Mama, this is too crowded," I protested.

"The funeral is in one more day, so all of us can be crowded for one day. I also want all of you to get your clothes together for tomorrow. I want our minds on Roland and not on little things like what were going to wear. Lisa, why don't you also run home and get yours and the kids' clothes for tomorrow."

When Mama saw their dirty clothes, she told Lynne and me to make sure we washed them good and to put hang in the bathroom so they would dry faster.

"Miss Tracy, my kids don't have any presentable shoes to wear for tomorrow!" Lisa said, and started to cry again.

"Don't cry Lisa, we'll work it out. We're family, so were going to make sure you and my grandkids are taken care of. Liz, you and Lisa take the kids and run downtown to the store where you work and get them a nice pair of cheap shoes. Here's a little money. We have to have Roland's kids looking good for their daddy's funeral."

As we were getting in the cab, Miss Elaine drove by and said, "Hi Liz. I heard about your brother. I'm so sorry for your loss. If there's anything you want me to do, just ask. Don't be afraid to ask okay?"

"Okay, Miss Elaine," I said.

"Is that your sister?" she asked, glancing over at Lisa.

"No, she was my brother's girlfriend."

"Oh, I see. Nice to meet you child."

On the way downtown, Lisa began bugging me for a new dress too. "No, we better keep looking for your children's shoes. We don't have enough for a dress too. We just need to stick to the plan, okay?" I said. "Lisa, we'll make sure you look real nice for tomorrow, okay?"

We found the kids shoes and got another cab home. As we were getting out, we ran into Shawn. "Hey Liz. Hi Lisa. What time is Roland's funeral again?"

"It's 11 o'clock tomorrow."

"Oh, thanks, I forgot. Lynne told Ricky, and Ricky told me. But I forgot. Me and my family will be by your apartment later on, okay?"

Lisa looked scared. I guessed she was still scared of Ricky, afraid that they were going to hurt her family or her brother.

"Lisa, you don't have anything to worry about. My mother is going to talk to all of them and try to squash this whole thing once and for all. Let's just go home."

"Okay Liz. I trust you and your mother. I hope you are right about this whole thing 'cause I know somebody is going to try to get them back, whoever did this! I'm just glad she was able to get my kids some shoes for tomorrow. That meant a lot," Lisa said.

"Sure, that's what grandmothers are for," I said.

After we got back upstairs, she told Lynne what Shawn said. "I'll sure be glad when the funeral is over so all of our lives can get back to normal. Well, I guess it will never be the same as it used to be, but I can try to go on."

We all tried to get some sleep that night. It was hard though, thinking about tomorrow, what it would bring and what emotions would we would feel. I tossed and turned all night and so did Lynne. Finally, I found myself drifting to sleep. I might have gotten about two hours of sleep. Early the next morning, I heard a baby crying. I didn't open my eyes to see if Lisa woke up or not but I figured she did, as the baby stopped crying. Mama got us up early. I don't think she got any sleep either.

The funeral limousines driver would be picking us up at 10 o'clock sharp, so I wanted to make sure we were all ready to go. When he came, we were trying to figure out who was going to ride with whom. There were two limousines. "I want all of my kids to ride together," Mama said.

"Okay, Mama, we'll do it like that." Lynne said.

So many flowers came they were all over the apartment and in the hallway also. People from the neighborhood were also dropping food off to us, all while we were trying to leave. A lady came up to Mama and told her, "Tracy, I can collect the food for you while you are gone." She smelled just like old stale wine.

"Liz, hurry and run upstairs and ask old lady Mae if she could collect the food for us, okay? I don't trust this drunk as far as I can throw her! That drunk won't get none of my food, that's for sure," she mumbled.

"She and her kids might be hungry, but someone in HER family needs to get killed then she can get her own food. This is a wake, not a family reunion! Girl, all of these people are dirty and crazy. You gotta watch them. Terry, do you need me to take something, any flowers or cards?"

"No Tracy, we're okay. Just go. Everybody is waiting for you," Terry said.

"Okay. Terry, this is my cousin Kathy. She's going to watch the apartment with you."

"That's fine, Tracy."

"Kathy, please help me put all of the hot food in the oven, and put all of the soda and cold drinks on ice."

Mama was still standing outside the limo, watching people take everything upstairs. "Tracy, stop worrying. Go ahead. Everybody is waiting for you. We got this. It will be okay," Kathy said.

Mama started to cry. I got out of the other limo and took Mama's arm. "Come on Mama, get in with us."

All of Roland's friends were already at the funeral home when we got there. They all had their heads down and were quietly crying. We sat in the first row in front of them.

About five minutes after the preacher started his eulogy, Lynne jumped up, yelling, "ROLAND, I MISS YOU AND I LOVE YOU! DON'T LEAVE ME!"

Ricky ran over, grabbed her and held her. Mike also ran over to me and hugged me tight. Tears started rolling down my face uncontrollably. I couldn't hear the preacher anymore or see the people around me. Mama stood up, ran to the casket and tried to hold Roland. "MY BABY, MY BABY!" she cried.

Aunt Rose ran up, grabbed her arm and hugged her tight as she walked her back to her seat. I was still crying loudly.

When the funeral was finally over, I couldn't remember what the preacher had said. At the gravesite, the preacher said a few words over Roland's casket and we all lined up to put flowers and dirt on the casket.

All of a sudden, a girl named Carolyn ran past us and tried to jump in the casket with Roland! Lisa ran up to her and tried to push her into the grave.

Mama yelled, "LISA, control yourself. Go back to the car. We'll be right there!"

Lisa went to the car while Carolyn was over at the grave trying to pull Roland up out of the casket!

Mama yelled, "What are you doing? You leave my son alone and let him rest in peace!"

The preacher started shaking his head. "I've been doing funerals for 40 years now, and I've NEVER seen anything like this before in my life!" Mama told him that this was the first person she had ever buried.

We turned around and we both started laughing hysterically, an emotion I did not expect to have at a funeral.

Chapter 11

On With the Show

"Lynne, who was that girl named Carolyn?" I asked.

"She said that she and Roland was going together."

Lisa yelled out, "That's a dirty lie! She's a lying bum!"

Mama heard all of the commotion. "Shut up, the both of you! What has happened, has happened."

"Where did she come from?" Sharon asked.

"Who knows?" I answered.

Sharon started to giggle and I started to laugh.

"Liz, I told you to shut up about this," Mama said.

"Mama, you have to admit it's funny. I bet you've never seen anything like this before, have you?"

Lynne chimed in, "Only in Harlem would you have us putting our brother in the grave and some girl trying to join him! This really needs to be on TV."

Lisa was still crying. Mama held her and rocked her to soothe her. Lynne was holding the baby and Sharon was taking care of Lisa's little boy. John stood nearby with his mouth poked out, trying not to cry, and Lisa's little boy kept playing with his tie. Neither understood what was going on.

I saw that John was getting ready to pinch Lisa's little boy. "You leave him alone John! Don't you pinch him. He's only a little boy."

The limo took us back home. I still wasn't crying, though. It was as if I was still on automatic pilot. I had to make sure that everyone else was taken care of. The old lady upstairs called to us. "I'm on a fixed income, do you think you can send over some food or a little money?"

Mama said, "I can give you some food, but that's all."

"Okay, that will be fine," she said.

Ms. Terry, my mother, her cousin and her husband, were all sitting in the living room drinking beer. "Girl, we have so much food, you're gonna need to take some home," Mama told Ms. Terry.

"Okay Tracy, don't forget to give it to me before I leave."

My mother chimed in," Liz, you go take some food to the little old lady upstairs."

I went into the kitchen, got some rolls and a few pieces of turkey, some greens and potato salad. Lynne and I took it upstairs, and when I handed it to her, she said, "Thank you." Then she added, "Honey, do you have any cake and pie and maybe a big soda?" I couldn't believe she was asking me now after I had already trekked up the steps to give her the food. I was the one in mourning.

Lynne said softly, "Let me see." We trekked back down the stairs and got her some cake and four cans of soda.

"Some of the people in the building gave ya'll some money," she said when we handed it to her.

She reached in my pocket and pulled out $10 and handed the envelope back to me. When we went back downstairs, I told Mama what happened. Ms. Terry said, "That's one crazy old lady!"

"You didn't give her my money did you?" Mama asked.

"I gave her what she asked for—some food, some cake and pie, and four cans of soda," I said.

Mama continued, "I didn't think I would have to pay somebody for keeping our food for us till we got back! Child, this world is really a mess! Ray, do you want another plate before you go, or you can take it home with you."

"No, Tracy, do I look like I need another plate?" he started to chuckle.

Mama continued, "Ray, you better take some of this food now, I don't know if I'll have anything to offer you whenever you come back."

"That's okay. I have to get ready to leave y'all nice folks anyway."

Ms. Terry said, "Ray, I'll walk you down the hallway."

As we closed the door, we heard another knock. "Who is it?" Mama asked.

"It's Ricky. Can I speak to Lynne please?" Mama let him in and called Lynne.

"Where have you been all day?" Lynne asked him.

"At my house with Lament and Randy."

"Umm, hmm. Where is Lament now?"

"He's with his girlfriend, Angie."

Lynne continued, "Isn't that the same girl Charles used to go with?"

"Yeah, but that's old and dirty now." They started to talk about other things. All of a sudden, Ricky sat down in a chair, put his head in his lap and burst out crying. Lynne started crying too and watching them started me up all over again. I went into the kitchen, away from them, and wiped my tears. I looked around to see if there was anything I could do. I began putting the dishes away when the phone rang.

Sharon got it. "Liz, it's for you."

I took the phone. "Hey Liz, its Mike."

"Oh, hey Mike, what are you doing?"

"Well, I just woke up from a nap and I thought about you, and was wondering how you were doing."

"Oh, I guess I'm doing okay. I don't really feel like talking right now. Would you mind calling back later, like tomorrow afternoon?" I was hoping that he would understand.

"Oh, yeah, okay, that's fine. I'll talk to you tomorrow, then."

"Okay, thanks for calling."

"Sure."

I lay my head down on the pillow and cried so hard I thought I might have a breakdown. I kept thinking about Roland and how we used to play together when we were all little. We loved to play games like dodge ball and basketball. He was only 19, four days shy of his 20th birthday! His life was cut so short! I thought. Moreover, he was the father of two children. Finally, facing the wall, I fell asleep for a few hours. It wasn't a peaceful sleep though. I tossed and turned until I woke up Lynne.

"Girl, don't forget, you're not the only one in this bed!" she mumbled.

"Oh, sorry Lynne. Just go back to sleep." Soon, my pillow was so wet that I put it on the floor, then the sheet started to get wet. I tried not to move around so much because Lynne's stomach was touching my back and I didn't want to wake her up. I cried silently.

We didn't go to school the next day so I slept late. I woke up to the sound of Lisa's baby crying. Lisa was trying to feed her little boy.

"Lisa, do you need any help?" She looked at me, her face was wet with tears. I couldn't understand what she said too well, because her voice was cracking. I went over, took the baby and started feeding her. Mama came into the kitchen, took the little boy into the bathroom and gave him a bath. Lisa managed to get a few words out to me though. "Liz, can you give the baby a bath too, and comb her hair?"

"Sure Lisa. The least I can do is help you to take care of my niece and nephew, the children of my late brother."

"Thank you, Liz," Lisa said.

Mama came over. "Lisa, you go lay down now. You're totally exhausted and you need some sleep. By the way, where is your mother and what does she have to say about all of this?"

"Nothing. She drinks all the time and doesn't pay me or her grandchildren no mind. She also said that Roland was a drug-selling bum on the street corner, and if that's the guy I want, then it's my business, but don't bother her with the problems that are going to come, and she's not going to take care of my kids either. I still have to pay her rent for my room."

"My goodness Lisa, I'm really sorry to hear that. Unfortunately, there's nothing I can do for you right now. You're going to still have to pay your mother rent till we can come up with something else."

"Yes, Miss Tracy. I understand, but, she wants all of my money!"

"Well, Lisa, you and your mother are going to have to work this thing out. I have no extra room. I didn't even have room for Roland before!"

Lisa turned her head away because she didn't want Mama to see how sad she was. She managed to tell Mama she didn't even have money for food for the kids.

Mama said, "Lynne, give Lisa a couple of dollars so she can get some milk for the baby." She turned to Lisa and said, "Lisa, you're going to have to get a job, you know?"

Lynne said. "I'm going to have a baby too."

Lisa sat on the bed and started crying again. She said she felt hopeless. She didn't have anybody to care for her or the kids. Lynne later told Lisa she would try to help her anyway she could, maybe by babysitting and giving her a few dollars here and there. "I can't give you the money Ricky gives me to save up for the baby though."

"That's fine." Lisa said.

"Lisa," Mama said, "That's the first step in getting your life together. You'll do just fine."

As Lisa continued to talk, the phone rang. It was Ricky. "Lynne," I yelled out. "Phone for you."

Mama looked at her and shook her head. "You girls are having these babies so young, and they don't even have a daddy so, they don't have any mature parents at all. You all have to think before you do things!" I went over to her to calm her down when somebody touched me on the shoulder.

"Liz?" I jumped. I didn't hear Mike come in or anyone knock on the door, for that matter.

"Hey Mike. You scared me to death!"

"Oh, sorry. Hey, what are you doing today?"

"Nothing, why?"

"Well, me and my friend are still making plans for the prom."

"Oh, my goodness, I forgot! The prom is this week."

"No, stupid, it's next week."

"Okay, Mike, don't call me stupid again."

"No, Liz. I was just saying that you forgot when the prom was, that's all."

"Mike, let me tell you something, I just lost my brother and I'm not thinking about any prom right now." Then, I started to cry, something that I *didn't* want to do in front of Mike.

"Liz, I'm sorry I said it like that. I didn't mean it." He held me and wiped the tears from my face.

"I'm really sorry, Leah."

"Leah!? You really are getting your friends names mixed up lately! Why did you call me that?"

"I'm sorry Liz. She called me to see if she could go to the prom with me. She heard about your brother, so I guess she thought you weren't going anymore. I told her that we were still going to the prom together. So, don't try to start anything."

"Um hmm, yeah, I bet you sure did tell her that!"

"I did! What? You don't believe me?"

"No, Mike. I really don't!"

"Whatever, Liz. I did. Let's talk about something else. Were going with four other couples. One couple is my best friend

108

Robert and his girlfriend Ashley. Carl and Erica are going with us too. We have to get there before 9:30. That's when it starts."

I only heard half of what he said. I was still hurt that he called me Leah. I didn't want to bring that up again but I did ask him about her. "Was Leah your girlfriend?"

"Girl, that's old news. We used to like each other but, she's so conceited she thinks everybody is supposed to like her."

"Mike, do you really want to take her to the prom?"

"Oh my goodness, no Liz, I want to take *YOU!* Why are you talking to me like that?"

"Because, I saw her all in your face, laughing and talking to you."

"So what! Sheron is also my friend, but that doesn't mean that I like them like I like you. Actually, I was hoping we could be more than just friends."

"You mean boyfriend and girlfriend?"

"Well, I was hoping to see where this took us."

Lisa yelled out, "I know what it's going to get you. Say, a baby!"

Mike turned to her. "Lisa, please don't talk like that to me. You don't know me at all."

"Yeah, but I know guys. Believe me, I've kissed plenty and they all tell you the same things. Lies. Girl, you're going to fall for some of them too. So, Liz, get ready to cry about those lies Mike's going to tell you."

Mike walked away. "I have to go, I have something important to do. I'm not going to sit here and argue with somebody who doesn't know what they're talking about. I'll call you around three tomorrow, okay? I have some more planning to do. I'll see you tomorrow at school."

"Okay, Mike." I was so confused. "Oh, no I'm not, I'm not going to school tomorrow."

"Oh, when will you be back?" Mike asked.

"I'm not sure but right now, school is the last thing I can concentrate on."

"I'll call you tonight then, okay?"

He left me mumbling to myself silently. Lisa came in the room. She said, "You know, Mike *DID* go with Leah. He used her and she used him. He caught her kissing Shawn's cousin at some school dance. Now, Mike can't stand to look at her. Besides, I heard Shawn talking to Randy and Roland. She's supposed to be having a baby too. She is so stuck up, too. She thinks that everybody wants her."

"Lisa, I didn't believe his stories about him and her. Everyone keeps telling me that they went together, and I better watch myself around Sheron, and I am," I said.

"Girl, you better be looking at this thing realistically and not in a fantasy world. Your heart can be broken into two, and that Mike can do it fast. So, you better watch him at the prom. Anybody can have a baby, if you know what I mean. You better pray about your feelings for him, and let Mike know that you aren't his fool or his nasty girl."

Mama chimed in, "You tell her Lisa, because she thinks he is all peaches and cream. He's just like those other boys. They didn't ask her to the prom. Mike did. Lisa knows, because she's seen all the messes, and look at the mess she's in now. No baby's father, no job to feed her kids, and a mother that drinks and doesn't even care about her or the kids. Liz, no man can take you out of Harlem. I never found a good love to help care for me and my children and take us out of Harlem."

"I know what you both are saying."

Lisa asked, "When are you going back to work?"

"I think Tuesday. I think I'll go back to school that day too."

"That's good."

Mama said, "Liz, I want you to clean the bathroom, and put clean rags and towels in there.

"But Mama, Lynne is still in there."

"Well, she's not going to be in there all day."

"That's right, I'm coming out," Lynne said. "You're just mad 'cause Lisa and Mama are talking about Prince Charming!"

"No, that's not true! I'm going over to Ms. Terry's house to help her with some of the food."

"Okay, Liz, did I burst your bubble?" Lynne said.

I answered, "No, but I know the real truth."

"Oh, you are so perfect, no one can talk about Mr. Perfect."

"Well, at least I'm not pregnant and I don't need to look for my baby's father, and that's the truth.

"Shut up Liz, and make sure it don't happen to you, and if it does, you better be married, have your own house and car and not living in Harlem. Don't forget, before you go over to Ms. Terry's house, you have to clean the bathroom so Prince Charming won't have to use a dirty bathroom!"

As I start to clean the bathroom the phone rang. "Liz it's for you," Lynne said.

"Who is it?" I asked.

"I don't know, but it sounds like Leah." I grab the phone.

"Hi Liz, this is Sheron."

"Sheron, what do you want?"

"I wanted to see if everything was okay with you, since your brother just died."

"No Sheron, you just wanted to see if I was still going to the prom with Mike or not, and HI LEAH! I know you're on the phone too."

"No Liz, I didn't call you for that reason."

"So why are you calling me now? You had a whole year to call me. And, how did you get my number anyway?"

"From Charles and Niecy."

"Oh, no! Now you and Leah got my number. Well, cut it up, and never call me again!" I slammed down the phone and went to Ms. Terry's house. I had to clean the bathroom later, I was so angry. Once I got there, I told her about those crazy girls and what happened.

"Girl, you should never talk to those two again."

Well, I'm not. They are not my friends and they mean nothing to me," I said.

"You're right, Ms. Terry said, "They aren't your friends. That should be obvious."

"I know, Ms. Terry. They're just upset since me and Mike started talking."

Ms. Terry said, "They're just being nosey. They want to see how long you can keep him! Girl, I must admit that Mike is fine, and he can dress good too, but all eyes are going to be on you and Mike on prom night. I'll make you up, you know, your make up and everything. So, make sure you get some jewelry to go with your gown that will make the color of the dress stand out. I'm going to take some pictures of you and Mike."

As she was talking, my mind started to wander. "Girl, keep your mind on wrapping this leftover food and not other things." We started to laugh for the first time since Roland died. Well, the second time, the first was when that girl tried to jump into Roland's grave. "What time is the prom and what day is it?"

"You know, I'm not sure. With everything happening lately, I really forgot. I think next week."

"Did you get your dress off of layaway yet?"

"No, not yet, because I still owe more money on it, and I need to get my shoes and a matching pocketbook."

"Won't you have to work really hard this week to get these things before next week?"

"Yeah, I know. I do. But, Lisa is over at the apartment with us, her and the kids, and she needs pampers and stuff all of the time. That's why I don't have any money. Man, they need to go home! Roland didn't leave her nothing but some hungry kids!" I started laughing again.

"Girl, that is the real truth. If your Mama and I didn't work, we would have some hungry kids too." As we were cracking up, Sharon pushed the door open. "Liz, Mike is on the phone for you."

"Sharon, watch your manners when you come in. You don't forget to knock when you come to my house, okay?"

"Okay, Ms. Terry."

"I'll see you later Liz, and come back to get the rest of the food, okay?"

"Okay, thanks." I got the phone again. "Hi, Mike? What do you want?"

"Well, me and guys picked up the tickets and paid for the limo. Can you put in $100?"

"Well, no Mike. That will be my whole check, and I still have to get my gown and the things that go with it."

"Oh, okay. I'll see if I get it from my grandmother. Do you think you can at least give me half of it?"

"No, not right now. Maybe my next payday."

"Okay, that will be fine. Just make sure you give it to my grandmother."

"Tell her you'll be paying her back." I got off of the phone and stood there scratching my head.

Mama heard the whole thing. "Liz, don't start borrowing money from his grandmother. If you go to the prom, I will try to help out as much as I can. I really don't know this woman, and I really don't want to know her. I don't want my daughter owing her any money."

As we were talking, the phone rang gain. Miss Maxine, Mike's grandmother, and Mama were talking. "I'll be giving Liz $50 toward the prom, okay?" Miss Maxine said.

Mama said, "Okay, that's fine." They talked a little bit more, and then Mama said. "I'll talk to you later."

"See Liz. I told you. That old lady is nasty. That's why I didn't want you to ask her for that money. Besides, she thinks her grandson is too good for you. That you are lazy and waste his time. So, don't ask that lady for nothing, okay, child?"

"Okay, Mama."

The next day, I returned to school. It was the first day back in a long time. I saw Mike up the hall and yelled to him, "Hey Mike! What happened? You didn't pick me up for school."

"Girl, I am too busy these days to do that." Oh, so now you have a job, or is it you're too busy period to talk to me?"

"No, Liz, that's not it. I'm really busy since I graduated. I'm here to see some of my buddies that I miss. Well, I gotta go, I'm going to the gym to play some basketball. Hey, do you work today?"

"Yes, I do."

"Well, I'll see ya' later."

"Okay." I was thinking, *whatever.* I was on my way to my first period class when I ran into Sheron. "So, y'all really are just friends, huh? Not boyfriend and girlfriend?"

"That's none of your business what we are!"

"Leah said she told you that Mike has a thing for every girl he knows."

"Leah," I said, "don't need to speak to me about a thing. Some things you can't hide. So, please don't talk to me about things you don't know about." I pushed past them and walked away. Sheron's mouth dropped. I left her standing there by herself looking stupid. I didn't need any of her mess anymore today, I thought.

I turned around, "Y'all need to stay out of my business and my face!" As I was walking to my class, I shook my head. The whole day seemed to drag along. Since it had been awhile since I had been there, I had to get used to long days again.

Finally, school was over and I headed to work. The first person I ran into was Steven. "Liz, people left you something."

"What is it?"

"Go to your department and see."

I went to my department, opened my locker and picked up an envelope with money in it. I guessed everybody collected it when they heard about my brother. I looked inside and counted over $100! I was so grateful. That with my paycheck would be enough to get all of my stuff for the prom.

I started my shift an hour early so I could get off early get my stuff. Right after work, I went to the shoe department and got my shoes and pocketbook. Then I got my gown off of layaway. I didn't have enough money for my jewelry, but I was still satisfied and very grateful. I took the rest of the money and took a cab home.

When I got home Mama's face lit up. "Oh my goodness! Where did all of this come from?" I explained to her what happened. "That's so wonderful! Your coworkers are nice people. Why did you take a cab though?"

"Well, I had a lot of packages and I was afraid that someone was going to try to take something from me, since it was so much, so, I took a cab with the rest of my money. I wasn't able to get my jewelry though. Mama, do you have a little bit of money for my jewelry?"

"Girl, I already paid Mike $50 for this whole thing so you wouldn't have to get it from his grandmother. I told her never mind. So, I'm all tapped out. Go ask Ms. Terry if she has anything that you could use."

"Oh, okay."

I called her. "Come over and bring everything you bought and we'll see if we can find something." I gathered all of my stuff and went over. "Oh girl, that is a beautiful gown!" Ms. Terry said. "The shoes and pocketbook go so good with it. Red is definitely your color. I have some white pearl jewelry that would go so well with that. I'll also find some good smelling perfume for you too. Girl, you're going to be the star of that prom. Now, all you need to do is wait for the day and Mike to pick you up."

I thanked her for everything and went back home. Lisa asked me if she could see my dress. "Oh, it's so pretty, and it's going to look pretty on you too. The dress and shoes go perfectly! You're going to blow Mike's mind! Please don't let him see the gown before the prom, okay?" she said.

"Okay, Lisa."

When the day finally came, I was so excited! I went to work at 9 AM so I could get off early. My hair appointment was at 2 PM. I made sure my white slip fit me. I had forgotten to try it on before. I got out of the hairdresser at 4 PM, and ran home to get in the tub. I took a nice, soothing bubble bath. I wanted to make sure I was ready on time so Mike wouldn't have to wait. He promised he would be here at 8 PM.

Ms. Terry came over around 6:30 to help me get ready. Lisa, who staying with her mother by this time, came over to help look out for Mike's limo. Mama kept saying over and over to make sure I watched Mike carefully. "Watch what he's saying and look at how he's acting, and make sure he gets me a cab home," she said. (Whatever that meant.)

As I got dressed, I put on Ms. Terry's jewelry. I panicked when I saw that one of the pearl earrings were broken! "What am I going to do?" I yelled.

Lynne said, "I'll be right back." She ran to the corner store and got a cheap pair of white earrings for me. They weren't the same, but they would do.

Mama gave me some elegant, long white gloves that she had stored in the bottom of a drawer. "I wore these gloves at my wedding to your father. I think they will bring out the white in your dress." I didn't know what to say. I felt so honored that she would trust me with something so precious. All I could say was, "Thank you Mama." I gave her a hug.

"I hope I live to see my little girl get married. I just lost the dream of seeing my son get married," she said.

Lynne said, "Mama, *please* don't start about Roland, this is supposed to be a happy time for Liz." But it was too late, Mama's tears started down her cheek.

Mike called and Mama wiped her tears and talked to him. "Is Liz ready yet?" he asked.

"Yes, Mike she is. What time is the limo coming to pick her up?"

"8:15."

"Okay, she be ready." I put the perfume on and unwrapped my hair.

"Tracy, Liz looks good!" Ms. Terry said.

"Yes, Terry, she sure does."

"Okay" Ms. Terry said. "Let me take some pictures of you." As I smiled and posed, Ms. Terry said, "Girl, show it off!"

Lisa ran into the apartment all out of breath. "The limo is here!"

"Oh, I have to go now." I gave everybody a kiss and walked out of the door. Mike met me in the hallway. "Liz, is that you?"

"Yes, it's me, not Leah." I started to giggle.

"Wow, you look...you look *GREAT!*" then he leaned over and gave me a kiss. Mama came out into the hallway.

"Y'all hurry up. Mike, where are your other friends?"

"They're down in the limo waiting." He was talking to Mama, but his eyes were still on me. It made me feel good that he found me so pretty that night.

Ms. Terry whispered in his ear, "Isn't this the bride you would like to marry someday?" I didn't know if he heard what she said because he didn't say anything, he just kept staring at me. He took my hand and led me outside.

Lisa said, "Here comes the Prince and Princess!" As we got to the limo, Robert opened the door for us. Ms. Terry got a few more pictures of the limo and we left. We headed downtown where we were going to the Temptations Show before going to the Prom. I was so excited that I was going to see the

Temptations in person! We had front row seats! I couldn't believe it. Then, the curtains came up and they came on stage. David started singing *My Girl,* and I went crazy. That was my favorite song! I kept yelling *"David, David"* and hitting Mike on the arm, the one that I was holding!

Melvin was singing backup and Ashley, who was Robert's girl, started yelling and hitting Robert on his arm too! Ashley said to Robert, "Boy they sure can sing!"

Robert said, "You both are going to break our shoulders and arms!" We started giggling and I glanced at Mike. He wasn't smiling. "I'm sorry Mike, but, this is the first time I've been to a show like this."

"Maybe it's the last too, well, with me anyway." I looked at him, hurt, and looked down.

"Mike, leave her alone." Ashley said. "She came to have a good time, so let her."

"Yeah, but she's out with me, not some hood in the neighborhood."

"Whatever," I mumbled.

Robert hit her in the hip. She looked puzzled, shook her head and kept dancing. After the show, we jumped in the limo and headed to the prom.

Mike took my hand and led me inside. The boys walked us to the table then left. We figured that they went to the bathroom. We were sitting around talking, waiting for them to come back so we could dance with them. They kept going in and out. Ashley went over to Robert and said, "What are you guys doing?"

"That's none of your business," he said.

"Yes, it is my business. You're my date for the prom and I didn't come here to sit by myself."

"Okay, okay, we'll be right there in a moment."

We decided to go to the bathroom to freshen up, but the bathroom was so full of smoke I walked out. I looked over and saw Mike talking to one of his classmates. Somebody tapped me on the shoulder.

I turned around. "Charles, what in the world are you doing here? Where have you been?"

"Around. Girl, I knew you were pretty, but boy you look great tonight. I wish you had come with me." I was surprised that he said that, and I started giggling.

Mike came over. "What are you two doing?" Charles shook his head and walked away. "Liz, what's up with you and Charles?"

"Nothing Mike. What's wrong with you anyway? I'm sitting at the table talking to these girls that I don't even know very well."

"I'm sorry, Liz." We headed across the room to get something to drink. "Do you want to dance?"

"Yes, I do."

We went out on the dance floor and started to slow dance. He started kissing me right there on the dance floor. "Mike, why are you kissing me now in front of everybody?"

"Because that's how I want to do it." Then, he started whispering nasty things in my ear. "Mike, are you drinking?"

"Come on Liz. Let's take some pictures for my grandmother." He completely ignored my question so I put on a false smile for the pictures. After the prom, Robert and Ashley were arguing with each other and Mike and I had nothing to say. Suddenly Mike looked odd.

"Mike, are you okay?" He ran to the bathroom, throwing up before he could get there. I couldn't believe it. My beautiful night ruined! When he came out I helped him into the limo. He started talking nasty to me about a girl he 'scored with' and how easy it was. I turned my back to him and didn't say anything. We stopped at Central Park to walk around, but that wasn't fun either because Mike was stumbling over everything.

The limo dropped us off at the restaurant for breakfast and left. Ashley and Robert took off, saying, "Y'all want to stay here with these drunks it is fine with me but, I'm leaving." Carl was so drunk that Erica sat him down in the restaurant seat. I went to call my Mother to let her know that I was okay, but inside I was sick. I came back to the table and found Mike asleep, his head on the table! I wanted to cry. I looked over at Erica and saw she was hurt too.

We paid for our food and Erica caught a cab. I couldn't believe this had happened to me. I got a waiter to call a cab for us, and I spent what little money I had left. I dropped Mike off at his apartment, and I walked to mine at 2 o'clock in the morning! What they all said about Mike was definitely true.

Mama said she wanted me home before 2:30. I had told her that everything was over at 2 o'clock. "That's good," she said. "That way I won't worry about you all night." I finally reached my house, climbed to my apartment and went inside, but I dared not tell Mama that I walked home. She would have Mike's head on a platter!

"Did you have a good time?" she asked when I got home. I never said yes. Instead, I started talking about how great the show was and how we had to pay for a lot of stuff. I couldn't tell her that Mike treated me like all of his nasty girls. I was so hurt. *I wish this day had have never come!* I thought.

Chapter 12

Liz's Heart Aches

I couldn't sleep that night after the prom. I was still thinking about how drunk Mike got and how he fell asleep. I couldn't believe I got stuck paying for breakfast and the cab back home.

Lynne was up listening to the radio when I went to bed. I knew that Lynne knew something was wrong by the way she looked at me. I acted as if I was too to talk and wanted to go to bed. My heart felt like it was broken in two. I wanted to fall asleep fast so I was hoping that she wouldn't ask me anything about the prom.

I woke up to a nice sunny day. It was unusually hot for May. As I got up to wash up, the phone rang. Sharon yelled out, "Liz, it's Mike."

"Tell Mike that I'm in the bathroom and I'll call him back later." Lisa was in John's room with her kids. I started getting dressed, hung up my gown and put my shoes back in the box.

"So, Liz, how was the prom?" Lisa asked. "How did he dance? I've never been fortunate enough to get a nice guy to take me to the prom, or one who stayed in school that long."

"Well Lisa, the first thing I liked was the *Temptations* show. It was great! We even got to meet David after the show. I also met Mike's best friends and their girlfriends. Once we got to the prom, Mike really didn't want to dance fast, so we slow danced. We took pictures at the show and at the prom."

"Aww, that sounds great! Tell me more about David!"

"Well, he kissed the hands a lot girl's that were sitting in the front row. Girl, he kissed my hand too! I started to beat on Mike's arm, 'because I couldn't believe it. Mike looked at me like I was crazy!"

"Did he sing My Girl?"

"Yeah, he did, and it sounded good too. Mike said, "Why are all of these girls yelling for nothing? He's a man, just like me!"

Lynne chimed in, "Yeah, that's what he thinks, some of these yelling girls are going to be with him at the hotel."

Lisa continued with her questions. "Did Mike kiss you?"

"Yeah he did but, that's all he did. Mike got some beer and brought it to the prom and he and his friends started acting stupid and silly."

"And, and? Lisa asked.

"And, that's it. I told you, nothing else happened."

Mama yelled out, "That's good, 'cause I don't need any more problems."

Mama started fixing breakfast for all of us. "Liz, do you work today," Mama asked.

"I'm not sure." I went into the room to get my work schedule. "Hmm, let me see. Yeah, I have to be at work at 1:30 today until closing." I ate breakfast and did a few things around the house, put on my work clothes, and ran out the door and down the stairs to catch a cab to work. On my way, I ran into Ms. Terry and her boyfriend.

"Hey, Ms. Terry."

"Are you on your way to work?"

"Yeah, I'm trying to hurry so I can catch a cab."

"Well, come on I'll take you to work."

"Thank you, I really appreciate it. Oh, by the way your jewelry is at the apartment."

"Okay, I'll get them later."

I got to work 15 minutes late. Janice was the first person I saw. "Girl, hey! How was the prom? You should have a smile all over your face!"

"Well, the prom was nice. The Temptation's show was great! David kissed my hand, and I went crazy!"

"Where was Mike sitting?"

"Next to me of course."

"Oh man, did he get mad?"

"No, he just thought all the girls were acting crazy for nothing."

"Maybe he should have kissed Mike's hand. That would have been really crazy!" I started.

"Well, I'll see you later Liz, I have t get these clothes tagged."

"Okay." I ran back to my department. Mrs. Elaine greeted me. "Liz, did you get your pictures back yet?"

"No, the prom was just last night."

"Oh, okay. Well, did you have a good time? Oh, by the way Liz, this is Peggy. She's new and I'm training her. Peggy, this is Liz. She's the one that you go and pick up the clothes from after she's done with them. Liz, she goes to college."

"Oh, that's nice." What else did she want me to say, I wondered. I sure wasn't impressed.

"You girls have more programs available to you than I did when I was growing up. "Yeah, but we all might not qualify for the programs we want to get into." I said.

Mrs. Elaine looked funny. "This is your chance to get into college any way you can. This stupid old world is finally seeing us as a people that should have some privileges in this world. So, we need to try to accomplish our goals with these things."

I listened but didn't hear much of what she was saying. I was still thinking about yesterday. I was tired all day because I hadn't caught up on my sleep yet, and I wouldn't get off till 10:30 PM.

Finally 10:30 came and I slowly put my supplies away. I looked up, out of the store window, and saw a young man looking in our window. I really couldn't see who it was though. I continued downstairs to get my stuff so I could go home, and I heard someone calling me. It was Peggy. "Liz, do you have a ride home?"

"No Peggy, I have to take two busses home."

"Well, I'm going your way. I live on 124th Street."

"Oh, okay. I can stop at one of your bus stops."

"Okay, that would help out a lot. Thanks, I really appreciate it." As we were walking, I heard someone calling me. I couldn't make out whom it was though. When I finally got to the lamppost I saw it was Mike.

"What in the world are you doing here?"

"Liz, I am sorry about yesterday."

I chimed in. "Peggy, this is my friend Mike." They exchanged hi's. "I guess I'll be taking the bus, Peggy."

"Okay. I'll see you later. Are you sure you'll be okay?"

"Yes, I'll be fine. Thanks for asking."

Then Mike started in. "Liz, I know I got drunk on you last night and I'm sorry but, you have to remember—this is my last year with my friends and I wanted to have a good time and really celebrate this year. I hope we can still be friends."

"I don't know Mike. We went to the prom together, first I had to take you home and then I had to see myself home alone all dressed up too. Then, it started to rain, and my gown got all wet and dirty and I had to spend money to take it to the cleaners!"

"I'll pay for your gown being cleaned, okay?"

"Well, that would be nice."

"So, can I take you to the movies this Friday?"

"No, because I have to go to work this Friday night and Saturday."

"Oh, okay." We walked to the bus stop and waited for the bus. It was late because it was running slowly. As we were waiting, we watched as a bunch of guys knocked down an old lady and took her purse. That was enough for us.

"Liz, let's get a cab." Mike said, so we flagged one down.

However, once we told him where we were going, he didn't want to take us. "I'm not going in that bad neighborhood. I'll drop you about four blocks from there."

"Okay, that's fine." Mike said. "As long as we can get away from here."

Mike paid the cab and we walked the rest of the way.

"Liz, give me your purse." I gave it to him, and he put it under his jacket. "See how I care about you by protecting you from the bums on the street?"

"Yeah, but you're all bums!"

"Oh, is that supposed to mean me too?" I started to giggle and looked down shyly. "Oh, that's okay, Liz. I do one thing wrong and now I'm a bum. He started to smile. I never told him how I really felt and what I was thinking at the time. My heart started beating so fast it was actually painful. He really hurt me that he took my feelings for granted.

Mike looked at me and said, "Elizabeth Rosemere, would you be my girlfriend?"

I felt as if I had just had a heart attack. Words wouldn't come out. I couldn't say all of the things I always wanted to say to him about being his girlfriend. He looked at me and started rubbing my hand. The tears started to fall, but just in my heart. I felt lost. I knew what my heart wanted though. I wanted to be Mike's girlfriend but I didn't want to tell him that I had never been someone's girlfriend before. I didn't know what to say to him.

"Mike, I don't know right now. You're going away this summer to basketball camp and then going away to college. So, that wouldn't be good for me to be your girlfriend right now."

"That's true Liz, but we can be together when I come home from school. People go together away from home all the time."

"Well, I have to think about this a little longer."

"Okay, I won't rush you." We said goodnight and I went to my apartment. I cut the kitchen light on, and saw Mama was waiting there in the dark. "Child, its 1:00 in the morning. What time did you get off of work?"

"Mama, I closed tonight. I got out at 10:55, and I had to take two busses. They were running slow since so it late. Fortunately, Mike came to meet me. As we waited for a bus, an old lady got robbed. Mike suggested we catch a cab, but the cab put us out four blocks from here and we walked the rest of the way."

"My goodness. Liz, you need to keep some cab fare with your bus money just in case. Don't take a purse either."

"Mike kept my purse in his shirt."

"Well, that's good, but keep your cab money in your shoe and your bus fare in your pants pocket. That old lady could have been you!"

"Okay Mama, I'll keep that in mind."

"Good, 'cause Mike won't be with you at all times. Besides, I never want you to depend on him. He's a young man and y'all are just friends. That was nice of him to see you home. Liz, you have to remember Mike has a lot of goals to meet and he's looking to meet them all. One of his goals is not to be married right now to anybody."

"Mama, I know his not ready to be married yet, and neither am I. He did ask me though about being his girlfriend." It came out before I wanted it to.

"Well, what was your answer?"

"I told him I had to think about it."

"Well, Liz, you need to find out who you are, and what you want out of life first," Mama said.

"Well, I know I want to go to college upstate and get an apartment to live near the campus."

Mama said, "So then you need to see Mike as a friend and not a boyfriend. Both of y'all need to meet your goals in life. Liz, think about it. If you get pregnant, your goals are gone. Down the drain! You need to keep working, and planning. Saving money to help accomplish this goal of yours, and keep your mind clear. So, you have to keep thinking in a positive way about you and your feelings. You need to sit down and write down on a piece of paper what you want out of life and look at the positive and the negative. You have to figure out what you don't want, and make sure it doesn't happen. Keep your job and think about what you want for the future."

"Mama, I work full time this summer. Right after school is over."

"Oh, that's great to hear. Let's get some sleep and we'll talk about this some more tomorrow. I'll see you before you leave for school tomorrow. I'm really tired right now."

"Okay," I told her. Mama turned out the light in the kitchen and went to bed.

I went in my room, expecting Lynne to be asleep. Instead, she is sitting on the side of her bed. "What's wrong Lynne?"

"My stomach hurts and my back hurts too."

"Oh" I said, and pulled the covers back and went to bed. I tossed and turned until I figured out that it was because the lamp was on.

"Lynne, can you please turn that light out! I can't sleep with it on."

Lynne rose up and said, "Okay, Miss Precious, if it will help you get some sleep!" but she didn't get out of the bed. "Liz, I'll cut the light out but, I can't right now."

I put the pillow over my face and hoped I could get some sleep. I was angry with her. She said I had no compassion, whatever that meant. I finally fell asleep but the rain was hitting the window so hard it woke me up. I got up, looked out of the window and decided to close it.

"Liz, I need some air."

"Well, what does that have to do with me?"

"Because you gotta remember, you don't sleep by yourself!"

"I sure wish I did, though, so I can open and close my window whenever I wanted to!"

"Well, for right now," Lynne continued, "You're sharing a room with me and it won't hurt you to leave the window cracked."

"Well, Lynne, if that's the case you need to change side beds so you will be over here by the window."

"Fine Liz, and take your smelly pillow and your greasy nasty head rag over there!"

"Whatever." I felt better. I don't know why we didn't think of this before.

"Lynne, did Lisa finally go home?" I asked.

"Yes child, her and her kids went home. Man, those kids were making me sick! They ate up everything and they always smelled sour even though we always tried to keep them clean. Lisa was really nasty too. Somebody tell me why Roland couldn't find a better girl than her! She's dirty and ugly! I hope she don't come over here for a while. I don't need a smelly stinky woman around, and her stinky children either."

"Well" I said, "She didn't have a good mother to show her all of that stuff I guess. Roland used to talk about his dream girl, remember?"

"Yeah, but that is not the one he was talking about! He went into detail about his dream girl. Lisa doesn't even have the shape he was talking about! She's skinny and dark-skinned, her clothes are big too. She left with a pile of my clothes. I'm never going to see those clean clothes again. The only reason why I'm not too upset is 'cause I need maternity clothes. I told her I might need those clothes back after I have the baby. But really, she can keep them. She smells too bad and I know that smell is not going to come out. Yek!"

We continued talking about Lisa until it started getting light outside. I asked her the next day (because it was still on my mind), "Lynne, do you think Roland would have married her?"

"Girl, I don't know. Probably. He really loved her. But I would hope not. For his sake. If they did, she would hopefully spend her days cleaning the house or cleaning the kids. She's not the type to work, so I can't see her doing anything else. That would have been a sad marriage too. In the future, her children might come looking pretty, but for right now, they both have her looks. I'm so sorry that Roland got her pregnant those two times."

"Yeah, me too."

I finally got up around 6:30 to get ready for school. I was sleepy from not getting any sleep, but I was kind of excited. This was the last week of school before the summer.

Mrs. Banks, my homeroom teacher looked at me and said, "Elizabeth Rosemere, you sure are looking pretty this morning. Boy, and you go with the most popular boy on the basketball team too!"

"No, Mrs. Banks, Michael is just my friend. He's not my boyfriend. He asked me to go to his prom with him. That's why we were together."

"Oh, okay. Hey, have you seen Charles Smith anywhere? I know you two are close."

"No, I haven't seen him lately. He moved from my building not too long ago."

"What about his sister?"

"She moved with them, I guess."

"Those two are two sad young people. Charles needs one more class to get his diploma and he will be done, but I don't think he will do that. He likes these crazy street corners better. He thinks he can get a better education there, and that's sad."

"Yes, Mrs. Banks, it makes me sad too. I really like Charles as a friend but his lifestyle scares me."

"Liz" she continued, "You have to be careful whom you trust as your friend."

"Well, my mother is my best friend."

"Well, that's great to hear! If you can respect your mother and your father, then you can respect other people too. If you don't respect your parents, it's going to be hard for you to respect other people. That's the biggest problem today. People, especially young people don't respect each other or older people also. Especially when you go in the work force.

"When you get a job, you have to listen to your boss. That is their business, and they have a right to hire, and fire you too. Also, having the right attitude helps a lot too. They want to make sure that you can follow the rules and regulations without any problems. Just like this boss. I have to listen to the principle, and I have to do it because I have a family, and I like my job too. Let me stop babbling. Liz, have you thought about college yet?"

"Yes, I would like to go but I really don't know how I'm going to pull it off yet. It's one of my goals though."

"Well, you need to keep that as a great goal. I hope you meet them. I also meant to tell you how sorry I was to hear about your brother."

"Yes, thank you. It's hard, because I really miss him everyday."

"Well, hang in there and keep in mind that the better your grades now, the better your chances of getting into a college you like and want."

"Okay, Mrs. Banks, thanks a lot. Oh, by the way, my sister Lynne is going to have a baby."

"Your sister Lynne?" She continued. "How did your mother take that?"

"Not too well. She struggling with her own kids. She said she doesn't have time for another baby too."

"Well, where is your father?"

"In jail, where Lynne's baby's father is going to end up too. Either there or in the grave."

"Honey, that's another story altogether. That girl will never finish school. Now, it's going to be hard for her to get a job to support her child.

"Elizabeth, please make sure you make your mother proud. The problems that your brothers and sisters have caused are weighing your mother down a lot. Make sure you finish school, get and keep a job that will make you proud. Just watch out for the boys, especially the popular boys."

"I am, I am. Believe me, I know how popular he is and how he treats girls." I said.

"Right, you don't want to loose your goals for yourself, or cause him to loose his goals for himself also. That wouldn't be a good relationship for a good friendship. I hope you see that it wouldn't be a good marriage for the both of you. Michael is a good basketball player, but not a good boyfriend. He's also a typical young man. He likes the way girls go after him because of his looks and his talents. That's the way it's going to be when he goes to college. For all of the girls that he didn't see in school, he'll see in college.

"There are much more over there, as you all will find out when you go. So, please Elizabeth, don't get your heart set on Michael. He'll be gone soon, and you need to know who you are, and where you are going, and how you are going to get there. Keep in mind you need a good job and a good education. Next year you need to concentrate on your grades so you can have them high enough to get a scholarship to a good school."

I replied, "Mrs. Banks, I'll keep this in mind."

"You need to listen to your elders, they have good advice for you, even if you're not crazy about what they are saying."

"Thank you, Mrs. Banks, I appreciate your advice."

"You can pick up your report card after last period, before you go to work, okay?"

"Okay." I kept thinking about what she said. She made a lot of sense. I really had to think about it some more. The day seemed to go by quickly. I guess when you have a lot on your mind, it does. Finally, the end of the day came, I got my report card, ran down the hall, ran downstairs, outside past the schoolyard, across the football field and the alley, to the corner to catch the bus going downtown to work. I caught it just in time.

I went to the back of the bus and I saw Lisa and her baby. "Hey Lisa, what are you doing on the bus?"

"Going downtown. Hey Liz, do you have a few dollars for some pampers?"

"No Lisa, I can't buy you any pampers and I don't have any money. Don't tell me about how I got a job because I know that."

"Liz, why are you telling me that for?"

"So you can stop asking me for money. That is my dead brother's baby, not my baby."

"Yeah, but I need you guys to help me with the kids."

"Yeah, but what about helping yourself?"

"But, I can't find a babysitter."

"Well, that's none of my business. I can't find one for you either."

"Oh, I forgot, you think you're cute since you went to the prom with Mike." She said.

"Lisa, that doesn't have anything to do with it. I'm tired of you asking me for money. My brother was a bum and you knew what type of person he was when you got with him. I'm not taking care of them, they are not my children and I'm not supporting you either. Your best bet is to go down to welfare and leave me alone. I have enough problems, and I have to help with my family with what little bit of money I have. I can't take on another person."

"Well, fine. Bye Miss Cutie!"

"Bye Dirty Lisa!" She kicked at me through the doors, but the bus driver closed the door and pulled off. Boy, that skinny nasty dirty bum, I thought. People were laughing at us so I sat in the back in my seat until my stop came, embarrassed.

Someone came up and touched me. I turned and saw it was Janice. "What was that all about?"

"That stupid girl has two kids by my brother. He's dead and now she wants us to take care of her and her kids. She keeps those kids dirty and smelly. She knows that I work at a department store and she wanted me to get some clothes for the kids. I came to work to take care of me and my family, not her. I don't mind sometimes giving the kids some clothes, because they really need it, but I want to give them when I want to, not when she tells me to. I'm not going to jump up to give her my hard-earned money.

"She sits on her tail all day asking people for money. She has my sister's clothes on. Now it is diapers, then clothes, next it will be food, then rent, gas, and electric. I have to nip it in the bud before it gets too far."

Janice looked sad and disgusted. "Girl, these lazy nasty stinky girls always seem to be looking for handouts. They never go to look for a job or get into a program for them or their kids. That girl looks like she needs plenty of help."

"Yeah, but, I don't have anything to give her. Her sister Jackie got this job for me. I appreciate her helping me, but you can see what type of family she comes from. Jackie was always drunk and smelling like alcohol all of the time even when she came to work. That's why she lost her job. She never came in, and when she did, she was drunk. "Our stop came, we got out and went in to work.

133

Chapter 13

Goodbye to a Friend

After the fiasco that happened that day, Lynne was exhausted. She cried herself to sleep. She also complained that her stomach was hurting again.

Mama came in the room. "Liz, is Lynne asleep yet?"

"Yes, Mama."

"Oh, that boy Ricky causes my daughter nothing but pain, besides being pregnant with his child. See, Liz, what a man can give you!"

Sharon said, "Mike can give you a baby, Michelangelo!"

"Shut up Sharon!" I said. "You're just like the rest of them. Always talking about something you don't know about. I can see what can happen."

Mama said, "Well, just as long as it's not you."

John ran up. "Liz, Mike's grandmother called about the party next week."

"John, did she tell you where it was going to be?"

"No. But she did say for you to call her because she wants you to get there early."

"Okay, let me check my work schedule. I have to see if I work that day."

Mama said, "Liz, please let your boss know that you need that time off next week. Don't wait till the last minute."

"Okay, Mama. I'm going to need a new outfit for that day and a new hairdo."

John blurted out, "Oh, like you needed to get a dress for Mike's prom."

"No, stupid!"

Mama didn't like me calling people names. "Liz, you don't have to call him names."

"Okay, but Mama, your children keep asking me about my business!"

"So what! That doesn't give you reason to call John stupid."

"Okay. Hmm, let me see if my job has a sale on a pants set or a nice summer dress. I need some casual clothes that look nice. Well, while I'm thinking about it, let me call Mrs. Maxine." I picked up the phone and called her. "Hello, can I speak to Mrs. Maxine?"

"This is she."

"This is Liz."

"Oh, hi Liz, I just wanted to know if you could come early to the party to help me set up at the recreation center down the street from your school?"

"Yes, I wouldn't mind helping out."

"Okay, so I'll pick you up at 3 o'clock on Saturday, okay?"

"Sure, that's fine."

"Okay, I'll see you then." I hung up as Lynne came out of the room.

"So Liz, are you the personal service for Mike's party now?"

"No, Lynne, I'm just helping out."

"No, Liz, you're going to service them and afterwards, clean up. That's just like Mrs. Maxine to take you as a little fool."

Mama chimed in again. "Stop calling names in my house, you know I don't like it."

Lynne continued. "But Mama, why go to a party all dressed up to service Mike and his friends? She is supposed to be his friend too. Remember that lessen when you deal with Ricky's friends too."

I just went into my room puzzled by what Lynne said. I wanted to be Mike's special girl and I wanted to go over there to help out.

Lynne came into the room. "Liz, you let Mrs. Maxine know that you came to the party to have fun too. You look at her straight in the eye when you tell her that!" I didn't say anything. Mama called me into the living room. "Liz, I wanted to talk to you. Make sure you remember this date, on Saturday, one month from now. Ricky's sister is giving Lynne a baby shower."

"But Mama, I don't even know her."

"You're always at work when she comes over here. She seems to be a nice girl, not at all like her brother Ricky."

"I hope she doesn't sell drugs or got a boyfriend selling drugs either!"

"Now Liz, that's not the right attitude to take."

"I know Mama, but Ricky's family is coming up here. We don't know them at all."

"Well, we'll just have to see. Oh, you can invite your friend Peggy."

"Oh, thanks Mama. That would be nice if she can come."

"Well, she seems like a nice girl. Just make sure you go to your boss to get that date off. I really am going to need you that day to help out."

"But Mama, Peggy might not be able to come."

"Well, just tell her about it, the time and date, and maybe she can come."

"Okay, Mama. I'll make sure I ask her. Man, Lynne is going to need a lot of baby clothes."

"Well, that's why Ricky's sister is doing this. Just please make sure you get off that day."

"Mama, I already asked for this coming Saturday off."

"Well, you have a whole month in between times. That shouldn't be a problem. Well, enough of that. Let's clean this nasty house. Where is Becky?"

"Downstairs with John," I said. "Sharon, go downstairs to get them."

"Oh, Mama! Liz is standing right at the door!"

"Sharon, your mouth is going to see my fist in a minute!" Mama said.

"Okay, Mama, I'll go down to get them."

Mama continued to distribute jobs to us. "Liz, get the end of this couch, and I'll get the other end, and we'll move it forward. We must have lifted it too often because it fell to the floor and the arm came off of it.

"My poor couch, it just fell apart. Liz, go downstairs to the yard and bring me a brick so I can prop this arm up and I'll go get a clean sheet to cover it."

I went out in the yard and saw something behind the garbage cans! When I looked closer, I saw it was a dead man! I immediately run out front, grabbed Becky and John's hands and ran upstairs.

"MAMA, MAMA, I just saw a dead man behind the garbage cans!"

"What? Where are my children?"

"Becky and John are right here with me."

"Did my babies see anything?"

John said, "No, Liz just grabbed our hand, and we ran upstairs."

Mama continued, "Did you see the face?"

"No, Mama, I just saw his feet and his hands. Maybe he was drunk. I didn't stand around to see if he was drunk or dead but he sure looked dead. I just thought about my sister and brother and got them."

"Well, thanks Liz, for thinking of your family. Where is Lynne?"

"On the phone, Mama."

"Tell her that she needs to make an appointment for her doctor or be ready to call the clinic. Oh, my. Liz, you need to get your bus to work. Come, I'll walk you to the bus stop."

I was puzzled. "Mama, don't you need to call the police?"

"We don't have time for that. She'll miss her bus and be late." When we started down the steps, we heard people talking. When we got out of the building, we saw the police. One police officer came up to us.

"Ma'am, did you see anything? You do live here, right?"

Mama whispered to me, "Just keep your mouth shut."

"Yes, we live here. But, we just came out so we don't know what happened." We pushed past the police and the crowd that had gathered around. Someone yelled out, y'all better never answer those police or you'll be dead too."

Sharon was with us. "This is a scary place to live and I don't like it here anymore."

Mama looked at her. "So, where are you going to live? Not over my sister's house. She don't want you or me over there to live, and I'm her sister. Don't think I haven't asked her to let us live there so I could save money to get a better apartment for us. She always gives me the same excuse. "I'm not your mother and they are your children, not mine. No, Tracy, I'm not starting with that.

"I wish she could care enough for my kids to help them out, like with school clothes. But, she keeps saying that I'm the mother and they are my responsibility, not hers. I have to live where my money can take me, and it can only take me so far. So, we have to live where we can afford it."

Becky said, "I'm tired of walking."

Mama said, "Okay, Liz, just get the next bus and that one will take you straight downtown. I have to get the kids back home."

I thanked them for walking me to the bus stop. I was happy that Mama took the time to walk along and talk with all of us. I kept thinking of that man in the yard though.

When the bus came I thought, the next time I see something like that, I hope I'm not living here. My children will not be raised like this in this rat hole! I thought about Mike. His future seemed good. Maybe he and I could get married one day. After all, we talked all the time and we did share a kiss. I hoped that this would turn out to be a good dream. Hopefully, my heart wouldn't kill me from the pain that he might someday cause me. I cried about my family all the time, and hoped and prayed that no one I knew would die.

"Hey Liz." I was so engrossed in my thoughts that I didn't even see Peggy come up to me as I was walking into the store.

"Oh, hi Peggy. Hey, are you still going to the party this weekend?"

"Yeah, as far as I know."

"What are you doing four weeks from now on that Saturday?"

"Nothing that I know of, why?"

"My sister is going to have a surprise baby shower and I want you to come to that too."

"Well, this is really too early to be able to give you an answer right now."

"Well, at least put that date in your book. The time is 4 o'clock."

"I'll call you if I can go, okay?"

"Okay, that sounds good. Hey, let's eat lunch together."

"Okay. What are we going to eat?"

"I don't know. I hope it's not chicken!"

"Well" Peggy said, "Let's look at the menu.

Do you want a hamburger and salad and a piece of cake?"

"Well, that sounds good, but it's still the same old menu. Why don't we go to the soul food restaurant down in the hood and get some cake and pudding?"

I thought she was crazy. "Peggy, you're really going to drive all the way down there?"

"Yeah, why not, Liz? I'm not scared of everything!"

I said, "The restaurant is all dirty, and everything."

"Yeah, but the food is good and plus, I like their greens and their sweet potato pie. It's just enough down to the restaurant."

As we were getting out, I heard somebody say, "Hi Liz."

I turned around and said, "Hey, Lament. What have you been up to? The last time I saw you was at Roland's funeral."

"Well, I kind of got in some trouble and now I'm living with my cousin down the street and across. Did your sister have the baby yet? You know, this isn't Ricky's first baby!"

"Well, they're together, aren't they? That's the main thing. But no, she didn't have the baby yet."

Peggy hit me on my side. "Let's go, Liz," she whispered.

"Well Lament, I have to go now. I'll see you later.

"Wait, who's your friend?" I just looked at him silently, waved goodbye and walked away. I couldn't give Peggy's name out because I thought of Lament as nothing but a lying bum.

"Thanks for not giving him my name, Liz."

"Don't worry about it. He's nothing but trouble anyway."

Peggy started getting her money out. "Liz, you have your money ready?"

"Well, Peggy, I only have ten dollars."

"But your order came to eleven dollars and forty five cents."

"I'll give you the dollar forty-five next week when I have it, okay?"

"Liz, this is your food. You have a big order here, you and Janice. I didn't ask for ya'll to give me money for gas and my time. I do expect you to give what you owe, though. That's not right."

"You're right, I won't do that again and I'll make sure you get all of your money." She didn't say anything. I knew she was a little angry but I guess she was more hungry than angry so we got our food. I couldn't resist the smells that were coming from the bags. "Boy, this sure smells good. I hope it's as good as it smells."

"Well, we'll find out in a minute. Liz, Mike's party is tomorrow evening, right?" Peggy asked.

"Yep," I said.

"What time do you go to work?"

I replied, "At 8:30, and I should be home around 2:30. It's only going to be a half a day for me."

Peggy said, "I'm coming in from 10 o'clock to 6 o'clock. Did you tell Mrs. Elaine, that you only have a half a day?"

"Yes, she knows about it."

"But you know you have got to remind her again about tomorrow. I'm working with her in the office today, so, I'll tell her." Peggy said.

Janice met us in the parking lot. "Liz, are you working a half day tomorrow?"

"Yeah. Now let's eat. I'm starving."

Peggy said, "Hurry, let's get this food out of the car and into our stomach's before I pass out. Janice, you owe me nine dollars for your food."

"Thanks, Peggy. Here's you're money. Liz, you sure eat big for a little girl."

"I'm really hungry and my stomach is growling." We headed down to the cafeteria to eat. Steve came around begging for food. We started laughing at him. He seemed so pitiful! He pulled out his so-called lunch. Janice teased him. "Steve, take that smelly sandwich home."

"Please, y'all give me something, I'm starving and that soul food looks good."

Peggy asked him, "Are you going to clean up after us when we finish eating?"

"Yeah, don't worry about that. Just give me some potato salad and some spare ribs." I gave him a piece of my pie.

"Liz, you just gave me a little bite!"

"That's right. I bought this for me and my hungry stomach, not your stomach." He didn't like that too much.

Peggy asked me what I was doing later on that night. "Are you getting your hair fixed at the hair dresser?"

"Yeah"

"Girl, I can do your hair at my apartment."

"Can you do it here?"

"No, stupid. I'm not going to even answer that question. You can wait for me if you want a free hair do."

"Well, I really don't know."

"Hey, I'm giving you a free hair do. Your hair will need to be washed. Bring some curlers and wash your hair before you come. I can blow-dry it on my lunch break. I can teach you how to work with your hair from now on."

I agreed and went to work. We were all in the locker room when Peggy came back from her car. "My car still smells like soul-food. We ate that three hours ago."

Janice said, "Peggy, three hours ago that food smelled like my feet when it's wet." We all laughed.

"Well, it isn't a good smell, that's for sure." Peggy took both Janice and me to our bus stops. When I got out, I said, "See you, smelly old lady," to Janice.

"Start with you first, Liz, old smelly thing!" We all started to laugh. I said my goodbyes and ran upstairs to the apartment.

Lynne greeted me at the door. "Liz, remember that dead man you were talking about behind our trash cans?"

"Yeah. I had almost forgot about it."

"Well, don't go to sleep yet. You need to sit down."

"What's going on?" I started to get worried. Lynne had a funny look on her face. "Liz, it was Charles. Charles' father told Mama about that happened." I was shocked. I couldn't believe what I was hearing. I jumped out of my chair and started sobbing.

Mama came in saying, "Liz, Liz, please baby, don't cry like that. It will be okay!"

"Mama, Charles was my friend and to hear that he died, it just breaks my heart!" I just couldn't say anything else. Mama and Lynne held me in their arms while I cried uncontrollably.

"Please Liz, don't cry so loud. It will be okay, you'll see."

"But, Charles was my friend." The pain of my heart was so terrible! No one knew what had happened. All anyone knew was that Charles started hanging out with some bad boys at his aunt's apartment building. She said she saw him early that morning with a boy named Rocko. Then, she didn't see him anymore that day.

I moaned and thought, Now I won't see him anymore either! I just lay there in my mother's arms.

"Baby, just go to bed. We all are tired so try to sleep now."

It was already midnight but the tears wouldn't stop coming because the pain of loosing Charles was just killing me inside. I went in my room and just lay on my bed. I didn't bother to get out of my clothes.

"Let me help you take your clothes off," Lynne said. She got my new gown and slippers and put them on me. I grabbed her arm and cried against it.

"Liz, don't worry, tomorrow will be a better day. You can call Mike and talk to him and maybe that will make you feel better. Right now, you need to go to sleep. Let me get you some warm milk."

Lynne continued to try to make me feel better about the whole thing with Charles. "Liz, please take this warm milk. It will help you sleep."

I shook my head no and pushed it away. She picked my head up, took a warm washrag, wiped my face and kissed me on the cheek. I took a couple of sips of milk, and lay down. I could hear my little sister and brother asking Lynne if I was all right.

Lynne answered them, "She's alright, she's just a little sad right now. She just needs to rest. So, you guys go back to sleep." Instead, they went into their room and sat in the dark. Back in my room, I tried to sleep, but all I could think about was who might be next in this building to die. Somehow, I fell asleep for a few hours. As soon as my eyes opened, I thought about Charles and my eyes started to fill with tears.

"Liz, the phone is for you," Sharon said running into my room.

"Sharon, tell them I will call them back later."

"But, it's Mike."

"Oh, okay. Hey, Mike. I guess you heard what happened."

"Yeah, I did. Why Charles is what I want to know. I just don't know why it happened, Liz! Hey, do you want to get together today?"

"No, Mike, I have to work today."

"Oh. Well, what are you doing this evening after you get off of work?"

"Well, I'm supposed to be going to this party with Lynne."

"Well, that's really nice. That will keep your mind off of everything."

"I guess so, but his memory I'll never forget! He was the first boy I met when I moved here."

Mike started thinking back too. "Yeah, he was the one that introduced us. That was a real nice thing for him to do. I'm very glad he did. Well, Liz, I guess I'll see you tomorrow if you have off."

"Okay Mike. That would be nice." We hung up, and I noticed that my face was wet. I guess I was crying when I was talking about Charles on the phone with Mike and I didn't even realize it.

Lynne walked up. So Liz, what party are you going to tonight?"

"I'm going to Mike's party, but I couldn't tell him that. He would know about the surprise. You're coming with me, right?"

"Yeah, I am."

"But you're not going to help out, right?"

"Yeah, you bet! I'm going there to eat and party in my shape!" We talked a little more, and then I got ready for work. I really didn't want to go to work, but I didn't want to stay home either, with everybody trying to make me feel better. Plus, I had to get my hair done. When I left my apartment, it was very hard to pass Charles door. I ran past and out of the front door.

"Liz, Liz!" It was Miss Mae.

"Yes?"

"I'm collecting money for the boy that died. Spread the word."

"Okay." Then, I ran up the street to catch my first bus.

When I got to work, Peggy wasn't there. Janice said, "Let me see if your thick hair is clean."

"Janice, a tragedy happened last night so I didn't get a chance to wash my hair."

"Oh, I'm so sorry to hear that. Are you okay?"

"No, but I'll get through it."

"Well, meet me in the bathroom at 12:30, okay?"

"Janice, I get off at 12."

"So, if you want a free hairstyle, just stay around here and wait for me."

Twelve thirty came fast. Janice saw me waiting for her. "So, I see you stayed around and waited for me."

"That's right, Miss Janice, you see me waiting so give me your curls and warm them up in the coat room!" I start laughing for the first time since yesterday. She finished my hair up in the coatroom. "It looks good and I really like the style, Janice. Thanks."

Peggy walked in. "Let me see," she said. She looked closely at my hair. "I can smell a lot of grease in your hair!"

"Peggy, my hair is not fried, okay? Janice is a good hairdresser plus, she didn't let me down. You said you would do it but you weren't here."

"I was running late. There was nothing I could do about that."

"Whatever, Peggy." I thought she did it on purpose but I didn't say anything. I thanked Janice again and went upstairs to get dressed. I missed one of my busses so I decided to catch a cab. The streets were crowded because it was the Fourth of July weekend. Fortunately, I got home before 3 o'clock, hurried and threw my clothes on, and just as I finished, I heard a honk outside. I grabbed my purse and ran out of the house.

"Thank you for being on time, Liz. I got everything for the party except the decorations and the balloons." We stopped at a store and I ran in and got all of the decorations. Once we got to the recreation center, she introduced me to her son Melvin. I said hi, and started to help fix the room up. "Mrs. Maxine, who will be bringing Mike?"

"His friend Robert."

"Oh, okay. I met him before."

"Okay, we'll put the food on one table and the canned soda into the cooler so it can stay cold." We started putting the decorations on the wall and around the tables.

"Liz, here. Put my apron on so you won't get that pretty pants set messed up." She put on the music, Smokey Robinson to start, and I started singing to myself.

Mike's uncle asked me to dance. I told him I only wanted to hand dance and not slow dance. Slowly everyone started coming in. His cousin Kate and her boyfriend Willie and other friends of Mike arrived. Mrs. Maxine started putting the food and the cake on the table. Suddenly the lights went out, and someone said that Mike was coming. Robert came in with Mike behind him, we popped out of our hiding places and yelled SURPRISE!

Mike's mouth dropped open. "Oh my goodness, all of this is for me?" Everybody started to laugh. He was still was in shock. We started to dance and I started passing out something to drink.

Robert came up to me. "Hey Liz. What are you doing over here? You should be over there with Mike?"

"Hey Robert. I haven't seen you since the prom. Where is Ashley at?"

"Oh, me and Ashley ain't together anymore. I'm just playing it solo right now." As we were talking, I saw Sheron and Leah come in. Mike started talking to them then dancing with Sheron.

Leah came over to us. "Hi Liz. Are you going to dance with Mike tonight?"

"Not right now. I'm helping out with the service at the party."

Leah walked away. I knew she wanted to start trouble. After they finished dancing, Mike went over to his uncle and his cousin. As I got closer to Sheron and Leah, Leah dropped a cookie on the floor and asked me to pick it up.

I looked at her like she was crazy, went over to the cookie and crushed it with my foot. "This is how I pick up your cookie. Now, it's good enough for you to eat!"

Kate, who saw the whole thing, started laughing at Leah.

Leah looked angry and said, "I see you are Mike's personal servant!"

Kate looked at her, and said, "No, I guess she sure showed you!" and started laughing all over again. I started to laugh with her, and we both walked away from them.

Finally, Mike came over to me. "Liz, I thought you said that you and Lynne were going to a party tonight."

"Yeah, I did go to a party tonight. Yours! I just told you about Lynne to throw you off about your own party."

"Oh, I get it now. That's crazy, girl!" We talked for a few more minutes and then he said he would be back. He went over to talk to Willie about what happened to Charles. "Boy, that really hurt me, man!"

"I know Mike. That was one of your main guys in school!"

"Yeah, he was, and I miss him too!" They talked some more, and then he came back over to me. "Liz, come on, let's dance."

"Okay." I thought it would make me feel better and it did. My favorite record was playing. We started dancing close and he stole a quick kiss from me. "Thanks for helping my granny out tonight. She really appreciates it."

"That's okay, Mike. After all, it was your graduation party."

"I'm leaving for college next week, so I won't be able to go to Charles' funeral even though I really wish I could just to support his family and other friends. Before I leave, though, I'm going past his aunt's apartment to leave a sympathy card for the family. Please make sure the family receives it, okay?"

"Yes, Mike I will."

"Hey, are you having a good time tonight?"

"Mike this is your party, are you having a great time?"

"Yes, I am, because you are here." That made me feel really good. It was then that I realized I was going to really miss him! Now that Charles was gone, I was going to have no one to hang with anymore. I was fighting back the tears. I didn't want to ruin the good feeling I had at the time since Mike and I were talking and dancing to my favorite record.

I started to help his grandmother clean up when the guests started leaving. His uncle came over to me again. He asked me if Mike and I were together. "I don't know, because he is going to leave for college next week."

"Well, he better take you there with him! If he doesn't, then someone else will snatch you up quick!" I started to giggle.

Mike came by. He heard what we just said. "Uncle, that's my girl," and started laughing.

"Hey, ain't no harm in trying to find out." We all started to laugh again.

We finally cleaned everything up and put the trash out. Mike's grandmother came over to me. "Liz, can I take you home?"

"Granny, I can take Liz home. Liz, are you ready to go home now?"

"Yeah, if you are." I was so glad that he stayed around me at the party and danced with me in front of everybody. I wanted Sheron and Leah to see that I wasn't Mike's nasty girl like they said. Mike and I started slowly walking home and talking. We got quiet as we passed Charles' apartment.

As soon as I got to the door, Lynne asked me, "Liz, how was the party?"

"It was great. I had a really good time."

"Did you and Mike dance together?"

"Yes," Mike said. "Lynne, that's why she came to my party, to have a good time and dance with me."

"Liz knows why I asked her that."

"Well, what's going on? Liz didn't come to have a good time?"

I just answered. I could see where this was going. "Yes, Mike, I had a great time." He kissed me in the hallway before we went inside my apartment. I thought to myself, I'm really going to miss him kissing me goodnight, talking and walking with me when it gets late at night. I slowly closed the front door.

Mama came into the living room. "Liz and Mike, Charles' funeral will be this Wednesday from 10:30 to 12:00.

"Oh Mama, Miss Mae says she is collecting money for our building to give Charles family."

Mama said, "Old Lady Mae is making a career out of collecting money and she gets some money and some food for the month. Not this time. She's not getting one dime from us! We need to find out for ourselves where the family will be taking the food and card money from friends. We don't need to give that woman a cut of our things!" We all fell out laughing! Mama continued. "Lynne, did you make an appointment to see the doctor?"

"Yes, Mama, it's Monday at 10:30."

"Well, I can't go with you. I have to work. Where is that worthless man of yours? You make him go with you to the doctor. Oh, is he working that day? Standing on his favorite corner? Lynne, you really got yourself a bum and I hope you don't marry him. Before the marriage could start it would be over."

Lynne started to get angry. "Oh boy, here we go again."

"Girl, you need someone to tell you these things. This baby is with you for the rest of your life!"

"I know, I know. You're telling me the truth, but sometimes I just don't feel like hearing all of that. Plus, I'm still trying to see who came to the party."

I chimed in. "Lynne, you don't know anybody who was there."

"I bet you Sheron and Leah came!"

"Of course. Granny invited them."

"Aww, come on Mike, I know that Leah and you used to go together."

"Yeah, when I was fourteen. That was about four years ago. She still likes me though, even though she knows I like Liz."

Lynne looked at Mike funny. "Mike" she said, "Did you tell her that?"

"Lynne, what's with all the questions?" I asked.

"I just don't want my sister looking like a fool!"

Mike started getting angry. "Lynne, aren't you pregnant by a bum? Don't that make you a fool too?"

"No, because I didn't go with Ricky for no four years!"

Mama came back in the room. "Alright, that's enough of that. Somebody's about to get their feelings hurt. We should be praying about Charles' family."

"Liz, I'm going home. I don't need to be talking about this nonsense, especially with your sister," then he left. I was angry.

Just because Mama yelled at Lynne, didn't give her the right to take it out on me and Mike. "Lynne, why is any of this your business? This is causing me nothing but pain in our relationship."

"NO girl, Mike going with you causes me pain! Besides Liz, you have to look at the facts. I don't want you to get hurt anymore than you already have. He's leaving for college in a week! You know, once they get there, they never look back. There are girls there just like you in his college that will be with him, so your relationship will not last very long!"

"Lynne, it still isn't your business. That baby in your stomach is your business, and also the bum that is called the baby's father!" I ran into my room and slammed the door! Only a few more weeks until this stupid baby shower!

A few weeks afterwards at work, I was looking for a nice gift for the shower. Janice was helping me. "Liz, this is pretty. I always use these things as a gift for a baby shower. Hey, have you heard anything from Mike? It's been two weeks?"

"No."

"Oh." She didn't say anything else about it. Peggy walked up as we were looking through baby stuff. "I usually like to buy baby sleepers for the gift. They really come in handy for the baby when it's born. Hey Liz, are you feeling okay? You don't look too good."

"I don't feel good. I just want to get to the shower and sit down."

Janice said, "Liz is lonely and she just misses Mike a lot."

I looked at her. "Maybe that's true," I said, "but, he didn't even give me his phone number or his address at school so I could write him a letter. I don't know why."

Peggy said, "Girl, he'll call you sometime this year. He's having too much fun!"

"Whatever!" I said. I didn't want to talk about it anymore.

The next day, I was supposed to be with Lynne all day and lead her to the party. I was supposed to have her back home by 4:30 that afternoon. We went looking for baby clothes, ate some lunch, then we took the bus home. As we were walking, I heard someone say, "Hi Liz." I turned around.

Lisa said, "Lynne, don't say nothing to that nasty girl."

"Oh, Liz, she has the children with her so why shouldn't we speak to them," Lynne said.

I stood there looking at her. I picked up my niece and gave her a kiss. I still didn't say anything. "You're holding my child, and you can't say anything to me?"

"This baby don't have anything to do with me saying anything to you."

"Okay, if you feel like that, then that's fine." I started walking and talking to Lynne. Of course, the kids were dirty and smelling sour like they usually do. I didn't want to bring them to the house though, because of the party.

We walked up the stairs and Lynne opened the door. 'SURPRISE, SURPRISE!!!' Everyone yelled. Lynne's mouth just dropped open. "This is for me?"

"No," Mama said. "This is for your unborn child!" We all started laughing. When Mama saw that we had Lisa and the kids with us she pulled me to the side. "Girl, hurry up and clean those nasty children up. I got some clothes in the top drawer for them and Lisa can go in Lynne's drawer and get some clothes."

"No Mama, I'm going to my drawer and get some clothes for her."

"Okay, but hurry." I pulled Lisa aside and told her, "Lisa, let me tell you something. Just because you had my brother's children, don't mean anything. You can find clothes all by yourself! I'm only giving you clothes that I don't want and that I was about to throw out. My sister Sharon is one size under me, so please make sure this isn't your only stop!"

"Liz, don't say those things to me!"

"Lisa, I really want to kick you out of my house, just like when you were showing off on the bus and tried to kick me!" Lisa looked at me funny but didn't say anything.

I washed her sour-smelling kids up and put baby powder on them so they would smell good. Someone knocked on the door and opened it.

"Hey, Peggy," I said.

"Hey Liz, this is Karen, Ricky's sister. She's the one who gave the shower."

I said hello and came out of the room with the kids. Mama introduced me to everyone else. "Liz, these are Ricky's parents and Ricky's aunt is over there. Her name is Louise."

She told jokes all night, making everyone laugh. Then, there was his other brothers, Kevin and Jim, and his older sister Rachael. We all had a good time. Ricky looked like a proud father sitting up there with Lynne opening up all of the presents. My mind though, kept going back to Mike. I really wished that he were here. Lisa was doing the usual, trying to eat everything up.

Mama shook her head. "Poor children, and they are my grandchildren too." she said in a low voice.

Ricky and Lynne were watching the kids too. They were trying to get into the gifts. I went over and tapped Lisa on the shoulder. "Lisa, didn't forget, these kids are your responsibility, so watch them."

She went over, grabbed them and sat one on her lap and the other on the floor besides her. Mama said, "Okay, everyone twenty-one and older can have a beer." Ricky came up to her. "I would like one please."

"You are still two years from twenty-one."

"But Miss Tracy, I'm close to it."

"Sorry kid, you and Lynne have to wait till you're old enough." She started laughing and so did everyone else who heard her. Then, someone turned the music on and people started to dance. I grabbed John and we started to dance crazily. Miss Terry tried to dance but she said the new music and the new dancing are not for her! We started to crack up.

Mama came up to her. "Girl, we are too old for this. We need to be sitting down playing cards and talking. Let's go over there and talk to Ricky's parents."

Mama looked over at me. "Liz, make sure someone cleans up after those kids. They're making a mess."

"Okay, Mama."

I went over to Lisa. "Lisa, you need to clean up the mess your kids are making."

"Okay, Liz, then we're leaving."

"That will be fine with me."

Peggy started laughing. "Why did you give those kids the whole cake?"

Lynne looked over at her cake and then at Lisa. The kids had put their fingers in the cake and their fingerprints were all over it! Lynne went over to Lisa. "Lisa, you have to go now." Then, she calmly went back into the living room and cut the cake.

Lynne said she had a good time even though Lisa tried to ruin it. Peggy and I went back to the kitchen and we were looking out of the kitchen window, talking. All of a sudden, we heard someone laughing and screaming. We look down and saw some children in a U-Haul truck, sitting in chairs. We started shaking our heads.

Peggy said, "Those poor people. They're moving their children as well as their furniture. Now, that is ghetto."

I started shaking my head again and laughing. "Liz, that's nothing to laugh about!"

"Peggy, I hope these people don't bring their problems with them!"

Peggy started laughing. "Girl, this is Harlem. All you have here is problems."

"I know that people will have problems wherever they are, but here in Harlem, they bring their drug trade and their bums like to hang out all night on the stoop. See Peggy, you don't live here. You live in Brooklyn," I said.

"Liz, we have drugs and bums there too, you know."

Ricky's parents came past to help Lynne with her gifts because they were about to leave, and since it was getting late, everyone else was leaving too. Peggy went to the bedroom to get her coat. One of Lynne's friends, Toya, came up to her. "Lynne, you got some nice gifts." Lynne started to smile.

"Lynne" I said, "Don't forget to thank everybody for their gifts."

"Oh yeah." She stood up in the center of the living room, and said, "Thank you all for coming and I hope and pray that my baby will be born healthy." I glanced over at Mama. She had a big smile on her face. Mama also thanked Ricky and his parents and friends for coming.

Peggy finally left and I started to clean up then headed back to the bedroom. Sharon asked me where I was going. "I'm going to bed, I'm so tired! I'm glad this evening is over!" I could hear Mama and Miss Terry talking in the living room. They were talking about how nice everything went. My eyes were closing as they were speaking and I fell fast asleep. I didn't even have time to think about my problems tonight.

The next morning Lynne had an appointment at the clinic. I stayed in the bed. I was still tired but I also knew I had to go to work later on this afternoon. When the phone rang John yelled, "Liz, the phone is for you."

I slowly got up, trying to guess who it could be. "Hello?"

"Hi, Liz. It's Mike. Hey, are you going to Charles' funeral today?"

"No, I can't. I have to work today."

"Liz, the funeral is at 10 o'clock this morning. I can pick you up with Granny's car."

"Okay, Mike. Let me go so I can get dressed."

"Okay, see you soon."

Mama yelled out, "I want to go too."

Then Lynne rushed out of the bathroom to tell me that she was going too. I asked, "Who is going to watch the kids?"

Mama said, "Sharon is here, she can watch John and Becky."

Lynne chimed in, "Sharon is going to senior high this year. We were watching our brothers and sisters when we were nine."

Sharon looked angry. "Oh, why me?"

Mama said, "Well, you'll watch them. Don't leave my apartment, okay?"

"Yes, Mama." Sharon mumbled back. A half an hour later Mike beeped his horn. Lynne left her appointment slip upstairs. Mama said, "You must go to your doctor's appointment!"

"My appointment isn't until 12:30 this afternoon."

"Okay, that's fine." Mama yelled up the steps to Sharon, "Sharon, don't let anybody in my house and stay off of my phone!" Poor Sharon, I thought. She was so angry that she couldn't go to the funeral that she didn't answer Mama.

We all got into Mike's car. Lynne hurried to get in the front seat. Mama stopped her. "Lynne, that ain't your man, so take your pregnant tail and come back here with your mother."

"Mike didn't say anything!" Lynne said.

"Lynne, he didn't have to say anything. He came to see Liz."

Then Lynne started to talk smart. "I don't remember him asking you to come!"

Mama said, "I don't remember him asking you either. Now, please shut up before I ask Mike to put you in front of the clinic two and a half hours before your appointment!" Lynne looked at Mama and got in the back. I opened the front door, got in, and Mike took off. When we got there we saw all of Charles cousins and his girlfriend in the car in front of us.

As Mike parked Sissy and Niecy began knocking on the window. Niecy was carrying her baby. Mike rolled down the window. "Hey Mike. Are you staying after the funeral? We need two more pall bearers."

"That's fine Sissy. I can do it.

Mike said, "He really was a good friend to me, and that's why I'm here. I flew right home from college when I heard."

When we pulled up to the church, we heard a woman crying loudly, "That's my son laying in that casket!" A man was hugging her. Everyone in the car—my mother, me, Lynne and Mike, felt terrible. We loved Charles and really missed him, especially Mike and me. I started crying against my mother's shoulder.

Mama said, "Ya'll be ready, so when they call our row, we can view the body." Mike took my hand then hugged me around my neck as we were walking. Tears streamed down my face.

"Hold on to me," Mike kept saying to me. He kept pushing me along though, because he could see me I wanted to sit down. Finally, we stood in front of the casket. I wanted to look at him quickly but instead I reached out and rubbed his cold face. I walked back to my seat with tears on my face and pain in my heart! Mama was hugging Lynne.

As the funeral director started the service, we heard a noise outside. I ran to the window and saw Niecy lying in the alley kicking, screaming and crying.

Mama said, "Let's go home."

As we left the church, Mike and the other pallbearers were still at the front of the church. We were walking down to the subway when someone yelled out, "Tracy!"

Mama turned around and asked Mr. Roy., "What are you doing here?"

Mr. Roy said, "My best friend's nephew died. I decided to go to support him. Are you headed home?"

"Yes," Mama replied.

"Well, I can give you a lift," Mr. Roy said.

He left us at our front door and we thanked him. When we got upstairs we heard Becky and John talking. Mama had a funny look on her face. "Where is Sharon? On the phone? Where did you two get candy from, anyway?"

"The old man that lives three doors down from us gave it to us."

"Don't you ever take any candy from anybody you don't know! And get up off of the hallway steps! What are you two doing in the hallway anyway?"

They looked back at Mama with a blank stare. Mama went up the rest of the steps, opened the door and ran over to Sharon. She snatched the phone from her and slammed it down. She slapped her in the back and yelled out, "You are supposed to be watching my kids, not talking on the phone! So, when I leave, is this what you're going to do?"

Sharon ran into her room crying, saying, "Nobody minds me anyway!"

Mama was really mad! "Lynne you get ready to go to the clinic, and Liz, you get ready to go to work."

"Okay," I said. "Mama, if Mike calls, can you tell him to meet me at my job, please?"

"Okay." I got dressed and ran out the door, tears still on my face. I kept thinking about how much I missed Charles. Whenever I thought about everything, which was most of the time, I got a chill all over.

When I got outside, Peggy pulled up. I get in but I was too choked up to speak, and the tears were still coming. Peggy reached over took hold of my hand. "Did you go to Charles' funeral today?"

"Yes." That's all I could say. I wanted to say more but the pain in my heart was too bad.

Steven was outside puffing on a cigarette. Peggy said, "Hi Mr. Steven." I couldn't say anything, so I rushed past him.

"What's wrong with Liz?" Peggy asked.

"She just doesn't feel well today. One of her good friends just died and she went to the funeral today. That's why she is crying. So Steve, please be kind to her today."

"Well, just don't ask me to do her work 'cause she is sad."

Peggy turned around and hit him on his arm and they both started laughing. I went to the locker room to put my pocketbook away. I didn't say anything to anybody, and I was hoping that nobody would ask me what was wrong. I just wanted to be left alone. I wanted to go home so I could lie down. This was going to be a long night though, because I had to fill in for someone else in another department. I also had to close tonight. I called home to see if Mike called.

Lynne said, "Not yet."

"Well, if he does, ask him if he could pick me up tonight in his grandmother's car after I get off of work."

"Okay, I will." Then she hung up.

Later on that night, on my break, I felt a little better. I looked for Peggy so I would have somebody to talk to. Unfortunately, Peggy left early. I had to close with that stupid Steven! I must have said it out loud, because he said, "Girl, don't remind me!."

He was making my night longer with his stupid jokes. I put some trash in the lobby and put all the supplies up front so Steven could put it away. Mr. Carl, our supervisor, called to Steve in the back but he didn't come.

"Liz, tell him to hurry up. I want to go home," Mr. Carl said. I went in the locker room and found him sound asleep!

"Steve, Steve, wake up! Mr. Carl wants you to help him put the supplies on the truck in the back!"

"Okay, Liz. I hear you. I'm up. I'm going there now." He jumped up and ran up front. After a bit, he called me up front too. "Come on, Liz. Everything is done."

"Okay, I'm coming now. Let me just cut out all of the back lights, and grab my coat."

Just as I was heading out of the door, Steve called me. "Liz, wait for me. I'm going your way too."

"Okay, Steve, but I'm not waiting long." As we left the store I saw Mike in the parking lot. I asked if he could take Steve to the bus stop.

"Liz," he whispered. "I don't know him!"

"Well, let me introduce him to you."

"Okay Liz, whatever, I'm tired," Mike said. I called Steve over and he got in the back.

"Hi, I'm Steven."

"Hi, I'm Mike, nice to meet you." He didn't say much to Steve and he dropped him off at the bus stop just as Steve's bus came.

"See Mike, you did someone a great favor. Hey, how did you know I worked late tonight?"

"Your sister Lynne called me and asked me to pick you up. Girl, I was laying up in my bed looking at TV when she called."

I looked at him funny. "So Mike, you don't like me anymore, or you just came up here for the funeral?"

"No, Liz! I was going to take you to lunch tomorrow but, were spending time together now." I looked at him but didn't say anything else. Once we got to my apartment, he kissed me goodbye and said, "Liz, I'll see you tomorrow, okay?"

"Okay, Mike." I rushed up the steps and opened the door.

"Did Mike pick you up from work?"

"Yeah, he did. Thanks for calling him. I guess you could see that I was going to get home really late."

Sharon came out of her room. "Liz, were going to go back to school in a couple of weeks, and we need some clothes."

Chapter 14

Lynne's Pregnancy

I was still thinking about what Sharon said about Lisa's kids living here with us. I started to cry silently, hoping no one would hear me. I thought about all of the people already here in this tiny apartment. Now, living with Lisa's kids would just be crazy! I was supposed go to the movies with Mike tomorrow, so I tried to get my mind off everything by planning for that. The next morning I was still tired and sleepy from yesterday but after I got myself together, I put all of the dirty clothes in bags to take to the Laundromat. Mama asked me to take the clothes to the laundry and told Sharon to bring it back when it was finished.

As I went downstairs, the cart kept making a crazy noise. Sharon said, "Liz, I hope this stupid cart makes it down the stairs. The wheel looks like it's about to fall off right now!" We made it to the laundry without it falling off. I put all of the clothes on the floor and separated them. I asked Sharon how much Mama gave her to wash the clothes.

"Mama gave me six dollars."

"Girl, that's not enough for us to wash all of this stuff!"

"Liz, that's all Mama gave me."

"Well, let me go to the store to get some more change."

On the way back to the laundry, I saw several crazy looking teenagers hanging out in the front of the laundry. As I got closer, I realized that it was Sharon and a few of her friends. I went into the Laundromat to find that Sharon had left some of the clothes in the washing machine.

I yelled out to Sharon, "The rest of the clothes aren't outside, are they?" Then, I grabbed Sharon's arm to pull her inside with me.

She told her friends, "Aww, don't pay my stupid sister no mind."

"Girl, I'm gonna leave you here when my clothes get dry, and you'll have to tackle this by yourself, including that stupid cart. Where did you find those slum bums?"

"Liz, you have no right to talk about my friends like that. Plus, you live right across the street from these so-called 'slum bums.' By the way, his name is Jeff and his sister is Kelly."

"So, those are your so called friends?"

"There you go being Miss Perfect again!" Sharon said.

"Just shut up, and help me put these clothes in the washing machine." Later on as we were drying the clothes, a red car went down the street."

"There goes Mike driving his grandmother's car," Sharon said.

I just said "Um, hmm."

Sharon continued, "Liz, he didn't pass here to pick you up."

"So, if he would have seen me, he would have picked me up."

"So, what about me?"

"What about you? Sharon, those little slum bums aren't nothing but trouble, and baby makers!"

"So, is that your way of thinking of Mike?"

"Little girl, you better move! Let me put these clothes in the cart. You can help me and just shut up!"

We loaded up the cart and started for home. The wheel on the cart looked like it was going to fall off at any minute. I told Sharon to take the heavy bag and I would take the rest of the stuff home in the cart. When we got in front of the building, I told Sharon to run upstairs to get John so he could help us get the clothes up the stairs.

"Liz, you go upstairs and get John, I'll stay with the cart, okay?"

I ran upstairs to get John but he could not find his shoe, so I ran back downstairs to get the clothes myself. As I get downstairs, Sharon was talking to her slum bum friends across the street again. I grabbed my clothes and left her. I figured she could take the rest of the clothes upstairs since she wanted to talk so much. I went inside and told Mama what she was doing.

Mama yelled out the window, "Sharon, come up here and separate your clothes!" Sharon ran upstairs with the rest of the clothes and pushed past me as she went inside.

"Let it happen again Sharon, and I'm gonna punch you in the face!" I said.

"Aww, keep your emotions to yourself!" she yelled back.

We were folding and putting the clothes away when the phone rang. I said, "Hey, Peggy. What's going on?"

Peggy said, "You tell me? What happened last night with crazy Steve?"

"Well, Mike picked us up."

"Oh, that was nice of him." As I was talking, Lynn came out of the room, obviously listening to my conversation.

"Um hmm, who called Mike last night for you?"

"Hold on Peggy," I said.

Lynne continued, "Well? Who called him for you?"

I moved Lynn out of the way with my hand. Mama came down the hall.

"Lynne, stop doing that to Liz. By the way Liz, you can tell Peggy how things are but not how things is! Get my point?"

"Yes Mama, I do." I got back on the phone with Peggy and Mama moved Lynne to the side.

Mama asked her, "Lynne, what is wrong with you? That is very disrespectful to do that when someone is on the phone! Don't let that happen again on my phone, you got it?"

"Oh, I forgot, Ms. Liz is your special child! She don't say or do anything wrong in your eyes!"

Mama started to get mad. "Little girl, let me tell you again, this is *my* phone, and you will respect anyone that calls on it!"

Lynne just rolled her eyes, sucked her teeth, and waved her hand at Mama as if to say *whatever.* Mama, who could not take her being disrespectful anymore, jumped over me and slapped Lynne with all her might! I jumped between the two of them and dropped the phone.

I yelled, "Sharon, run and get Ms. Terry! Mama, Mama, don't hit Lynne! I got between the two of them, and instead of Mama hitting Lynne, she hit me by mistake. That blow hurt and tears started running down my face. Lynne was trying to hide her face but Mama hit her in her mouth and a little blood started to trickle down her face.

Ms. Terry came running in. "Tracy! Stop before you hurt her baby and go to jail!"

Mama just said, "Let me go. I have a lot of anger in me today!"

"NO! Tracy, please stop!"

I tried to push Lynne into the other room and Ms. Terry tried to push Mama in the other direction. Mama yelled, "Terry, I am going to slap that girl until she respects me in *my* own house!"

"No Tracy, just let her go!" Finally, Mama let her go. John and Sharon helped me push Lynne away from Mama. Ms. Terry got Mama to go to her apartment to cool down for a while.

I lay down with Lynne on the bed. She started crying, "My stomach hurts!" I started rubbing her stomach so she could go to sleep.

All of a sudden, Mama came back in the room and started yelling again. "You go find that bum boyfriend of yours and go live with him!" Tears streamed down Lynne's face.

Sharon ran and got a washrag. "Is it clean, Sharon?" I asked. "Yes, Liz, it's a clean rag!" I wet it to put on Lynne's face. Lynne just kept crying about her stomach hurting and I started to worry. I told her to lie back down. She lay down, but she was moaning in pain. Finally, after about forty-five minutes, she fell asleep. I told everybody else to keep quiet so she could sleep.

I ran upstairs to Ms. Terry's house to see how Mama was doing. "Liz, I told your Mama to go in my room and get some rest."

"Oh, okay. Well, is it okay if I go to the movies with Mike?"

"Well, I guess so. What time are you coming home?"

"After the movie is over, so I should be home around 9:30," I said.

"Well, okay. Just be back before 11. Your mama should be back home by then."

"Okay. Ms. Terry, please tell her tonight after she wakes up, when she is calm, okay?"

"Okay, Liz, I will. Oh, before you leave, go check on your sister to make sure she's okay."

"Okay, I will. Lynne was asleep when I left to come here." I ran back downstairs and found everyone in his or her rooms.

The phone rang. Mike asked, "Liz, are you still going to the movies with me?"

"Yes Mike. What time does the movie start?"

"Around 8:30."

"What time is it over?"

"I guess around 10:45."

"Okay, but I have to be home at 11, okay?"

"Okay. I'm going to pick you up and we can go out for a snack around four o'clock, okay? Granny let me use her car today so I'll see you soon."

"Okay, that's fine. See ya' soon."

As I was hanging up, Sharon came out. "How's Mama?"

"She's okay. She's over Ms. Terry's house, and she's lying down over there. So, please don't go over there today, okay y'all? And, don't go over to those new kids' house either or bring them on our steps making a lot of noise, waking Lynne up."

"Yes, Liz. I love to hear your rules and laws."

"Girl, you are really asking for your feelings to be hurt today!" I tried to ignore Sharon's smart remarks. I started to separate my clothes from the laundry, hoping I could find my nice pants set so I could iron it and wear it tonight to the movies.

Lynne got up to use the bathroom. She left the door open. I went in. "Lynne is everything okay?"

"No, my stomach is still hurting. I need to call the clinic so I can go in there tomorrow."

"Who's going with you?"

"Well, I guess me, myself and I."

"I can leave school early to go with you."

"No, that's okay. I can get Ricky's sister or Ricky to go with me."

"I can go with you if it's first thing in the morning, 'cause I have to get to work early so I can have some extra money on my paycheck next week. Well, I need to use the bathroom so I can get ready to go with Mike to the movies this evening. He's picking me up early so we can get a snack or something, and then were going to the movies.

I went in the bathroom to wash up and comb my hair. When I was done, Lynne went into the bathroom behind me.

"What happened to all that soap that was in there?"

"I just finished washing up. I lathered my body with the soap, that's all," I said.

"How are we going to wash up tomorrow? That was our last bar and you almost used the whole thing!"

I asked John to go next door to Ms. Terry's house and ask if she had a bar of soap. Sharon heard the conversation and chimed in. "I know you want to be all pretty and smelling good for Mike, but now you use all that soap up to be pure?"

"Shut up Sharon! It's none of your business what happened to the soap."

"Well, what do you need all that soap for?"

"If you must know, miss nosey, I washed up. Is that okay with you, Ms. Sharon with the slum-bum friends?"

"Liz, you just need to shut up! You only got one friend, that's Peggy, and Ms. College is all stuck up and she thinks she's all that too!"

"That's right Sharon. I don't need the neighborhood bums to be my friends because Peggy is all the friend that I need. That and my job. All of y^all girls in this neighborhood are going to end up just like these boys around here!"

"Oh, so I guess you think you're really going to end up with Mike?" Sharon said.

"That might or might not be true, but at least I'm looking for the best this neighborhood has to offer!"

"You know what Liz? Mike is smart and he's going to college but he likes nasty girls as his girlfriends."

"What, Sharon? That's okay. Mike and me aren't getting married or anything anyhow. I'm not looking for a marriage in the future anyway, just to be his girlfriend."

Sharon said, "Well, take that thinking with you to the movies and see if Mr. Mike doesn't drop you like a hot potato! Just like all the rest of those girls he been with."

Just then, we heard a honk outside. John looked out the window. "Liz, it's Mike in his grandmother's car, here to pick you up."

"Okay John. Go tell him I'll be right down."

"I'm not running up and down all those steps for that!"

"John, I'll pay you fifty cents if you do it."

Sharon butted in yet again, "John, I wouldn't go downstairs for a jive fifty cents if I were you!"

"No Sharon, you wouldn't go downstairs for fifty cents, because I wouldn't even ask you to do it!"

"That's right. I'll be thinking about you when I go across the street with my 'slum bum' friends!" I just waved my hand in front of her face and walked past her.

"Y'all two girls are making me sick with your stupid crazy arguments!" Lynne said.

"Lynne, Liz thinks she is all that. She thinks she is the smartest and prettiest in the whole neighborhood and she thinks that Mike is the king of the neighborhood too! He's probably been with all the girls in the neighborhood too! She's going to be his next nasty girl." Sharon said.

She was making me mad! "Sharon, if that's what you want to think, then fine! You go ahead and think that. The truth is that you are just jealous of Mike's friendship and me! I'll see y'all two bums later."

Lynne yelled out, "Liz, you better be back by 11 tonight. Then we can see who the real bum is."

Mike decided he didn't want to take his grandmother's car downtown, so he dropped it off and we headed for the bus. Once we got downtown, we decided to stop at McDonalds to grab something to eat. Just as Mike was putting his cheeseburger to his mouth, he dropped it on the floor. "Mike, what's wrong with you today? You're acting funny."

"Liz, I just have a lot on my mind. I go back to college soon, and I'm just trying to get adjusted to everything. It's a different world over there! Even though I've been there for a few months, I'm still getting adjusted to campus life and it's way different than living in Harlem, I'll tell you that! I don't want to leave Robert and my other friends behind. I'm also worried about Granny. I don't like the fact that she will be alone now."

"But, Mike, you've prayed for this for a long time. You've always wanted to play Pro Ball and live a better life for yourself. Well, this is the road to that life so you better take advantage of it."

"Yeah, that's true but you have to remember I was raised in that little two-bedroom apartment. It's all I know."

I looked over at him. "Mike, think of all of the horror stories that we have heard about people that never made it out of Harlem and their lives went to waste. I know you don't want to end up like that, do you? I sure know I don't. I'm getting out of Harlem if it takes everything I have in me!"

"Boy, Liz, I'm going to miss you most of all. I really want you to be my special girl."

"Well, I don't know about being your special girl. Just concentrate on your dream and we'll deal with that later. I'll be here. We can see what happens later when you finally come home from college."

"Okay, Liz. Hey, do me a favor. Please check up on my grandmother from time to time. I know how people treat old people around here when they live by themselves."

"Okay, I will. Hey, we better hurry up and finish so we can catch the bus to the movies. That's the only bus going to that theatre." We grabbed our things, stuffed the last little bit of food in our mouths, and ran out the door just in time to catch the bus. We sat in the back.

Mike slid his arm around my shoulders. "I'm a lucky guy today. I'm spending time with a cute girl on 124th Street." I started blushing.

"I see you blushing over there!" he said, smiling. I was embarrassed that he could tell and I started to giggle. We got off in front of the theatre and I ran across the street with him holding my hand. Mike paid for our tickets and we sat in the back of the movie. The movie was just starting. Mike slowly put his arm around my shoulder and started kissing me on my neck and talking to me softly. "Mike, we can't do that. I don't want to become your nasty girl."

"Liz, don't we really care for each other? That's what people that really like each other do."

"Yeah, that may be true, but I'm not that kind of girl. I'm really glad you like me and you want to spend time with me but, I'm not going to do that." He put his arm down and scooted over to the other side of the chair, as far away from me as he could.

I started to feel nervous. Would he still take me home? I remembered what my Mother told me about taking emergency carfare with me. I looked over at him and saw he looked disappointed. I got up and went to the bathroom. As I was getting up, I asked him if he wanted something to eat or drink. He mumbled "No Liz." I went up the dark isle to the bathroom. Once there, I glanced at my face in the mirror. I looked as confused as I felt.

I took a seat next to the wall and started counting my money to see if I had enough money to catch the bus back home. I decided that I had at least enough to go take a bus to my job and ask Peggy to take me home, or I could get some money from Janice or Steven. I pulled myself together and went back into the theater.

"Mike, do you want me to leave?"

"Liz, why in the world would you ask me something like that?"

"Because of the way you're acting."

"No Liz, you just confuse me about our relationship, that's all."

"No Mike, I'm the confused one. I want to know why you brought me here in the first place."

"Well, because I wanted you to be my special girl."

"I'm not going to be your special girl just to become your nasty girl. Remember, I have dreams too. I want to leave Harlem without a baby. I want to finish school in one piece."

By this time, the movie was over and he hadn't answered me, so we caught the bus back home. Once we got on the bus, Mike didn't have much to talk about. He even sat across from me instead of beside me. When we finally got back to my apartment, Mike blurted out, "Well, I'll see you later Liz."

"Thanks for taking me out today. I hope you're not mad with me."

"No Liz, I'm not mad with you."

"Well, you have a good night and I hope you have a safe trip back to college."

"Thanks, Liz. I'll be coming back and forth to see Granny." We said goodbye, he left and I went upstairs.

Mama was in the kitchen making a sandwich. "So, how was the movie?"

"It was okay, nothing special."

"Oh, by the way Liz. Roland's kids are going to live with us for a little while."

"A little while will turn out to be forever!"

"Well, the kids have a social worker and I'm going to stay home to take care of Becky, so I can take care of them too."

"But, Mama, they are your grandkids!"

"That's right Liz, they are. What do you want me to do about it? Remember, you might need me to help you with *your* kids in the future."

"Remember Mama, Lynn is having a baby too."

"Yeah, and I'm not going to tell nobody that I'm going to help her with her baby!"

"But Mama, where are all these people going to sleep in a little three-bedroom apartment!"

"Liz, we could always get another apartment in this building."

"No, Mama, we need a house!"

"With what money can we afford to pay for one? Besides, I don't have to pay a security deposit for another apartment here."

"Okay Mama, if that's what you want to do. But, I'm still in school and only work part-time."

"That's fine Liz, but this is my battle. Don't worry so much. By the way, could you be on the lookout for some nice school clothes for your brother and sisters?"

"Mama, what about my school clothes?"

"Look Liz, you have to help me out with their school clothes. Or, just help me with laying away their clothes and yours."

"Okay, Mama, but don't forget even though I get paid every two weeks, I don't want them to take my whole paycheck."

"Well, that's not a problem. I can give you the money the first of the month. We need to get started now. John's size is 10 regular and his pants are 12. Becky's dress size is 10 and shirt size 12." She began to run down the sizes of everybody in the house as if I was going to remember.

"Mama, Sharon can wear my clothes that I got last year for school, cause I wear a size eight."

"No Liz, she needs some new clothes, like you."

"But, she wears my clothes to school now! By the way, who's going to buy their shoes?"

"I am going to buy their shoes with the last pay check from my job before I quit." I just looked at her hard, but careful that she didn't see me looking at her that way.

"I'm going to bed," I announced to everybody.

Lynne heard me. "You're slower than my baby. It's going to be here in six more months. You take longer than that."

"Shut up Lynne! I know you better take care of those baby gifts that you got, or ask that bum father Ricky to buy the baby some clothes!"

"Liz, you call every baby a bum."

"So, why are you picking with the truth?"

"Liz, that's all you talk about, you and your friends, y'all is bums too."

"Well, what is the little clown's name going to be?"

"Well, I know it isn't going to be a pink color clown."

"Well, Lynne, I don't know what that's supposed to mean, but, let me name her."

"Who told you it's a girl?"

"Nobody, Lynne, but let me name her."

"No Liz, it's my baby, and I want to name her."

"What about Ricky and his family?"

"What about them? I haven't heard from them since the baby shower! See, these bums needed a free meal for that day. Please, I'm not worried about them at all! So, how was the movie anyway?"

"It was okay, me and Mike just got to know each other a little better."

"Liz, if that was true, then I was there at the movies with you!"

"Why do you keep getting in my business about Mike? You know the Doctor said the baby will be here in less than two months, so you need to welcome your pain, because having that baby will be painful."

"Liz, the pain doesn't last forever!"

"I guess that's right, cause Lisa wouldn't have had two kids for Mama to raise and keep forever."

"Yeah, but they are Roland's kids too."

"Yeah, that's what the flea said, that they were Roland's kids."

"Liz, you all are always calling her a nasty name!"

"Yup, that's right, cause she's always trying to get something over on other people."

"Girl, you just hate Lisa with a passion!"

We both wound up in bed talking. Lynne was lying on my bed with her stomach against my back.

"Lynne, I'm not ready to hold your baby yet!"

We laughed and giggled for a while, then drifted off to asleep. Before we knew it, it was morning. The sun was barely up when Ms. Terry knocked on the door. She said that her daughter was having an asthma attack and she asked Mama to watch her son until she got back from the hospital.

Mama said, "Just bring him over and he can wear some of John's old clothes."

John looked at me, and said "Oh no, here they come again. First Lisa's children get my things and now Ms. Terry's son!"

I decide to try to find something to eat. I suggested to Mama that we go put the clothes on layaway. She said "Okay Liz, that sounds good. Let me get breakfast made and we can go after that.

Sharon and Becky came over and Sharon said, "Liz, make sure that Mama gets us enough clothes for the school year."

"Well, lets see what we can afford. We still have to live somewhere," Mama said, then she went into the bathroom washed up and got ready. She told Lynne and Sharon to watch the kids until she got back.

We ran out of the apartment to the bus stop. While we were waiting, Mama mentioned to me that Lynne was always complaining about her stomach hurting and she was worried. She was also worried about having Lisa's kids in the house. We talked about a lot of things while we were waiting for the bus. It felt good to talk to my mother like this again because I didn't get the chance very often.

When we got off the bus, the first person I saw was Janice. "Liz, aren't you off today?"

"Yeah, I am, but me and my Mama are going school shopping today. Is Peggy here today?"

"No Liz. She comes in later this evening. I'll see you tomorrow, okay?"

"Okay Janice," I said. Mamma and I went upstairs and started looking at the sale-priced rack. She put everything she liked in the cart. Then, we went over to the children's department and looked for some clothes for Roland's kids, but she knew we wouldn't have enough for everything.

She looked over at me. "Liz, can you put some money toward the bill?" She was hoping that I could use my store discount to help reduce it. "Ma, I just have twelve dollars in my pocket."

"Well, let's see how much we need to put down on layaway." The layaway bill came to over a hundred dollars so, with my store discount of twenty percent, I put seven dollars down on everything. She was at least able to get some underwear for Roland's kids, which she paid for. That left me with five dollars, so when we were done, we stopped at McDonalds for lunch. After we got our food and sat down, Mama asked me where Mike and I ate.

"We ate here, Mama. Mike dropped his burger on the floor, though. He said he was nervous about the whole college thing, and he asked me to promise to call his grandmother sometime."

"That would be nice of you to call her sometimes and see how she is doing, but she still has relatives here that can look after her too. You need to be worried about finishing school yourself and getting ready to go to college next year. Let me ask you this, when you go to college next year, is Mike's grandmother going to call me when you are away to check up on me? No, I don't think so. So, don't listen to everything Mike tells you. Right now, his life is changing drastically. It would be nice to call her, just don't go out of your way to do it, okay?"

"Okay."

"No, Liz, I really mean this. This woman really has high hopes for her grandson, which is good, but I guarantee you, all of the people that she knows, when her grandson makes it professionally in basketball, she probably won't even be speaking to them. All of that money Mike will be giving her will put her in another class of people, or so she will think, and it won't be anybody from Harlem. She'll probably get a nice apartment in upper Manhattan and we will never see her again. Liz, don't give all of you, okay? Let his other friends call her."

"Mama, I see what you mean."

"Good. Now eat your sandwich so we can head back home." I slowly finished my food. My mind was on what Mike said to me at the movies and how he was acting. I wasn't ready to tell Mama about that though, so I didn't say anything.

We caught the bus back home and got off at our corner as usual. Mama brushed up against Sharon, who was standing next to the building talking to her friend Jeff.

She looked at Jeff and said, "When you get tired of looking at Sharon's behind, you take your tail across the street. And Sharon, you can get off of my stoop because you didn't do anything in that apartment, I'm sure!" She started pushing Sharon upstairs, and mumbling, "They are always in your face!"

Sharon was trying to tell Mama that John and Becky were still downstairs too. I went downstairs and got them. When we got inside the door, Lynne was telling Mama that Sharon and John were picking on Roland's kids and had them crying so she sent them outside.

Mama looked angry and said, "Let me tell y'all kids something. You all leave these kids alone because I will slap you three children to the floor if I catch any of you messing with them again! These are your brother's children and I would think that you could show them a little love! Y'all go to your rooms and clean it up."

Later on that day, Ms. Terry came over to pick up her son. She was at the hospital with her daughter all day long, and she was very tired. John had picked on him all day. Mama said, "I hope I don't have to kill those three children of mine!"

Ms. Terry said, "Girl, please! They are getting so noisy and smart mouthed and lazy. John is acting like those kids across the street. I guess he likes to feel strong and I bet you he can beat all of those little kids, so you need to jump on him now, because I can see all the problems that will come already. John is only 12 years old, and he already is acting so big and bad, with a smart mouth too."

The next day, Sharon was in my room giggling about something. She was whispering something to Lynne. Lynne said, "Tell it to Liz."

"No, Lynne you tell it to Liz," but I just sat up in the bed, angry with them for waking me up.

"Y'all girls don't have enough sense to see that I'm still asleep?" I yelled.

"Sharon got something to tell you," Lynne said.

Sharon said, "No, Lynne you tell her."

Sharon started talking. "Well Liz, Mike was driving his grandmother's car last night."

"Me and Mike took the bus to the movies last night. When did he get his grandmother's car?" I asked.

"I don't know but Sharon said she saw Mike driving his grandmother's car with Wendy in the front seat.

I asked, "How do you know Wendy, Sharon?

Sharon said, "From seeing her with Sissy."

I said, "I don't believe you. Y'all just starting something with us."

"No, Liz. I am telling you the truth. Ask John. John, come here and tell Liz who you saw last night when we put out our trash."

"I saw Mike with a girl in his grandmother's car."

"Who was it, John?"

"That girl that use to go to school with Sissy."

"Y'all sit up in my face and tell a lie."

"No we aren't, Liz. After he let you off in front of our apartment about 11:30 we took out the trash and he came driving past us fast but we seen her."

"Y'all like keeping trouble with us by saying these things," I said.

"No Liz. I believe them because Mike is no angel," Lynne said.

"Lynne, you would say something like that. See, you call yourself picking a slum-bum, see Mike as a bum too."

"See Liz? Here's something to learn, Mike is a man and his needs come first."

My heart dropped into my stomach. I began to quiver and feel sick on my stomach. I turned over in the bed and so as not to face them. I was hoping Mike would call me or come over. I wondered, would I be able to tell him what I've heard? He and Charles called Wendy a nasty girl. Mike wouldn't dare be caught talking to her. How could he be with her now? I felt hurt but I lay there in silence.

Mama asked, "Liz, do you work today. No? Could you watch those two kids for me while I go to the market with Ms. Terry. I left them breakfast and make sure Sharon helps Lynne wash them up and finds them some clean clothes."

I got the baby and fed her first. Lisa's little baby wouldn't eat and started to cry. I put the girl in the chair and picked the boy up. My mind looked back on Roland's baby picture. Lynne picked up Lisa's little girl and I tried to get baby Devon something to eat. I felt sorry for him, being so young and not having either one of his parents. I held him on my lap. John put the toy truck on my lap, then John put the toy on the floor so Devon could play with it, but the little baby kept crying. Sharon came over to wash him up while I started to clean up his mess in the kitchen.

Lynne came into the kitchen to eat. "Liz, seem like you going to be mad with us, seem like forever."

"I don't want to talk about that again."

"But you really need to face the truth."

"Okay but not right now." I got up and went into my room.

"Liz don't forget you got these kids."

"I know that! Don't holler at me Lynne. Girl you don't need to be starting no argument."

"That's not what I am doing."

"Then you need to stay out of my business."

"That will be just fine Liz, but let me tell you next time you find out something about Mike, you will find it in the street. That is okay with me."

I got the children and put them in my bed while I listened to the radio. They seemed to be content and they went back to sleep. I was watching them sleeping when Mama called us to get her groceries out Mr. Melvin's car, Ms. Terry's new boyfriend. This man was kind of old for her, I thought out loud.

"He's old enough to be her father, and I wondered where she found this man." Mama had overheard me.

"Well Liz, that should be none of your concern or your business."

"Hmm that is real true, tell that to Liz."

Mama said, "Shut up Lynne. I don't need a mocking bird." I cleaned up all my clothes and looked at what I was going to wear to school that year. Mama looked at John, Sharon and Becky's school clothes. Suddenly there was knock on the door and I rushed over and opened it.

Lisa was standing there. "Liz, can I see your mother?"

"Mama! Come out and hi to Lisa."

"Hi, Mrs. Tracy how's my kids?"

"Well they are sleep right now, but I can go and get them."

"No. Mrs. Tracy. I just want to talk you."

"Since your son died, my whole world just died with him. I am not able to take care of my children, because my apartment is so expensive here and I don't have a job, not much educated, and it looks like nobody's trying to hurry to marry me to be my children's daddy..."

"No, Lisa. It's not like that. Nobody's going to take care of your children. That's your responsibility as a mother.

Lisa said, "I want you to know that I love them. I show my true love by giving them to someone that really care for them. I will be in court tomorrow."

Mama said, "Well I plan to get those kids and I'm hoping you will get your life together."

Lisa replied, "When I get my life together, I will go back to court to get them. I still live with my drunk of a mother. I didn't want to raise them there."

I rushed back to my bedroom and gathered up some of my old clothes. "Here Lisa these are some of my old clothes."

Lisa said, "Thanks, I needed some clothes." Then she said, "So I will see y'all soon."

As Lisa was leaving, Mama said, "Thank you Lisa, for stopping past to tell me all of this."

Lynne stared after Lisa and said, "I won't be giving my baby up."

Mama said, "You have to have a baby first. You will feel it in your stomach moving but you have not yet had a baby and the problems and stress that one can bring. Don't ask about it, okay? I hope you won't bring another one for me to take care of."

I gathered the kids and put them in the front room with Mama. I went back in my room and lay around until the next morning. I got up, washed up and rushed to work without eating anything, hoping to pick up my check to cash it.

I went to get my layaway out, which took almost all my money. Peggy said, "Liz, what are you doing, going on a shopping spree?"

"No, this is school clothes for my sister and brother and me. I hope you can fit it in the trunk of your car."

"No, Miss Liz. Your clothes will junk my truck up."

"Please Peggy, school opens one week from now."

"Okay, Liz. I am going to surprise you by stealing y'all school clothes."

"No, your surprise is Big Tracy. And she will be down here with a surprise with her fist." She started to laugh.

I stomped upstairs with the bag and opened them up, then John came over to help me.

"Where is Mama?"

"She's over to Ms. Terry for a moment.

Sharon came over and I gave her the clothes. She said, "Liz, is this all we got? Didn't I tell mama I needed more clothes for school?"

"No. Why, Sharon? Because you don't have any money to buy any more. John said this is a real nice pants and shirt."

Then Mama came in and Sharon asked her, "Is this all?

"Yes. This is all I am going to buy. You get those clean clothes that we got, separate them, and mix the old and the new."

"Where are our shoes?"

"Sharon, when I get my money you will get your shoes, so you need to get your Sunday church shoes and wear them back to school. You don't go to church anyway, so now my shoes won't go to waste if you wear them.

"But these clothes are casual. Those shoes are dressy."

Mama said, "But who's looking at your feet, and if they decide to look at your shoes and they don't like them, tell them they can buy you a new pair."

"Mama, you got to pay me my money back," I said.

"Okay Liz. Get my wallet out of my pocketbook. Besides, Sharon, you are just going to go across the street to those bums' apartment, so you don't need a new pair of shoes. Next thing you need is to find you a job. You are fifteen years old. Ask Liz to find you a job with her."

I said, "No, not while I'm there, Sharon won't be working with me."

"Y'all got a thing about calling people bums but not looking at yourself."

"No. I was just telling you that people are referring to us as Harlem bums. We are all bums because we live in Harlem.

"Girl, you listen to all that garbage because you aren't doing a thing with your life, and so you are on the same line to being a bum with a baby. For one thing, you wouldn't stay in school and get a good education so you can get your child the best for his life. And your child's father is on the corner in Harlem. You need to look at your future, not everybody else's. This is the only place I could afford. I am only one person. Besides Liz, nobody go out their way to help us. You better change your life course so you won't be called one of those bums from Harlem.

Lynne got mad with me and Mama but I just ignored her. I didn't believe people really had to live in Harlem for the rest of their life. I know they can try to work themselves out of here. Some are new to the program for low-income people but if Lynne is willing to get in it after she has the baby, she can make it. The pregnancy only lasts nine months. Going with Ricky is just like going nowhere but she still has her dreams, I thought. I am trying to stay in school and look for me a better job, unless I'm accepted at a college in upstate New York.

I went into the living room to talk to Mama. She asked me if Mike was still here. I said no, he should have left yesterday to go back to college.

"Are you still in love with him?"

"Yes, but I still don't know how his feelings is," I said.

"One thing you need to know is that love might not last forever and you need to keep your feelings in check. I know that, because your dreams and goals got to be for you, and you will have a trying time with that goal. With a goal, there is pain, sweat and tears. Everything you get out of life is a pain."

We went in the kitchen and cleaned up the dishes.

"You know, Liz. I think Lynne is in a high-risk pregnancy and she and her baby is stressed out. She don't understand the type of pain she is experiencing and I am afraid she might not make it. She put her hands over her face and started to cry.

"Mama. Please don't cry. Please! We will pray and ask God to help us." She kept crying about losing Roland and Charles until I started crying. Losing Lynne would be too much for me to stand, losing her baby would hurt me too.

Mama said, "I can ask Lynne to go to her clinic appointments regularly so they can watch her and her baby. But she don't like the clinic and won't keep her appointments, she said she was tired of the doctor tell her all the time. But Liz, that is all part of her pregnancy, being checked up and down her body. But seeing her not wanting to go to the clinic, that is really upsetting, 'cause I can't go with her. Her baby's no-good father don't stay around long enough for me to tell him what is going wrong with Lynne. Maybe he can go to the clinic with her and help her with some money and clothes. Right now the baby gets very little money but it won't be enough money to take care of them."

I kept to myself all that my mother said about Lynne. Mama told me to take Sharon to school tomorrow. I told Mama that Sharon had to be on time and that I was not taking Jeff and his sister Kelly with me. "If she is going to wait for them, she will have to make her own way to school and to her classes."

The next morning we got up early and got something to eat. "Sharon, hurry, hurry! You won't make me late for school," I called out. "They might make me stay after school for being late, then I will be late for my job. I have never been late for either one of them. I will be leaving at 7:45 and it is now 7:25 so you got twenty minutes to get dressed and be ready to head out the door." I got my books, put a headband on my hair and looked in the mirror to see if everything was okay.

Lynne said, "Liz, you look okay this morning. Help Sharon with her hair."

I got a headband out of the hair box and put one on Sharon's hair. I was finished and Sharon would at least be decent the first day.

Chapter 15

Liz Meets a New Friend

The noisy children across the street came over to walk to school with Sharon and me. I didn't speak, just I stared at them silently. They kept playing noisily as we went down to the bus stop. Jeff had pushed Sharon out in the street, so I stopped and looked, then said, "Hey little children. You need not to be so rallied up this first day of school."

They gave me a nasty look and said, "We can find our own way to school."

I said, "That's fine with me but, Sharon Yvette Rosemere is coming with me. Okay!"

Sharon said, "Liz, we can find the way to school from here." The bus was coming anyway, so I pushed Sharon up on the bus with me and the children shoved past the crowd to get on the bus with us.

I told Sharon, "You need to just sit right here so I can make sure you get off at the school stop with me. I'm not worried about your hoodlum friends." Sharon pouted but when we got to school, I took her to her homeroom class.

Sharon shuffled her feet. I said, "Sharon you never been to Harlem Senior High School, so you need to stop acting like you so big, 'cause we already have enough gangs here. Now is your opportunity to find your way home because I'm leaving to go to work at 2:15. You and the bums can go back home together."

"Liz, here you are calling us bums in school."

"That's right, because I put up with enough this morning coming to school. And another thing, Sharon, you don't let nobody push you out in the street. Girl, you already acting like a little fool. My last year is going to be rough on me with you being here, so if you start a fight or end up in a fight, that is your behind. I never have any problems with anyone here, so the rule is, if you start it, you take care of it, if they don't kill you first. You need to leave Jeff with his friends before you two get into some serious trouble, because I am going to leave both of y'all and go to work."

As I went to my class, I saw Leah in the hallway. Leah said, "So Liz, did you have a nice summer?" I slammed the door in her face. She laughed and her friends looked at her with a crazy look. I went to my seat and put my book and pencil on my desk.

That's when someone touched me on my shoulder and said, "Hi! My name is Regene."

I turned around and said, "My name is Elizabeth Rosemere, but they call me Liz." She told me that she just moved here from Flatbush.

I said, "You know, I was raised over there with my grandmother before she died."

Regene said, "Girl, it is so bad and dirty!"

"I know, because we moved from there to over to Harlem and it is real bad."

"So, do you have any friends?"

"No, not really, because I don't have time to hang out. Besides, I work in the evening downtown at the department store.

"That's real nice to have a job."

"Yeah, but I'm trying to help my mother out."

"That's nice. At least you got a job somewhere. That's what I need. So what do you do at your department store?"

"I'm a clothes rack girl."

"You like your job?"

"It's okay I guess, but I need the money. Besides, it's not that hard."

"Is the pay good, and is training hard?"

"I guess the pay is okay, but I'm just part time, and the training wasn't hard at all. The clothes you take out of the boxes is heavy, but I guess I'm just used to doing it now."

The teacher came in and told all of us to take our seats. She said, "My name is Mrs. Thompson, I am your math teacher, and this is your homeroom class. You all need to come up here and get your class schedule, but first tell me your name so I can put it in my roll book. Start with this first row."

The new girl got up and said, "My name is Regene Dudley," then I got up and said my name. After everybody had introduced themselves, the teacher gave more orders.

"People, open your book and take down your drill assignment and your homework. After that, here is your emergency cards to be filled out and your lunch ticket applications."

Regene touched me again and said, "Girl, she seem like she is real sharp and firm in this classroom."

The teacher said, "Girl, please sit down in your own seat, stop leaning on her shoulder, and stop talking to her, okay!"

I enjoyed talking to Regene. When we was leaving to go to the other class, Regene was looking at her schedule. I came up behind her and said, "Let me see your schedule." I said, "We're in all of the same classes so you can just follow me until I leave at 2:15 to go to work." We were going down the hall when I saw Sharon move with a crowd of girls.

"Sharon, are you finding your classes?"

"Yes, big sister, I can find these classes," she said as she was giggling with some of those girls she met.

"That sister of mine can sure find a friend, but I can be sure of them not being good people. I have a sister named Lynne and she finds the worse type of people. Those girls Sharon was with seemed the type of people that were just seeking trouble, but I thought, she wasn't the first thing on my mind.

"Regene, are you going to eat in the cafeteria?" I asked.

"Yes Elizabeth, but does the food taste good?"

"Please call me Liz, because if you keep calling me Elizabeth, people won't know who you are talking about."

"Okay, then you can call me Jean, because my family and friends call me that. So please call me that too."

I started to giggle at her. "So the both of us got a nickname. I've had my nickname for eighteen years." Jean told me she has had her nickname for eighteen years too.

She said, "My aunt gave me my nickname because she didn't like Regene."

"My daddy that I never saw gave me my nickname. Well that's the story my mother told me. She said I was named after his great grandmother."

"I never saw my father either."

"I heard about my daddy being in jail."

She said, "Seem like we got the same pattern in fathers."

Finally, lunch came and we sat down to eat. Sharon came over to ask me for some money. I said, "Sharon, I know you ain't begging me for my money after Mama gave you some."

"But Liz, I left my money home on your dresser when you was doing my hair."

"Here's the other part of my sandwich, you can have my cookie and milk and you can ask some of your new friends for some help. What about your friend Jeff?"

"Jeff don't have any money."

"Did you give your money to him? Girl, take yourself back over there with your giggling classmates. I will see tonight if you gave your money to your friend."

"That little sister of mine drives me crazy. First thing in the morning today her and her noisy friends was playing and started to push her in the street."

"Oh Liz! That is dangerous. What if a car would have hit her?"

"Tell that to Sharon. That little girl don't see nobody but the bad children across the street. She calls them her friends."

"Girl my sister is just like that, she got a baby by the next door neighbor." He was her friend until she got pregnant. Now she all by her lonesome. Nobody looks at her as a friend now. That's just like people. Before they get you in trouble you got lots of friends."

"Jean, my sister looks like she going down the same road," I said. "My older sister is pregnant and she never see Ricky anymore. That's her baby's father. She met him thru my dead brother Roland, and he was a drug dealer, so you know what type of person Ricky is. But she seemed to be drawn to those types of guys."

"Liz, that is the worse thing they can get into. Boy, those girls don't know what happened to their life."

The bell rang so we cleaned off the table and left to go to our English class. After classes, Jean said in a low voice, "I'll see you tomorrow."

I said, "Yeah, we we'll see each other tomorrow. Goodbye." As I left, I thought she seemed lonely like me. This was the first friend I had met this year. I got off the bus in front of my job and ran into Peggy.

"Hi Peggy, you been here long?"

"No I just got here a little while ago. So, how was your first day?"

"It was a real nice day. I met a new girl from my old neighborhood. She seem to be nice but she's also lonely like me because I don't hang around nobody here. Those people in school are most definitely nothing but trouble and they all are in gangs. They got a gang from every different neighborhood. I never fit in with all that and I believe I never want to."

"Liz, that's a relief to hear that you met a friend to talk to instead of arguing with your sisters all the time."

"I'll just keep my ear open to see how Jean turns out as a classmate first and then we might can become friends."

"Liz, you need a friend to talk to in school but you also need to be careful in choosing the right friends."

"That's right, Peggy. This is a life and death situation." Peggy laughed loudly.

"Girl, you are sweet, but on the other hand you are real crazy."

I left her downstairs laughing, punched in and started to work. It seemed like it was going to be a long day for me, working and going to school too. When I got home, I was going to have to put out my clothes and iron them. Now I had to look for a dress for senior day. I wondered what type of shoes I was going to wear. I know, I thought, *I need some type of heel, but what color dress am I going to get? I need to match my shoes with it.*

Then I started thinking about Sharon and wondering how I was going to find out whether she left her money at home or gave it to her friends. Because if she did, we were seeing the real Sharon. I thought, *if that little girl is going to buy her friends, she needs to at least buy some good ones.* But I knew that wasn't the real Sharon.

Peggy hollered, "Come on Liz, if you want to get a ride home."

"Okay. I've got to put everything away."

When I finally got downstairs, Peggy asked, "What took you so long?"

"I was daydreaming about someone."

"Oh, Mike! Girl you haven't heard from him?"

"No, not yet. He's one of my thoughts but that's not the person I was thinking about."

"So who might that person be?"

"My sister Sharon, she is really off the hook. She found some bums and they put their hooks in her."

"Liz, you really got a way with words and I don't want you to explain that to me."

"Peggy, it would really take a complete twenty-four hours to tell you about my family, especially my sisters Sharon and Lynne. It seems like their lives are all over before they gets started."

"When is your sister going to have that baby"?

"The last Lynne went to the clinic it was due at the end of October. But she's always complaining about her stomach hurting."

"That's not a good sign, Liz."

"I know Peggy, but what can I do if she won't go to the clinic, to see about herself." It took a half of day to talk about Lynne's problems. The other half was about Sharon and her bummy so-called friends. "That silly girl went to school only one day and found another group of bums."

"Girl, let's get in the car." Peggy said.

"And let me turn on the radio so I can relax after this day."

The next day Jean was in homeroom.

"Hi Liz, did you work hard last night?"

I said, "No it was a good night. I got a ride home with my girl friend Peggy. She goes to college and she's a sweet and kind person."

"That's good Liz, we all try to have a good friend." Then Mrs. Thompson came in class and asked, "Do everybody have their homework done? The first person in this row, stand up and explain their homework to me.

Jean got up and started to say something about her homework. Mrs. Thompson burst in saying, "Little girl I don't know what you are talking about! Are you sure you copied your homework correctly?" Then I got up and started to explain my homework to her. She told me, that it needed a lot of work. The teacher said, "Math and numbers mean something, this was a simple assignment, you could have asked your parents for help."

A boy named Melvin got up and said, "Mrs. Thompson. My parents is dead and my grandma is 79 in years. Who do I have to ask for help?"

She replied, "You and some others can stay after school for my help." Then she said, "I am here until 4:15 and you will earn your own grade in my class"!

I turned to Jean and said, "Girl, I work after school."

She said, "Liz, you need to tell her now, but me, I need to stay after school everyday and probably at night too."

"Jean, this the first week of the school year. Things will get better. Besides, we will get a chance to prove ourselves so don't beat yourself up about it."

"Well Liz, I'm hoping to get into college."

"Who's your counselor?" I asked.

"Mrs. Jones."

"Mrs. Jones is my counselor too," I said.

Then Jean suggested that we hurry to the next class so that we wouldn't be late." I told her that we could run up the back stairs.

"Jean, the more I be around you the more I like the way you talk to me."

Now, all we had to do was see how our grades were going to affect us. I prayed that mine were good because my goal was to go to college. When the day was over, I told Jean that would call her that evening.

Regene said, "Umm, how are you suppose to do that? You don't have my phone number?"

I gave her my number, then I told her, "I don't have time to get to those nasty broken-down lockers."

She said, "At least you got somewhere to put your coat in the winter so nobody will try to steal it."

"That's right, Jean, we need to keep everything we got. We need to lock it all up."

We ran downstairs and right into Sheron and her friends. I rolled my eyes at Sheron and said, "Those two girls will never be my friends." She looked at Jean.

I said, "I really like Jean." We went our separate ways.

When I got to work, I had to rush to punch the clock. It was a long night but it was finally over and I was glad. Peggy was waiting for me outside. I got in her car and turned the radio on. "Miss. Liz, all you do now is turn my radio on, and it's too loud."

"Sorry Peggy, but my life is getting better since I found a good friend."

Peggy said, "You must really like Jean."

I said, "Yeah, we talk and walk together to our classes."

"That's real good and I'm really happy for you because once you get someone's phone number, you ring their phone off the hook."

I told her, "I get the picture." She put me out and I went up stairs.

Mama said, "Liz, a girl called for you. Her name was Jean."

I told Mama that Jean was a new girl I met this week Mama said, "Liz please be careful about these new friends."

"Okay, mama. I'm checking her out."

The light was on in the living room. Lynne said, "A new girlfriend? I thought Mama was talking about a new boyfriend."

"No, that girl's name is Jean and she just started to our school. By the way, did Sharon leave some money on our dresser yesterday morning?"

"No, Liz. Sharon put that in her pants pocket. I saw her do it myself."

I said, "That little liar! Sharon was begging me in school for some money. She must have gave her money to that bum friend of hers that is really messed up and she really makes me sick."

"Liz, don't be too hard on that girl. She's a new teenager and has boys looking at her now. We all been there before."

I told Lynne, "That might be right, but she better not ask me for any more money. My answer will be NO!"

"Lynne, you are getting bigger and bigger each day." I fear that Lynne is going to have her baby any day now. "Please don't have it tonight. Please, because I am too tired." Lynne told me not to worry, that the baby wouldn't be coming anytime that night.

I laid out my clothes for every day that week, turned out the light and said my prayers. I prayed that Mike would not forget me, that he would give me a call or send me a letter. I thought, / *might call his grandmother this week and ask her about Mike.*

By the end of September, Jean and I were close friends. She helped me cope with assignments and she made sure I got the information that the teachers gave. She was the friend I needed and she often called me on the weekend to talk.

The first of October, I called Mrs. Maxine and asked her how she was doing. She said she was fine, and then I asked about Mike. She said, "Mike is doing fine. He's busy and you need not be worrying me or calling me for some information on Mike. He's got your number and he's got your address, so you should not be calling me." Then she hung up on me.

My feelings were hurt. I asked myself, *what did I do to Mrs. Maxine? I respect her, and Mike and I are friends.* I put down the phone and sat quietly in the chair in the front room, sad and afraid.

The phone rang. My mother picked it. I was hoping it was Mrs. Maxine, calling back to say she was sorry.

"Hi, Liz this is Jean, what are you doing this Saturday?"

"You tell me."

"I could come over…well that's why I'm calling."

"Jean, you are welcome over at my house but we aren't doing too much over here."

"That's okay. I just wanted to get out of this apartment and this neighborhood for a day."

"So can you come at one o'clock?

"Okay Liz. I'll see you."

I put down the phone again after talking to Jean and got my pants and shirt out to iron. I told Mama that Jean was coming over. Mama said that it was okay and asked me if Jean was a nice girl.

I said that she is a very nice girl and I told Mama how she copies down all my homework assignments and gives them to me before I leave to go to work, then she calls me to give me the last class assignment.

Mama said. "She seem to be nice. Are you going to get some snacks?"

I said, "That's a nice idea, I'll go to the Chinese corner store and get some."

Mama said, "Liz, you need to watch those people. They will cheat you in a heart beat."

I just said, "I'd like to get a big bottle of soda."

Mama told me that we needed toilet paper. I said, "Mama, I just got two arms so send some of your other children. They can come with me."

Mama said, "Baby, that's okay. Me and Ms. Terry is going to the market tomorrow. Just bring one big soda."

I got my jacket and walked to the store. "Liz, can I go?"

"Yes John, you can come and help me." We ran into Sissy, who was big and pregnant.

"Hi Sissy, are you pregnant too?"

She said, "What does it look like, or who do this look like?"

I walked straight past Sissy and her friend. I told John, "I could just slap her down."

John was afraid and told me to keep going and not to look back. Then he asked, "Please Liz will you buy me something?"

"Yes John, but my purpose for going to the store is to buy me something, not you."

"Okay Liz, but just this time." I told him he would not be charging me anything for him going to the store with me. Besides, I reminded him, I didn't ask him.

John said, "I know, but I got a taste for some ice cream."

I said, "But your taste can't buy you nothing, so let me tell you something before we go into the store. I will pick the type of ice cream I can afford. I'm having company over, so you need better not get into Jean's face, okay John?"

"That is not a problem if you are getting me some ice cream."

"Boy, shut up. This is my money."

We got the snacks and walked home with Sissy and her friends' eyes on me and John. I kept on going into our apartment. Sissy started to cross the street with her drunk boyfriend, Anthony. When I opened up the bag, Sharon asked me if I brought her something.

I said, "No, not particularly for you."

Lynne laughed and said she wasn't going to try to ask me for anything. I put the ice cream in the freezer, the soda in the refrigerator and put the potato chips and cheese curls, my favorite snacks, in the cupboard.

There was a knock on the door. I ran to open it. I invited Jean in and introduced Jean as the new girl in my class. "This is my mother and her name is Mrs. Tracy. These are my two sisters. This is pregnant Lynne."

"Just call me Lynne, I'm not going to be pregnant forever," she said.

"And you already met Sharon in school. This is Becky, my youngest sister, and this my little brother John."

Jean said, "Hi everybody. Glad to meet you."

Mama said, "Honey, sit down and rest yourself. So you are in Liz's class."

She said, "Yes ma'am, we sit together in all our classes."

"So where you live?" Jean told her that she lived at 1202 Reese Street, apartment 3D, in Flatbush area.

Mama said, "Did Liz tell you that's where she was born and raised?"

Jean said, "Yes."

Mama said that she was leaving and for us to sit down and talk with each other and that it was nice to meet Jean. Jean replied, "Same here Mrs. Tracy." I brought out the soda and chips but I had to call my mother because Lisa's greedy kids tried to eat it all.

Jean asked, "Liz, who kids are those?"

"They're my late brother's kids and it would take a whole month to tell you about him and his life. But I really love and miss him."

We talked, laughed and giggled the whole evening. When it was time for her to go, John, Lynne and I walked her to the bus stop. Jean said, "Thank you for inviting me over and walking me to the bus stop. Here comes the bus now."

I was talking to Lynne when she turned around and saw Sissy staring at her. Lynne said, "What's the matter with Sissy, peeking at us?"

"She and her friend tried to start a fight with me today but I went around her and went to the store. She's messed up. Look at the clothes she got on."

Lynne told me, "Find a big stick and beat that fool up, and I got your back."

I said, "Lynne, you might got my front, but you don't got my back." She said I was crazy.

We went back to the apartment, I put my jacket down and went to the kitchen to clean, wash, and put away the dishes. Then I swept the floor and put things away. I was so tired I put my nightclothes on and went to sleep.

Chapter 16

Lynne's Baby

When Lynne got up, she complained that she had some aches and pains in her stomach and in her lower back. "Lynne, this is the day," said Mama.

John rushed in and asked, "Is the baby being born here?"

"No, John. The baby is being born in the hospital. Let's see what time the baby gets here." As Mama explained this to John, she showed little excitement. Lisa's kids looked confused and everybody was milling around.

Mama started to give orders. "Sharon, you can go to school, and Liz you can go too."

"But Mama! Who will watch Lisa's kids?" I asked.

Mama said, "Ms. Terry and Cousin Katie will look after those kids."

I told her that I would keep calling to see when she has the baby. I told Sharon, "I'm not going to school with those hoodlum children across the street."

Sharon said, "Liz, that's okay with me and them." She left before I did.

I gave Lynne a kiss and said, "Girl, take that pain like a woman."

She told me, "Please Liz, I don't need to laugh right now because these pains are very serious." I ran out, got on the bus and went to school.

I sat next to Shawn. I asked, "Hi Shawn, where have you been these days?"

He said, "Well, I try to stay cool and quiet."

I said that was nice and then I told him, "You know my sister's having a baby today."

Shawn said, "Alright! Ricky baby number two. You know I used to like Lynne but I can like you now."

I said, "Let me tell you something before I knock you on the floor, Shawn, I thought you were ugly then, and you are horrifying now." The people on the back of the bus started to laugh. I got off the bus and started walking the block to school. I thought, *that ugly boy is real crazy if he thinks I like him. That drug dealer! I really feel sorry for Lynne having Ricky's baby.*

As I sat down in my homeroom class, Jean came up to me and said, "Hi Liz. How was your morning?"

"Jean, my sister is really in pain. Today is her time to have the baby."

She said, "That's good Liz, her having the baby and all. I hope and pray that the baby will be healthy."

"That's what I hope for too, Jean." After lunch, I called the hospital. Lynne still hasn't had the baby, so Mama said to call before I go to work. She also reminded me that I needed to call my job if I wasn't going to work. When the school day was over, I called the hospital to see if Lynne had her baby yet. They said that she was still in labor. I decided to leave work at 5:30 to go to the hospital.

I told my boss, Mrs. Randy, that I would like to leave at 5:30. She said that first I needed to put all my clothes and tags up at 5 o'clock, to leave the rack for the other girl, and to clean my area up. I thanked her.

She asked me, "Well? What is the occasion?"

I said, "My sister is in labor."

She said that she hoped my sister had a healthy child. I thanked her again for letting me leave work early. Then she said,

"Remember what I asked you to do. Neither one of us need to get written up."

"Oh no, ma'am, we sure don't need to lose our jobs."

Then she said, "Let me tell you from experience, it was very hard to find this job. Please take care of this one because you will need a reference in the future. As a black person and your supervisor, I'll tell you it's hard to get good people to help you, so now you go back in your department and start work."

At 4:30, I called the hospital front desk from the cafeteria phone at work and asked for my mother. "Is Mrs. Tracy there?" Mama answered the phone, "Hi, who is this?" "Mama, this is Liz, did Lynne have the baby?" Mama replied, "Yes child, yes child. It is a fat little girl." I asked how Lynne was. Mama said she was still in the delivery room. I told Mama, "I wanted you to know that I will be there at the hospital at 6 o'clock." Mama said she would see me then. I left the cafeteria, ran and told Peggy that Lynne had a little girl.

Peggy said, "Let's see how fast you leave this place." I said, "Girl, I got my running shoes on and I leave here at 5:30 this evening."

I rushed back in my department and started to put things away. I put the rack out on the floor, put my clothes on, and I punched out. I started to walk downtown to the hospital. I got there at 5:45. I was excited about having a niece. I got a nametag and went up to the fourth floor. I asked for Lynne Rosemere.

The nurse told me that her mother was in room 412. I opened the door and saw Mama was crying. Worried, I asked, "What's wrong, Mama?"

She said in a faint voice I could hardly hear, "Lynne died...but the baby lived."

Not understanding, I asked, "What are you saying?" I rushed to the nurse's station and asked, "What is my mother talking about!"

The doctor turned to me and said, "I am sorry about you losing your sister."

I screamed and I fell to the floor. I was kicking and screaming when Ms. Terry walked up, helped me up and was hugging me when the nurse told Ms. Terry that my mother's child bled to death. She said my sister never came in to the clinic so they couldn't follow her pregnancy.

Suddenly Ricky came in with some candy and flowers. Ms. Terry said, "Let me help you Liz. Let's get you in that room where your mother is.

Ricky turned and said, "What's wrong Liz, what's wrong?

Ms. Terry turned around and said, "Lynne died this evening."

Ricky was helping me into the room but he suddenly dropped me and ran out into the hall. He ran up and down the floor and then back, collapsed on me and I fell again.

Mama kept pulling on me and she said, "Please stop, Liz. I can't help you and Ricky. Boy, this is a long night for me."

No one went to check on the baby. We asked the nurse if we could see it. The nurse said, "Yes, and we wanted to talk to y'all."

Ms. Terry said, "This really isn't the time. They are all in shock right now."

Then the nurse asked, "Are they taking the baby home?"

Ms. Terry looked at Ricky. Then the nurse asked, "Who is the father?"

Ms. Terry said, "He's over there, but he's in no shape to talk to no one."

I was still trying to get myself up off the floor but I started to crawl into the bathroom and bumped my head on the wall. The blood ran down off my head into my face. Ms. Terry grabbed me and called the doctor. He and the nurse ran in. He said, "We are giving her a shot of medication to calm her down and then we are going to give her some pills to put her to sleep.

Mr. Ray grabbed Ricky and helped him put the candy and flowers on Lynne's bed. Ricky said, "Goodbye baby. I love you." and he started to cry on Mr. Ray's shoulder.

Mr. Ray said, "Come on son, let me take you home."

We started down to the car but I was so drowsy I couldn't see much. Ricky jumped out of the car and ran up his street. Mama cried on Ms. Terry shoulder, all the while hollering, "Why me, why me, to lose two children so far in my life. I had them, I loved them and I tried to take care of them. But God probably loved them more than I did."

I was crying with my head on my mother's lap. I was sick and worried and wondering how it could have happened. *She just had a baby, she died and the baby lived.* My mother knew something was wrong, but she never expected that it would be the death of Lynne.

"Who will take care of Lynne's baby?" I started to scream from the back of the car.

"Child, please stop screaming before the other kids hear you," Mama said softly. Then she said, "I'm not going to tell them right now. I hope God will give me strength to tell them later, because I can't tell them why it happened. I will tell them how much I loved Lynne and am going to miss her. We will take care of the baby she left us."

Mama told everybody to sit down. I told them that Lynne had a baby girl, but Lynne didn't make it. John asked, "Why didn't Lynne make it?"

I said, "Because she was really sick and needed more care before she had the baby."

Sharon pushed me down into the kitchen chair and started running, hollering, and shouting, "Not Lynne, not Lynne!"

Mama rushed over to hold her. Lisa's kids began crying also. Their little faces were soppy wet with tears. I knew they didn't know why they were crying. Maybe they were afraid of all the noise. Sharon ran out across the street to Kelly, crying and telling them about losing her sister today. They asked about her baby. Sharon sat in their front doorway, fainting and falling into their hallway.

Mama went over, grabbed her and started to walk her back to our apartment. Mama said, "Please baby, please let's go home." Jeff and Kelly pushed by Mama and held Sharon.

Kelly said, "Come on Sharon. Don't scream like that."

Sharon started to push everyone. She didn't want to go home. She kept saying, "Leave me alone and let me walk! Okay guys, I need to walk! She started crying and walking off by herself. Mama called to her, "You could cry at home!"

"No mama, I want to cry here, here and now!" Mama said, "But all our neighbors want to know what is going on."

Mrs. Mae came out and asked, "Is your sister okay, or is the baby okay?"

"No," I said, "My sister died this evening."

She turned to my mother and said, "Oh, please! Not your family! You all were through enough tragedy in your home." Then her hand went up and down and no words would come out.

Sharon was walking up and down the street crying. I got Jeff, Kelly and Keith to walk behind her to talk to her. I left, went back to the apartment and started to say a silent prayer. I asked God to help take us through this day, this nightmare. I got out our old picture album. I saw us when we was young. There was Lynne, Roland and me in the park. We were playing ball and running around. We were Mama's first set of children. My grandmother was playing with us in some of the photographs. I needed to see what a family was supposed to be doing. It shouldn't be dying like this.

I lay on my grandmother's picture and cried out loud. I really missed her. She kept us while Mama was at work. Grandmother took good care of us. She was the first person to take us to school. Now all the people in this picture were gone. My grandmother, my sister, my brother, all gone. The tears came down so hard that the pictures were getting wet. My tears then turned to rage. The picture was smeared and when I looked, some of us in the picture were gone.

Mama came in and started to cry with me. She said repeatedly that her beautiful two children were gone, so I sat beside her and held her, rubbing her back. We couldn't believe that we were going through this. I said, "We shouldn't hurt in this way—it's not fair! They just wanted to live too. They had a dreamed to be filled."

Now we had their children to love and to care for. I wanted their children to know that I loved them. Mama said that they would know. Mama took the children and gave them a bath.

The phone rang. Kelly said, "Liz, can I speak to your mother." I gave the phone to my Mama.

Mama said. "Hi honey. Oh, yes. Sharon can spend the night. But she got to come home tomorrow."

I started to wash Lisa's kids. I put them in my bed on the side that Lynne slept on, but I couldn't sleep there. I could still smell Lynne's perfume. I came out of the room crying.

Mama said, "Liz, I will sleep with them tonight."

I got ready for bed, but I just couldn't sleep at all so I got up to call Peggy.

"Hi. Is Peggy home?" It was already 10:45, I said to myself. The person who answered got Peggy, who was already asleep. I said, "Peggy this is…I lost my sister today."

She asked, "Is this Liz?"

"Yes, it's me."

"What could happen to your sister? She just went to the hospital to have a baby!"

"My sister was very sick and she bleed to death."

"Okay girl, this is just killing me, you losing your brother, nine to ten months ago, and now it is your sister. Oh Liz, you got my love and sympathy. So how is the baby, is she doing okay? Y'all got enough children in that little apartment to take care of."

"That's the truth, but it is still my family."

"Girl, you really did wake me up."

"I'm sorry, I needed to talk to someone."

"Is your mother okay?"

"No, not really. She got to make the funeral plans. That's painful enough to do. You think we will be on this earth forever."

"I see it is just for a short time."

"Ain't that the truth."

"Liz, have you heard from Mike?"

"No, I hope he's finds out or hears about Lynne's death. Maybe he will give me a call or stop past."

"I hope so too, Liz, because you really need to see and talk to your closest friend."

"That will lift my spirits and help me get thru this trying time."

"Did you call Jean yet?"

"No, not yet. I'll call her tomorrow."

"Well, sleep is a must so I will call you in the morning to see if you need any help."

"Please call tomorrow so we can go see the baby at the hospital."

"What time do you want me to call you?"

"Around about 10 AM. I should be up. Goodnight, Peggy, I'll see you tomorrow.

"Okay, you'll hear from me."

I hung up the phone and started to get sleepy. The next day when I woke up the sun was warming my leg. When I turned over someone touched me but I couldn't see who it was. I heard "Liz, Liz." I made out the voice, rose up and said, "What, Sharon?"

Sharon said, "I tried to see the baby last night. We tried to sneak in but the guard kicked us out.

Surprised, I said, "You went to see the baby last night!"

She said, "Why not! My sister is never going to see her again."

"Sharon, we don't need anymore hurt."

"I know that, but my mind isn't clear right now. I loved Lynne." She started to cry. I put my arm around Sharon and thought to myself that we needed to learn to be at peace with each other. Lynne was her favorite sister and they had the closet relationship. She held me around my waist, crying until my gown was wet from her tears, which was okay with me.

Mama came in the room and told me that Peggy was on the phone. I said, "Hi Peggy."

"Good morning Liz. Are you ready for me to come over?" I told her that I wasn't dressed yet but that she could still come over and help my mother. She said that she should be there at 11 o'clock. I told her that was a perfect time. I hung up the phone and went in the bathroom. I rushed around in the apartment, looking for my clean clothes in the laundry bag so I could iron them for today. I phoned Jean who asked me if she could come over and see me today. I said yes, and told her to come over at 12 o'clock in the afternoon. I kept on ironing and putting my clothes out. Mama asked me to iron the children's clothes and dress them. I did that while Mama braided Becky's hair. Sharon went to sleep in my bed.

I cleaned up the kitchen and made a list of snacks to pick up at the corner store. I was ready to go out as soon as I put on some clean clothes. I rushed outside and headed for the corner store. I could feel eyes on me. I turned around and saw Sissy and her boyfriend. He hollered out and said, "I'm sorry to hear about your sister." I turned my head and didn't say anything to him. In the store, at the counter, I started to cry. I asked the man at the counter if I could have a minute. I went into the back of the store and wiped my eyes. A lady asked me if something wrong but I ignored her and went back to pay.

"Liz, Liz, I'm really sorry about Lynne."

I looked up and saw Sissy. I remembered she had lost a person before, a brother, Charles. I thanked her for caring about me and my family. Sissy looked like she was going to have that baby right there and now. She asked me when Lynne's funeral would be held. I said, "I really don't know, Sissy."

She said, "If I don't have my baby, I will be there."

I said, "Okay, it's nice to know that you care enough to be there."

She then said, "I'm sorry to hear how she died, and I hope everything will be okay when I give birth to my baby. Please let my boyfriend know when the funeral is."

I said okay, but I wasn't going to that nasty pot-smoking apartment. I ran home to get there before my company. I ran past Mrs. Mae's apartment, past Charles's old apartment and into my apartment. Peggy was there, sitting in the front room talking to Mama.

Mama said, "So what store you went to?"

I told her, "I went to the corner store, but I ran into Sissy, and I was talking to her."

Mama said, "Okay. I just wanted to know what happened."

Someone from the hospital called for Mama. I told them that someone would be there later to check on the baby. Jean came in and I introduced Peggy to her. We were talking when Mama came in and asked me and my friends to go to the hospital to check on the baby. Peggy drove and we went straight up to the OBGYN floor.

When we passed Lynne's old room, I started to cry. Peggy and Jean held me, telling me that it would be all right. We went to the nursery and I asked for the baby of Lynne Rosemere. The nurse asked us to put on a gown and facemask, then brought the baby to us. I took the baby in my arms and started to cry. I kissed her and I told her, "I will take care of you." The baby was crying so I patted her on her back and rubbed her face.

Peggy asked if she could hold her. She took her and asked, "What is her name"?

I said, "I'm naming her Ralynne. The R is for Ricky, and the other part is for Lynne. I asked the nurse if the father came past today.

The nurse said, "Nobody came to see the baby, but tomorrow at 11 the baby will be released, so someone must be here to get her."

I said, "Me or my mother will be here to pick her up." The baby spit up on me so I put her down and looked for something to clean myself up. Jean gave me a napkin.

Jean asked, "Liz, do you work tomorrow?"

I said, "Yes, but I'm calling the job in the morning." I gave the baby back to the nurse and we all walked toward the elevator. I said, "Believe it or not, I'm feeling like a mother."

Peggy said, "Yes Liz, and I believe in my heart that you will be a good mother, even if it is Ricky's baby and not Mike's, you are a mother."

I said, "Girl, the ugly and sick drug-selling fool, I got to see how he's going to act when we go pick up his baby."

Peggy picked my mother and me up at 10. Peggy said she was glad to do it because she knew we were in need of her. She said, "but please sound like it's nice to hear me."

I hugged Peggy and Jean. Peggy said, "I know you are a proud mommy."

I smiled as we started toward the car. Once in the car Peggy said that she was hungry so we stopped at McDonald's. Peggy asked, "So who's treating."

I said, "I will treat y'all."

Peggy said, "You know Jean, Liz don't always spend her money."

I said, "That's because I don't always have money. So what do you want Jean?"

Jean said, "Whatever you get Liz."

I said, "So do you like everything I like?"

She said, "That will be fine Liz, whatever you get because I don't have any money."

Peggy said, "You are missing the point. She is treating us, so you can pick out whatever you want to eat. So look at the list and get the biggest on there.

I said, "Next time Miss Peggy, you foot the bill and we can get it in the large."

We all started to laugh and giggle. Peggy said, "Let me tell y'all something after I eat all my food."

I said, "Why we got to wait until you eat all that food."

She said, "Because I need my stomach to be full."

"Yes, Peggy we can wait until you eat all the food I bought."

"Now that's right, Miss Liz, because you gave me a full stomach now I am going to put you out in front of that corner right there."

"Well, Miss Peggy, on your empty stomach you would put me out in front of my apartment."

"That's right Liz, ha ha. Let me stop at this corner."

"See Peggy, you always put me off in front of my apartment," I said demandingly.

"Not today, baby!"

"Remind me in the future not to feed you, because when you got a empty stomach, I get chauffeured in front of my apartment. Girl, just take you and your full stomach home."

"I'm just joking with you Liz."

"But next time the joke is on you."

Peggy swung open my door. While laughing she said, "Now the joke is on you, get out!"

I said goodbye to Jean and told Peggy to take my friend home. I told them that I had a good time and that I really needed that little piece of humor in my life. "Thanks Peggy, for all the crazy things you said. Bye, I'll call you."

"Remember Liz, I'll be at work at 3 o'clock. So don't forget to call Mrs. Bailey before she goes home at 5 o'clock."

"I won't forget I need my job!"

I left Jean and Peggy and went in my apartment. For a moment, I had forgotten my sad situation. Some time later Mama talked to a funeral home about burying Lynne. Mama told me to put the kids in the back while she talked to the man. She asked if they ate.

I said, "Yes. I just finished feeding them."

"Please clean up their mess." Then she started talking to herself, "Okay. But tomorrow is a new day and my joy will be to see Lynne's baby and bring her home."

I put the kids in my room and cut the TV on. Then I decided that they needed a bath because they had food all over them. Becky came in and hugged me. She knew that something was wrong. She never talked about it but the tears just started to roll from her eyes.

I told her, "I understand your pain." I hugged her back and I started to cry with her, remembering that we lost my brother and sister. I knew this pain from our sister's death was not going to go away for a long time. I knew my mother would never forget it. These are her children...were her children.

I washed the children up and went to bed for the first time since Lynne died. I found the medicine the doctor gave me and took it. Soon I found myself drowsier than ever and I fell asleep. The wind blew against my window so hard that the cold air brushed against my face, sending a freezing cold chill up my spine. I jumped out bed and rushed to shut the window. After all, it was November, I remembered. It was supposed to be cold. I went to sleep again. I slept so soundly that I didn't hear anything. When I finally got up it was after 2:30 that Monday afternoon. I washed, got dressed. I wanted to fix some pancakes but I needed some eggs, so I went next door and asked Ms. Terry where my mother was.

She said, "Oh, you don't know? They went and got the baby. You looked so tired your mother decided to leave you here and take all the children with her."

"Oh my GOD, I really forgot!"

"But they should be back soon. They left at 10:30 this morning."

"Let me try to catch them!"

"Liz, your mother should be back by now."

I asked Ms. Terry for two eggs and I went back in the kitchen to finish fixing my pancakes. Suddenly, Mama pushed the door open.

Mama said, "That smells good Liz."

I asked, "Where's the baby."

"Well, Liz the baby has a little fever so she had to stay overnight."

"So what are you going to name her, Mama?"

"Well, you can name her."

"Well what name did Lynne pick?" I asked.

"Lynne wanted a boy and she had all boy names picked out. She only had one girl name picked out, Andrea. That sounded like a boy's name too."

"I wanted to name her Ralynne—R for Ricky and her name Lynne."

Mama said, "Girl y'all young people with those names. What happen to Elizabeth?"

"I will never name her my name. That is either a old name or a dead person's name."

"Remember your name came from a relative."

"That's why I hate my name."

Mama said, "Okay, that will be fine for you to name her. Now, let me go get her clothes out for her tomorrow. We will see if we can pick her up. Let me see if she is doing any better tonight."

I ate them some pancakes and asked Sharon to clean up the kitchen. She poked around and said in a sad voice, "I will, Liz."

I asked, "How you like the baby? Is she cute?"

Sharon said, "I wanted to be with Lynne and let the baby see her mother again."

"Well Sharon, let us just get through this right now, okay? Please try, because it will kill mommy and she is all we got."

Sharon said, "I know that."

Then there was a knock on the door. "Is Sharon home?" It was Kelly and Sandy.

"Yes, wait a moment and I will get her."

Sharon told them to come in and to go in the kitchen. She made them some pancakes. It was already 6 o'clock. I said to myself, *if my Mama wasn't so worried, those bums would have never come in to her apartment and then got a free meal. That never would have happened.* However, my mother's heart was on the funeral and the baby. Sharon got away with a lot. She never asked for permission to let her friends come in. They giggled, laughed, talked and played around in the kitchen. I didn't want to cause an argument so I just kept my thoughts to myself. They finally left at 10 pm. It was a school night so that wasn't supposed to be permitted in my mother's house.

The children were asleep when I remembered that I forgot to call in. Peggy answered.

"This is Liz, Did they know about me losing my sister?" Peggy asked, "Did you call in?"

"No, because I forgot."

"Mrs. Bailey was at work and I told her about you losing your sister."

"Okay, Thank you Peggy."

"Liz, you got to bring a death slip in."

"Okay, I will Peggy, when I come back."

"Don't forget Liz, we need a girl for your position if you don't come in for more than three weeks."

"Okay, what about Jean taking my place?"

"That's right, and I can train her."

"To be honest, I don't know when I will be coming back, because right now the baby got a fever and she is still in the hospital."

"So when is your sister's funeral?"

"I don't know. Let me ask Jean about working and you can ask Mrs. Bailey tomorrow."

"I don't work tomorrow 'cause I am working this weekend. Girl, I got to get off this phone."

"Okay Peggy, I will call you later."

We hung up, and I went in my room, stretched out on my bed and looked at the ceiling. John hit me on the leg. "Liz, Liz Mama want you."

I ran in the kitchen. Mama looked at me and said, "The baby is ready to come home."

I smiled and said, "Oh boy! That's good."

Mama ordered me to go and get the clothes that she would wear home. Mama grabbed the sleeper and the hooded sweater set that I held and said, "She will be released at 11 o'clock today. First, we gotta go see her social worker at the hospital, Mrs. Osborne. After we pick up the baby we will get a cab." Mama reminded me to get the baby's receiving blanket as we were leaving. I also grabbed a piece of toast with some margarine and ran out to catch the bus with Mama.

We met Mrs. Osborne in her office. She gestured to us to sit down. "You know you might not be able to take another child."

Mama answered, "Oh, yes we can because my daughter here is going to take the baby. She is only five months from graduation. We want this baby, and the only way she's going to be well is if she gets a good start."

She asked, "How will you support this child?"

Mama started, "Well Mrs. Osborne…"

I anxiously interrupted. "I got a part time job, and I get paid by the hour. I can use that to take care of her.

Mrs. Osborne said, "Okay, what about education?"

"I am a honor student."

She continued, "That is a real positive. We can try and see how well you are doing, and we will monitor the child's progress. Remember, someone gots to take her and make an appointment to see the doctor."

Mama said, "That will not be a problem. The other kids will be in daycare this month."

Then the social worker asked, "How old are they?"

Mama said, "Devon is three years old, and Shevon is two and she is potty trained." She added, "Children's Welfare can help out with the bill, my fee is only $60 a month and it is with bus service.

"When is the funeral?" Mrs. Osborne asked.

Mama softly answered, "It is Saturday at 11 o'clock."

"I already called upstairs and Dr. Schwartz is up there waiting on you."

Mama said, "Thank you for seeing us."

While we were leaving, I asked Mama, "Mama, do she know that I am going to college in the fall?"

Mama replied, "Fall ain't here yet, is it."

"But if she keep nosing around she might come and take the baby," I said.

"Well remember this Liz, she isn't my relative and she isn't my God. Once we get my baby home that will be none of her business. Besides, I can take care of Ralynne alone. There won't be any problem."

Chapter 17

Liz and the Baby

The nurse gave us a little box of supplies and then took us into another room. To our surprise, the room was filled with people and there was a table in the middle of the room piled high with baby items. People started coming up and hugging us and telling us how sorry they were about Lynne's death. Mama and I both started to cry.

On the table were cards with money, a little coat and hat set, a car seat, stroller and all kinds of toys. The staff had given the baby a shower. We couldn't stop crying because this was more than we could have asked for. On another table, there was a cake with some ice cream, salad, chicken, and ham plates, all kinds of cup cakes, some juice and some sodas.

The nurse asked me what we named the baby. With my voice quivering, I told her, "Rolynne Sherry Rosemere."

Mama looked at me and said sadly but proudly, "You changed her name from A to an O."

"Yes, O is Roland and now Rolynne, because I believe her mother loved her brother very much. She would be proud of that."

Mama said, "Okay, lets try to get those things home in the cab."

A lady came over and whispered in my mother's ear, "A good start for that baby, eh."

My mother hugged the nurses and doctors and said, "Thank you all from my daughter's baby, but now the problem is, how am I going to get all those pretty things in a cab?"

Rolynne's doctor stood up and said, "I will take you home." I cried as I thanked him. Mrs. Osborne smiled at us. A nurse put Lynne's baby in my arms and I held her close to my heart, then handed her to Mama. This surprise would stick with me for the rest of my life. I had experienced losing my sister and gaining a newborn baby within three days. I believed that there was a God that looked out for the people in Har-lem-and thanked him.

The nurses wrapped the food up. The janitor helped me put it in a bag. they got a hand truck for the large box and they took me and Mama down on the freight elevator. Dr. Schawrtz held the baby so Mama could sit down. Mrs. Osborne took me and Mama in her car, while Dr. Dr. Schawrtz took all the boxes in his truck. Mrs. Osborne told me to call home and make sure that someone would meet us.

Sharon answered the phone. "Hello Sharon. Listen, we got the baby and we need someone to help with the baby shower gifts. You and John can help."

She said, "Becky went to school so who will keep the children."

"Bring them downstairs."

"But they're sleepy."

"Put both of them in the crib. But as soon as you finish, meet us downstairs and wait for us."

"Okay, I'm doing it now." I hurried back to the car. I prayed that Sharon got it right and met us at the front stoop. I got in the front. I was so overcome with emotion that I couldn't say anything.

Mama gave her the directions to our apartment. We saw Sharon playing with John and a little boy named Frankie who lived on the first floor apartment. We got out of the car as the truck parked in front of our stoop. The doctor opened the door and pulled down the box.

Mama told John to go upstairs and get Ms. Terry. Sharon's mouth dropped wide open until I said, "Sharon! are you going to help me?"

She answered, "Okay, okay Liz. I am." But Sharon didn't know where to go first, to the truck or the car, so I went over and put some things from the back seat of the car in her hand. Frankie got some things out the trunk of the car. Ms. Terry came over and got some things out of the truck.

Mama said, "Please, don't reach over the baby. Someone might hit her."

It took us almost an hour to haul all those baby things up the stairs. Our apartment was so full of everything. They were in the front room, the kitchen, Mama's bedroom and my bedroom. I realized that the apartment really was too small for all of us. Sharon asked, "Mama, where all these baby things come from?"

Mama replied, "The hospital staff and doctors and nurses gave us a surprise baby shower. Boy, this is unbelievable. Look how nice these gifts are. So now you got the honor of helping us put it all away."

Sharon said, "Yes, yes, because I want to open up the gifts."

I said, "No, Sharon, we need to move the gifts out of the way."

Ms. Terry hollered, "Girl, what happened? Tell me that again? The staff and hospital gave a baby shower for the baby? Girl, this baby will never wear all these things or use them all. Tracy, be smart and save some of these clothes for the next grandbaby."

Mama said, "Those big size clothes are going to Shevon first. But for right now we going to have a party with this food."

Ms. Terry told John to go to her apartment and get her two kids. Mama unwrapped all the food. After Ms. Terry's two kids came over, Mama locked the door. "Now the only people that get some food is the people that help us. So Sharon, don't call your hood rats over here."

Ms. Terry said, "Tracy don't talk so loud, because we don't want old Mrs. Mae to hear us. She will try to call or come up to get a free plate. Besides, I'm gonna work for my plate. But I do need a nice cold beer."

Mama turned to her and said, "Terry the food is free. You can buy you a cold beer. But I am just going to enjoy this good food. I hope this food will last me for the rest of this week because I won't have any money for two weeks and Liz haven't been working." They talked, laughed and joked until 9 PM. Mama told Sharon to clean up the kitchen and to put the food away. I held the baby and looked at her for a long time.

Mama said, "Please don't spoil that baby because you are going back to work soon and this baby will be with me, okay? So listen. Put her down and clean off the bed."

"But Lisa's kids are asleep in the crib."

"So let us get the box with the bassinet in it and open that up. That's where the baby will sleep. Liz, if you want to watch her sleep you can let her sleep in your room."

The phone rang and I said, "This is Liz."

"This is Mike, I heard about you losing your sister. When is the funeral?"

I told him, "It will be 10 o'clock Saturday. We just picked up the baby today."

Mike said, "Liz, I want to be there for you."

I replied, "I hope so Mike, because I really need a good friend right now." When we hung up, my heart was full for the second time that day.

I went back in my room and checked on the baby. She was asleep and looked peaceful so I let her lie in her bassinet. I gave her a goodnight kiss then I took a hot bath. Suddenly I heard someone push on our front door. I put on my robe and went in the front room. The person tried to push again as I tiptoed into the kitchen and turned the light on and then tiptoed into my mother's room and woke her up. I said in a low voice, "Someone is trying to get in our apartment."

Mama jumped up and grabbed a baseball bat. The baby started crying about that time and whoever it was ran away. Mama ran over, put the night lock on and said, "Someone saw us bringing some of the new baby things in. So this is the plan, tomorrow we'll get a heavier lock, and then I'll call my sister Rose, get her husband's truck and put the boxes full of paper on the truck. We are going to get some tape and call Ricky to help us. Tonight the plan is this: we keep the light on in the kitchen and in the front room, and tomorrow I am going to Ricky's house and let him know what the plan is."

We went back in our bedroom but I couldn't sleep so I sat up in my bed and watched the baby sleep. The next thing I knew, John said, "Liz, Liz the baby is crying." I went into the kitchen to make her a bottle. Mama called the children and her sister Rose. The plan was to start at 5 o'clock. Mama took Sharon with her to find Ricky.

Mama came back and said, "Ricky will be here at 4o'clock, him and his boys." I said that this was a better plan than the one she had last night. Mama continued to order, "So y'all get all those things out of those boxes." We started to tape them but we ran out of tape, so I called Peggy.

Peggy said that she would be there at 4:15 with the tape and she would haul some of the boxes in her car. Mama said, "So that will be just fine, having another car in our plan. So you will go with Peggy, Liz."

Then I reminded Mama, "We can't park on this side of the street at this time of day."

Mama said, "That's right, we want the other side of the street where Anthony and your bum friends are."

"Why blame my friends for this incident," replied Sharon.

Mama answered, "Now we aren't blaming your friends, but those people was sitting on the stoop when we pulled up. Let me tell you Sharon, I will slap you in your mouth if I hear you tell anyone about my plan. Do you hear me Sharon? No one. Not even one of your friends. Okay, Sharon?"

"Yes, Mama I hear you."

Mama gave another order, "So finish taping those boxes. In the kitchen under the counter where Calvin is, is some old paper. When Ms. Terry come in this evening, we can ask her for some of her old newspaper. So let me get the phone and call Rose again, to ask her to bring some of her newspapers."

I told mama that the baby was wet and she needed to be changed. Mama told me to bring her in her room.

At 2 o'clock in the afternoon. Ricky knocked on the door and said, "Liz, let me in to see my baby."

I opened the door and said, "Ricky, we know whose baby this is." Jokingly I said, "And now you are going to support her."

Ricky answered, "Yes that is why I am here, to support and hold and kiss my baby."

I asked him, "Did mama tell you her plan?"

He said, "Yes, that's why I'm going to help her. That is my baby's things. And I don't like Anthony and Sissy, that dumb sick bum."

I told him, "Mama say we aren't here to fight. We just here to surprise them and make sure that they won't break in our apartment." Mama came over and said, "Remember, Ricky you take the baby to my sister's apartment and later Liz will bring the baby back home. Okay? Take that box of baby clothes for Liz and mark it. Leave it at Rose's apartment. That's the plan. And you can disappear again until we call you with another problem."

"You could leave me some money?" I asked.

He replied, "Okay Liz, since you are already begging me." He kept looking at the baby sadly and said, "I wish her mother was living. Everybody need a mother and love."

Mama asked Ricky, "Where your mother at?"

Bluntly, he said, "Mrs. Tracy, my mother left me for her boyfriend and my aunt took me and my sister in."

Mama asked, "So who was at the baby shower?"

Ricky said, "I call her my mother, but she is my aunt, and my uncle, I call him my father. But I got a lot of problems. And I guess their plan is to throw me out."

I butted in and said, "Ricky I can see why."

"You know, that's right Liz."

Then I told him, "You can stay on that one corner seem like forever doing your business."

Peggy came to the door with the paper and Ricky put the baby down and went outside with John. I started upstairs with the box of paper.

The second knock was Ms. Terry. Mama took her in her room but I still could hear their conversation. Mama said, "Child, I knew that those lazy bums were looking and you are going to be in this plan." Soon all the boxes were finished.

The third knock at the door was my aunt and uncle. Sharon ran cross the street and told them to park there. Ricky's friends came up to help with the boxes. The same people were on the stoop along with Sharon's friends. They asked if they could help her but Sharon bluntly said, "No one need to help me and my family."

Jeff and Kelly looked puzzled. Ricky got in Peggy's car after putting the baby in the car seat, and then Peggy took Ricky home. Peggy took me over to my uncle and aunt's apartment to stay until Lynne's funeral.

Mama called me and said it was Anthony and Sissy trying to break into our apartment. I asked, "How you know?"

She said because Sissy was cursing about how she don't have any baby clothes and she was going to have her baby soon. She started to curse Anthony out about it. She asked him to buy her some baby clothes. He told her, "Your baby clothes were in the box and it up and went with the father at his house. I tried, but it just didn't work."

Sissy asked, "So why can't you get a job or something." Anthony told her, "You live here free, it smells bad but it's free, so don't ask me for nothing, okay? I am not stealing *your* baby some clothes." Then he pushed her away from him. She went in her dirty, stinky, smelly apartment, looking sad and hurt.

I said, "Mama, I told you Anthony and Sissy try to steal everything. I never trusted her and we need to work hard to get up out of that apartment. But the only apartment that will be vacant is on the third floor, apartment F, and it is real big but it's not my ideal apartment."

Mama said, "I told you we need to move, because this is not my ideal apartment for us. We need to move and get a house. This idea sounds nice, but it's not real. No money is coming in like that, you know, that we need to pay for a good house."

I asked, "What about low income apartments?" Mama answered, "You mean those high rise apartments? And you call these people bums. You're really going to be looking at a big community of bums. That is more of a problem. And the children will have no place to play. We need to get our money together to pay rent in this apartment."

I told her, "Okay Mama, but I still don't like it."

"Okay Liz, you learn to live with this. When you get your home, then we can live with you. But for right now the responsibility is on me."

I hung up the phone and my Aunt Rose said, "Amen, that is the truth child. Y'all need a house. You can only be here until Saturday. These games are not to be played forever." Everything always got silent when my aunt talked. Her neighborhood was a little better. Besides, it had a security guard in it all the time. My uncle still worked there as a maintenance man after thirty years. When he is off he also helps people go to the market or move furniture into their new apartment and set it up.

My Aunt Rose is my late grandmother's youngest sister. She helped care for us. She used to work in the same building as a maid. She would bring us some good clothes from the rich people she use to work for. Her two sons are on disability and my grandmother cared for them too. She was used to them not talking and their odd way of walking, but my sister Lynne and brother Roland made fun of them. Now both of them are gone and my two handicapped cousins are still here. Now Becky is in the same position. The world will label her as something to throw away, I thought, but I love her and she still is apart of my life.

The baby started to cry so I rushed over to check her and saw she was throwing up. Her stomach was always upset. It was too late to call the doctor so I held her and tried to comfort her.

There was knock on my bedroom door. Aunt Rose said, "Child that baby can't keep on crying, because she isn't on this lease. Try to keep her quiet because I could get put out of here. The people that own this building promised me and my husband we could live here if we follow their rules. My two sons doesn't talk or cry, so the people next door wouldn't know that someone else is here. These people is old and nosy and can listen good with an ear aide, tell someone or get you in trouble with the landlord."

I got up and walked the baby around the room, hoping she wouldn't cry. Soon she went back to sleep and I fell asleep too, but soon woke up again. It was so peaceful and quiet in that room. I heard the phone ring. My aunt was talking to someone but I couldn't hear their conversation.

The next morning when I woke up, Aunt Rose was standing over me. She said, "Child you can't sleep all day with the baby. You need to wash yourself up, get the baby clothes out and wash and boil her bottles. And you need to remember this is your baby and how well you keep it will tell how well you carry your responsibility. That responsibility was left on you and your mother. That isn't your fault or the baby's fault. But someone has to carry this. This is a very defenseless person. Now let me get some of those clothes so you can give her a bath.

Liz, do you know how to give a baby a bath?"

I said, "Yes, I think so."

She replied, "Girl, this is a small baby so you should know how to give her a bath. Sit down, Liz. First thing is to get all her clothes together. Second, get the things you need to wash her with. You need her washrag and towel and soap. Get some lotion, baby oil, baby powder and a pamper. You got to watch how you handle this baby, make sure you got a big towel to protect you, and a mat to put on the floor. You need another towel to cover her so she won't get cold. Make sure your room is warm, then put the baby towel on your shoulder so as you finish washing her you can dry her. This is so she doesn't catch a cold. Are you ready to wash her? Let me get a big boiling pot, because I don't have anything else to put the water in. You are too far from the bath sink and too close to the bath tub."

We washed her right in the bedroom. I put some newspaper on the floor to set the boiling pot with the warm water on. Aunt Rose continued with the directions, "Never wash the baby in cold water as that will make her sick too. It would be easier to wrap the baby up and place her in the center of your bed and get some more warm water. Hold the baby's head and widen your legs so the baby won't fall. Wipe and dry her head last, and then put some oil on it. Put a cap back on her head. That also helps her from getting sick too. Now you are finished. Get the baby bottle warm. Now she is nice and clean and ready to eat."

I gave the baby to Aunt Rose so I could wash up. I finished cleaning up everything, washed the dirty clothes and put them on the radiator so they could dry. I put everything away. My cousins just stared at the baby. They seemed to enjoy looking at her.

My aunt told me, "Liz, don't leave that baby around my sons. They haven't been around a baby before, so please watch them. They are really little children in men's bodies."

I said, "Okay, Aunt Rose, I will watch them around this baby."

She said, "Liz you missed breakfast, so here is your lunch."

I said, "Don't fix anything. I'm not hungry right now."

Aunt Rose said, "Well if you don't eat lunch, you might as well eat dinner. You need to go to the store for me. I need some fish from the fish market downtown. You need to get on the bus. Do you know how to get there?"

I told her, "Yes I work around the fish market. Will I need to get a five-pound fish?"

"Yes honey."

I got the fish and as I was going home, I heard someone call me. It was Jean. "Hi Liz."

"Hi Jean, so you're going to work?"

"Yes."

"How do you like my job? its not hard, but it does get busy for the holiday."

Jean said, "Liz, when are you coming back to work?"

I told her, "I don't know right now. But I really need the money."

She replied, "I know that is right. Well let me get in and punch the time card."

I said, "Okay. I'll see you, Jean and hope to see you in school." I got on the bus just to find out I was on the wrong one, so I had to walk nine blocks to my Aunt's apartment building. As I was walking, I ran into Steven coming from work.

Steven asked, "Are you going to work?"

Irritated, I said, "No fool, Steven I am not going to work."

He said, "So, where are you going?"

"I'm going to my Aunt Rose's apartment. I'm not living with my aunt, Steven."

Then he asked, "Can I walk with you?"

All of a sudden, he reached down and kissed me. I took my hand and wiped his kiss off my face. I said, "Look Steven I don't like you and I don't want you to kiss on me."

I began walking up the street. I didn't look back at Steven. I ran up the street and went into my aunt's apartment.

She said, "Liz, what took you so long? Did you clean and cook the fish?"

I told her, "No, I ran into all my coworkers and started to talk to them. I don't eat dinner at midnight anyway."

Aunt Rose said, "The baby been throwing up so I called your mother. She is going to take the baby back to the hospital tomorrow." I reminded her that Lynne was ready for the viewing so I needed to go over there.

She said, "But don't be coming back here no five or six hours later. This is you and your mother's plan. But my plan was never to be worried about this baby."

I responded with, "Okay, Aunt Rose, I'll go to the viewing of the body at 12:30."

She told me, "Your mother will be here at 11:30, so you might want to take the baby."

I informed her that this was still wintertime so the baby didn't need to be out in the cold and that she was already sick. My aunt said that she would keep the baby until we got back. She added, "But I am not keeping this baby all day and all night! Okay?"

She cooked the fish and we ate with the baby sitting on the center of the table. She didn't cry. Aunt Rose pulled her cap close to her eyes to block some of the light shining in them. I could see that she was getting attached to the baby. I smiled at her as she talked about her two sons when they were babies. If anything came from this, it is that she shared a memorial with me, I thought.

After I ate, I washed the dishes and cleaned the kitchen, then I went in the room to find the clothes I would wear to see my sister for the last time. My eyes started to fill and tears started to fall. I wiped my face, then I asked my aunt to watch the baby while I took a bath and got ready for bed.

She reminded me, "Liz you need to get the baby washed up and ready for bed too. After the baby's bath, I'll put her to sleep and then you can take a bath. However, remember, the baby comes first. This way she can sleep and you can take a bath in peace. Liz, a baby can be a lot of work and take a lot of time. So you need to get it in your mind how this is going to effect you in your life.

"I know you told me about your plan to go away for college. You need to tell your mother that just because she just lost that baby's mother, trying to make you the child's mother, that isn't right. Your future is your future, it's not your mother's future. That needs to be discussed now, because this might hurt you later in life. We all need to know your stand with this situation."

I listened to Aunt Rose, then turned around and went to bed. I was so tired that I left my clothes on. Suddenly the baby started to cry and I jumped up, fed her and laid her on my chest. She seemed to be very content with that. She had one eye open while falling asleep. I softly talked to her until I started to cry. I rubbed and patted her on the back.

I was up but dragging the next morning. I didn't want to see my sister laid up in that funeral home, but I knew my mother counted on me and needed my support. I hoped my heart could stand it. I got the baby's clothes together and put them in the baby bag. I put my clothes in a plastic grocery bag. I'll try to relax tomorrow after the funeral, I said to myself.

Someone called me to the phone. "Hello, Liz. Get anything that belongs to the baby together. Do you want me to bring your heavy coat?" Mama asks.

I said, "Yes, bring my heavy coat."

She said, "Well, be ready at 11:30."

I said, "Yes, Mama I'll be ready."

Then she told me, "Liz, Mike has been calling for you."

Excited, I replied, "Oh my goodness, I forgot about Mike!"

She said, "You can see him at the viewing or if you go to the funeral."

Aunt Rose got on the phone, "Tracy, I'm going to keep the baby until you get back from the funeral." Mama thanked her. I got up, washed up and got dressed for the funeral and then I sat at the window for the moment. Then I made sure all the bottles were made up. Aunt Rose told me she would wash up the baby.

A blue car pulled up with Mama, Mike and all the kids except Becky. Lisa's kids were also in the car. I ran outside and got in the front seat. "Hello Liz."

"Hi Mike" I thought to myself, *Maybe I can get through this with Mike's help.* The lady at the funeral home directed us to a room. Lynne had on a pretty dress that Ricky gave Mama the money to buy. All the neighbors in our building were there.

I started to sob. Mike held me and said, "Liz, I'm here."

Mama cried, stroked Lynne's hair and started repeating "My daughter that I lost. Please honey, what happened to my pretty little girl?" Ricky held Mama and led her back to her seat. Her tears soaked his shirt.

As the funeral started, a guy started to cry loudly. I looked over Mike's arm and saw it was Gary. I suddenly thought *Lynne's baby looks like him more than it does Ricky. The little girl has brown eyes. Oh, my sister, both of these men here crying for you. Both might think that they fathered the baby.*

Ricky looked at Gary angrily. Mama hit him on the arm and whispered, "Please! This is a funeral, not a night club. You can fight over a girl later. I want peace in life."

Gary kept sobbing over Lynne until Mama told the funeral director to close the casket. As soon as the service was over, Mama started to move the crowd to their cars. We all made our way to the burial ground.

Ricky ran out to Aunt Rose's to get the baby to take to the burial ground. Aunt Rose came with him. Peggy came too, but she drove her car. I took her in the back room and said, "Look Peggy, both of Lynne's men are here crying."

She said, "What! Girl? Oh please don't let it be like your brother's funeral when the girl jumped in the casket."

I told her, "No, these two are going to kill each other instead."

Peggy replied, "As long as they got too do it, let me get in the car. Then they can kill each other all they want."

My family took Mike, Aunt Rose and the baby. Ricky got in Peggy's car. When we arrived at the burial ground, we found Gary there first. He put a pink rose on Lynne's casket, and then he stood there crying. Ricky was getting angrier so Mama took Gary's hand, rubbed his back and started to talk softly to him, then she escorted him out the gate.

Ricky cried out, "WHY LYNNE, WHY?" Mama escorted Ricky, holding his baby, and Peggy. The preacher shortened his prayer and everything was over. I thanked Peggy for being there and I thanked Mike for bringing my family to the funeral. Mike was lost for words.

Some people came with us to our apartment. I asked Mama what happened to Ms. Terry. She told me that she stayed at our apartment to collect the food. As we turned the corner, to our surprise again, Gary was still sitting in front of the gate. As we drove past, he went back into the burial grounds. Mama said, "Let him have his final respect."

Ms. Terry ran up and started talking to us. "Tracy, my cousin Katie came so I got a friend to bring me to the funeral."

"Okay, Terry, I'll meet you at my apartment."

As Mike reached our street, Mama thanked him, "Thank you baby. Are you coming in to get something to eat?"

"Yes Ma'am, I would like to have something to eat." I interrupted them and directed Mike to an empty parking space. He walked up the stairs with me, hugging me around my neck.

I unwrapped the food. Katie helped me fix a plate for Mrs. Mae. who came up beside me and asked for some potato salad, greens and chicken. Then she asked if she could have fried chicken and barbeque chicken too. Mama said, "No, please give her just the fried chicken."

"Can I have some sweet potato pie and chocolate cake?"

Mama says again, "No Liz, give her one or the other."

Mrs. Mae said, "That'll be fine, thank you for my dinner."

I told her, "I'm not fixing you a plate of food for your breakfast too."

"Thank you, child, for giving me something to eat. You're not only a neighbor here today."

I fixed Mike a plate of macaroni salad, greens, and some bar-b-que chicken. He took it into the front room to eat.

Now that all the neighbors were leaving, old Mrs. Mae had the nerve to ask, "Anything y'all like to give away?"

Mama told her, "No, Mrs. Mae, you ate everything we would like you to have."

"Okay, Tracy, I see you tomorrow."

"Okay Mrs. Mae, I see you in our passing." Then Mama shut the door. Ms. Terry, Katie and Mama were dividing the food. Mama cut the ham, wrapped it up and put it in the freezer for the future. The leftover potato salad wasn't seasoned well so they seasoned the salad like it was suppose to be. The cake was all gone, and the only thing left was the string beans, so Mama gave them some of that. "Girl if all the neighbors were like Mrs. Mae, I wouldn't let her in my apartment to eat at all. She's a diabetic, but I'm not here to feed her sugar."

Ms. Terry went on to say, "Girl, Tracy if you are going to have another funeral, God forbid, please have it somewhere else."

Mama said, "I know what you saying, Terry. Katie is a very sad person, she never say anything. What happen to her is this. My father's brother beat her so bad that she doesn't say too much. All that drama make her slow. She got one grown daughter and her name is Ruthie Mae and I can't stand her 'cause the way she treat her mother, as if Katie doesn't have enough problems. Katie was in the kitchen cleaning up. She's nice, that's why I keep up with her and tried to get her here to help me, and this way she earns a little change in her pocket. Besides, she the only relative that will help me. She always do for me, even if it isn't no money involved."

"That's nice of you Tracy."

Mama asked, "Mike, would you take Katie home please and Liz could go with you."

I said, "Who'd watch the baby?"

"Whoever got the baby now is who is going to watch her." So I got our coats and went toward the car. Katie got into the back. As we were driving off, we saw Robert, Mike's friend. Mike rolled down his window to holler at him. He said, "Hi man, where you going?"

"Downtown, man."

"Jump in Robert, and after these ladies go home you and me can hang out."

"That sound nice to me man." Mike dropped Katie off first, then me next. When I was getting out Mike said, "I'll see or call you later Liz."

"Nice to see you Robert. Okay Mike. Will I hear from you before you go back to college?"

"I hope to be with you before I leave."

"Okay, Mike until then, I'll see you."

I ran upstairs and opened up the door. Ms. Terry was saying, "People, you carry it to the grave. Especially about the truth in Lynne's case."

Mama said, "She died and the baby look like Gary."

"I can't believe that, Tracy. You know that ol' saying, *Mama's Baby and Daddy's Maybe.*"

Mama continued, "I asked her who the baby's daddy was and she say Ricky is the baby's father. But two drug dealers at that. One of them got brown eyes and the baby got brown eyes. Gary gotta high forehead and the baby gotta a high forehead. In addition, the baby has a round face just like Gary. Please let me find something of Ricky."

Ms. Terry said, "Yes, his last name, that the only thing that baby got. There's no question in my mind, she deal wit' both of them at the same time. Now we just gotta hope they don't have kill each other over this baby. You know wit' her looking like that wit' that last name."

Mama replied, "That's not nothing I am going to say, cause I'm just her grandmother and I love and care for this baby."

Ms. Terry said, "That is a pretty baby, looks like Gary, with a father named Ricky McDonald. A common name for a complex situation."

Mama said, "We just take these names to the grave." Mama and Ms. Terry just shook their heads and said, um uh.

Mama told me to get a diaper. "I know you heard us talking. Please never tell anyone. These things can get a person killed." Mama continued, "We just going to give her love and support from our family. Besides Ricky love this baby, so we just let him love her. But we got to hope and pray Gary never come into the picture. We need to keep this a family secret—never tell it. We need to keep this little one in our life."

Finally, Ms. Terry shut up and left for the night. I washed up the baby and put on her sleeper and matching hat to keep her warm. I washed myself up and got my PJs on but for some reason I couldn't sleep so I decided to turn the radio on. Marvin Gay sang a medley, *Distant Lover.* I started reflecting on my relationship with Mike and how distant this love was and sadness came to my heart. I laid my head on my pillow and found myself falling asleep.

I woke up and saw Mama picking up the baby. For just that moment I forgot there was a baby. She took the baby, went in the kitchen and got a bottle of milk. I stayed in my bed until the sunlight crept to the top of my bed, then I got up and went in the kitchen.

"Good morning Mama. What's wrong with the baby?"

She said, "This baby is still vomiting and has loose bowels. I am calling the doctor this morning 'cause she is sick." Mama gave the baby a bath and got her ready to take her to the emergency department of the hospital.

I felt sad for little Rolynne because she is so young and so sick and she needs my love and my attention. I asked Mama if I could go with her. Mama said, "No, you got to watch the other kids. But you could go and get a cab for me."

I put on my clothes in a hurry and ran outside to find a cab. Mama got in the cab with the baby and told me to make sure the kids got something to eat.

Chapter 18

The Shadow of a Man

I went back upstairs and I looked to see if there was any food, like maybe bacon, thawed out. I looked in the cabinet to see if there was any more cereal, but the only thing I saw was a molded piece of bread. I looked around the apartment to see if there was any money, but the only money I found was a five-dollar bill. Well, I thought, it can buy oatmeal and all of us will have something to eat.

I needed milk and sugar so I went to see if Ms. Terry was home. I knocked on the door but I didn't get any answer. I thought to myself, It's Sunday morning. I guess they still asleep. I ran back to my apartment, looked around again and I found one can of milk. It was still early but I knew Lisa's kids always get up hungry and go to bed hungry, so I needed to get their breakfast started. I went to the corner store and asked for a box of oatmeal. The clerk said that it would be $3.49 for a little box and the larger one was $4.80."

"And how much for five pounds of sugar?"

"$2.99."

"How much is a small sugar."

"$1.79."

"I only have $6.22 so can I bring back thirty-seven cents?"

"Bring back thirty-seven cents. Remember bring back and I going to give you large oatmeal and two pounds of sugar."

"Yes, I will remember to bring back your thirty-seven cent when my mother comes home." I couldn't believe these people, I thought. First, they were more expensive than the supermarket and the food was not as fresh. I just shook my head and went home. I knew it would cost me more money and take longer to go to the market on the bus.

When I passed Ms. Terry's apartment I could smell something burning. I knocked on the door but there was no answer. Suddenly I saw smoke coming from under her door! I kicked the door open and screamed FIRE! A man ran up the stairs and we both kicked at the door until it flew open. I knew Ms. Terry and her children were asleep. The apartment was full of thick black smoke. The man grabbed Mrs. Terry and I ran and grabbed the two children. I fell to my knees and dragged them toward the door, then pulled them out in the hall. The man helped me drag the kids on down the hall out of danger. I couldn't stop coughing and was gasping for breath.

Sharon came running down the hall, saw what was happening, then ran back to the apartment and called the fire department and the rescue squad. By the time the fire department got there and put out the fire, the walls and the furniture were burned. Everybody got out safely, but they were coughing and choking from the smoke. The emergency people checked us out, and then I went to our apartment and dropped down in the front room chair. Sharon got Mama's robe to put on Ms. Terry and Becky's coat to put on Ms. Terry's little girl. The Emergency team ran in and out of our apartment. The hallway was full of water and wood and old burnt clothes.

One of the firemen thanked me for getting the family out. He asked me if they smoked. I still couldn't talk without coughing. He said, "That's alright little lady because you really is that family's hero."

A woman firefighter asked Sharon some questions about the fire. I told Sharon, "Don't say anything to them, because you really haven't seen anything to tell anyone."

She said, "But Liz! I did smell the smoke."

"But Sharon, you didn't go up to see what happened. Only thing you did was call 911. So Sharon, please don't be calling our apartment building the news station. What you see and tell, you might cause yourself some problem or somebody in your family. I know Sharon, how you and your friends like to see some action but where we live, this is enough. We see people get put out. We hear loud guns firing. People get banged in the mouth. Young and old ladies fight over a bum. So Sharon, you don't need to be in the 'know' of everything."

I continued, "If it happens to someone you know, you can drop a dime in the telephone booth, but please don't be the one that everyone can get the info from. People tell who the nosey persons in their building are and then the police will target you for information about everybody's business."

Irritated, Sharon just said, "Okay Liz."

I started thinking about Rolynne's two daddies. I thought, I know Ricky hates Gary and Gary hates Ricky but I don't want anyone to get hurt or killed over this baby. Sharon and her friend will probably have a field day over this lie. She wants the truth but she won't get it from me or my mother and Lynne took the truth to her grave. I am going to do the same thing.

I thought about how much I love my niece and decided I was going to honor her mother's life just the way she left it. I did disapprove of what she did, but I respect her point. I made a promise to myself to take care of my dead brother and sister's children. I realized I am now the oldest, so my mother needs my shoulder to lean on and for me to help her take care of all my family.

Sharon said, "Liz, Liz. Who was that man that helped kick in Ms. Terry front door?"

"Sharon, I really don't know who he is."

Sharon said, "I hope Mama gets here soon so we can tell her about the fire in Ms. Terry apartment."

"Well, let's sit down and pray that this won't break Mama's heart." I said.

Sharon said, "Ms. Terry didn't look too good."

I reminded her, "Her condition could be serious. Now we gotta see how her children gonna be now even though those kids get on my nerves. John, can you get those kids off the table and clean up that mess of theirs? Becky, get your shoes out of the kitchen. Now let's clean the hallway at Ms. Terry's. Y'all get the trash bags. Water is running into our apartment."

I opened the door to see how much trash and water they left us. Sharon was complaining, "Liz, these firemen put out the fire and when we shut our door all this water run all over these third and fourth floor apartments. We might as well have had the whole apartment building on fire. This is a big mess. People on this third floor need to clean up too."

I asked her, "Please Sharon, do you really think these people care about cleaning? Look at their filthy apartment door and their mess they leave in the hallway. Nasty writing on the walls. Scratches on walls, door and hallway. Please don't let me get started about the beer bottles and cans in the corner of this floor."

Sharon said, "We need to put the trash can in the hall and drill it up against the wall with a chain."

I said, "Please, Mama would have to pay another increase in her rent for that mess."

Sharon said, "But Liz. They need to paint and mop the hall, and the stair railing need to be fixed. The window is always broken."

All I could say was, "I know what you are saying Sharon, but this is where we live at for right now. Just pray to God to bless us with another house or better apartment building."

Sharon continued, "You know Liz? I was afraid that Ms. Terry and her family was dead."

"Me too."

John jumped in and said, "I really like her little boy. It would really hurt me to hear that he die."

Becky bowed her head sadly. I know that she liked those kids a lot. They listened to her and played with her everyday. We know Becky is slow and acts and talks like a five to seven year old, but they make her happy when they take the time to talk to her. I know what she is trying to say to me by the expression on her face.

John ran to the back yard to take the trash out but he came back so fast I said, "John, I know you didn't throw the trash out, you put it in front of our apartment building."

John said defensively, "No I didn't Liz! It was a young man that carry the trash out."

"Well, here some more trash you can take outside." He was back again even faster. He immediately said, "See Liz. He did it again," as he was laughing. I looked down over the stair rail, but the only thing I could see was a shadow of a man. "John, this man must be a ghost."

"No Liz, he just a young man that was willing to take my trash out." He said this while still laughing.

I told him, "This time I am going to take the trash out." As soon as I got to the second floor, I saw the door to 2-B close. I never did see anyone. I told John, "That ain't funny. I never seen him."

He told me, "He don't like you Liz, because you always tell us what to do. He must hear you talk to us and he want me to be his friend."

I said, "Oh boy, just get some more of that paper that Peggy left under my bed."

I heard a Mama coming. Concerned, she said, "What happen here, cause all the neighbors looking at me in a funny way."

I said, "Oh, sit down first." I told her about the fire in Ms. Terry apartment and that they were in ER at the hospital. Her mouth dropped open. She put the baby down and ran out the door without saying anything, I looked out the window and saw her getting on the bus that goes downtown to the hospital. I picked up the baby, who was asleep, and took off her snowsuit. I laid her in her bassinet.

Mama left before she could tell me how to give the baby her medicine so I read the directions on the medicine bottle. One medicine was supposed to have been given to her an hour ago. I woke the baby up and put two drops in her mouth. She was still crying I rocked her back to sleep. As I was laying her down, John said, "See Liz, that man came upstairs to mop the hallway."

I said, "John, you don't know him."

He said, "But I like what he do for me."

I told him, "I am going to tell Mama about that man tomorrow. Besides, where he live at in this building?"

John said, "I don't know that, Liz." I questioned him, "Do you know his name?"

"No Liz. All I know is that he do my work for me and I want him to be my friend."

"Okay John, but until then you keep away from him. Do you understand that, little boy?"

"I hear you."

I then told him, "So shut our front door."

John asked me, "Where did Mama go?"

"She ran back to the hospital to check on Ms. Terry and her kids." Sharon bumped John and said, "You watch yourself around him. You and your unknown person! Nobody never see him or talk to him, so please don't put us in danger with that person nobody know." John said, "Sharon, this is the truth, he help me." Unconvinced Sharon continued, "But you just met him, John. He just put the trash out and mop the hallway. Okay, but you need to find out who he is. You should introduce us to him first before you call him a friend. Besides he is an older man."

John said, "Okay. I listen to you and Liz."

The phone rang." Hello is Liz Home."

"This is Liz. Hi Mike, are you home?"

"Yes, but I'm going back to college tonight."

"Is your grandma taking you back to college?"

"No, I am going on the train. I'm calling to see if you going be home around 3 o'clock."

"Yes. I will." I hung up the phone and started to clean up. I told everyone what to do. "John, straighten up your bedroom and Sharon, please clean up Roland's kids."

Sharon said, "Liz, don't be rushing us because Mike is coming over in an hour. Mike probably get some lunch."

I said, "Girl, we ain't talking about food but I am going to the store to get a soda and a big bag of potato chips."

Sharon said, "I am not watching that baby and those kids too."

I told her, "Move, Sharon and let me pass." I went to the store and got in line to pay for my order. "Your bill $3.60."

"No, my bill is $2.95."

"No Miss. You owe me thirty-seven cents plus tax on your bill. Bring up $3.60." I moved to look in my wallet for some change. The man said, "Here your bag." I turned around to see who paid my bill but I couldn't see anyone. I went outside and looked around to see who to thank. I only have twenty-cents in change, I thought, those chinks didn't forget when I owed them thirty-seven cents.

On the way back to our building I kept turning around to see if anyone was following me. I never did see anyone but as I was going up the stairs, the front door to the building closed again. I looked down through the stair rail, but the only thing I saw was the shadow of a man. I started to stop and knock on Mrs. Mae's door but I knew her motor mouth would never stop. She would want to know everybody's business and she would gossip about everything.

I ran up to our apartment. Inside, Mama was crying and saying, "At least Ms. Terry and her kid will be home. Nothing left of her things though. Liz. Fix some tuna fish sandwiches for everyone." Mama wouldn't eat anything. I cleaned up the kitchen.

There was a knock on the door. "Hi Mike. Come in."

Mike asked, "What in the world happened to Ms. Terry's apartment?"

I said, "She had a fire and the whole apartment burned."

Mike asked, "Did anybody got hurt?"

"Well, they went to the hospital for the smoke but they was talking and explaining that she left a cigarette in the kitchen and forgot about it and went to bed."

Mike said, "That's good that nobody got burned because that apartment is a mess and a loss."

We went into the kitchen, still talking about Ms. Terry. The phone rang and Mama answered. All I heard was "Okay. That will be fine."

Mike was telling me that he left his address and telephone number at his college. He stood up, kissed me and said, "Liz I got to get the 4:30 train to college. You got my information already. Call or write me sometime." He said goodbye, went out and I shut the door.

Sharon came by and said, "John, we can eat all these sandwiches because Mike is gone again."

I came in the kitchen and took the sandwiches from them. "No, you will not eat all the sandwiches and drink all the soda because Mama haven't eaten anything and some is for her. Now sit down and eat a sandwich and drink a glass of soda."

Mama called me in and told me that Ms. Terry was coming home. I asked, "But Mama, where is she going to sleep at?"

Mama said, "I guess she gotta live here until she can get a new apartment. You might can live with Aunt Rose."

I told her, "That few days drove me crazy. Her son move around me at night. No, I never do want to come over there and stay."

Mama then said, "Liz, they are strange, especially her husband. That man got a crazy way. Daniel always doing something to Rose. She got three crazy persons. Liz, as long as they didn't hurt you or my grandbaby that would be all I worried about. See if any small clothes of John and Becky laid around here. Tomorrow, Ms. Terry and Linda is coming home but the little boy got to stay there for more physical therapy on his arm. It got burnt pretty badly and he can't use it too much. Let me try to find extra sheets for tomorrow. Mr. Roy going to pick me up too and pick up Ms. Terry and her little girl. I can go to the used clothing store before I got to be at the hospital. Do Lynne got any big tops?"

"We gave all those small clothes to Lisa but let me see if any more clothes laying around and I'll put it in a trash bag or empty box." I started to look. "Sharon, look in y'all room and see if any clothes too small for Becky. Mama, I thought that you didn't have any money."

"But Mr. Roy is her man and if he can't help her now, she don't need him. Let's see what he really gonna do for her now that she don't have anything. My heart go out for her, but my life is already good and full of problems. I don't need any more.

The next day Mama got a phone call from Mr. Roy saying he was on his way. She told him she needed to stop past the used clothing store to get her some clothes. He said, "Okay, that will be no problem."

Mama told him, "Roy, you need to know I don't have any money."

He said, "That's okay, I got a few dollars."

She said, "I will be downstairs in front of our building."

"Liz. Here's some change to get a loaf of bread. I'm letting Roy drop me off at the market because I don't have any food."

I said, "I can testify on that behalf, Mama."

As I was going to the store, I passed a man sitting on our stoop. I said hello. He was looking down and he didn't answer. As I was coming back from the store, Mama was sitting at the front of the stoop. Mrs. Mae came out and started to ask questions about Ms. Terry. Mama just said, "Not now Mrs. Mae. I got someone come to pick me up."

Mrs. Mae just continued, "Is Terry coming home today?"

Mama bluntly asked, "Did you call the hospital to see if she coming home?" Mrs. Mae went back into her apartment without saying anything. Mama said, "That nosy lady called the hospital and asked questions about Terry. Liz, hurry upstairs and see about the baby. Sharon sleep hard and she will not hear her."

As I was going upstairs to my apartment I saw the shadow of that man at apartment 2-B again. I asked John what he looked like. "John, is he cute?"

John looked at me strangely and said, "He look like a young man. Besides I don't look at a man and see if he cute."

Sharon got up. "He must be a monster."

"No Sharon," John said. "He just a nice man."

Sharon said, "I am going to knock on his door this afternoon."

I jumped in and said, "No Sharon, don't be ignorant."

Sharon then said, "But Liz, I don't really care about him. He just John friend, not yours."

I told her, "No, because everybody in this building know each other."

Sharon intervened and said, "That's not true because there's people that we don't see that live here and we don't know them. Like the crazy neighbors that drink at the end of our floor."

I said, "That's true Sharon, but this man is funny and I never did see him that night when he helped me get Ms. Terry and her family out of her apartment." We were talking and eating an egg sandwich when the baby started to cry. Sharon got up and carried her in the kitchen. "Bring the bassinet."

Sharon said, "Liz, you better hurry, those hungry children is woke and ready to eat."

I got their breakfast, the last of the oatmeal. Sharon told me, "I'm going to feed Rolynne and give her a bath and put on a cute outfit."

I said, "I need to do that, Sharon."

She said, "No Liz. I can do that. She is my niece too."

"Okay, I'll test that bath water." I ran warm water in her baby tub and helped Sharon get all her clothes and her accessories.

Sharon fed her and said, "This baby got brown eyes and she don't look like Ricky at all." I didn't comment. Then she said, "Well, we can at least be sure that she is our niece." The baby woke up. Sharon started to clean her up while I got her medicine and put two drops in her mouth.

I thought, she is getting older and she won't be sleeping as much. Sharon was talking and playing with her, then Rolynne went back to sleep. Sharon said, "You know, Christmas is here in a couple of weeks."

I told her, "I know we ain't getting a lot of stuff. We been through a lot of problems and we are trying to move."

The doorbell rang. John said, "Ms. Terry and Linda is here." He was looking for the little boy. I told him, "Oh John, Ms. Terry son's still sick." John didn't say anything but his face said it all. He was disappointed his playmate didn't come home.

Mama told me to put the food in the fridge so she could cook it later. Ms. Terry sat down and cried for a while. Mama said, "Terry, think of this. You might not have anything, but you do have you and your children's life."

She looked up and said, "Thank you, Liz, for saving my life." I walked over to the couch, sat down and started to look at television. Then Ms. Terry picked up the baby and kissed her on her cheeks.

Mama asked, "Terry? Who was that man in your apartment with you when the fire broke out?"

She said, "Oh, Tracy that was Willie. That my man too."

Mama was confused. She said, "I need to call Willie to pick you up. Not Roy. That was who paid for the clothes and food." Ms. Terry looked back and said, "Both got a wife."

"What lie did you say to Roy?"

"I told him I was asleep and left my cigarette lit and it drop and burn the apartment."

"Girl, you are cutting your life a little too close for me."

"Yeah. I thought about that when I see Roy."

Mama continued, "Roy a nice guy and he care for you."

Ms. Terry replied, "That might be true, but my whole life stays in a uproar. When I need him and then his family want to be with him, he leave for weeks, sometimes a month. He got four weeks vacation. He and his family stay out of town. He got a pretty nice house uptown in Manhattan. He never leave his wife. Neither is Willie. He been married for 22 years."

Mama was shocked. She just asked, "Terry, why do you keep your life like that?"

Ms. Terry just kept talking, "Paul wasn't all that much but he was separated until he went back to his wife. Girl, when I need these men they never there."

Mama said, "When I see my life with my husband fall apart, I stay by myself and I haven't found a good one yet. Besides, when I tell them I got six kids—conversation stop."

"See Tracy, I always have a man in my life. Whether he married or single."

"That might be true, but you still live here in the slum. If these men didn't put you in a better apartment, make you their "wife," you still are by yourself. The little time they spend with you is just playtime. Let's see who pay your rent and take care of you. Girl, I hope you can see the real picture. I know I am a little older, but you are a woman that got children and where is your baby's father?"

Terry, sounding a bit embarrassed, answered, "He got married on me and left me with nothing."

Mama said, "Girl, you are cutting it close. What if both y'all die. Or one of you did? What lie are you going to tell? You didn't know him, you woke up and he was in your burnt bed?

Terry looked at Mama and said, "Girl that is really something to say."

"Terry, I know that would be a problem." Mama laughed and said, "Girl you are acting Trashy!"

"You know that's right Tracy. I was afraid."

Mama reminded her, "But not today. You just spent Roy's money."

"Girl, I gotta change my life. After this episode I am afraid."

Mama also told her, "You know, I just love you and care about you as a friend. Terry, I never want anything to happen to you or your children."

Terry answered, "I know that you really care about me 'cause I have nowhere to go."

Mama told her again, "That's right. Remember that, Terry - nowhere. Those men bought their wife a nice house. You don't have anything out those relationships."

"I love you, Tracy but this is the only life I know."

Mama said, "Your life was almost over. Let me get up from here and make us some soup."

Ms. Terry went into the bathroom to wash up again and washed the clothes too. Those used clothes were making her itch.

Mama came out of the kitchen. She said, "Let me make a bed for Linda and Terry you can sleep on the couch and I got some old clean sheets."

"Thank you again for taking in me and my kid."

We all ate and went to bed. We were all cramped up. There were people everywhere in our apartment. Wednesday I went back to school and to work. Mama didn't need me. Ms. Terry helped Mama with Becky and the children.

After school was over I went downtown to work. I gave my supervisor my filled out funeral slip. Peggy came up to me and said, "Girl we really need you back here."

I asked, "How Jean doing?"

She said, "She doing okay, but I'm just used to seeing you around in the rack department."

"Girl, I am glad to be back."

Peggy reminded me, "This is the Holiday rush. Those people was outside early this morning ready to shop. Now the store opens at 8:30 AM and closes at 11 at night and you gotta work this holiday schedule and its always in a rush.

The day was slow and I forgot a lot of the department numbers. I went into the office and I started talking to Peggy. Peggy got the list of numbers and copied a sheet for me. Peggy sarcastically said, "See Liz? This job is still the same even if you should leave it for a year."

"I know, but I forgot some of the department ticket numbers."

"Well here's one list to keep." I left and ran into Steven. "Hi Steven, you still here?"

He said, "Yes Liz, where am I going?"

I giggled, "I guess nowhere. Believe it or not, I don't have nowhere to go either."

Steven said, "Why not work here Liz? Besides who put up with me."

I just said, "Now look at you Steven. You know that's the truth."

He laughed and hit me on my arm. I left him and went to punch out. As I was going to the time clock I ran into Janice. "Hi Janice, I missed you."

Janice started with, "Girl let me tell you about your friend Jean. She like that crazy Steven."

I told her, "No Janice, Jean is a nice girl."

She said, "Yeah, but she is going to be a nice FOOL for Steven. They get on the same bus and go home together."

I was so shocked, the only thing I could say was, "Girl I can't believe this. I should warn her about that fool Steven."

Janice said, "That's right Liz, 'cause she must not know about him being a father of two kids and not paying child support." She said, "Your friend can be another mother on the list to not be getting child support from Steven. I hope its not too late for you to help her."

"Oh Boy, not my girl Jean." I rushed over to find Peggy. "Peggy, what's this I hear about Steven and Jean?"

Peggy said, "Girl I wanted to call you to tell you what was going on at the job but it wasn't none of my business. She is your personal friend."

I told her, "But when I introduce her to you I want her to be your friend too."

She said, "Well Liz, I like her but she isn't my friend. She is your friend. Besides I am not looking for a friend in high school."

I immediately started thinking about what Peggy said. To my surprise, Peggy had just gone along with me and Jean as if she really liked me and her. Because she is in college, she really didn't care for us. I asked her, "Is you still going my way home?"

She said, "Yes Liz, you can still get a ride." I opened the car and got in. Right at that moment Jean and Steven came by holding hands. I looked, waved my hand and hollered out, "I see you in school tomorrow Jean."

Peggy looked disgusted. She said, "That couldn't be me walking with that worthless Steven. He need to be kicked in his butt."

But I said, "Peggy, I like Jean and I respect her feelings, so we just have to deal with that."

She said, "Not me Liz, that is your friend and I'm not dealing with her anymore."

I said, "I am real sorry you feel that way. See Peggy, we look up to you."

Peggy said, "I know that might be true but your parents is your role model."

"That's not what I'm saying."

"What are you saying?"

"That our parents haven't ever finished no school and so we learn from college folk how to act and talk, and maybe we can use some of your experience."

She said, "I am not your parents. They got the best experience you can learn."

I could see where Peggy comes from. I decided not to say anything else. I got out at my apartment building and thanked her. She didn't speak. I shut her car door and said goodnight. I was sad that Peggy did not like Jean and because of what I said, she probably didn't want to speak to me any more either. I realized she wasn't a real friend. I liked Peggy but I was not kissing up to her just because she has a car and goes to college. I am going to college on my grades. I will earn a scholarship on my on merits, I thought.

I opened our apartment door, passed the front room and looked around for the baby. I could hear Ms. Terry snoring. I tiptoed into the bathroom, got my washcloth and wiped my tears. I was sad because Peggy and I had been through a lot. I decided to look at this whole situation and see it in another way. Is she or isn't she my friend? I asked myself. I went to sleep with my heart heavy.

The next day was trying to get ready for school but everybody else was trying to get in the bathroom. I started hollering at them.

Mama said, "Liz, wait your turn."

I said, "But I gotta get ready for school and for my job."

Mama told me, "That's alright Liz, but Ms. Terry gotta take care of some business this morning."

"But who'll drop off the kids this morning?"

Mama said, "I guess Terry will."

"Is Linda okay for school this morning?"

"I guess so because she is going."

"John, hurry up."

John yelled back, "Liz, wait. I got in here first."

"John, I got to get to school early this morning."

John told me, "That is okay, but you didn't get in here early."

"Boy, just hurry. Do not worry what order we woke up."

"Stop yelling at me Liz!" Mama said, "John, you be washed up fast before I come in there to wash you up."

He open the door, shoved me and rolled his eyes. He said, "Liz, you are so mean."

"That's okay, John. How you feel this morning? Just leave the bathroom."

"No, you are mean everyday."

I hollered back, "You left this bathroom a mess."

"Clean up while you are in there."

I threw his rag in the tub and put his pajamas behind the bathroom door. I was thinking, his pajamas smelled bad and he needed a bath, not a wash up. I got my clothes on and ran out to catch the bus. I was hoping I could get to school early to talk to Jean.

When I got on the bus I ran into Leah. She didn't speak. I moved in the back of the bus and sat down. My school was the next stop. Children were laughing and playing loudly, I forced myself through the crowd. As I got out, someone tapped me on my shoulder. I turned around to see Jean.

"Hi Liz, glad to be back to school?"

"Hi Jean. I want to talk to you."

"About what?"

"You know what I want to talk about. It is Steven that I want to talk to you about."

"Oh that. I know what everyone is saying about us."

"Jean, I know what I seen. Steven try to go with everybody there."

"I know that but Liz, I am different. Steven is about twenty-five years old."

I told her, "I know his age. Steven got two babies, Jean, and he's not taking care of them."

"He told me all that."

"Jean, you just met him Thanksgiving week and this Christmas you are going together. Let me tell you something, I am not worried about the people on the job but I am concerned about how you got to that level. Now that man isn't any good. You are eighteen years old this month. Now you can handle this situation. You need to finish school and decide what is best for your life. We all talk about going to college. You let all your dreams float away just for one month meeting Steven. Girl, you are crazy. Why didn't you get a guy in your neighborhood? At least the whole job won't know and start talking about you and him. Besides, he just clean and help us with the rack. Is that your future? Man, your outlook on life is going to be a mess. You need to try and find a decent person to date. Your past can mess up your future. Besides, Steven never finish school, so who will take care of who. I see you as a trusted friend and hope this can get you back on track. Jean, do you see what I'm saying?"

Jean seemed a little shocked and said, "Yes, but he say he really care about me."

"Girl, that stupid fool care about every girl until she get a baby by him. Don't let you be baby number three."

"But I really care about him."

"What's his game? Because he never have any money and stop that stupid mess on the job, holding hands. Remember I got you that job so when they talk about you they talk about me."

"Okay Liz, I will stop talking to Steven on the job."

"Girl when you call to get a promotion on the job, you never get anything for being a fool around Steven. Steven 24 years old and he still is the lowest money on the payroll and been there for six years, because he always joke and play around like a little child. There gotta be something wrong to keep acting like that. He cute and all but that is a crazy fool. You don't need someone like that. He will cause you to ruin your young life and then the whole world will see you as a young fool that didn't finish school."

The school bell rang. Jean said, "I am very sorry Liz, and I hope we can be friends again."

I told her, "I didn't want to lose you as a friend but to let you see how this situation look. If Peggy never speak to me anymore that is fine with me. Jean, I guess we was too young for her and I really think she wasn't our friend anyhow. It really hurt me but at least I know the truth, I won't follow her like a little puppy dog up on her tail. We just keep on moving on and I am sorry you wasn't told about Steven. Now we need to be even more tight. Now we will let each other know what's going on with each other. This way we can really talk about what is the best solutions to our problems. We need to have a good relationship because we only got each other. Seem like no one care about us. We stick together in school and on the job and we are never to let someone put us down in front us. Okay, Jean?"

She said, "Liz, I do agree that if we are friends we need to be there for each other, not talking gossip about each other or trying to hurt one another just to have our way."

Jean and I talked all the way to the job. "I'm sorry Liz, for this problem about Steven. Because me being lonely and he seem to be nice, but I just liked him. Now my heart is hurt and my feelings is hurt. Please forgive me and next time I will tell you about my male friend."

"Well Jean, I really don't need to know your life story but I need you to be honest with me when we are together because, being friends we need each other to do that so we could do things together."

"But Liz, I am going to be scared to go back to work."

"Did you do anything with him? He could go back and tell someone at the job."

"Well no, but we was close with each other."

"Did you do anything that will get you pregnant?"

"No, that ain't it. I told him about my problems and my family and it is a serious situation."

"Well, that is a relief to hear."

"But I don't want the world to know, I hope he won't tell anyone. This is embarrassing."

"Well, Jean please don't leave your job. You probably be sad and your feelings get hurt, but you do have a job when school out. It be out tomorrow, then we can go shopping and to the movies when we don't have to work."

"Christmas holiday is so busy. We will never have time, Liz."

"Christmas is not going to be here forever. After the holidays we can share our time together, okay Jean?"

"Well, it sound good to me because my family drive me crazy. They need money for everything now. They want a Christmas gift but my money go out my hand so fast. My stepmother want my whole paycheck but I tell her I need some of my money for me. She tell me my father don't take care of us. He out there gambling all his money. I told her she should leave him."

I told Jean, "Well girl, my life isn't much better. We got our next-door neighbor live with us, my brother's kids, my sister's baby and three other sisters and brothers. The apartment is crowded but I just have to live with that. Here come our stop."

We rushed into the department store and ran to the basement to punch our time card. "See you Jean."

"I see you later Liz." I went into our basement office to get the tag tickets.

"Hi Peggy, how are you doing today?"

"Okay Liz, how you doing?"

"Okay for right now." The phone started to ring. I left to get my supplies and my clothes rack. I dropped my ink pen on the floor and as I was picking it up I heard a voice."

How are you today Mrs. Liz?" I rose up to see Janice.

I said, "Hi Janice," in a cheerful voice.

She said, "How is Love Bird doing today?"

"Who?"

"Your friend Jean."

A little annoyed I said, "She is doing fine Janice. She just make a mistake."

"No Liz, that girl is hot. Look at what people are hearing and seeing on the job."

"What they saying?"

"That Steven slept with her."

"Well Janice, I wasn't there and you wasn't neither. I know what I hear about Jean but Janice, do you know the truth? Why do you listen to those lies people say on this job. They like to gossip and she still is new at this place."

Janice went on to say, "I know that Liz, but she still hot."

The manager came in. Irritated, she said, "Okay, y'all two need to be getting back to work."

I just said, "Okay, Mrs. Sherowski. We will."

She continued, "Y'all two have been talking too long of a time."

Janice looked at me as if to say, "Come on, is she serious?" We went back to work fast because my rack needed to be put out in each department. I kept working, until Steven came. Steven said, "Liz, you told your friend not to talk with me anymore."

Angrily I said, "That's right Steven. She is still in her last year of school!"

"I know that Liz, you really don't need to tell me that. Besides, that wasn't any of your business. Janice told me y'all conversation about me and her."

"What did she tell you I said?"

"Well she told me that you got mad with me messing with your friend."

"I didn't say that Steven, but I was upset 'bout what I heard that she is sleeping with you."

"What if she was sleeping with me? Isn't that none of your business."

"No, but the whole job don't need to know that. She is a nice girl. Too nice for you Steven, you won't do nothing but ruin her young Life."

"Girl, you really don't know that."

"I can be sure if she keep messing with you, she be in some type of trouble."

"You just stay out of it Liz! If that's what she want, then let her tell me that but for you telling me all that, I'm not listening."

"She is not your friend. She is my friend who I got a job, not you, so please stay out of my face with this foolishness. You jive around with her feelings. Move and leave me here with these clothes and shut the door behind you!"

"Y'all girls are something else."

"Just leave me alone."

He finally left and left the rack too. I kept working and then Janice came over and picked up a rack for the Children's Department. She was grinning and whispered to me, "Steven is mad with you Liz." I just kept putting tags on clothes tickets and flashed a smile.

Peggy hollered, "Liz do you need a ride home."

"Oh, yes Peggy, I need a ride." Jean came behind me and asked if she could ride with us. "Don't know. This is Peggy car."

I rushed toward Peggy and Jean rush up behind me, Peggy looked up at Jean and said, "I'm sorry but I said Liz."

I said, "But Peggy, she need a ride too." Jean face dropped. I then told Peggy, "I'm staying here with Jean."

She said, "That's okay, suit yourself, but I'm leaving."

"Thank you for asking."

Jean didn't say anything and Peggy got into her car. I thought to myself, I really needed that ride, but Peggy don't like Jean anymore. Tonight I am going to get home real late but she didn't have to act like that to her. I never did say anything to Jean about Peggy. We walked through the lobby and out toward the bus stop. Steven was at the corner watching us. He said, "So Miss Liz, you don't have Peggy to take you home."

"She asked me, Steven, but I decided to catch the bus with Jean."

When the bus came, all three of us got on. Steven asked Jean to come and sit with him. Jean said, "No Steven, I'm going home to Liz's house."

I thought to myself, how she gonna come home with me and she gotta go to school tomorrow, but I just stood there and listened to Jean. I didn't ask why she told him that and wondered how she was going to get home.

I ran off to get my second bus and she followed too. "Why did you tell Steven that you are going to my house."

"Because Liz, he told everybody on the job he slept with me." Then she started to cry. "And it's just a lie and he told everybody," she said hysterically.

I said, "Jean, I know he told a lie and everybody believe him and now you just be more careful about who you talk to on the job."

"But it really hurt me. They call me a young trashie girl."

"Now, how are you going get home Jean?"

"I catch a cab from your house."

"But it is already too late for you to find a cab."

"I know that Liz. We can call one."

"In Harlem, that cab take a long time to come but because you is here, I'll call one."

A blue car was parked in front of our apartment. "It looks like Ms. Terry's boyfriend, Mr. Willie here. Let us run upstairs to see if he will drive you home." When we reached my apartment and opened the door, Ms. Terry was sitting in the kitchen talking to Mr. Willie.

"Hi Mr. Willie and Ms. Terry. Could you take my friend Jean, home?"

Ms. Terry said, "Liz, why didn't she catch the bus home."

I told her, "A man on our job keep messing with her."

She said, "Okay, me and Mr. Willie going to the market so we can take her home this time. She will pay Mr. Willie for driving her home. Okay miss, are you ready?"

"Yes ma'am, I'm ready."

I said, "See you tomorrow at school."

"Okay Liz, I will be there."

They all left and Mama called me back to ask me what was going on with Jean.

"See Mama, Jean met a man named Steven on our job and he started to tell people he was sleeping with her. Now everybody treat her dirty and talk about her in a really trifling way. Even Peggy, she won't take her in her car. She said that Jean act like a skank, and she ain't hanging around those types of people, and she isn't going to ride her in her car."

Mama said, "Well Liz, Jean is your friend. You treat her kind and let Peggy do what she want in her car but don't treat Jean bad because they don't like her. You let her know that she is a good person and she is your friend. If she still feel like that, she doesn't want to be yo' friend. Then don't get in her car. You never treat people bad, because of another friend, and you won't be around her acting like that. You never know how folks really is but be respectful with both of them and let me tell you something. Don't listen to Peggy. It can cause a problem for y'all, especially by embarrassing Jean right in her face but don't you go and instigate trouble for neither one of them. You know Peggy and Steven. You don't have to fight."

"But Jean scared Steven will bother her after work."

Mama told me, "She gotta keep her some carfare so she can get a cab or pay someone to pick her up."

"But Mama, Jean live with her stepmother that take all her money and her daddy gamble all his money away all the time and a lot of times she be hungry in school right after payday."

Mama said, "Poor Jean, these parents are not caring about their children or their feelings these days and their problems being teenagers."

"I really gotta get ready for bed and where is Linda gonna sleep at?"

Mama told me, "We'll put Linda on the couch until her mother come back. Now we need to see if we got that apartment on the third floor and Ms. Terry can have my apartment if the rental said so. There is a bad wire in here that can cause a fire in this apartment but Ms. Terry going talk to them tomorrow. When her son come from the hospital, they could have somewhere to live. Then this apartment would be more crowded. Only room I got left is in the window sill with a chair and pillow and hope drug people won't bother him for doing this."

"Him see something? That be another problem but I got to try see if we can do this exchange, my apartment for the third floor." Mama just kept talking, but I understand what she was saying. She continued, "Now I would have to pay more money for it but I could put a bed in the walk-in den. Have a small room just for John. We could really fix it up and if they ever fix the extra bathroom-that might work for us."

I stopped Mama before she could say anything else. "Right now I need to see my bed."

Mama said, "Okay Liz, I see you in the morning."

When morning came, it was drizzling. I knew this was the last day of school before the Christmas holiday but I messed around in my room moving everything around instead of getting ready. The baby started to cry and kick in the bassinet so I went over to get her. Sharon busted into my room saying, "That baby always crying. Liz you aren't even dressed for school yet."

"I know that Sharon, but I am so tired. I got in late last night from my job."

She said, "Are we getting anything from you on Christmas."

"No Sharon, not even one gift—no one. Not even Mama or the baby. The baby got more clothes than I do. No to her too. Is Ms. Terry here this morning?"

"No, I didn't see her this morning. Besides I got to take Linda to school, I gotta leave now or be late for school." I got up and started to wash up and put my clothes on. Mama hollered for me to hurry up. I rushed to pull up my pants and jumped to my feet.

Mama said, "Liz, look down at your feet."

"Okay Mama," I said, "I got the wrong socks on."

Mama said, "One is white and one is pink, you sure are a working girl Liz."

I asked Mama where was Ms. Terry. She told me, "I don't know, but I do know she was with that worthless Willie. When she come in, I'm going to the rental office and inquire about that apartment cause I can't go through this too many families in this one apartment thing. Especially two women raising children, my stand is different but y'all young women don't get the picture. What kids see in their home, they will act on it."

There was a knock on the door. I asked who it was. "It's Terry, hurry. I got food in my hand."

I rushed over, opened the door and took the bags. Mr. Willie had a big turkey in his bag, Mama tried to find room in the freezer. She wrapped the ham from the funeral and left it on the table. As they were talking about the meal for Christmas, I got the correct socks on. I ran and got my books, touched Mr. Willie on his arm and asked him if he could take me downtown to school.

He said, "Yes, I'm going down that way."

Mama said, "Let's hurry up there because I got to be at my lawyer office in an hour."

As we were leaving, Mama pulled me to the side and whispered to me and said, "Sit in the back of that car."

I told her that's what I was thinking. As we were getting in the car he asked about Jean. "Is Jean doin' okay?"

"Yes, she's doing fine the last time I talked to her." He said, "She is a pretty little thing and a scared one too."

I told him, "She just got problems like other teenagers."

He asked, "Who does she live with?"

"She live with her parents."

He said, "You really can sit up here with me."

"My mother told me to sit in the back and if anything goes on in this car, I'll jump out and call the police and then they will take you from there."

"No honey, I am not trying to get fresh with you."

"I just let'n you know what the deal is when I am in your car by myself."

He changed the subject, "So, how far from your school."

"Two blocks up the street, make a left at the corner and put me out at the corner."

I thanked him and went into school. I went into the office and got a late pass then went to first period, I looked around my class to see if Jean was there but I didn't see her. It was the last day before the Christmas holiday and there was a lot of noise. I was thinking, I hear a slam of the lockers, running and playing up and down the hallway. We really don't need to count the people, cause the noise will always excel here.

I got out of school at noon. I knew the teacher wished that we could stay out for two whole months. The life here is a curse for a black teacher. The students were throwing paper across the room, running up and down the hallway, dancing, kissing and boys feeling on girl's butt. I left and went down to catch the bus to work.

It was so crowded it smelled like musky underarms and onion breath on the bus. If I was driving, I would pass out from the odor on the bus, I thought. I got to work and went into the basement office to punch in. Peggy look at me, but she didn't speak. I said, "Hi Peggy."

"Hi Liz, there your rack over there, waiting for you."

"Okay, I will get them in a moment. Is Jean here today?"

She said, "No, I haven't seen that bum today." I stopped and looked at her then I said, "Peggy, I understand you don't like Jean but she is my friend and you probably never liked her from the first place."

"That is so true Liz, and how so true."

"Let me tell you something Peggy. I don't really care who you like. Especially how you don't like her. She is my friend, as for me being your friend, well I just don't want to be yo' friend."

"If though you can make that mistake."

"Okay Peggy, forget college. I mean, don't make that mistake because you could really use their intelligence."

"Liz, take that messed up rack of yours and get out of my office before I call a security guard on you."

I told her, "I'm glad it took that to see what type of person you are."

Peggy was being so sarcastically nasty, "Oh, one incident of this and now you try to get all up in my face."

I told her, "You can raise yo' voice, you don't like Steven either."

Peggy asked, "What is the problem?"

"Okay, I forgot we don't meet up to your standards. You don't meet up to my standards either, Peggy!"

"Honey, you people never do have any friends anyway."

I snatched the rack and left. Peggy was still yelling, she said, "Do me a favor and never come in my face again."

I yelled back, "If I do, you gonna need those security guards, 'cause they will be taking me out of here." That night on the job was so long. We had to put out even more than the usual amount of clothes on the rack but somehow I got through it. Jean and I punched out and left to go home. Janice was with us. We all walked to the corner and Janice started talking about what she heard.

"I heard what you say to Peggy."

I asked her, "Where was you, in back?"

She didn't answer me but just kept on talking. "You told her right, and if she kept on talking, and fussing, I was gonna call the security guard on her."

Chapter 19

Christmas

I started thinking about Steven and Jean but I didn't say anything to Janice. I didn't want her to start gossiping on the job about them or about the discussion Jean and I had. I waited for Jean in the cold, all the time praying for my bus to come. Janice's bus came and she waved goodbye. This was our last day to work because Christmas was just two days away. Jean ran up to me and asked if I was going to buy some gifts for my family. I told her, "To be honest, I don't have any money. Mama needs my help to pay the bills and we don't have a Christmas tree to put gifts under any way."

Jean said, "We don't have no tree either, Liz and the sad thing is, we don't have a lot of love either, even if we do give each other a gift. My father will try to get the value of the gift and take it and sell it and drink it up."

I told her, "Yeah, this year we had two deaths and a family friend that almost died and now lives with us. My money don't extend that far. I can answer that question. No, I won't be giving gifts this year. This is a bad year and I just came back to work. Here comes yo' bus Jean."

"I see it, I'll see you Liz, and I call you tomorrow.

I suddenly heard the loud screech of the bus's brakes. I hollered for it to wait. As we passed the corner, I saw a lady and a man sitting on a car kissing. To my surprise, it was Ricky and some girl who looked like Janice, but I couldn't see her face. She had on clothes like Janice's—blue wool coat, green corduroy pants, black boots and a green cap. My eyes were glued to the window until I they were out of sight. I thought, *If that was Janice, she ain 't got noth 'nbuta dope-selling bum.*

As I got off to catch my next bus, a man got off with me. Suddenly, he pushed my hand off the door. I turned around to see a man with a slim body who was wearing gray gloves. Before I could see any more of him, he disappeared into the crowd. I walked over to the sub shop on the corner where I could watch for the bus. I lay back in a chair, hoping to see who pushed me. It was a strange feeling, knowing that someone was watching me from the crowd. All I wanted to do was get home, even if the apartment was full of people.

I ran up the stairs to open the door. Sharon was combing Linda's hair and Linda was yelling that Sharon was hurting her head. I asked Sharon where Mama and Ms. Terry were. Sharon said that they went to the market. I said, "Sharon, don't kill the girl."

Sharon said, "Liz, this hair is nappy and Ms. Terry tell me not to put a perm in it. Her hair is just like steel wool. We could use it on the Fourth of July, if we really want to see something that sparkle and give off a bad smell too. She want me to put it in some braids. Girl, this little miss need a perm bad. She might be little but her hair is as old as some steel wool."

I laughed and said, "Girl, please hurry up. She got to go to bed with that loud mouth." Sharon was trying to finish her hair but not before telling me that combing Linda's hair was just like going outside to fight a gang of boys. That's how tired she was. I went to my room and saw that all the children were lying in the beds. I moved some clothes and found that someone had wrapped a coat over the baby.

I ran and asked Sharon, "Who put a coat on top of that baby?" She said, "I don't know."

I told her, "You could suffocate that baby." She told me to go and ask John.

I woke up John and pulled him out of bed. He fell to his knees and then started to cry. He screamed, "What are you doing, Liz?"

I asked him, "Did you put a coat over that baby and wrap her up?"

Trying to stop crying, he said, "No I didn't Liz, please stop bothering me, I'm sleepy."

"Let me tell you something, any person put a heavy coat on top of a baby and cover her face is trying to suffocate her and it could cause her to die."

John said, "Leave me alone Liz, I told you I didn't do that."

"Well, who did it John?"

"I don't know who did. Maybe the mystery man downstairs did it."

I slapped John on the head and told him, "No, little boy, that didn't happen." He climbed back to his bed.

Sharon started to laugh. "Boy, he got you good, Liz. I know you are scared of that man and he lives in this building too. You beta' watch yourself 'cause he's watching you!" and she just continued to laugh.

I said, "Girl, I am too tired to talk about that." The key turned in our apartment door and then it opened. Mama, Ms. Terry and Mr. Willie came in. Mr. Willie asked, "Why are y'all stand'n there look'n like y'all seen a ghost?" Sharon started laughing again.

Mama said that Ms. Terry got our apartment and we got the third floor apartment. Mama said, "Liz, you need to bring your pay stub home. I can bring it to the rental office."

I asked, "Is the apartment in my name?"

"No Liz, they just want to see if we make enough money to pay for that apartment."

"We got to pay more rent in there? Boy, Mama. More money."

Mama said, "Starting tomorrow we need more boxes." I said, "We should have kept the boxes that we gave to Ricky."

"We sure should have," Sharon said, but Mama said, "That's not the case. They are all gone and I know Rose didn't keep hers. She is too clean of a person to have boxes lying around her apartment and I am not going to ask her. We must go to the store and get some. Liz, when do you get paid?"

"Saturday morning, but because Christmas is Saturday we might get paid Friday morning."

Mama told me, "We'll call on your job and find out when you get paid."

"Mama, I'm off two days and start work Monday, and then work right until New Years."

"That's why I tell you to call your job to ask your supervisor and then you can ask her to write a letter telling them how much time you work and what your pay is. As soon as your supervisor tells you, Peggy can type it."

The only thing I could say was, "Oh, that's beautiful, just perfect. Peggy will be delighted to know my business so she and Janice can talk about it."

Sharon, trying to be nosy, said, "You and Peggy ain't friends anymore. Not you and the college girl."

"Shut up Sharon, I don't need you to be teasing me. Now you think you funny all night, trying to tease me about that mystery man and all."

I told everyone goodnight, went in my room and moved all the stuff they put in there. This room is a junkyard, I thought. I moved Lisa's little girl Shevon into the middle of the bed and put a pillow on the other side of her. I wanted to make sure she didn't fall off the bed. I put Devon in the bed with John, who woke up and whined for me not to put Devon in bed with him. I asked, "Why, he already asleep.

"I know that Liz, but he wet the bed and smells funny."

"You do too, John. Leave the little boy alone and if I hear him cry, I will be back to put you on the floor to sleep." I groaned loudly as I put his shoes in the bathroom because of the lack of space. I went back to my room and changed into my nightclothes. The baby started to cry loudly. I was thinking, boy, she didn't need to wake up now while I was trying to go to bed. I checked the baby and she was wet. I wiped her off and changed her clothes. After I got her dressed, I took her into the kitchen with my mother. I said, "Mama I'm trying to sleep tonight and really don't want to watch her."

"Okay Liz, I can watch her."

"Mama, I changed her and fed her."

Ms. Terry say, "Bring her here, me and Willie can watch her while y'all get some sleep. Okay Tracy? She will be fine with us."

I changed into my pajamas and I put some old socks on because my feet were always cold. I lay down but Lisa's little kid kept moving around in my bed. I let out a sigh and then I fell asleep. The next day I awoke to the sound of the children moving around. I tried to open my eyes but instead, I went back to sleep. I heard the phone ring, then John ran in and said I had a phone call. I put on my robe and got the phone,

"Hey, Jean."

"No, this isn't Jean."

"Who this is?"

"A good friend and someone you haven't heard from in a while."

"And who might that be?"

"Think for a minute." I was getting mad. I said, "I don't know you, and you say you know me?"

I hung up. I told the kids, "If someone call me and don't say who they are, y'all hang up." They all just looked at me like I was crazy.

John burst out saying, "It's the mystery man on the second floor."

I said, "John you need to be the mystery man and get lost." They all started to laugh. I thought about the person last night at the bus stop. I was thinking, / *really don't need this problem. Now we going to be moving, I don't want to move in the same apartment building, but what can I do but stay here and take this mess like a little sissy. Now Sharon is on my back making fun of me. She don't understand I got to catch the bus at night from my job and it is always late and dark. She don't even have a job, to be going outside in the dark. Now I gotta give up my money for an apartment I don't even want to live in.*

"That's why I hate this place we live in," Mama heard me say out loud.

Mama said, "Well Miss, do you have any more money than what you are giving me for these bills?"

I said, "No Mama, I don't have any more money."

She said, "That's why we can't move into better neighborhood and a better apartment." She came over to me and hugged me. "Child, I do know what you are feeling and I know how hard you work."

With tears in my eyes, I told Mama, "I am always under stress, try'n to give it my all."

She pushed me away from her and looked into my eyes. "Liz you keep that dream to get a better house and better education because my dream of better is gone. All I got is y'all. I don't have anything, but all I have to give is my heart and my words. My life experience wasn't good. You can get a good husband and good life and a future.

"Liz, years come and go, but dreams last forever and can come true. Even if it don't, you will know how you feel and still know what you want. With your goals in life, you can move in that direction. But Liz, learn from what you see and learn from what you been through, but have true love for God, your family, and your heart. Never be content with the life you have now.

Look at me Liz, I love you and want to be there for you as I see my little girl grow up to be a beautiful lady."

Mama started to cry on my shoulder, her tears causing pain in my heart. She said that she failed me as a mother because she didn't prepare us for life. She said, "The only thing I got from my mother was the real world. She never hold or hug or talk to me about life. She worked in the school system cafeteria as a server. How we prayed for her to bring their rolls, buns and cookies home. My father never talked to us either, because he worked out of town fixing holes in the road."

We sat down in my bedroom with her holding me. Ms. Terry came and closed the door. Mama said, "See Liz, I'm already 38 years old and trying to work and never could promise a better neighborhood. Life has a purpose but I don't know my future anymore. A dream about a big house in Long Island wouldn't be real for me. Or even moving into another city. I have never prepared y'all for moving to another city 'cause I stopped wanting things. This is the only thing I see right now. I am still grieving over the children I lost. My hope is to raise their kids and if you have kids, I will love and assist you in being a mother."

Tears kept coming. "But Mama this is my life."

"Yes Liz, this is yo' life now but who say this is your future. It is between you and God how your life gonna turn out." Then she kissed me and went into the bathroom.

I know I upset her but I am tired of living like this. I lay in the bed with my hands over my eyes. Suddenly there was a light knock on the door and someone called my name in a soft voice. I didn't answer because I was still crying. Jean entered and said, "Hey Liz, do you want some company?" I sat up slowly and shook my head yes. "Can I ask what's wrong with you?"

I told Jean that my mother and I had a heart to heart talk and now I was sad, hurt, and angry. She said, "Well I came over to see if you want to go to the mall."

"Yeah, I would like that. Let me go in the bathroom, wash my face and change my clothes. What are you buying?"

"Some gifts for my new nephew."

"Oh, your sister have the baby?"

"Yes, last night. Just after I left you to come home. She still at the hospital."

"What are some things you gonna buy?"

"Just things newborn's wear." We talked back and forth from the bathroom.

Ms. Terry called to me and said, "Liz, your girlfriend buying newborn things? See if you can sell some of Rolynne's new things. That will help yo' mother out with food this week. I can go down and get a pizza and one of those sodas for y'all to drink."

I told her, "Okay, that sounds like a good idea."

I asked Jean if she would like to look at some of Rolynne's presents. I told her, "She got three baby showers. If you like some you can buy some of them. The new ones got the tags on them." I pulled some clothes from under the bed and spread them out. She picked out a snowsuit, some gowns, a sweater set, a bottle, footies, washrag set, and enough baby supplies to keep a baby clean. She spent $110. We gave her some gift boxes to put it all in. I put the money in an envelope and put Mama's name on it.

We went into the kitchen where Ms. Terry had bought a pizza for us and I gave her some money for it. Jean said, "Thanks, Liz. We can take these things over to my house. We can catch a cab after we eat and still hang out in the mall."

I said, "Girl, that sounds okay with me but I have to ask my mother." I got up after we ate and went in to Mama's room and put the envelope on her pillow. She was still asleep. I asked Ms. Terry to tell my mother where I was going. We left to catch a cab and while we were waiting, Robert beeped the car horn at us, rolled down the window and said, "Where y'all gorgeous young ladies going?"

I said, "Jean, let me handle this."

"Well Robert, we're taking these things over to my girlfriend Jean's house. We left some of the things behind the door for John to watch while we try and find a cab." He asked us to jump in.

We got the baby gifts John was watching and John pushed his hand out. "Oh, I forgot to give you something. Here is a dollar. Now you can leave us alone."

At Jean's house we put the stuff under her sister's bed, then we cleaned up the apartment for her sister to come home the next day. I asked, "Where is yo' step-mama?"

"Who knows, she probably running after my father to make sure he don't mess up his money?"

"Do she work, Jean?"

"Yes, she work at the state building and make good money as a typist."

"Why she want that crazy-acting drunk?"

"That's why mother left him, before he kill her." We finished cleaning up and putting things in order. We caught the bus, pushing each other and giggling at each other. She tried to step on my feet and I tried to do the same to hers. We ran to the back to sit together. I asked her what Janice wore Wednesday. She said, "Well, she had on a wool coat and green corduroy and pair of boots and a green cap."

I told her, "I seen a girl and boy kissing on a car as the bus passed them. It looked like Ricky, my niece's father, with Janice."

"No Liz, you sure you seen that?"

"Yes, I know I seen both of them."

"Well your sister is already dead."

"Yeah but she was always claiming that her man is good material," I said.

271

"Not Ricky, cause he danger material. He sell drugs and get high, and run with different girls. Liz, don't be willing to get involved with that mess. It will never solve anything. Okay, my best friend. We don't need to lose our goals or our lives over this. Let it be, if that what she want let her have it. She will see what type of person he is. Who knows if she don't already know what he is. If it don't take a lifetime to find out about those types of guys."

The bus stopped when we got to the mall. I told her about the incident with the man wearing the gray gloves and how he tried to push me off the bus. She asked, "Why would a person want to do that to you, Liz?"

"I don't know, it happen when I got off to catch the next bus to go home."

"Now all we need is a gray-gloved man to come and push us off the bus.

We looked at the new clothes on display in the stores and we laughed at the customers pushing each other in the line." Hey Jean, what does this remind you of?"

"Our job Liz, those people almost ready to fight for those sales." Now we got ready to go home. I bought a blouse and a pair of pants. Jean was upset because she had spent all her money on her nephew.

When we were finished, we went to McDonalds to get a hamburger. When we went to catch our bus Jean started saying the gray-gloved man was after us. I ran to get on the bus quickly to try and get away. Jean was laughing so hard, and saying, "He just got to catch you first, to put his hand on you. Girl, you need to be on the track team." It was already 8:30 PM when we got to our bus stop. I told her that I needed to catch my bus straight home. "That's fine with me Liz. If it is too late for me, I will catch a cab."

I reminded her, "That will be a fortune."

"I know, but I don't want go home too late." My bus came first and I got on. I told Jean that I would call her tomorrow. She waved goodbye. I sit in the front behind the bus driver. I asked him if he could tell me when East 124 Street came up.

He asked, "What block, miss?"

"The one-hundred block sir." I lay my head back on the bus seat and then someone tapped me on the arm.

"Miss, miss. This is the block."

"Okay. Thank you mister." I got off and ran down the street and into my apartment.

"Liz, why are you running so hard?" Mama asked. I told her about the incident of the man pushing me off the bus. "He wore gray gloves on his hands."

"Liz, there is a lot of gloves like that."

"Not the gray gloves that tried to push me off the bus."

"You need to put it in your mind that a man accidentally pushed you to get past you. It was a crowd on the bus, Liz. A lot of people will be pushing others to catch their next bus home or get to their job. You need to take that out your mind now, okay?"

"Let me thank you and hug you and Ms. Terry for thinking of that idea about selling the baby clothes. It really did work. I needed it to help me pay for the security deposit on that apartment. The baby already got nine snow suites and twelve sweater sets in all types and colors."

I told Mama, "There's a girl in my class, Mayria, and she is pregnant. Her and her boyfriend come to our store to buy some baby clothes but I haven't seen them lately. She looked sad, I guess she isn't buying any more things but she need some baby clothes."

"Liz, I am not giving it away, I want to sell them. Besides there's a friend on my job named Betty. Her daughter is going to have a baby on the first of next year. I'm going to give her a call right now."

I went to get the baby from Ms. Terry." Ms. Terry, you love this baby."

"Yeah, she put me in the mind of when Linda was a baby. Now I hope I be here to see her grow." I played with the baby. I w rubbed her cheeks and she started to smile. Mama got off the phone and said that Betty would be over here tomorrow. She said that Betty wants to put extra clothes away for when the baby gets here.

"Girl, y'all started me to be bold now and ask people. I need $400 and I got $270 now. We need to get $130. I know this is Christmas but I don't have anything to give y'all, but after the holidays we can go to the movies."

John put his head down. Sharon stomped in my room and started to cry. She hollered, "But Mama we never get anything. The last time we got some clothes it was school time. Now we need winter clothes. We have nothing."

Mama said, "Yes you do, Sharon. You got a place to eat and a warm place to sleep. Please John, Becky, Sharon, forgive me for this Christmas, for not giving you a gift."

I went into my room to go to sleep but Sharon was in my bed. I put the baby in her bassinet and she went to sleep. I moved Sharon's hand, turned my back to her and went to sleep. The phone rang, but the only thing I heard was, "I see you this afternoon."

The baby started squirming back and forth, and then she started crying. I got up to feed her. She was wet. I put the receiving blanket on my lap and changed her. She cooed and smiled at me as if she missed me.

Sharon woke up crying again because she wouldn't get anything for Christmas. I got over Christmas a couple of years ago. I would make a list but the only thing on my list I got was a gift from my mother. Once I got one gift from Santa Clause but he was sleepy and smelled like a drunk. Once he almost dropped me. I had never talked to Sharon about any of it. There was one more day until Christmas. I thought, *If I get up tomorrow morning, I can catch the early special sale at my store.*

The next day I whispered in Ms. Terry's ear and told her what I was going to do, then I ran into the kitchen. I made some toast with jam then I ran out to catch the bus. I jumped on and sat in the back.

"Hi, Miss Liz, are you working today?"

"Oh, hi Janice. No, I'm not working today. I'm going downtown to our store to catch a sale." We both got off in front of where we worked at 7 o'clock in the morning. The store was already crowded. I pushed my way all the way in the back. Janice showed me where the rest of the sales were. On a back rack, I found a pair pants and shirt for John. Now I looked for some clothes for Becky. I got her a nightgown and some slippers to match. I got Linda the same thing. I got Lisa's little boy a truck and a pants set and I got the little girl a doll and tea party set.

That took all the money I had left but there was a four-piece pant set at home in my room. I would tell Mama that I would pay her later for it. Now I had to find something for Sharon. I suddenly remembered that I bought a pants and sweater set at the mall with Jean. I decided Sharon could have that. I could put all these gifts in the boxes from the baby gifts under my bed. The cashier ringing up my stuff said hello to me.

I replied, "Oh, hi, Mrs. Louise."

"Your bill is $92. 82 but I know you are going use to your twenty percent discount."

"Yes, I know it."

"Okay, your bill is $60.90. This is my gift to you Liz."

"Oh thanks. I needed this, 'cause this is all I have."

"You know, we used to exchange gifts here, but these people was bringing old gifts they got from their parents and grandparents. People was ready to fight them over those bad gifts they was bringing to work to exchange. They had to stop all that drama." I laughed. She then told me, "Girl get out this line and go home and enjoy your Christmas."

I was still laughing while I was putting my money in my wallet. Janice came up to me and asked, "Why you laughing so hard?"

"Mrs. Louise was telling me about y'all exchanging gifts."

She said, "Yeah, these people used to get so mad they wanted to fight. One incident started with Mr. James and Ms. Ester. She gave him a big bottle of cologne two days before Christmas. She was just bragging about how big his gift was. He said that the cologne that she gave him broke him out and he demanded his gift back. She started to argue with him about it. He said his skin was dark, and now it's red. The manager said that they couldn't exchange gifts anymore, because their exchanges was fighting words in themselves."

I thought, *I have to call my Aunt Rose to see if I can bring the gifts to her house and pick them up tonight.* I went to the basement and asked Peggy, "Hello Peggy, can I use the phone please?"

She said, "Yes Liz, and hurry up with it." Aunt Rose said that it would be okay if I left the gifts over at her house. I hung up and thanked Peggy, and then I left and caught a cab. The street was crowed with cars, everybody was trying to go home. I decided to call Ms. Terry and see which one of her men came over.

Ms. Terry said, "Who is this?"

"This is Liz. I'm downtown with a lot of gifts. Could I get one of your friends to pick me up and I will pay them."

"Yes, Roy is talking to me now. I'll tell him where you are." It seemed like forever before they came to get me. My legs were hurting before I saw his blue car slow down. I waved them down. They pulled over and I got in." Girl, you must be cleaning those sales out."

"No, I just used my twenty percent discount."

The car bumped up to the street to Aunt Rose's apartment. We put the gifts in her closet in the front room. When we got back to our apartment, Mama asked me, "Why you get up so early?"

I whispered in her ear, "I went Christmas shopping and left the gifts over at Aunt Rose's house." Mama told me that was a real nice thing, but the day was still cold and there was no Christmas spirit in our little apartment. It was so cold and calm that I fell asleep in the front room chair. Then the phone rang. Ms. Terry answered it. She told me my aunt Rose wanted to speak to me. I was asleep, I could hardly open my eyes but I got up and made my way to the phone.

"Liz, did you forget yo' gifts are over here in my apartment?"

"Oh my God, I did forget!"

"Well Liz, you need to get someone to pick them up tonight, especially if you plan'n on putting it under the Christmas tree for tomorrow morn'n."

"Okay, I will be there to pick them up."

"Liz, it's already 9:30 at night. What time are you planning to come over here?"

"Well, I gotta see who can take me?"

"I guess I see you when you get here."

I hung up and went into the kitchen where Mama and Ms. Terry were cooking. I said, "Ms. Terry, can one of your male friends take me to Aunt Rose's to pick up my Christmas Presents?"

She told me, "Wait, let me see who is home." She got her telephone book and started to dial their numbers. She came in and said, "Yes, Paul is coming over to get me, I'm going to ask him to take me to the supermarket and then ask him to take you to your Aunt Rose's house."

"Let me go get my shoes on."

"Liz, I got to get in the bathroom." She washed up, and then she got dressed in Mama's room. She came back in the front room to look out for him.

Mama came in and said, "Terry, I thought Paul was dead in your life. I thought you said that Paul went back to his wife."

Ms. Terry say, "He did Tracy, we are just good friends."

"All of them are married."

"Well Tracy, Paul come past here to go to work."

"Girl, if you don't have sins!" Mama sarcastically said. She continued, "Just get you little black book, you can count your sins by the number of married men you got in your life, and if you had to confess them to a priest you would probably be dead right about now. Ms. Terry started to giggle lightly, as she slowly turned her head away from my mother. She bowed her head as she left the room. She didn't say anything but I could see she was embarrassed. I went outside. I didn't want to hear all that old-folks talk. I remembered when my grandmother used to tell me that.

I looked up and down the street. A man walked up and said, "Hi Liz."

"Hi, Mr. Paul."

"Is Terry upstairs?"

"Yeah, she's in my apartment." We both went upstairs. When we went past her apartment, he turned around and said, "Did Terry have a fire?"

"Yes sir."

"Did everybody get out unharmed?"

"No, her little boy still in the hospital." I got in front of him and used my key, but before I could finish turning the key, Sharon opened the door. She had the baby in her arms. Ms. Terry came over to Mr. Paul and said, "Hi Baby," then kissed him on the lips. I was shocked because she had not seen him in over a year and a half. He kissed her and asked her what happened to her apartment. She told him that she was smoking, that she fell asleep and the apartment caught on fire.

He asked, "How's your little boy, is he doin' alright?" She said that he was doing fine and that he would be home for the Christmas holiday. She added that this holiday was going to be a sad one. Ms. Terry called her niece and told her that she had a ride and that she would be there with Linda in a little while. Mr. Paul came in the kitchen, "Hi Tracy."

"Hi, how are you doing?"

"Oh, I'm fine." Mama said, "But the last time we talked, Paul you were getting laid off from work."

He said, "Tracy, I got me another job in a plant. Then they cut my wages but they kept us working. That's why you need to be a good worker."

Mama started telling Paul about herself, "Well, I lost two of my kids and got their children to raise. I left my job, so you can see I need some help."

He just said, "Well we all need that time to time."

Ms. Terry went in the kitchen and told him she was ready to leave. Mr. Paul said, "Terry, I gotta be on my job at 12 o'clock, and my watch say 10:20 now, so you got a hour to get it all done."

She got Linda's things and told me to get ready. I put on my coat.

In the car Ms. Terry said, "First person you are dropping off is Linda at my niece's house. She only up the street."

He drove without saying anything to us. At Ms. Terry's niece's place, Linda got out and rang her bell but she didn't seem to be home. Ms. Terry got out and started ringing all the bells until a young man stuck his head out a window and asked, "Who is it?"

Ms. Terry asked, "Is Wendy home?"

"She at 2-D bell, miss."

"Could you kindly knock on her door and tell her Aunt Terry is outside waiting for her."

"Yes, just this time miss." She and Linda waited. A young lady hollered, "Aunt Terry? Is that you?"

"Yes, Wendy, It's me and I'm still standing here in the cold waiting for you. Are you going to let her in?"

"Yes, wait I'm coming." She finally come downstairs and opened the door. Linda went in the building and Ms. Terry came back to the car. Mr. Paul looked at his watch and asked, "Where to, Terry?"

I said, "She lives downtown near McDonalds, those apartment building there on the left side. They are the Belair apartment buildings." Aunt Rose was watching for me out the window and came down to let me in.

She said, "Liz, if you were fifteen minutes later, you wouldn't see your gifts until tomorrow. Girl, I gotta get some sleep, not stay up and wait for you."

I told her, "I am sorry but Ms. Terry got me a ride to your house, and I ran up the stairs." Aunt Rose said that the gifts were in the closet where we put them. I took all the gifts out. I noticed it looked like someone had been playing with them but I just kept moving fast. I took the big box first. Aunt Rose called Ms. Terry to come help me. She grabbed the small box. Mr. Paul came up to help too. With all the boxes in the car, we started back to our apartment. He drove fast so that he wouldn't be late to his job.

He got us back home and I ran upstairs. Mama opened the door before I could, and she came downstairs to help us. We put the gifts in the front room. I said, "Mama, when I went in the closet in Aunt Rose's house, it look like someone messed with our gifts."

Mama said, "You know Liz, those grown men are playing with their toys. They love to play games and things."

"Boy, look at the mess they made." Mama continued, "Liz, they aren't normal people."

I was putting everything in order when I saw a light blinking on and off. On the table next to the sofa was a little wilted Christmas tree. I asked Mama where she got that tree from.

She said, "From the used store. And the bulbs too."

I put the gifts under the tree. Mama baked a cake and brought some ice cream and beer. All the food that Ms. Terry and Mama cooked smelled good. Mama put on some old records, got a big glass of Hennessey, her favorite drink and started singing Unforgettable. She started to cry as she drank her beer and sang. Mama kept on playing the same record over and over again.

Ms. Terry and Mama started thanking God for helping them go through all the pain and hurt and live to tell someone about it. Ms. Terry put up her glass of Hennessey and started to say, "Thanks, for letting me have such a good friends, Tracy and my men."

Mama said to Ms. Terry, "You thank God for those three married men? You must be drunk." They kept laughing. They were getting drunk but I just laughed at them. Soon their conversation started to slow down, and Ms. Terry lay down on the couch and fell asleep. Mama was singing herself to sleep. I started to cut the record off, but she said, "Liz, I will cut it off!"

As I went into the bathroom, I heard my mother crying to herself. She was moaning about how much she missed her family, how her life was a lonely one, she prayed that she could leave Harlem one day, and how she wanted to be proud of what she had become.

I looked in the mirror and cried, hoping my life wouldn't be like my mother's and Ms. Terry's. I would be proud as a nurse or lawyer. I finished washing up, put my pajamas on and put the baby on her stomach in the bassinet. I cried myself to sleep. Soon I couldn't hear the record that was playing anymore. That

Christmas morning, I awoke to a lot of movement and noise and the phone ringing. No one would answer it. I jumped up out of bed and stomped to the phone. I said a tired, "Hello."

"Merry Christmas, Sweetheart."

"Who is this?" I said in a big bold voice.

"This is Mike, Liz."

"Oh, Mike, Hi!"

"Did you forget me?"

"Oh no, I just wasn't expecting you to call."

"Well, I'm over to my uncle's and I'm gonna try to get over there some time today."

"Please Mike, not this morning. My mother is asleep and I got to feed these kids and clean up their mess." We hung up the phone, and I went into action for the day.

I called everyone for breakfast, got the kids in the kitchen and fed them. The baby was screaming so I picked her up, fed her and washed her. John was playing with Devon and his truck. I told him to watch them while I gave the baby a bath and I told them not to go outside.

As I was washing the baby, I noticed that she had a red mark on her nose so I put baby lotion on her and powdered her down. I put her clean pants set on her, brushed her hair, sat her in her swing and put a baby pillow beside her face. I put Devon in the bathtub, washed him, dried him off and put clean clothes on him.

Next, I got Shevon and put her in the tub, washed her up, dried her off and put her green and white corduroy pants set on. I got the comb, brush and grease and started to comb her hair, but she kept fighting until I let her go. I told her to go and play with her doll but instead, she went over to John and laid her head on his shoulder.

I wondered where Ms. Terry slept. I guessed that she went out. Sharon came into the kitchen where I was washing the dishes. I asked her if Ms. Terry left. Sharon said, "Yes Liz, she left last night. Mama was playing her dead records all night. It was to the point where I went there to try and cut the record player off."

She ate her pancakes. The door opened and Ms. Terry came in. She said, "Good morning Liz, and Sharon. This gift is for you Liz." I couldn't understand why someone sent me a gift.

I got everything cleaned up and ate some toast and jelly. I heard Mama say, "Come on in and Merry Christmas." I hurried to finish washing up and then got dressed. To my surprise, it wasn't Mike. It was Lisa coming past to see her kids. She gave Mama some money. Lisa said that it was all she had. Mama said it was thoughtful. Lisa tried to play with her kids but they ignored her and played with each other's toys. Sharon thanked her for her gift and Ms. Terry came over and gave me a kiss.

Mama said, "Don't kiss that drunk."

Ms. Terry say, "Tracy, you got a big nerve, you was feeling good too, last night."

"Terry, I hope that God forgive me for my spirit, 'cause I have drunk Spirit." And both of them laughed. The baby was crying so Sharon brought her in the front room and put her in my lap.

I said, "I will appreciate it if you watch her and comb and braid Shevon's hair."

Lisa said, "Liz, I can do that. Where is the comb and brush?" I got the comb and brush and I gave it to Lisa. She grabbed Shevon and started to comb her hair.

Mama asked, "Liz, are you going to look at your gift?"

I moved over to the Christmas tree to open it. In the box was a blue gown and robe and a pair of slippers to match. In a small box was a gray glove. When I saw that, I threw the gift down.

Mama ran over and asked, "What's wrong?"

"Mama, there are some gray gloves in there. The same ones that man that pushed me had on his hands."

"Oh Liz, you saying a man ran over here to give you a gift so he can continue pushing you? Liz, when the company manufactured this, he didn't just make one glove."

Ms. Terry told me to give her those gloves. She said, "I am going to make some money off it. You going to keep that gown, robe and slippers? What's going to happen when they start to push you?"

Mama said, "Please, you are going to drive me crazy with that foolishness." Sharon laughed and said, "You are really something."

I put the gift to the side and Lisa started laughing. She said, "I hope you don't think all that's true."

The phone rang and I went into the kitchen to answer it. I said, "Hello."

"Is Liz home?"

"This is she, who this?"

"Its Jean. What you doing later?"

"Mike supposed to be coming over here this evening. Are you coming over?"

"Yeh, I would like to come at 2 o'clock."

"That'll be fine Jean." I went into my room and listened to the radio. I tried to gather all the baby bottles to wash them, but one of the bottles dropped on the floor and shattered into pieces. I hopped around in my bedroom trying to clean up the mess but I looked down to see my foot was cut and bleeding. I called my mother who came in, looked around and called John to bring the broom.

She started to clean up the glass. She said, "Liz let me get a clean rag." Then she cleaned up the wound under my foot. She told me to just sit for a moment while she got the first aid box. There was a knock on my door and Jean came in. She had a gift in her hand.

"Here Liz, this a gift for you from me."

All I could say was, "I'm so sorry Jean, I didn't get you a gift for Christmas. My money is short and I couldn't buy you one."

Jean say, "That's okay Liz. Is Mike coming over?"

"I don't know, 'cause he say that he gonna try. Jean do you got Robert's number?"

"Yeh, he gave me it that night you introduced me to him but, I never call him because I was scared too. What type of person is Robert?"

"Well Jean, he is smart and goes to community college here and he used to go with a girl name Ashley but they broke up. He was a little wild and a little crazy at his prom."

Jean said, "Girl, on my prom I'm gonna go crazy and wild too. We aren't doing anything, let's call Robert."

"Okay Jean. Give me the number."

"I don't have it with me."

"Okay, I got his number somewhere. Let me go look in my last year's notebook. I wrote it in there. Oh, where's John. He got that notebook. John give me your notebook."

He turned and looked at me for a moment, then he say, "For what!"

I said, "Just bring it here please and I'm not paying you it!"

The number was faded a little bit but I could still see it. Robert came on. "Hello, this Robert."

"Do you know who this is?"

"No. Who are you? If you want to play games on my phone, I going to give you the dial tone."

"This Jean, Liz friend."

"How you got my number?" I hurried and put Jean on the phone. She said, "From that day we met. You gave it to me. What are you doing today?"

"I'm going to see some friends this evening and hang out. What's your plans?"

"Right now I'm over to Liz house talking to her. Did you see Mike today?"

"No, not yet. Well if nothing don't go out as planned, maybe we can all go out."

"That's a good suggestion."

He said, "But right now I need to get off the phone."

She told him, "Okay, I'll see or hear from you later." She hung up the phone and she told me she was so scared.

She said, "This the first boy I talked too like this."

"Well Jean, this is probably not the last time." We were sitting on my bed talking about how we really liked Robert and Mike. We really would like to picture how our future with them would be. We were listening to the O'Jays on the radio and thinking about what our futures would hold, who we would marry, and if we were going to get a job and leave the slums. We talked until about 11:30.

Mr. Willie was in the kitchen drinking some beer. He was going to go to the hospital to pick up Ms. Terry's son, Andre. Ms. Terry said that he would take Jean, and Mama said that she and Ms. Terry were going with her. They left me to watch all the kids.

Mike and Robert never showed up. As I cleaned up, I realized this was Christmas day. I thought to myself, it was a sad and lonely one. Everybody that wasn't asleep were looking at TV except Becky and Sharon, who were reading a book together. Mama and Ms. Terry went out. I decided to take off my dirty clothes and go to bed. I was not really sleepy but lonely and sad. I looked over at the baby, and then my eyes went closed.

Chapter 20

The New Year

The day after Christmas, I got up early and cleaned up all the gift-wrappings thrown around the apartment. Somehow, I couldn't get it out my mind that Mike never called or came over the day before. After all, it was Christmas day when people usually share their time with their loved ones and their family. I thought that in reality he must not love me.

Ms. Terry came into the kitchen, "Good Morning, Liz."

"Good Morning, Ms. Terry," I said.

She asked me, "Well, what's on your schedule for today Liz?"

"Well I gotta go to work this afternoon."

"Well, you know Liz, I gotta go over to my niece's and pick up Linda and you know that pants set you got her for Christmas? That is what she is wearing home. I want to ask my niece to keep Linda for another couple of days so I can spend some time with my son. He still gotta go back and forth to the physical therapist for his arm but I already know her answer, that she got to work. I really don't need to ask her but I just got to try."

I smiled at her as Mama came into the kitchen. She said, "Someone fix me a strong cup of coffee and put a couple of slices of bread in the toaster. Put me some butter and jam on that toast."

Ms. Terry rushed over and got the coffee and toast ready for Mama. Ms. Terry got the last piece of bread so she got dressed and went to the corner store to buy another loaf. I sat in the kitchen chair, not saying too much to anyone.

Sharon came into the kitchen complaining that the kids made a mess in her bedroom. I hollered out to Sharon, "Stop complaining and clean it up."

She picked up Mama's toast and coffee, sat down at the table with it, and began eating. She said, "First thing, stop hollering at me Liz. You're not my mother and this isn't your apartment."

Mama came in, stood in the kitchen doorway and just looked at me. She told me, "Okay miss. You need to stop hollering first thing in the morning and where is my toast and cup of coffee?"

Sharon said, "Oops!" and put her hand over her mouth. "I'm sorry."

"I know you are sorry, Sharon. You never supposed to eat anybody's food until you ask first." Mama pushed Sharon out of the room, told her to put on her clothes, go to the store and get another loaf of bread, and to bring back a bottle of milk with it."

I told her that Ms. Terry went to the store to get a loaf of bread. She said, "That is fine Liz, now we will have two loaves of bread."

I looked straight at my mother and asked her, "When we suppose to be moving?"

She said, "In fact, it is this week."

"Oh boy, I hope so. Mama this place is crowed. It stay dirty and messed up. Mama, where is the gift that have the gray glove in it?"

Mama giggled, "Maybe Ms. Terry got it on." The door opened up and Ms. Terry came in. I asked her if she had the gift box with the gray glove."

"Yeh Liz, it's at the end of the Christmas tree in the corner of the table."

I looked while Ms. Terry went into the kitchen to talk to Mama. I looked all over but couldn't find it. I went in the kitchen and asked Ms. Terry, "Did you put the box in any other place?"

"No Liz, the gift was left under the tree." She got up from the kitchen chair, came in the other room and looked for it. Ms. Terry teased, "Oh no, Liz, did the man come back and got his glove?"

Mama started to laugh. I looked at her and started to laugh, then looked at them both with a puzzled expression. I said, "Wasn't anybody else here?"

Mama said, "Lisa and your friend Jean."

"But Mama! Jean was in my room talking to me, and when she got ready to leave she went in the kitchen to ask for a ride, never going in the front room at all."

"Well the only person left is Lisa," Ms. Terry said. "She did look rather bad yesterday."

Ms. Terry said, "At least we had a Christmas this year. Even though we didn't have a man or a job."

Mama said, "Liz, are you going to help me put your things in the boxes for us to move?"

"No Mama, I got to work this afternoon."

"Girl you betta hurry up in that bathroom. I got to give those kids a bath right after they finish eating their breakfast."

I ran up and got the ironing board. I pressed my apron and pants set then John came in asking what I was ironing and said that Lisa got those gloves.

I asked how he knew that.

He said, "When she looked at the gift, she opened the box, took the gloves and put them in her coat and then she left."

I slammed the iron down, went in the kitchen and I told Mama that John told me how Lisa stole them out of this apartment. Mama turned around and said, "Liz, that is fine, it was Christmas for her too."

"Yeah, that might be true, but everyday isn't Christmas here. Besides, she needs to stay out of here until next Christmas. Who need her stealing from me? Mama, you gotta watch Lisa and her hands and her coat."

Mama just looked at me, "And she paid for them too, and what you say'n is the truth but she do have two little children here."

"Mama, she can come and get them and keep them until next Christmas. That will be fine with me."

"Liz, you really know how to express your feelings about people, but remember…I take care of them and that is not how I am willing to treat them. She is a young girl with children that she can't take care of. You know these are Roland's kids, Liz."

I said, "That's what she tell us. Lisa look like she been around with other guys."

"If he took his love for his children to the grave and believe these was his, I'm going to take my beliefs about these kids until I go to my grave, Miss Liz. Please get ready for your job, and I will let Lisa know that if this keeps happening, her stealing from us, she will not be welcomed in my apartment."

I got ready for work but the phone rang as I was going down our hallway. I answered it.

"Is Liz home?"

"Yes this is Liz."

"Hey, this is Robert."

"Hello Robert, what are you doing today?"

"That's why I'm calling you, to see what you are doing?"

"First thing, I got to go to work."

"Do Jean work today?"

"Yes she do."

"Let her know to give me a call."

"Let me call you back Robert, I can call jean to see what her schedule is." he hung up and I called Jean.

"Hello, is Jean home?" The person on the other end said, "No, she already went to work."

"Okay, thank you." I got dressed in a hurry and caught the 12:15 bus downtown. I ran downstairs and across the street but the traffic was moving so fast, I couldn't catch the bus. I hollered, "Oh Boy, That's All I Need!" The bus stopped and waited as if someone asked the driver to stop for me. As I was going between the lanes toward the bus, I looked around and saw there was no one on that corner…I jumped onto the bus, paid my fare and found a seat.

I couldn't understand the bus stopping just for me. My mind stayed on that one for a while. I figured I wouldn't mention it to anyone. When the bus door opened, I saw my other bus pull up. Next to it was Peggy in her car driving to work. She never spoke to me anymore so I knew not to wave her down for a ride. While I was waiting for my next bus, my hands were freezing. I thought, Those scary gloves would have really helped me out right about now. I wound up getting to work early.

I ran around looking for Jean. She wasn't in her department so I asked Mrs. Ester, "Did Jean come to work?"

She said, "Yes she did. She in the bathroom." I rushed toward the bathroom as Jean was coming out."

"Jean! Guess who asked about you?"

"Who, Liz?"

"Guess, Jean."

"I don't have time to guess."

"Robert, Jean. He called this morning asking me what are we doing today and I told him that I got to work, and then he asked about you."

Jean jumped up and down with excitement. She questioned me. "Girl is that true? Do you think he really like me?"

I told her, "Well, he wouldn't be asking about you."

Jean said, "Well, let me give him a call."

I warned her, "Not while Peggy is downstairs. Peggy seen me on the bus stop, and she never did stop and ask me do I need a ride. But that's okay, Jean, 'cause I don't need a phony person like Peggy as a friend anyway."

Jean agreed, "That's right Liz, because we are good friends. Just because she is going to college, she thinks she can treat people just any type of way. That's no way to treat other people."

Jean and I ran up to the lobby giggling. I dialed and asked for Robert. He told Jean that he would be picking her up at 8 o'clock tonight when she got off from work. When she hung up the phone, she fell back on the wall, held her heart and closed her eyes. "He is a really cute guy, and going to college too. Just what I need. Someone smart and handsome."

I brought her back to reality, "Don't forget about me in your dreams, Jean. I know you with all those emotions."

"No Liz, how could I forget you?"

I came upstairs and asked Mrs. Ester if I could I get off at 8 o'clock." "Yes, but a lot of these things goes downstairs, so let that girl know what time you are leaving." I went down to the basement and said, "Hi Peggy, I'm leaving at 8 o'clock." Then I went out, leaving her with her mouth open.

Janice peeped in and looked at Peggy's shocked face, and then she came in the back room and laughed. "Liz, you are giving that college girl the blues." I just looked at Janice, shaking my head but not saying anything."

I turned back and said, "I am just tired of getting home late and not enjoying the Christmas holiday, 'cause I got to work here late everyday and every weekend. The person that makes the schedule need to know this, that I need to enjoy my life too."

Janice agreed by saying, "That's right Liz, me and my man is going to get married soon." She went back to her department, leaving me with my mouth open.

Those words stuck in my mind. I just hoped that Ricky wasn't my niece's father. I hadn't seen Ricky lately, but he did go to jail a lot. But if that's the type she likes, I thought, God please help her because she is going to need it. Ricky is a low life and is a really bad case for even a loser but if that's what nice want, that's just what she is getting.

I kept looking at the clock because my patience was running short. I hopped that Robert was picking up Mike so we could be two couples instead of one and a tag a long. The time seemed to be going slow, and customers kept bring back gifts or looking at sales. The cashier was overwhelmed with ringing up purchases and answering questions. The line just kept getting longer and longer. Mrs. Ester told me to bag some of the items from the registers so she could take a break. I went over to help Carol. She looked so tired. She told me to take the hangers off the clothes and put them in a bag. I rushed over and got all the hangers, cleaned up the paper wrappings off the floor and put it all in the trash can.

She was so busy that she didn't realize she was throwing away sales slips from credit cards. I put all the credit card sales slips in her moneybag and started to help her with the customers. She was trying to show me how to work the cash register. I told her she was too busy and we didn't need to cause me to lose my job. She said, "Liz, you are great at handling the register. Now you need to start knowing how to use the department numbers and codes. This is very easy and I know you can do it. Don't you want to learn?"

"Well Carol, with this line full with customers…we need to get these people out of here. I am getting off at 8 o'clock tonight."

Carol asked, "But can you help me with these customers?"

"Okay Carol, but I am leaving you. I am not staying over. I got somewhere to go. You got one hour." I was so busy the time got away from me. I was bagging a customer's clothes when Jean looked at me and pointed to the clock.

"Okay Jean, I'm coming." I tapped Carol on the shoulder and said that I was leaving now. Mr. Carl stopped me and asked me if

I was leaving for the night. When I said yes, he told me to push my leftover clothes racks in the corner of my department. After doing so, I ran upstairs to the lobby and through the doors. Jean and Robert were in a black car. I jumped in and said, "Hello Robert. Where is Mike tonight?"

He replied, "I couldn't find him. I called his house but his grandmother said he wasn't home. I know his college has a game this holiday."

I said, "I hope we see him before he go back."

As Robert continued to talk to Jean, I sat back and listened to the slow jams on the radio. I was reflecting on my feelings about Mike and wondering why he didn't call me while he was home from school. I watched Robert leaning over close to talk to Jean. It had started drizzling. It was a cold day. It made me think about my life, take a good look at the choices I had made so far and my goals. If I had my wish, I thought, I would leave Harlem with my family. I couldn't think of anything better for my future. I thought, if Mike wasn't going to be in my life I might as well move on. Then Jean interrupted my thoughts with, "Liz, we're at your apartment building. Are you asleep, Liz?"

"No Jean, I was just in deep thought. Oh, okay. Y'all are already to throw me out."

"No girl, we are all going home."

"Well, Miss Jean, you give me a call when you get home tonight. Right now, my watch says 9:30. So, Robert, take care of this precious cargo."

"Okay Liz, I hear you."

"See if you can get in touch with Mike."

"Liz, I will try very hard to get in touch with my buddy."

"Okay, have a good night y'all love birds, and thanks."

"Okay Liz. We see you later."

I ran upstairs to my apartment and put the key in the door. Mama said, "Hold on Liz." She opened the door and said, "Liz, we need to get down to the new apartment with Ms. Terry and help clean up."

"But Mama! I'm tired. I just came home from work."

"I know that Liz, but Sharon and John is watching the baby and the kids." I went downstairs with her, pulled down the dirty curtains and saw a clean window and sill, the only thing in the room that was clean.

Mama said, "Liz, this your room." My room was grungy and dark so I got some rags and soap. The rug was filthy with trash piled on top of it. I put all the trash in a paper bag. I got the broom and tried sweeping it but it didn't do much good. I asked my mother for some more bags because I had used all mine.

Mama told me, "Tomorrow you gotta go get some more." She came in my room and said, "See Liz, you can get a new bedroom set and curtains or shades to put in your room and you really can fix this place up."

"This is nice, Mama, but then everybody will be in here anyway."

Mama said, "Let us see what we can do with this new apartment."

"Mama, your room is big and spacious."

"That room is mine but I'm going to have my bed and two other single beds in there. See that little room that leads into the bathroom?"

"But Mama that little room is just a big closet."

"Yeah, but I need more room for the kids as they grow older."

"That's why I was hoping for a big house."

"But Liz, you are going to be leaving to go to college. Let us just finish cleaning up the apartment."

Ms. Terry came in and showed us the dirty rags she was using and said, "This is not a bad apartment when you clean it up. I can see if the rent man can get us some paint."

Mama replied, "Let me tell you something, girl I need my money from the old apartment to be put towards our security deposit. I can put the rest of that money on next month's rent." We kept cleaning until four o'clock in the morning. Then I told Mama that I was sleepy. I put the trash outside of the apartment door and went upstairs to our old apartment.

Sharon was sleeping on my side of the bed. I didn't feel like fussing at the moment, so I got in bed on her side. Sharon was snoring so loudly that I couldn't fall asleep and I just lay there. I put my pillow over my head, hoping to drown out the noise. Soon Sharon was moved and got quiet. I stretched out and went into a deep sleep. I occasionally opened my eyes when I heard a noise but quickly fell asleep again. I woke up when John came in my room and said I had a phone call from Jean. I gave a beastly growl as I raised my head and told John to tell Jean that, "I will call her back when I WAKE UP."

John said, "Alright Liz, but you are going to owe me if I have to come back in here."

"YEAH, YEAH, PLEASE LEAVE!" As he was leaving, he slammed the bedroom door so hard the window shook. I used my last bit of strength, got up out of bed, ran up behind him and gave him a big pluck in the head so hard he started to cry.

I told John, "Next time don't shut my door so hard. The window almost broke. Those windows need to be fixed already. When it rain and the wind blow, those windows shake. Now we got to see what the new apartment windows do and this apartment only gets warm in the kitchen. My room and the bathroom stay cold. We got to sleep in our clothes on some nights."

"Well Liz, I hope your job can get us some more pajamas." Sharon said.

"That's not going to happen, Sharon."

Ms. Terry came in and told us that Mama needed Sharon and me to come downstairs and clean the windows and help put up some shades.

"Okay Ms. Terry, let me wash up and get some oatmeal, then I will be straight down."

Sharon was waiting for me to finish washing up and eating my bowl of oatmeal. When I finished, Sharon and I started down the stairs. Sharon said, "Liz, I was hoping we move into a house."

"I know. That's what I wanted too." We went down the stairs to the apartment on the third floor. I said, "Sharon, I got several paper bags of trash out of here at four o'clock this morning and put them in the hall. We need to take them downstairs."

I opened the door and Mama immediately started to give orders. "Get those rags and soaps, water, and clean those windows."

Sharon and I started to clean the windows and then I asked Mama, "Who took those bags of trash out?"

"I don't know what you are talking about," Mama said. She continued. "A neighbor could have removed them."

But my mind went straight to the shadow of a man I saw on the second floor. "That man scare me, Mama."

"That might be true that he scare you, but you are scaring me talking like that and now you got a name for him."

Sharon burst out laughing and she said, "Liz, that man is going to put you in your grave, not Mike."

"Stop teasing Liz, okay."

"But Mama, Liz's life is so funny, these things keep happening to her."

"You betta look out for her Sharon, because he could hurt her."

I intervened, "Mama I gotta leave to go to work at 3:30."

"Okay Liz, just go get the boxes with my clothes then you can go."

"But I got to go upstairs to tell Ms. Terry that Mr. Ray is coming at 2:30."

"Okay Liz, hurry up but your room is your responsibility to clean."

"After work tonight Mama, I'll get it clean." I ran upstairs and saw Ms. Terry sitting in the kitchen holding the baby. I told her that Mr. Ray was coming over at 2:30 today.

She said, Thank you Liz, I was wondering what had happen to Mr. Ray." I started telling her about the color shades I was putting in my room."

"What is that, Liz?"

"You never heard of beige? I want to put beige in my room. There is only four different color shades at my store: blue, red, white and beige. When I get to work, I'm going to see what other colors they have out today. I'm going to buy the shades and curtains from my store. I can use my discount, I'm really going to fix up my room. Tomorrow we are going to move in, but we going to put some of our boxes in tonight.

The phone rang and I picked it up. "Is Liz home?"

"Yes, this is Liz."

"Hey! This is Mike."

"Okay Mike. What happen to you on Christmas?"

"Well, my aunt moved to Rochester, New York, and I went up there to help her out."

"You could've asked me if I wanted to come."

"I am asking you this. Are we going to be a couple New Year's?"

"Yes Mike I will be with you on New Year's."

"We're going down to the waterfront to see the fireworks."

"What time Mike?"

"I'll be there at 9:30 to pick you up. I'll see you then Liz."

When we hung up, I ran in my room to get my work clothes. I

had to run to catch the bus. On my second bus, I moved to the back and I saw Jean.

"What happen Liz, why didn't you call me back?"

"Girl, Mike called me and asked if we could be a couple on New Year's night. At 9:30 we are going downtown to see the fireworks."

"That's what Robert said to me about New Year's." We both started to jump up and down and hug each other. We got off at the store laughing and giggling. I asked, "What time are you getting off?"

"At 9 o'clock."

"I am too. See you in the front of the lobby at 9 o'clock so we can get on the bus?"

"Sure." I went into the rack department. Later someone called me and said that I would be in the cashier department. Mrs. Baueburg told me that she would be using me as a part time cashier. She said, "And you will be training your girlfriend as a rack girl, your old position." We left the office, she showed me around the toy department and got me a key to the register. She showed me how to use the register and showed me where the price list was kept. I started cleaning up the toy shelves. The toys were pretty and colorful. I played around with them to see how they worked. Mrs. Bonnie came in and started training me on how to sell gift certificates.

My first customer had a big order. I got price list and rang up her sale. Mrs. Bonnie told me to watch my cash register. When I finished ringing up the customer and she left, I noticed she left her toys. Mrs. Bonnie told me to put the toys behind the desk with the customer's name on a sheet of paper along with the price of the toys. I followed all of her instructions. "Liz, did you ever work as a cashier before?" she asked.

"No ma'am, I've never been a cashier before." The night was finally over and I straightened up the area. It was time for me to punch out. I looked at some of the clothes as I was going to the basement to punch the time clock. I got my coat and waited for Jean to punch out. When she finally got back there, she told me that she got my old job.

"I know that Jean. I'm going to be training you."

"Where are you working at?" Jean asked.

"At the toy department as a cashier."

"We got an opening in my department."

"I know that, Jean."

"My cousin Gracie need a job, we were talking about getting an apartment together."

I told her, "Yeah but you need to get out of school first, so you can make more hours."

"I know but Gracie can get a job now, and get help from her baby's father in the service."

"He's not going to stay in the army forever."

"I know that, but with a job, it can help us get an apartment."

"Don't she got a little boy?"

"Yeh, that's right Liz, but she already out of school."

"Jean, do you got an outfit for New Year's?"

"No, but I'm going to the mall tomorrow. Do you want to go with me."

"Yeah, I don't mind going with you. I do need an outfit too." we left and caught the bus home.

When I got to our apartment building, it was already 10:30, but I still stopped in our new apartment on the third floor. I moved the paper out of the front room and then went into my room. I looked around a bit, wiped the windowsill off and washed the walls down. I saw that the closet needed some hooks but it really needed a good paint job first. I put some soapy water in a bucket and I mopped and wiped down the woodwork, but the water got so dirty that I had to throw it out and get fresh water again and again.

Finally, I stopped and just stood there looking out the window. There was frost on the outside of the window and the trees were blowing, flowing back and forth as if they were ballroom dancers. I looked back around the room pictured it as if Mike and I were married and this was our little apartment. I finally got the door locked and went upstairs to our old apartment.

Upstairs everybody was in the front room watching the Christmas Special Concert, but Ms. Terry was helping Mama. I started to move the boxes into the new apartment but I decided to go to my bedroom. The bedroom, like usual, was left in a mess. I moved the clothes off my bed onto the floor, put on my pajamas and tried to go to sleep. I put my head in my pillow, the room started to get dark, and I fell asleep.

The next morning it was snowing. The children were laughing and acting crazy. They were running in and out of my room and the apartment. I got up and made myself some pancakes. The children were still screaming about the snow. Mama and Ms. Terry were downstairs to the new apartment. Sharon and John were outside playing in the snow. The baby was sleep until the other kids hit the bassinet and woke her up. I picked up the baby and cleaned her up. The children were looking out the window. They were so excited about the snow that they didn't want to eat right now. The snow continued to drop, and it got colder outside, but I just sat in the front room with the kids and the baby.

Then the phone rung. "Hello is this Liz?"

"Yes, Jean this is her."

"Did you look outside?"

"Yeah it is snowing bad."

"Girl, I am not going to the mall."

"I know that's right because I'm not either."

"We got two days 'til New Year's."

"Maybe tomorrow it'll be a little bit better. Looking outside now, I think we are going to be in today but we could call Mike and Robert."

"It's 11 o'clock. You can call them Liz."

"I'll call Mike and you can call Robert."

"Okay, that sounds good." I called Mike but the number I called was out of order. I hung up and just sat there confused for a while. Then I called Jean back, but her line was busy. When I hung up, John came in and said that Sharon and her friend Kelly were coming up. I went into my bedroom and lay across the bed but Sharon came in.

"Liz, it is snowing and it is cold out there."

"Why you bring all that snow in here? You need to wipe your feet before you come in." I stayed in my room, lay the baby on my chest and we fell asleep together.

Mama came in and asked me if I was going to work today. I said, "No, Mama we aren't working in this bad weather."

"You need to call your job and see if you are working today." I got up and gave her the baby. The phone kept ringing but there was no answer. I hung up the phone, went to the kitchen and told Mama that no one answered. I put on my clothes and got my old rundown boots. I was playing with the little children when I saw Mike coming up our walkway. We started to throw snowballs at each other, then a car pulled up with Robert and Jean. They got out the car and joined in the fun. Mama called down to me and said not to come up but to go to the market to get some chicken, bread and potatoes."

I ran upstairs and asked her, "Do you got some money?"

"No, do you got some?"

"I got ten dollars."

"Use that, this way we all have something to eat." I got the money and the cart.

"Where you going with that cart?"

"Mike and Robert's car is going to get stuck in this snow. It is getting heavy." We all started down the street. This was going to be a long six blocks, Robert kindly mentioned, but because we all was together it wouldn't seem so long. We started throwing snowballs at each other.

At the market, a loudspeaker announced that the market was only going to stay open for the next hour. Jean and I ran down the aisle grabbing things. She got the bag of potatoes and I got two big packs of chicken. I got syrup, pancake mix and some eggs, and chocolate syrup to make hot cocoa. When we got to the bread shelf, there wasn't any left. I got in line to pay the cashier. The cashier said please bring cash, no food stamps. My bill came to be $22.69, but I only had ten dollars in my wallet. I asked Jean if she had any money." Yes Liz, I got six dollars."

"Let me see what the guys got." I asked Mike and Robert. They said they had nine dollars and some change. I gave the cashier our bills and change and we picked up our food, but now the snow was so heavy I had to leave my cart with the manager. I told him I would come back for it tomorrow.

Each one of us carried a bag as we tried to make our way back home. The snow was falling so thickly I could hardly see. Mike took my hand and Robert took Jean's. As we were walking up the hill, we heard a car crash. By the time we got home, my hands were cold and my coat was drenched with snow. We ran upstairs to my old apartment. Mama opened the door. "I was wondering what happen to y'all. Now y'all take your coats off and go down to the new apartment. And Liz, we need some help moving some of our furniture."

We all went down to the new apartment. I brought my radio with us. Mike sat on the radiator, and Jean and Robert sat on the floor. I went upstairs, got the potatoes, a pan and a knife, the chicken and some plates. I put oil in the pan and put the pan on the stove. After the pan was warm enough I started to fry the chicken. Then I cup up the potatoes and made French fries. Jean boiled some water to make hot chocolate. We finished cooking and started to eat.

Mike said the food was good. Robert fell asleep after he ate. We looked outside and the snow was still coming down. On the radio the newscaster called this the blizzard of 1975. We all sat on the floor talking until Mama yelled, "All y'all young people need to call your parents."

Everybody went back upstairs to make those calls. When they came back down, Mike started making jokes. Mama said, "Before y'all go home with y'all full bellies y'all got to help me bring down my furniture. They both said, "Okay, Mrs. Tracy."

Back in the apartment, Mike was sitting in my new bedroom. We were talking and kissing but Sharon came down and sat in the room with us.

I said, "So, why are you here?"

"Mama said for me to sit down here with y'all. Y'all aren't married and this isn't yo' apartment." I didn't say anything else. Mike and Sharon started to joke and play around. Sharon started to punch on him. Mike started to laugh at Sharon because she fell on the floor. Soon we all fell asleep. The next morning Mama came in and said, "Y'all had a good night, but I need y'all this morning."

"Okay, Mrs. Tracy we ready" Mike said. Everybody moved the boxes and furniture. When we finished, I got breakfast ready for them. They ate, and we all went outside to see if we could dig Robert's car out. We dug, then pushed, his car out of the parking spot where he was stuck. Jean left with them.

I went upstairs to call my job and a lady told me that the store would be closed until after New Year's Day. I got back downstairs to put up my bed. After I finished this, this day would be mine to go downtown and get ready for New Year's Day. When I finally got my room cleaned and bed up, I decided to go to sleep. I slept until 5 o'clock in the evening.

I got up and I washed up and put on my pajamas. I couldn't do anything but think of Mike and the night we spent together. Tomorrow would be 1976 and we were going out. We were sure hoping that this would be a better year. I went back to my room and straightened up the rest of my things. I started looking for my wool pants set that I bought last year. I found it in a box in my closet. I put my other things in my drawer and straightened out my clothes and put everything in order.

It was after 2 o'clock in the morning. Mama told Ms. Terry that she was going to the store to buy some beer and liquor to celebrate the New Year. Ms. Terry replied, "That sounds good to me, let's go and get some." I picked up the baby and put her in my bed. She smiled and tried to talk to me. I played with her until she went back to sleep, then I got in my bed. John was playing with Sharon and Becky. He pretended he was a ghost, hid in my room and made a noise. I told him to get out so I could go to sleep. John left my room laughing, I put the covers over my head and went to sleep.

The next morning was New Year's Eve. I was so excited all I could think about was being with Mike, Jean and Robert. I got up early. I could get to work, I told myself. We were only going to be there a half day anyway. I washed up and went in the kitchen to make some toast. I put butter and jelly on it, grabbed my coat and started out the door. Mama hollered, "Where are you going so early?"

"Mama I got to go to work a half day today," I answered. "Besides, I open up as a cashier today," I added.

"Okay Liz, I see you this evening." I ran out the door to catch the bus but when I got to the bus stop, the corner was piled up with a hu-mongous hill of snow. I tried to climb over it and my feet fell straight through. The snow was so high that it came all the way up to my knees. I was slipping and sliding, tripping and gliding. It was a mess. Thankfully, the bus driver waited for me. When I got up the steps he asked, "Is everything okay, miss?"

"Yes. I almost fell but I'm okay." As I was walking to the back of the bus, I could feel my soaked socks squishing in my boots. I said to myself, This is going to be a problem when I try to work today.

When I got on my second bus, I ran into Randy. He said, "Hi Liz. What you doin' up so early this morning?"

"I'm going to work this morning."

"Where at?"

"Downtown." I sat down and he sat beside me. He told me, "I was sorry to hear about Lynne's death. All the guys wanted to go wit your pretty sister."

"Yeah, one of y'all guys did go with her. Ricky."

"Yeah that's right. Here's my stop. See you later, Liz."

"Okay, nice seeing you Randy." I thought. That crazy drunk got two cousins pregnant at the same time. Boy, if Lynne would have went with him. She thought she was sick going with Ricky and Gary, she would have really been sick, and stressed out to death. All of them that went with Randy now all pregnant with his child and you best believe he ain't nothing to look at.

Mrs. Louise was waiting outside for someone to open the door. I went over and said hi.

"Oh, hi Liz, you know these sick greedy managers tell us to be on time and they don't even be here. They need to come in early to open up this door. I could've stayed in my nice warm bed for all of this. All they think about is all the money those sales are going to bring in. This is New Year's Eve, and all the fools are going to be out here. It is so cold waiting for someone to come open up this door Liz. They could have gave me a key and the alarm code, I'm not going to rob them. Besides I already spent thirty-nine years working for them and I am ready to retire from here. These people put you through a lot of crazy things. Being rich make them go crazy and make me crazy for working for them." I started to laugh.

I told her, "I'm going out this New Year's Eve."

"Girl you better go downtown. It be sounding like a whole bunch of car accidents, when people be up their screaming on

New Year's." Finally the supervisor came and let us in. She had the nerve to say, "It is really cold this morning."

As Mrs. Louise and I were going down to the basement to punch in, she said, "She up here saying its cold and I was the one that been out there for forty minutes freezing." She seemed a little irate. I just laughed. She continued, "Honey, I'm going to find me some coffee to warm my arthritic body. For keeping me out in the cold, I hope our supervisor get arthritis too." She left and I laughed some more.

Jean came in and said, "Hi, are you ready for our big night?"

"Yeah, you know I'm ready for tonight and we getting off early too. Jean, I really don't have any money."

"Liz, the guys are taking care of us for the night, so we can just sit back, relax and enjoy it."

"You know Jean, my mother told me to have my own money to go out with."

"I know that Liz, but the guys is not going to do anything. You know Robert and Mike well."

"You just met Robert and Mike at Thanksgiving holiday and now it's the New Year holiday. I am going to get some type of change in my pocket to get home. Even if they are treating us out to watch the fireworks. If I'm going to have some change you need to have some change too, Jean."

"I will have a little change Liz."

"'Cause if things don't work out we could need to get back home, or if we get lost in the crowd we could get back home," I continued.

Jean went over to the time clock to punch in." What time you get off Liz."

"Two o'clock today."

"I'm getting off 2:30 this afternoon but as long as I go out with you guys tonight that'll be fine with me."

People were still returning their gifts. Some gifts were damaged to the point that we had to return them to the company with a note attached. My last customer came at 1:50. I was hoping that she knew this was New Year's evening.

"Girl those people not interested in your time, you got to finish her up and I'll be glad to close out your register." Mrs. Louise said. "Girl just go home and I'll finish her up."

"Thank you Mrs. Louise. I owe you one."

"No you don't, but the company owe me for being in this store for thirty-nine years."

I giggled and ran downstairs to punch out. Our supervisor, Mrs. Goeawitz, asked me if I could stay on the clock to help her out on the floor.

"Yes ma'am but I'm going to leave at 2:30."

"That's fine the store is closing at 4 o'clock anyhow. If you want to stay until then you can make a little bonus for yourself."

I stayed and Mrs. Louise came over and said, "Liz, you really could stay at your own register." It was finally 3:50 and the store speaker was announcing that the store was closing in ten minutes.

Jean and I ran downstairs to get our coats. Jean ran upstairs to get her layaway out for tonight. I said, "Hurry up Jean. We are going to miss our bus!"

"Okay Liz, I'm coming!" she yelled back. I ran outside to catch our bus. The corner was so crowded. I asked Jean if she wanted to come over to my house to get dressed for tonight. She agreed and told me that her cousin Gracie wanted to tag along with us. I said that that was fine with me. She told me that she was going to call her and tell her where I lived so she and her boyfriend could meet us. Her boyfriend was back from the army and they wanted to go out.

Jean asked, "Who is driving?"

"I don't know, but one of them has to be driving."

"Could they pick them up?"

"I don't know but you could ask them." We missed the first bus and had to wait. We didn't get on our second bus until 5:45. We were glad it wasn't that crowded. Then we had to catch another bus anyway to get to my apartment. We got off that bus at the corner of my apartment building. We were giggling with excitement. We ran up the stairs and when we got to the third floor, Sharon and her friend were sitting on the floor taking up the whole hallway. I turned my nose up and said, "EXCUSE US!"

They got the hint and moved. We went inside the apartment and Mama said, "Now y'all two come and sit down and eat some black eye peas and rice. Its cold out there and y'all need to eat."

I interrupted her before she could say anything else. "But we need to get in the bathroom to wash up and get dressed for tonight." My feet were cold and wet so I took off my boots and socks.

Mama came in and said, "You can throw those smelly socks in the basket." And they really did stink. I washed up and got ready. Mama said that Mike was going to be over at 9 o'clock to pick us up. After I finished getting dressed I remembered that I needed another pair of boots. Sharon was the only one that wore the same size shoe as me so I asked her if I could wear her boots.

She said, "Yes, if you're going to pay me."

"Sharon, where are your boots?"

"On my feet, but they already wet." I shut the door in her face. She started giggling. I went into the kitchen and asked Mama if I could wear her boots.

"Yes Liz. My boots are too wide for your feet but you could use about two or three pair of socks with them." I ran in her room and got them. I had to put on three pairs of socks. Then it was already 8 o'clock when I started to curl my hair. Mama had reminded me to put on my hat and gloves. I put on my new wool hat and glove set that I got on sale at my job.

Mama said, "It is already 8:15 and now you and Jean come sit down and get your New Year's meal," Jean wasn't ready yet. she still had to curl her hair. I gave her a hat from an extra hat and glove set, but Mama commanded me to sit down and eat. Her cornbread was so good. As I finished eating we heard a car horn. Mama called both of us over and handed us some money. She told us to use it to catch a cab or the bus if things didn't work out. She continued, "Here's a thermos full of hot chocolate and now you roll this up in this wool scarf."

"Thank you, Mama." She was looking out the window waving to Robert and Mike as we got into the car. Mike got in the back with me."

"What you got there, Liz?"

"Some hot chocolate."

"Give me some." The next thing I heard was, "Give us some." I told them to wait while I ran upstairs and got them some in plastic cups. When I got back in the car, Jean was telling Robert about her cousin Gracie and her boyfriend who were over at Jean's aunt's house. Robert blew the horn. I started telling Mike about my New Year's meal of black eye peas and green rice.

"Liz, I bet your Mama put a hurt'n on that smoke neckbone and I'm going over there and get some later." Gracie and her boyfriend finally came down and got in the car. Jean introduced us to Gracie and Melvin.

We tried to find a parking spot closer to the area but it was too crowded. We parked all the way down the street from almost everything. It was 10:20 when we started out walking. We were rushing and pushing, people were hollering, laughing and drinking. Mike said, "Liz, stay with me and hold my hand. I don't want to lose you." We kept moving toward the singing and dancing.

Robert and Jean were so far behind us I couldn't see them. I just kept walking with Mike. When 11:30 came, closer to the New Year, Mike and I started to sing with the rest of the people. The crowd was pushing us from behind so I had to keep pushing to keep up with Mike. Midnight came and 1976 was here. They cheered with beer and wine and champagne and soda and the confetti fell on us as we kissed the New Year in.

People threw their cups up in the air and I was wet and cold from all the celebrating. I put my scarf on my head and around my neck, the one my mother had given me. We tried to make our way back to the car as we looked for Robert, Jean, Gracie and Melvin. We couldn't find them because the crowd was pushing and pulling us all around the place. Mike put his arm around me and said, "We got to find them, honey." It was after 2:30 in the morning when we found the car. Jean and Robert were there. Mike tapped the window on the side Robert was on.

"Okay, where is your cousin, Jean?"

"I don't know Liz, I thought they was with y'all." We drank our hot chocolate and waited for them. They finally came over to see if this was the right car.

"Where to, Robert?"

"I don't know Melvin, this y'all city."

Mike said, "We going over to Liz house for our New Year's meal."

"That's what I want to hear," Robert cheered.

There was a lot of loud music playing when we got to my apartment, To my surprise, Mama and Ms. Terry were having a party with some of the people from upstairs. Mama told us, "Y'all ladies go and fix y'all boyfriends something to eat." We washed our hands and fixed the plates. Gracie and Melvin started dancing. Mike and Robert came in the kitchen and started eating. Jean touched Gracie on the shoulder and told her to fix her man something to eat. When she stopped dancing, Melvin grabbed Jean and started swinging her around. Melvin was swing dancing like a pro. While he was "getting down," he was saying, "Go Girl Go, Let your New Year be Merry!"

Mama kept saying, "Hap-py Hap-py Hap-py New Year!" That was after she had another drink. Then Mike and Robert started dancing with me. Mike swung my arm around his back and brought me side to side. We kept dancing, and then we kissed. We finished the dance and started kissing everybody in the apartment.

We laughed at my mother because she did a split on the floor and couldn't get back up. We had to help. Ms. Terry was talking to Mr. Paul on the phone. A car horn blew, and as she was leaving she said, "Girl, my New Year's is not lost 'cause I got a man."

We were still dancing when we heard gunshots go off outside. It was after 6 AM then. Mama hollered, "Y'all gotta get out this apartment because I'm going to sleep. Liz, you clean up the apartment!" Gracie and I started to clean.

I said, "I wish this night would never end. New Year's Eve means we could be together for the rest of this year. Mike gave me a kiss and they left. I finished cleaning up the apartment.

The television was on in my room but the kids and Sharon were sleep. I turned the television off and put on my nightclothes. When I got in bed it was already 7 o'clock in the morning. This was the best time of my life because of Mike and my friends. I dreamed about our future together until Shevon came into my room crying. I looked at her for a second, and then put her in bed with me, but she kept moving around. I took her into the kitchen with my mother who was in there holding the baby. I went in the bathroom.

Mama called me into the kitchen. She said, "We had a good time this New Year's Day Liz."

"Yes we did. I wished that day never end."

"Liz, you need to know the truth about New Year's Day."

"What Mama?"

"New Year's Day is the time to be together with your friends and family but its really a celebration to reflect on the past year and hope for a better year. If Mike is in your future, that would be good. But if he isn't in your future that is a part of life. Remember your feelings is going to change and your life is going to change. You will experience life whether it's good or bad.

Remember you still got to live and love whether you with Mike or not, whether you have friends or not. Life will still go on." I listened but didn't said anything. I moved a pan off the stove, went into my room and lay on my bed. I thought, *What my mother don't understand is, I need something to hold on to because my life is in Harlem.*

Chapter 21

Back to School

The next morning was rainy and cold. Mama kept calling us to get up and get ready for school. I got up but Sharon was still in the bed complaining about it being to cold in our room and that she was too sleepy. I went into the bathroom to wash up. When I got out, I went into the kitchen for something to eat. Mama said, "I only got one thing and that's toast, but we need some jelly."

"Mama, that's okay, I'll get something at school."

She asked, "Do you get a free breakfast?"

"No, the only thing I get free is Lunch."

"Why don't you see if you and Sharon can get some free breakfast?"

"Okay, I'll try to ask my counselor this morning." I settled for some hot cocoa, and then I left to catch the bus. When I got to the corner, Kelly asked me if Sharon was going to school this morning. I replied, "I don't know, because she was still in the bed when I left, and I'm not going to wait for her this morning. I'm too cold waiting for the bus." Kelly came with me to the corner.

Kelly sat beside me on the bus. As we talked, we watched out the window for Sharon but she never showed up. As we got closer to school, Kelly said that Jeff was not going to school either. I asked, "Are those two getting together?"

She said, "I don't know but that's what Jeff said."

"I know. Mama better not find out."

"Oh, please don't tell her. Jeff and Sharon is going to be mad at me," Kelly pleaded.

"Miss Sharon was in on this plan."

"Well, let me tell you like this. It was Jeff's plan for Sharon."

"Umm hmm, when Sharon get pregnant will that be the plan for Jeff?" Kelly didn't respond. The bus put us out in front of the school and I went straight to the counselor office to talk to Mrs. Jones. The secretary told me that Mrs. Jones was not there yet, and then said, "But, what is your name and I can leave her a message. Please go straight to your class before you are late."

I waited for the bell to ring for first period. I looked for Jean but she wasn't there yet. On my way to English class, I saw Sharon.

She said, "Hi Liz."

I said, "Hi Sheron," and kept walking. I had not forgotten the trick that she tried to pull on me at Mike's graduation party. I in my next class, I waited to see if Jean was coming. I wanted to talk to her about Sharon and Robert. I wanted to know if they were a couple and if Jean was going to the same college as Robert. Neither Jean nor Sheron showed up. I was thinking, *Jeff's plan has been carried out and I know I am letting my Mama know what Sharon is up to.*

After school, I left to go to work. The bus was late so I started walking. It was a twelve-block walk, but if I tried to catch the bus, I knew I was going to be late. The bus went past me, in the process splashing dirty water all over me. I was glad I had another pair of shoes in my locker at work. I made it to work in the nick of time and hurried downstairs to punch the time clock. I looked to see if Jean was in but didn't see her so I asked Peggy, "Did Jean call in today?"

Peggy said, "No, but she should have called you. She yo' buddy."

"That is nice of you to know that, Peggy, but I am not her employer." I was not going to stand there and argue with her. Peggy was getting under my skin. I picked up the money drawer and went into the toy department. Carol told me that they needed me in the lingerie department. When I got there, I ran into Janice who asked, "Hey, how was your New Year's Eve?"

"Mines was very good this year," I said.

"What did you do, Liz?"

"Well, we went downtown to see the fireworks with some friends and Mike."

"Girl, my life was good that day! My lingerie that I bought was white you would've thought I got married in them."

I looked at Janice and laughed, and then I asked, "Boy, who's the lucky guy?"

"His name is Detroit."

"You know something? I thought that Ricky was your boyfriend."

"Oh no, Ricky used to go with my sister. Girl, my sister know Ricky from hanging on our street corner, and then she got mad with him and kicked him to the curb. That was over about three months ago. She went back with her ex boyfriend, Sherman."

"Yeah. Ricky be hanging on our corner now but he isn't nothing even to talk about." she left and went to lunch. I kept working while people were still coming into the store.

When it was time for me to go home, I went to the basement to punch out. I checked the time cards and noted that Jean didn't work that day at all. When I got home, I was going to call her, because Sharon didn't come to school today. The first bus arrived on time but the second bus was twenty-five minutes late. While I waited, the rain beat on my face. When the bus finally came, I was cold, tired and wet. By the time I got home from work, it was 10 o'clock.

I opened the door to the building and right away Mrs. Mae started telling me about my family. "I wish your sister and brother keep their friends out of this hallway."

"Okay Mrs. Mae, I will tell my mother."

She was still running her mouth as I walked up the steps. She was saying, "...because they leave candy wrappers and soda bottles all over this hallway. Besides I am the only one who clean this part of the hallway up."

I didn't say anything else. When I opened my apartment, the door Ms. Terry was holding the baby. Ms. Terry asked if they were hiring anyone where I worked. I told her that I didn't know but I would ask around tomorrow.

Mama told me, "That will be nice if you can get her a job."

I went into my room to find Sharon lying on my bed. "SHARON GET OFF MY BED!" I immediately ordered.

"Okay LIZ, you don't have to holler at me like that."

"GET OFF. Why didn't you come to school today?"

"I stayed home," she responded.

"I am going to ask Mama, Sharon."

"Liz, I got only one mother and you can ask her that."

"I don't believe you, Sharon."

"Liz, personally I don't care if you believe me or not!" Then she left and slammed the door behind her. I took off my wet clothes and went into the front room to sit down.

Mama came in. She asked, "What's the argument about?"

"I asked why she didn't come to school today."

"Well, Liz, Sharon stayed home with me while I went to the market."

Sharon added, "I told Liz I only got one mother. I didn't need her permission to stay home! I asked her could I be home."

Mama said, "Now Sharon is your sister, you don't need to know why. In addition, she don't need your permission. You can stop now. She know who y'all mother is."

I got up and took the baby from Mama. Mama asked, "Liz did you find out weather y'all can eat breakfast for free?"

"No, Mrs. Jones wasn't in today but I will try tomorrow." I played with the baby for a while.

Ah man, I thought, I almost forgot to call Jean. I ran to the phone. "Hello, can I speak to Jean?"

The person on the other end said Jean wasn't home yet. "Okay, tell her that Liz called." I put the phone down slowly as I thought about where Jean could be. The first thing that ran through my mind was that she must be with Robert. I went into my room. Sharon gave me a nasty look and turned her face towards the wall.

"Look Sharon, I had to find out if what Kelly was saying was true or not."

"What did Kelly say, Liz?"

"Well, she told me that Jeff was putting you in his 'Plan' of staying home."

"That lying little stinky snotty nose girl. I can't wait until I see that girl tomorrow. Because she telling lies on me."

"Look Sharon, you don't have to fight. This way you show her how you feel. You know, by not being her friend anymore."

"No, she need to be banged in her mouth."

"That is Jeff's little sister."

"I don't care!"

"No Sharon, don't put everybody into it."

Mama came into our room and I told her the story that Kelly told me. Mama told Sharon, "If you go over there and start a fight with her I'm going to bang you. You don't need a friend like that. You go to school with Liz tomorrow. This way you can stay away from them. Now you can see what type of friends you have."

Sharon's looked mad and disappointed. She sat up in her bed staring at the floor not saying anything.

I turned on the radio to listen to the old jams, but all I thought about was Jean. I got my clothes laid out for school, then turned the lights out and went to sleep. However, this dream about Mike and me having a life together kept popping up in my mind. I got up and quickly slipped into the front room. I got my books and started on my homework but that didn't seem to be clearing my mind. I was getting so sleepy that I gave up and went back to bed, hoping the dream wouldn't bother me too much.

The next thing I heard was "Liz, get up!" I got up and started to wash when Mama came and asked me if I wanted something to eat. I asked, "Well, do you got some jelly to put on my toast?"

"Yes Liz, I got oatmeal, cream of wheat, eggs and bacon. I also got some more bread 'cause my social worker gonna be here. Now y'all clean your room good."

I told Sharon, "Okay, Sharon clean your side of the room and make your bed."

"I thought I told you I got ONE mother."

I told her to move so I could make my way into the kitchen. I got Mama to make me some Cream of Wheat, then went into my room to straighten my side of the bed. I went back into the kitchen and ate. Sharon told me to "hurry up and come on." I got my books and left with Sharon to catch the bus. Sharon saw Kelly and Jeff and didn't say anything to them but I said, "Hi Jeff and Kelly."

They said, "Hi Liz, Hi Sharon." Sharon gave a pitiful little wave in the air and didn't say anything.

We got off the bus in front of the school and I ran to my counselor's office to talk to Mrs. Jones. When I got there, I asked the lady in the front room, "Is Mrs. Jones here?"

"Yes she is, what is your name young lady?"

"Elizabeth Rosemere."

"Okay, I will call her."

Mrs. Jones came out and asked me to come in. I told her that my mother wanted to know if we qualified for free breakfast.

"Well, do you get free lunch?" she asked.

"Yes."

"Well, then you get free breakfast. Elizabeth, your score was a little low in math. Didn't you tell me that you wanted to go to college?"

"Yes ma'am."

"Well, you need to enroll in our Saturday morning class. You really need to pull up your math scores. See, here is your score for the test we gave in December. It is very low. I am going to enroll you in a Saturday class for math, then we are going to give you a practice SAT test for college. This is for you and your parent to fill out. Now, your first class for math is at the end of this month. The time will be 8:45-11 o'clock. You need to tell your supervisor that you can only work after 12:30 on Saturdays." she gave me a late slip for class and a breakfasfAlunch ticket. I tried to find Sharon to tell her to get a ticket like mine but I didn't see her.

I heard someone calling me, "Liz! Liz." I turned around and saw Jean. "Hi Jean, why didn't you come to work? Was you with Robert?"

"No Liz, I was over Gracie's house."

"Well, is y'all a couple yet?"

"No, we friends like you and Mike but I did have a nice time." We went to our next class. We didn't talk about Mike or Robert anymore that day. Our day was no different from any other day in class, answering questions and writing down home assignments, then getting our coats and walking to the bus stop together.

"Jean let me tell you what the guidance counselor, Mrs. Jones said."

"What she say Liz?"

"Well, first I went in her office to talk about getting some free breakfast tickets. She told me that my math scores were low and that I need to go to Saturday school for a SAT test."

"Oh Liz, she never talk to me about my grades."

"That's what you should be doing, Jean. You can talk to the counselor about your SAT test. Here comes the bus Jean, let's hurry before we be too late."

When we got to the back of the bus, there was a sickening smell of body odor. Jean said, "It smells bad back here. It smell like every inch of their body is stinking." I laughed so loud that people started to look at me. Jean put her hand over my mouth but I was laughing so hard that I was falling out of my seat, unable to control myself. When we got off the bus, Jean pulled me down the street. She said, 'Girl stop laughing so loud. People gonna think we crazy or might think we making fun of them." I let Jean drag me to our job. When we got to there I stopped laughing but tears were still running down my face. I finally calmed down. I wiped my face and went to work.

Carol asked, "Liz, are you working over here today?"

"No, I'm back to my toy department."

"That is crazy. You change like everyday."

I told her, "Mrs. Louise told me that I'm a cashier floater. We need to ask them to let us see the new schedule."

"That's okay where they put me, Carol."

"Liz, I need someone to relieve me from my register so I can go on my break."

"Carol, this job isn't my problem yet." I let her stand there and wonder who would relieve her. I got my cash bag and started to take customers.

"Please lady, could you see if this toy on sale?" a customer asked. I stooped down to look at the list of toy sales and saw the customer put the toy under her skirt. I asked her where was the toy that she wanted me to check on sale. She told me to never mind. When she left the department, I called security and described as looking like someone's grandmother. The guard said that the lady had escaped out the back to the loading dock. I started snickering.

The security guard said, "She'll be back, they always come back," as he walked away. Carol turned to me and said, "Liz, I hope she don't come in my department again." When I thought back to this day later, and realized I was laughing for at least half of it.

Before I punched out, I ran upstairs to my supervisor Mrs. Bundy's office. I let her know that I would be going to Saturday class and asked her if she could put me on the schedule for after 12:30 on Saturdays. She told me that it wouldn't be a problem. "And since you are going to go to college, you need time to study, so you can come to work every other weekend," she added. I thanked her and ran back downstairs to punch out, but Peggy had already put the time cards in a pile to record. I asked, "Peggy where is my time card?"

"Here Liz, next time you call down here to tell me you going to be working over."

"Next time you check with the supervisor." I said. I went to the lobby to see if Jean was still waiting, but Jean had already left. Oh boy, I thought, now I will have to wait here all by myself. As I got to the corner, the bus came. It started as a smooth ride home but after three blocks and it broke down. Now I was thinking, this is going to be some long wait before I make it home. Carol came up behind me and touched me on my shoulder. I jumped and turned around, and as I was catching my breath, she said, "This is a real mess with the buses, especially at night. I got three kids and a sick mother at home. Let me see how much change I got to catch a cab."

"Yeah, me too." I looked in my wallet and to my surprise, I had five dollars, the same five dollars my mother gave me on New Years. I also had four dollars in quarters that I was supposed to use to wash clothes. "Carol, what way are you going."

"I'm going past 124th Street. Where you headed?" We got a cab and I told her that I would pay half. The cab put me off at the front of my building and I gave Carol eight dollars for my half.

As soon as I walked in the door, John told me that Mike called. I went straight to the phone and called him. The phone rang but no one answered. I guessed he had left to go back to college. I went into my room to change into my nightclothes. I asked Sharon where Mama was. She said, "She down to Ms. Terry's."

While I was getting some water from the kitchen, Mama came in. I told her how the lady at the store stuffed the toy in her skirt. "Mama that lady was dressed like someone's grandmother. She an ol' thief." Everybody that was listening to our conversation started laughing.

Mama said, "Liz, don't you try to protect their money. Give those thieving people that money. You don't need to get hurt over that money. Besides, that money is insured by their bank. You got these thieves all around you. Be careful and don't get involved with those types of customers. Don't give information about where you work or what time you come to work. I mean to nobody. These types of people always want to know where to get money from. They never willing to work, they hustle people and rob others. So, you look around you when you go to work or catch the bus, even in school. Someone might ask you, if you can give them a deal. You tell them, this is your job, and you need it and I would like to keep it. No deals can be made."

"I do understand this Mama," I said, as I was trying not to be bored out of my mind. "Liz, I want you to listen to me and not say you understand me as if this would never happen to you. Everyday these types of incidents happen to people you know, even if they don't tell you. This is a part of life and *it do* happen."

"And, another thing happened today," I said, cutting into my mother's speech. "My counselor told me that my score in math is low and if I'm going to go to college, I'm going to have to go to Saturday school. I asked my supervisor if they could make my schedule after 12:30 on Saturdays."

"Are you going to take this class?"

"Yes ma'am, I need this class and I will work every other weekend now. That'll give me time to study and go to the library."

"Okay Liz, but you still have your chores around the house to do."

"I know that Mama, I do my chores now, and I work."

Mama asked, "Did Mike go back to school?"

"I don't know. I tried to call but I couldn't get in touch with him. Maybe I'll call him tomorrow."

"Liz, you don't have to run after him. Let it be his will to come and see you. He know your number and he know where you live. Honey, please don't run after a boy, 'cause if you start now, your whole life is going to go down that path."

"I know that's right, I'm listening to you Mama," I said cheerfully.

I went into my room and got into bed. The sheets on my bed were soft and they smelled good. I felt like I was in the big warm arms of Mike. I drifted off into a deep sleep. The next day brought some snow in with it. There was still some snow left on the ground from before. I heard the children laughing and playing and Sharon was hollering out to John. I got up to see how much it had snowed. I opened the window and asked Sharon, "Is school out today?"

"Yes Liz, that's why we all out here playing, 'cause school is out."

I started to turn on the television to catch the news but my stomach sounded like a pack of bears growling. I got some hot cereal and sat at the window looking out and laughing at the children playing. Suddenly someone came and parked in the middle of our street. I girl came out with a baby. It looked sort of like Sissy but she looked old and worn out. She had no hat, a thin jacket, no boots, some little summer shoes on, and her hair was flying all over the place. For some reason I felt sorry for her and especially her baby. She was trying to walk through all this heavy snow but was about to fall.

I called down to John and Sharon to help her. Sharon sent John and his friends over. I knew she was alone and abandoned in that apartment where they were selling drugs. John got Sissy's bags and took her by the hand. When she got to the apartment safely, she waved.

I waved back, then left the window and called for Mama. However, Mama and the other children were over at Ms. Terry's apartment. As I was about to close the door to our apartment and head on down to Ms. Terry's place, the phone rang. I decided to answer it. "Hello," I said.

"Hi, is Liz home?"

"Yes, Jean, this is Liz. What is going on in your life?"

"Well, I am still talking to Robert and calling him."

"Mike did call here but I couldn't get in touch with him. Did you talk to Mrs. Jones?"

"Yes, Liz but I don't know if I am still going to college."

"Why Jean? Don't you want to?"

"Yes, but the problem is my grades. I need three classes to pick up my GPA. I don't have time to make up those main classes. She said that I needed to pull up my score in those classes now. I need to improve in those classes to finish school and get my diploma."

"I wish I could help you, Jean but I really don't have time to do that, you know. If I had the time I would try to show you how to do some of the work but I don't."

"That's okay, Liz."

"Well, if you want to do better in life you'll make the time."

"Do you think we are going to work today?" Jean asked as a way to get me off the subject of college.

"I don't know," she replied.

"Why don't you call them and find out?"

"No Jean, you can call them."

"Okay Liz, I'll call." Then we hung up and Mama came in the door.

"Oh good, Liz. You was up."

"Yeah, up here looking out the window at the children. Mama, you know this is Rolynne's first winter living here."

"Yes, that's right, and she is blessed to be with her mother's family. Those two kids over there is blessed too."

"That's right Mama, 'cause Sissy got out a car this morning. She was looking wild and deranged. She had on a thin jacket and some summer shoes. It is snowing out there! I asked my sister Sharon to help her on the walkway. I really felt sorry for her and that baby. She was alone and abandoned with a baby. Only time I see Anthony is when he want to use that apartment for selling drugs."

Mama said, "Ms. Terry got some old clothes she was getting rid of. Hold the baby and I'm going down there to ask her for those clothes. None of my girls can fit in them anyway." I took the baby to the window to see her uncle and aunt playing with Lisa's kids. Someone handed John two big bags. John went to Sissy's apartment building. I was wondering to myself, *why is John going into that building and leaving Kelly and Jeff outside playing?*

I told Mama what John did. Mama said, "I know Liz, because I told John to go over to Sissy's apartment and give her those clothes that Ms. Terry have. They smell a little smoky but Sissy can wash them. They smoke and drink so much themselves that those people won't know the difference."

The phone rang and I got it. "Hello Liz."

"Yeah? Do we work today?"

"The security guard said no, not today, but we can call tomorrow."

"Jean, we get to relax and sleep today. School is out so I am in today. Mama said Hi Jean." Jean told me to tell her hi and then she hung up. I started reflecting back on the conversation we had earlier about school. Robert is in college but she doesn't want to take the time to try for college. That job isn't going to help her in the future. I hopped into my nice cozy soft warm bed, and drifted off again.

The next three weeks flew by. The first day of Saturday morning school was cold and damp. It was like that throughout the whole apartment. When I got up it was still dark outside. As I was getting ready for school, I thought about how alone I was going to be in Saturday class. I wasn't going to know one person. After I finished washing up, I threw on some clothes, got my socks and boots on, then headed to the kitchen to grab something to eat. As usual, we didn't have any food. As I was walking towards the door, I was trying to decide either to go to the store and buy some chips and a soda or be on time for the bus. When I got to the corner, the bus pulled up. I had just enough change. The bus was so crowded I didn't have a place to sit. I quietly stood there until finally a man offered me his seat.

Now I was able to ride more comfortably but Jean was still on my mind. I was thinking about how Jean's heart was on Robert instead of college. I would keep talking to her about Robert and trying to convince her to change her mind about college. I tried to tell her that in the future having your own degree in something will really pay off, but all she could say in her defense was that he really cares about her, as if that really has something to do with her education and career. I keep telling her that her life does not guarantee a good job later on and by going to college, she would at least have something to look forward to in case her and Robert don't last. The only thing she says is that she already knows this, but this is HER future and HER feelings.

I wish that I could make her see through all those feelings. Maybe she'll be at work today, I thought. I can keep on her case about being in love and setting her heart up for pain.

When I got off the first bus, I heard someone call, "Lynne! Lynne! Where are you going?" I looked up and saw Mr. Paul.

"Oh hi, Mr. Paul. I'm not Lynne. I'm Liz."

"Where are you going so early this morning."

"I'm going to school. I have to take a class for math on Saturdays and my bus is here. I have to go catch it." I hurried for the bus stop while waving goodbye. He pulled off into traffic and drove away. When I got off the bus, I looked around the schoolyard, hoping there were no other seniors that I knew there.

The counselor came out and told us all to go in the office and sign in. Mrs. Jones sent me to room number 122. The teacher, Mr. Harris, was quick in telling us that we must listen, follow all his instructions and always be in his class five minutes early. He told us that if we miss three days in the whole four months that we would flunk and be put out of the program. He told us to make sure we have a binder notebook and a good pack of number two pencils. He added, "If you are not prepared, DON'T COME IN! Next Saturday you must be here and prepared ready to work. I will be testing you. This will show me if you're doing your homework and class assignments."

He asked all of us to sign our names to a sheet and pass it around. The guy behind me leaned over and whispered in my ear, "He looked like Bozo the Clown and his pants are skin tight."

I burst out laughing. "Is there a problem with what I am saying?" asked Mr. Harris.

"Oh, no sir. I was looking at my picture in my wallet."

"You need to let us see that picture, we want to laugh too."

"Okay, but its not that funny."

"Then we aren't going to be hearing you laugh again."

"No sir, you won't hear me again."

"I will not tolerate foolishness in my class."

After half an hour, we signed out to go home. Tim, The boy that made me laugh, came out and started talking to me. "Where you live at in Harlem, Elizabeth?"

"On 124th street."

"Do you have a boyfriend?"

"I'm not dating anyone and not looking for a boyfriend."

"I don't have anyone calling me right now. are you in this program to go to college?"

"Yes, I'm trying to get my grade up for the SAT test."

"Look, maybe we can work on our homework assignments together."

"No, my mother don't like boys to call our home. Besides how old are you?"

"I'm seventeen this month."

"You're in the eleventh grade and I'm in the twelfth grade ready to graduate. I don't have the time to spend being a friend."

"Well, can I walk you to the bus stop?"

"No. I'm going to the bus stop on the next street."

"Elizabeth, its 11:45 in the morning, Could I safely walk you to the bus stop?"

"Okay, but remember, we don't need to talk about you being my boyfriend."

"Okay, I'm walking with you."

"Besides, call me Liz because that name Elizabeth was my father's dead grandmother's name and I never met her, my father's mother, or even my father."

Tim told me that his father was in the service overseas. "And my mother is now divorcing him. Liz, how many brothers and sisters do you have?"

"I got two sisters and one brother but I lost one brother and one sister this year, my mother is a single woman trying to cope with all our needs. That's why I'm working, to help her keep a roof over our heads and food in our stomachs, but at the same time, I'm upset because my whole paycheck goes on my mother's bills. But I realize that I am helping her. What about you, Tim?"

"I work for a dealership cleaning cars on the lot, but all the money I get, my mother seem to give to her new young boyfriend. That problem is driving me crazy. My life is going all out of control. She doesn't do anything for nobody but herself. I got three brothers and I take care of all of them. My father left her 'cause she was lazy and stupid. She don't even have a job. she get an alimony check from my father. I get the money from her and take it to the rental office until her boyfriend, Boo Boo, hear about it.

"Me and that man is going to go at it if he touch me or my brothers. That man is sick, ugly and dirty and she tell me she love him. It's like someone pulled the wool right over her eyes. She too blind to see the truth. Besides, he's all big and fat, he don't got anything going on. That's why I have to stay out late every night over a friend's place. I don't want to be home, to see him coming in there."

I said, "Boy, I thought my life was out of control."

"Liz, if you a one-half decent person you got a good mother."

"Well, this is my stop. Thank you for walking me here."

"You seem like nice girl."

"Well, you seem like a nice guy."

"Be careful when you get off from work tonight, Liz."

"See you next Saturday in class."

"Okay Liz, I'll see you."

The bus pulled up and I got on. I was trying to move to the back of the bus but it seemed every time I tried to move, I was hit by shopping bags and big coats. I kept moving back, hoping someone would get off so I could get closer to the door. The bus smelled like someone was smoking and the ride was so bumpy, I was forced to get off two blocks before my stop and walk. At least this way I could clean that nasty smell out my lungs. I quickly walked those two blocks.

In the lobby, I bumped into Steven. He said, "What's been going on with your time Liz?"

"Well, I go to school on Saturdays now for math so I can take the SAT."

"Well, if that's what it takes, then take that time to do it. You won't like it here when you finish school. These people will wake you up early in the morning to come to work and my weekends is always theirs to use."

"Well, I got to punch in." As I went past the office I heard, "Good afternoon, Elizabeth."

"Hi Peggy, you know its still okay for you to say Liz," but she turned her head away from me. I took my keys and went into the locker room, then upstairs to my department. *That Peggy...there's not a word to describe her, not even college student,* I thought.

I started putting the prices on the toys when I realized that the store manager had everything decorated in red, and it wasn't even Valentine's yet. It would be another two weeks. The gifts could be decorated in red, I thought, but did they have to decorate all the toys red too? Red hats, red balls and pacifiers, I wondered if this was supposed to make them sell. Our memo told us to put everything red in front. I rushed around and put tags on all the red toys.

Now my mind turned to my conversation with Tim and how he felt about his mother. Boy, I thought, my life is a mess but his life is taking him down to the ground. I felt sorry for him and his brothers. I thought though, that the good thing was that he was working to feed them. God gave him a hard life, I thought, and still he is doing a lot of hard work and is showing love to others.

I was glad to talk to someone and he seemed like a nice guy. That's a little strange coming from a bad background like his, I thought. I remembered how they always say, *if you live like us you will be strong but you have to take the right course.* I thought, *but a teenager don't want to grow up like this. People make fun of where we live and talk about us on the news, about how people are poor in America.*

Listen at those rich people they act as if they own the world with all the money they spend trying to be something. The way they act is crazy, what if their life is messed up too. Their lives all out of control too. But I still believed that God gave us that hope of love that we can use to endure almost anything.

Carol touched me and said, "Liz, are you still with us?"

"Oh, Yes, humm, I was thinking out loud."

"Yeah Liz, I couldn't make out who you was talking to."

"Well, sometimes I got a lot on my mind."

"But next time you make sure you let the person know how you want them to respond." I started to giggle and covered my face in embarrassment. She continued, "Who do you want later on tonight? They could be ready to answer that person."

"Sorry Carol, but these things make me mad sometimes."

"Please don't go off on me when they do."

"No Carol, this time I will include you in it."

"Thank you, but you need to get on my register and let me go out for lunch."

I went to her department and was still laughing to myself. I asked Janice if Jean came in to work.

"No, I see that she was off from looking at her schedule. Your girlfriend's boyfriend Robert is sending her into another world. She rushes in almost late, or she's always on the phone. You need to talk to her."

I didn't say anything but I thought, Jean and Robert are my closet friends and her actions will affect me on the job if it gets worse.

I started waiting on the customers and took charge right up until it was time for me to get off. Mrs. Ester informed me that tomorrow I would be working with her. I went past Peggy to see the schedule and she said, "You are off on Sunday because you will be working all day Saturday, and you will close on the night shift."

I replied, "What about the rest of that!"

"Here's your schedule: Monday 4-9; Tuesday 4-9; Wednesday 4-9; off Thursday; Friday 4-9 and all day Saturday 2-9."

"Is Jean working with me?"

"Don't worry about your lost little friend."

"That really means you, huh Peggy?" I said as I pushed her out of my way and slammed the door.

Mrs. Esther rushed over and said, "Girl, watch yourself around her. You know that Peggy is the supervisor's pet."

"That might be true but she met the person going to beat her down."

"Girl, don't lose your job over that foolish mess," Mrs. Esther said.

"Peggy thinks because she got that job she can say anything to people."

Mrs. Esther told me, "I seen a lot of girls that got that position and lose it. It don't mean that she got much more than we all got because she goes to college. You get ready to go home, and I'll cover for you and talk to our night supervisor. That girl's jealously is making her crazy. She's always starting trouble with y'all but this time I heard the conversation. I'm going to go stand up for what is right." I went upstairs and left through the lobby. I caught my bus and went home.

That Sunday I felt miserable when I looked at all the Valentines gift and decorations. I watched most of my coworkers buying gifts. Some were buying candy and sweaters, others cards and teddy bears. I started thinking about how Mike and I were good friends and nothing more. I said to myself, *It would be nice to get something anyway, even if it's a card. At least that will show me that he really cares about our friendship.* I continued to daydream about what might happen on Valentines Day. I was looking forward to being off work on Friday. I knew that people would be celebrating Valentine's Day the whole weekend. I decided to call my friend and see if she would be off. We could go to the movies on Friday.

It was Wednesday and I was glad there were only two more days until the "Day of Love." I rushed to get dressed while I was listening to Sharon fuss about her socks being dirty. I told her, "This is no one's fault but your own. You the one that's too lazy to go to the Laundromat and wash them."

Sharon yelled, "I am not washing those dirty clothes."

"When you come home you have the honor of washing clothes, Mama intervened." Sharon poked out her mouth, stomped her way out the door and headed for school.

"Mama, why can't we buy a washing machine?" I asked.

"Do it look like we can afford it, Liz? Besides, you see how tiny this apartment is? I can barely afford this. When you get your dream house you can make sure you got a washer and a dryer."

"Mama I don't want to wait until I'm grown to get some convenient things in life."

"Well, all the things I want to be convenient for me would put us all in a worse hardship than this. Besides Liz, you need to hurry up and go to school."

"Okay Mama, I'm leaving now." I got my books and headed out the door. I knew I had to catch the next bus for school, as I wasn't out early enough for the first one. To my surprise, Sharon was still waiting at the bus stop. I told Sharon, "I thought you already got the bus."

"No, Liz I was waiting for Kelly and Jeff and their cousin Sally."

"You are telling me you are going to be late for school for your friends?"

"No Liz, the bus was crowded. Here come the next bus, and that's crowded too."

"But we are going to get on it, little girl. You need to be right here so we can push our way onto this bus." The bus driver pulled up with the door already open, and we made our way on. Sharon started complaining about the smell of the bus. I told her, "You need to stop complaining about the bus because this the only transportation the state gives us we can afford."

"Look Liz, there's a seat. You can sit there." I started to laugh, there was only one-third of a seat left because this big fat man had the rest of it.

I moved close to Sharon to whisper in her ear and said, "You got to be a baby to sit with him." We both burst out laughing, then got off to catch the next bus. "Liz, if that fat man opened his legs he would have had the whole seat."

"Sharon, that man's thighs big as two of Mama's and Mama is a full-sized women."

"Oh Liz, if Mama ever hear you say that she would hit you into tomorrow." We laughed all the way school.

When we got to school, we saw Jean. I hollered, "Jean, Jean." My English teacher told me not to holler in the building so I rushed up to her. She was talking to Herman.

"Hey girl, where you been, Liz?"

"You know I got me a new schedule." I asked, "Jean! why are you talking to Herman?"

"No Liz, you got it all wrong, he was talking to me."

"That boy got a face like Dr. Jekyll, and a body like Mr. Hyde and not to mentioned he talk like Mr. Magoo."

"Liz, you sure know how to describe a person. You telling me that Herman isn't human?"

"No, it looks like he's not from this planet." We laughed all the way to homeroom. Jean sat behind me and started writing me notes. She said that she and Robert were still seeing each other. She told me that she can see the two of them being married in the future. Mrs. Thompson came past and snatched the note from me. She asked us to stay after class.

When the bell rang, we were still in our seats. As soon as the last student left, she closed the door and started in on us. "Do we have time to send notes during class? Why are we exchanging notes in class?" Before we could come up with some type of excuse, she asked, "Who wrote this note?"

"Not me!" Jean looked at me all puzzled.

"I guess you wrote the note," the teacher said, but Jean didn't answer. "I already know who wrote this little letter but this is the last time that this little incident is going to happen in my class. If you are not doing your homework y'all better not write nothing else. Next time you will be suspended, then you can tell your parents what happened. Y'all better start thinking about something else like your class work." Then she told us we could leave and go to our next class.

As we were going down the hall, Jean didn't say anything to me. I asked her, "Are you mad with me?"

"No, but you didn't have to volunteer *who did it.*"

"Let me tell you something. I am not getting punished for being your friend. I am not getting sent home because you didn't want to say nothing. If you are mad with me, let it be that you are mad."

"Well, no Liz, I'm not mad with you. Weather you know it or not."

"Jean, this is our last year here, let us at least graduate. We been in school for twelve years and I don't know about you, but I am tired of Harlem Park Senior High. Let me see a better place to be in."

"That is the honest truth! I am tired of looking at this madness too. Liz, we got fifteen minutes left in this class." We sat in our seats and listened to the teacher until she told us that the class was dismissed for the day.

Everybody got their books and started to hurry, and Jean and I started out too. When Mrs. Thompson saw me, she told me to stay awhile.

I asked Jean if she worked today. "No. I am going home. I see you later Liz, or I will call you."

I said, "Okay Jean," then I went up to Mrs. Thompson's desk.

She asked me to sit down, then shut the door, "Elizabeth, you got a good opportunity to get a college education but you need to look at what type of friends you have. Jean seems like a nice friend but her mind is not on getting into college. Her actions tells me that she's not even interested in finishing high school. Her grades need to be pulled up to graduate. I asked her do she have the time today to get some help. I always ask her to stay after school so someone can tutor her. She tell me she got to work. Now, in your case you are sacrificing work to school on Saturdays. Liz, don't hang around a person that isn't willing to help herself and her own future. I know she not encouraging you to get into college. People that hang out around people like that start to take on some of their attitude and traits."

"Oh no, Mrs. Thompson, my goal is to get into college whether she is my friend or not. I want to buy my mother a house so we all can leave Harlem. That is a bad place to live, my goal is to go to college so I could get that dream house for us."

Mrs. Thompson said, "I'm telling you there is an opportunity to get a scholarship and you are working toward that. Whether you let your peers destroy it or not is up to you."

"No, Mrs. Thompson I am not letting my friend Jean take this away from me but I thank you for helping me see this problem."

"If you need any help please feel free to let me know. You can leave and go to work, Elizabeth." I thanked her again and left to catch the bus. Since I missed my first bus, I had to run to catch the next one. the bus arrived soon as I got to the corner. I started to make my way to the back but I saw Mrs. Ester and sat with her. She looked at me and said, "Girl, I seen the big boss about that situation with you and Peggy."

"What situation, Mrs. Ester?"

"That she going to lay you out about you asking if Jean was off."

"Oh, okay. That situation. I forgot about that conversation."

"And Liz, they will be talking to her. The big boss was telling me that she heard Peggy don't have such a great disposition with some of our coworkers."

I replied, "Now I wonder what Miss Peggy going to say."

"Now Liz, don't say anything to her, just watch her. Let's get off here Liz, at the corner. We can go in through the lobby." When we got to the lobby, I left Mrs. Ester and ran down to the basement to punch in. When she got there, she stopped and looked at me with a betrayed expression on her face. I looked at her a little sheepishly but quickly regained confidence and proceeded into the locker room.

Janice was laughing. When she found a breath between laughs she said, "That Peggy is going to drive herself out of a good job." I acted like that was none of my business and got my cash box and left. When I got to the toy department, Carol asked me to relieve her of her register. I told her that first I would have to see who was in my department. I rushed over and found to my surprise, that it was Jean.

I went over to her and said, "I thought you went home."

"My cousin came to school to pick me up. Then she told me that the job called and they needed me to come in. what did Mrs. Thompson talk about? Was she still talking about me?"

"Well, let me put it like this, It's nothing that I didn't already know." Then I left Jean and ran up to Carol's register. I started to ring up the customer's huge gift-wrapped boxes, added cute printed cards and tied weights to their balloons so they wouldn't fly away. The night was long because I was still wrapped up in ringing up people's purchases, at least until Carol came over, She told me that I could hang around in her department, but that I really needed to help Jean at the toy department.

She said, "The customers saying that Jean short changed 'em." I went over, got the receipt from the customer and rang her up. Meanwhile, Jean told me that she could handle all the money. I looked at the receipts and started to count the money in the drawer. I told Jean that she had shorted the register about $23.89.

"See Liz, I am not working over here anymore," she whined. All I could say was, "Okay, but you still need to pay the register now or you will have to later."

"Liz, I got $23.89 to pay it, but I never want to work over here again. I'm going to tell our supervisor."

"No," I pleaded. "Let me teach you how to work the register and how to read the price list."

"No, I don't have the time for this type of job."

"But they need more cashiers. That might be the only job you can get."

"I guess I won't have any job then." After hearing her say that, I could only think about how my teacher was right about Jean. Her whole life was about Robert and his education and not her own education. I snapped back into the present and touched Jean on the shoulder. I asked, "What are you doing this week?"

"Well, Robert was talking about going to the movies or going to a basketball game this weekend."

"Oh, I was thinking maybe we could go to the mall, me and you."

"I got plans."

"Okay, that's nice plans."

I continued to clean up all the mess Jean made with the register and the space around it. There was paper all in front of the counter. I told her to stay there, then I ran downstairs to the basement to get a broom. Peggy was standing in front of her office doorway with a nasty smirk on her face. I looked at her, sucked my teeth and ran back upstairs to discover that Jean had got her coat already and left to catch the bus home. I started to get angry and I thought, *that Jean is something else. She makes an enormous mess and leaves me to clean it up and wait on the rest of theses customers, ooh boy am I hot with her.*

I finished and put everything away. I punched out and looked for Janice. When I caught up with her, she said, "That Jean, you know your friend, got somebody to pick her up about a half-hour ago."

Janice, Mrs. Ester and I walked to the bus stop together. "Liz, what happened to your girl? She leave you?" asked Mrs. Ester.

"I know, but I wasn't ready to leave when Robert came."

Janice said, "But Liz they could have waited for you."

Mrs. Ester agreed, "That's right. What type of friend leaves another friend, not asking if they going her way." I didn't answer but my blood started to boil with anger.

I caught all my buses on time. I got off at the corner, walked up to my apartment, put my key in the door and took a deep breath. When I went in, I went straight to the kitchen, not stopping to take off my coat or to rest. I looked at the clock on the wall. It said 10:45. *Now if Jean had thought about me I would have been here at 9:30. She is sure 'nuff showing her real colors,* I thought.

I went in my room, moved everything off my side of the bed and put my pajamas on. It was a little difficult falling asleep because I was too angry, and still thinking about Jean. I put the sheets over my face to make the room darker. I rolled over on my side and I felt my body beginning to get heavy. I couldn't stop thinking about how I got hurt by a close friend today. I was thinking how she had given her heart totally to Robert. I rolled over again, trying to find a comfortable position to fall asleep. I thought, Jean acts as if nobody can see how blind she has become over Robert.

Chapter 22

A Friend Dies

The next day was like all the others. I woke up feeling very sleep deprived. I struggled to wake up and finally came to my feet. It was Friday. I was getting ready for another day of school but then Mama asked me if I could keep the baby while she took Becky to the doctor. "Oh Mama, I'm trying to keep my grades up," I whined.

"Liz, I need you to help out today and besides, I always ask Sharon to stay home from school. She need to keep her grades up too, you know."

"I know Mama, but she isn't in her last year of high school. And you know I'm really looking forward to my graduation," I said as I put on my coat and picked up my books.

"I know you are Liz, but you need to help me out at home as well." I stopped, took off my coat and plopped my books on the bed.

The baby was still asleep. I went into the kitchen to make myself some breakfast. Becky came in to get a glass of milk, walking with her head down, and bumped into me. She dropped the glass of milk, and it shattered all over the place, even hitting my feet. "You *stupid* girl! You almost cut my feet!" I hollered.

Mama rushed in and said, "LIZ, Becky got a problem, and you know she doesn't mean it! And, if you call her a name again, I'm gonna holla' and call you a name and see how you like that. Besides this is your little sister, not your child! I respect your feelings. You don't need to call names like that! While you living in my house, you need to have respect for everyone!"

"But Mama, it happened suddenly and those names just came out," I pleaded.

"Okay, but to remind you, she already sick and slow in doing things."

I turned around to her and said, "Becky, I'm sorry." But the tears were rolling down her cheeks and I knew her feelings were hurt. I stooped down, wiped her face with a napkin and kept saying that I was sorry, but Becky didn't react to anything I was saying.

Mama called Becky and said that she was ready to go. Becky rushed back into the kitchen and gave me a Valentines Day card, and hurried back to Mama. I was surprised that she took time to make me a card. I read it and laughed because the Valentine's heart was on upside down. I thought, it is the thought that counts. It showed me how she felt about me. Besides, she was in a special class in a special school.

I got the kids up. Lisa's kids would be going to school a half-day starting tomorrow. I was glad about that. Now my mother would have some time for herself. I got all the kids washed up and I gave them their breakfast. The baby was still asleep so I woke her up early for a bottle. Right after she finished her bottle, she vomited on me. I bent her head down to make sure the vomit don't go back in her throat. I wiped her mouth and rubbed her back. By then the kids were finished eating.

I rushed down to Ms. Terry's apartment, still holding the baby, to tell her that Mama had already left to go to the doctor's office. Ms. Terry came upstairs with me. The kids were in the hall playing on the railings. Ms. Terry was telling me about her new job. I told her that I was going to Saturday School. When we reached my apartment, we found a big box sitting in the middle of the doorway. Ms. Terry picked up the box and asked, "Whose gift, Liz?"

I answered, "I don't know because it wasn't here when I left to go to your apartment."

"Mike could have sent it to you."

"I don't think so, 'cause he hasn't called or wrote me since the Christmas Holidays."

"But it doesn't mean that he didn't send this big box of candy to you." Ms. Terry started to tear open the plastic. She said, "This is a pretty box of candy and a perfect gift for someone. And expensive too," as she popped pieces of chocolate in her mouth. In between chews, she managed to tell me, "It's real chocolate too. I'm gonna eat these until I get sick."

I quickly snatched the box from her hands, saying, "Let me get this gift from you so you won't get sick from eating it and, no one else can get any if you eat it all."

"Liz, that's what I needed you to say. I won't get out of control. That candy tasted so good and chocolate is my favorite. Now I can go back to my apartment. Since my energy is up, I can finish cleaning and moving things around. Did you see my old apartment? Boy, they're really trying to fix it up in there. That apartment was burnt down to the floor."

"I know."

I went back in my apartment and put the television on for the kids. I went in the kitchen and stopped right dead in my tracks. Those children made such a mess eating their food, I thought. I still had to clean the pots and pans too. After cleaning up the kitchen, I headed for the bathroom. I knew that it needed to be cleaned. I decided to do all that before Mama got home.

I needed to tell Mama that Ms. Terry was looking for her and that she would be home until it was time to pick up her kids from school. I went back into the kitchen to wash more dishes just to discover that we were out of dishwashing liquid. I needed to run down to Ms. Terry apartment and ask her for some but I knew nobody would be there to watch the kids. I saw my niece and nephew zoned into the television, giggling at the cartoons. I couldn't leave them unattended, so I went into the front room and watched the cartoons with them.

I got up after awhile and went into the bedroom, peeked in the bassinet and saw Rolynne was wide-awake, laughing out loud and talking to herself. I heard the door open and Mama called, "Liz, where are you?"

I hollered back, "I'm in my bedroom cleaning up."

"Where is the baby?"

"In my room in the bassinet playing by herself."

Ms. Terry came upstairs so I told Mama, "Guess what happen to me today. Someone sent me some pretty Valentine candy and left it in the front of our door. There was a pretty card too. There's no name on it or in the card."

Mama replied, "Do you think Mike sent it as a Valentine's gift?"

I said, "I don't know, but we need some dishwashing detergent."

"Here some money, so go to the corner store and get some."

On the way back to our apartment, I checked the mailbox. I went through the mail, hoping there was something for me. One letter was addressed to Elizabeth Rosemere. I walked up the stairs, opening the letter on the way. It was a Valentine's card from Mike. Excited, I gave the rest of the mail to Mama. I jumped up and said, "Mike sent me a card in the mail." Then I calmed down and thought out loud, "Then who sent me a gift?"

"I don't know Liz, but I am not going to talk about that mystery man. Hand me those pampers over there." I was wondering all day why someone would want to send me something. I went in my bedroom, shut the door behind me and tried to go to sleep but Sharon came in and started asking, "Who sent you a gift, Liz?"

"Who knows, Sharon?"

"Alright, I figured it out. It's a man in this building that likes you and wanted to give you a surprise."

"That's fine Sharon, but this man is scaring me."

"While he is scaring you, let me eat some of that candy that he send you."

It was a puzzling thought and a scary one too. I lay in my bed thinking about it. Mama came in my room and asked me if I had to work today. "No Mama, I'm off today. I should call Jean and see where she and Robert are going tonight but Jean is working until 8 o'clock tonight. I know if Robert is taking her out, she is not going into work. He is Jean's whole world." When Mama left I was still thinking, *now I will see my girlfriend hurt if things don't work out with Robert, but if me and Mike don't work out as more than friend's I will be hurt too.*

Suddenly I heard someone in the front room. I got up to see what was going on. I opened my bedroom door, and slowly went towards the front room with my mouth open. Ms. Terry was stomping towards our front room doorway. Her mouth was wide open but no noise was coming out.

Mama kept saying, "What's wrong Terry, What's going on, are you okay?" But she kept stomping her feet with her mouth open and her head turned up at the ceiling, her hands waving back and forth in the air. Mama held her up and tried to calm her down. When Ms. Terry started to hold her hands over her heart, Mama told me to call the ambulance. Finally, Ms. Terry stuttered, "Paul is dead! He died in a car accident coming home from work last night."

Mama asked her if she wanted to go to the hospital.

"No Tracy, I need to sit here for a while, but this is a shock to my heart."

"How do you know about this, Terry?"

"Well, Ben's girlfriend Lorraine called to tell me. Ben heard from Paul's wife. She called him this morning when he got home from work. She asked him to tell their boss and their coworkers."

"Terry, you scared me because the way you were looking I thought you were having a stroke."

"No, I wanted to die. Paul was my real love and I'm going to miss him."

Mama said, "Now you need to get yourself together, 'cause you have got to go to the funeral home to see him."

"I know, but I don't think I can get over losing Paul like that."

"Terry, I am going to send Liz to pick up your kids from school. You sit right here. You aren't in any condition to do anything." Mama said, "I liked Mr. Paul. He was good to me. He was the first personal friend of yours I liked. Him and you been there for me and now I got to say goodbye. This pain won't be leaving easy." They cried together.

I kneeled on the floor next to Mama and cried with them. Sharon came in asked, "What's going on here?"

I got off my knees, grabbed Sharon's arm and told her that Mr. Paul was dead.

"What, Liz? That was my buddy!" She grabbed me, laid her head on my shoulder and started to cry. I was afraid this death was going to drive me over the edge. I had seen Mr. Paul two weeks ago coming from work. I never thought that would be the last time I saw him. For a moment I forgot the kids, I asked Sharon to get them.

She said, "But...but, Liz."

"Hurry Sharon, you already late picking them up from day care." Sharon ran out the door. Mama and Ms. Terry were still sitting on the couch crying. Shevon touched my leg. She was crying and wanted me to pick her up. I tried to comfort her and said, "Grandma is alright, baby." I rubbed her gently on the back. Then Rolynne started crying too. She was awakened by all the noise. I tried to pick her up out of the bassinet but Shevon wouldn't let me put her down.

The door burst open and John came in. I called to him, "John, please be quiet. Mr. Paul died this morning."

He sounded irritated and said, "Oh no, not this again."

"By the way, get Shevon off me."

"No Liz, I don't like her because she always pulling on my shirt."

"Look John, she isn't going to kill you. Do it so I can clean the baby up." When I finished, I went back into the kitchen to see if Mama and Ms. Terry wanted something to eat or drink. I came in the front room and asked, "Do you or Ms. Terry want something to eat?"

"No Liz, clean up this mess in this chair."

"Okay Mama. Can you hold the baby?"

"Yes, bring her here and get a blanket to put on her. It's cold in this apartment. Then go to the stove and boil a big pot of water. It can warm this apartment up. It seems like the heat doesn't come on until 5:30 in the evening. Then we freeze until the next day at 5:30. I'm gonna call the rental office about this. I got young children and a baby in here."

I asked, "What do you want me to cook tonight?"

"Anything you want, as long as the kids eat." I looked in our refrigerator to see if she had any leftovers but there wasn't anything in there worth eating. There was one pack of pork chops in the freezer. I told Mama that I was going downstairs to see what Ms. Terry had to cook. Mama said, "Liz, Terry say she got some pork chops in the freezer and bring it up to cook for all the children. And she say that there's some potatoes and bread in there too."

When I opened Ms. Terry's door, it looked like someone had ransacked the place. Her things were all over the floor. There was nothing in her freezer. I ran back upstairs to tell Ms. Terry. She jumped up out the chair and yelled, "Oh my God, they robbed me while I was up here crying!"

Mama said, "Terry, you probably left your door open."

347

Ms. Terry agreed, "I probably did. Next time I will grieve in my own apartment. Maybe I won't get robbed. I walked Ms. Terry back to her apartment.

She started to cry again, saying, "I'm not even going to ask these dope-selling drunk people did they see anything because I might ask the person that did it. They didn't get any money, but they stole my food." I helped her straighten up. She continued, "Look Liz, I bet they took my cleaning supplies. Their apartment be clean now, 'cause they got my things."

She lay down in her bedroom. I cut the lights on and locked the door as she wept, then I went back upstairs. I told Mama what happened. Mama said "Poor Terry. If one of her married men die again, we might as well put her in a grave."

I helped cook and feed the children, and then I went in my bedroom and cried off and on all night. I was sad about how none of us could go to his funeral and how none of us knew his family to send them a card.

The day of Mr. Paul's funeral was one day that I dreaded. It was on a Wednesday, and Mama asked me if I was going to school. "No Mama, I'm going with you to the funeral."

She replied, "Well, let's hurry and get dressed. Katie is coming over to watch the kids. I want you to make sure everybody got something to eat and everyone is all washed up. The wake is from 10 to 11 o'clock and the service is 11 to 12 noon. We should be there between the wake and in time for the funeral. Liz, the plan is for me and you going to the funeral."

I asked, "Well, what about Ms. Terry?"

"Ms. Terry is going to be by herself. I am going to support his family. I went and got a card, Liz. Can you fill it out for me?"

Then there was a knock on the door. Mama said, "Come in Katie. Everybody in here. They all ate and the pampers are right here and there's bottles of milk in the fridge. Hurry up Liz, Let's go!"

I got my coat. We planned to catch a cab but we saw the bus coming. We put our change together and caught the bus downtown. "Mama, we are going to be late if we got to get on another bus now, even if we catch a cab."

"Liz, lets wait and see which one comes first." The bus came first. Mama said, "This bus will let us off two blocks from the funeral home." When we got off, I asked, "Mama what time is it on your Mickey Mouse watch?"

"It is 11:15. We is in time." I leaned over my mother's shoulder and asked, "You sure that's the right time?"

"Girl, you just love to see this cartoon mouse watch," as she put her sleeve over her wrist. I laughed. It made me feel good because my mother was playing around with me. When we got to the funeral home, the service had already started. They gave us a program and we sat in the middle of the chapel. As we were sitting down, Ms. Terry slipped across in front of Mama and sat in between us. She said, "Tracy, you left a little early I got Roy to bring me."

Mama didn't respond because she was looking at Mr. Paul's children. Mama started shaking her head as the tears fell from her eyes, but we all kept looking forward. Mr. Paul's wife stood up with their eldest son and started to walk down the aisle. When they got to our row...she stopped. She turned our way with evil in her eyes she said in a loud voice that cracked, she said, "Leave! This is *my* time for *my husband* to say goodbye! I know who you are! And *what* you are!"

The whole chapel got silent. Mama, Ms. Terry and I got up and left the funeral home. As we were leaving, Mama grabbed Ms. Terry's arm and said, "I got embarrassed for nothing. I came because he was a friend and you came as his lover. Now let's get something straight, this won't happen to me again because our friendship will stay in our apartment building. See how all of this reflects on me and my daughter! We never had nothin' but respect for Paul but you, on the other hand, you his lover and personal friend. Everybody in there thinks me and my daughter was going with him."

Ms. Terry looked as if she wanted to say something but Mama wasn't finished. "Look, we didn't come here together. We won't be going back together. Me and my daughter is leaving you here at *your* man's funeral."

Mama and I went outside and looked for a cab. Mama was still letting off all her steam, "Think, Liz. We already tired from walking. Now we are tired and embarrassed." We spotted a cab and Mama flagged it down. We jumped in, hoping that Mr. Paul's wife wasn't calling us more names. As I was about to shut the door, Ms. Terry jumped in. We didn't say anything. When we got home, Mama reached in her purse. She pulled out a sympathy card and handed it to Ms. Terry. Ms. Terry looked at her holding the card.

Mama said, "You wanted to be his wife, take the card. You were being a counterfeit wife. You'll only cause your own death." Ms. Terry was speechless for a minute, and then she found the courage to say she was sorry.

"I wish I could believe that Terry, but do we got to go through this again? Being embarrassed with your other two married men? These situations don't always affect just you, it affects other people too. Make sure you don't bring your nice and sweet men around me or my children no more. None of us need to be embarrassed or lose our lives because of your life style."

Mama turned to me and said, "That'll let her know that she won't be bothering us with this again. And this friendship is going to take a turn if she do 'cause I'm not going to get killed for her mistakes."

When Mama opened the door to our apartment, Katie said something about us being back early. Mama started to explain what happened but I couldn't listen. It really hurt me because we had lost a good family friend. I went in my room and let my mind shut down.

The next day I got up, went to school and to work. For three months, I let my life slip away. I was not saying much of anything to anybody. I was depressed. I didn't feel a part of anything or anybody. One day as I was leaving for school, I passed the mailbox. I didn't have the key but something urged me check to see if there was anything in it. I used a hairpin to open the box. An envelope, addressed to Elizabeth Rosemere and dated April 28, 1977, was lean on it. I opened it to find a birthday card and four tickets to Madison Square Gardens from Mike. The tickets were only good for two days.

I hurried to school. I wanted to ask Jean if she and Robert wanted to go but I didn't see her in homeroom. As a matter of fact, I didn't see Jean the whole school day. I tried to think of why. I had not called her or hung out with her for a while because I had shut my life down. I wasn't talking to anyone. I didn't want to know about anybody else's death. I wanted to move on from Mr. Paul's funeral and forget about losing a family friend. I was simply going to school, work and then back home. When I was off from work, I went to the library to study, hoping that no one would talk to me. I was lost for words and I wouldn't be good company, anyway.

I missed my dead family and friends. They would sometimes make me angry and upset me when they acted crazy, but I loved them and could live with their personality. They made my life full and complete. Now I felt all alone.

When I got to work, I ran to the basement to punch my time card and looked to see if Jean was already in. Jean had a sick slip on her card. Janice came up beside me and said, "Your girl sick again, and she will not be working today." Then she spoke softly, "You've been real sad lately, Liz."

I followed her lead and whispered, "This last year of school been very stressful. I'm trying to take the SAT test on Saturday at school. And..." Before I could finish my sentence, she pointed at Peggy.

She said, "Don't talk too loud, Peggy listening like always. She never speaks to us at all but listens to all our conversations."

As I was going up to my department, Mrs. Ester came over and asked me, "Is Jean that sick?"

I said, "I don't know."

Mrs. Ester said, "This is spring and she got the flu?"

"Well, Mrs. Ester, she is my friend and I just found out that she is sick. You know Mrs. Ester, I was depressed and didn't talk to anyone."

"I knew something was wrong with you but I was waiting until you wanted to talk to me."

"I got the prom, my graduation, then college coming up."

"And we all cheering you on in your future."

Chapter 23

Liz Graduates

We put up all the new stocks. "Liz, your friend needs to see a doctor because she really needs to know what is wrong with her. These sickening crazy bosses will be the ones to punch her card out—and permanently. And she definitely needs a sick slip from her doctor."

"Mrs. Ester, I haven't talked to Jean lately. My friend Mike sent me some free tickets to see him play at Madison Square Gardens and I got four of them. So I wanted to invite her and Robert to the game with me and my sister Sharon."

"That's a nice thing he did. Is that your boyfriend?"

"Yes, ah, I mean No. He is just a guy I like. But he is just a good friend, no plans for the future. But, Mrs. Ester I would like to see him play basketball. So this is a big gift."

"Well child remember there's all types of friends that's gonna be there. So please don't put a lot of hope in you being the only person that's going to see him."

"I know, because my mama constantly reminds me of this. She lets me know, he got a lot of new friends and not really looking at his old friends like that."

"Well Liz, here's 8:30. Let's roll out so we can catch the 8:50 bus home. The next bus come after 9:10."

We stuffed everything in a box and rushed downstairs to clock out. We met back at the lobby to wait where it was warm. Then we got on the 8:45 bus. I had caught my other bus at 9:05

and got to my building at 9:35. That was the earliest I had ever gotten home that winter. Mrs. Mae was outside complaining about John and his friends making noise in the hallway. When I got in the hall, Apt. 2 B door opened a young man said hello to Mrs. Mae. Guess he must have heard her yapping all the way in the hall. She said, "Hi Bruce."

I asked her who lives with him."

"His mother and his grandmother." Then she started laughing and said, "So those were some nice gifts from the mystery man. Oh yeah, I know about those strange gifts."

I left looking at her and saying, "I know you know everything until drug dealers invade our apartments. Then you don't see any thing and you can't hear a lick."

I reached my apartment and opened the door. I stopped, looked at Sharon, then it hit me, *"Oh,* the mystery man *is* BRUCE!"

Sharon jumped up and started pointing at me with her hand over her mouth, trying to contain her laughter. Mama and Mrs. Terry came in and Mama said, "So you finally found out who he is."

"No, Mrs. Mae told me, in a round about way. Old Mrs. Mae knew everything about the gifts."

Mama told me, "Okay, now you should say hello."

I let them know, "No, if he had killed me would I be able to say hello?"

"Well Liz, you are still living as far as I can see," Mrs. Terry added. I shook my head because it didn't happen to them.

Sharon said, "One thing, you didn't have to pay for any of those gifts."

"Okay Sharon!" They all laughed some more.

"It's not that serious, Liz. We all had secret admirers."

Mama said, "Well no, Terry, all of mine were bums. And I don't wish that experience on anyone."

Sharon asked, "So who you taking to your prom?"

"Ask Bruce, he should be available," Mama kindly suggested.

"His name is Bruce, but he got a face like Bruno the Dog," I reminded them.

"He's nice," said Mrs. Terry and "He's already gave nice gifts."

"Mrs. Terry this is not the fifties or sixties when your guy didn't have any money and there was a limited amount of guys to take y'all to the prom."

I went into the kitchen, talking to myself. "He never been that special to me. He got bad skin, fat and stubby hair, and he had to make his self a secret. And those gifts, I can throw back in his face."

Mama burst out laughing. Sharon shook her head, "You aren't that pretty Liz, so your choice of guys are limited. They aren't exactly knocking your door down."

"That's okay, but at least I will be the one to choose them to come to my door."

I called Robert and when someone picked up the phone, I asked, "Is Robert there?"

"Yes, this Robert."

"Sorry Robert, I'm still laughing about something Sharon was talking about. Robert, Mike sent me four free tickets for me to see him play basketball at Madison Square Gardens. Do you want a ticket for you and Jean?"

"That's great that you didn't forget me. Now are you going Liz?"

"I'm taking Sharon with me."

"Oh, 'cause if you didn't want to, I could see if my friend James wanted to go."

"I'm using the other two tickets. The game is Saturday at one. Would you pick me and Sharon up?"

"Okay, that wouldn't be a problem." We hung up and I started to get ready for bed.

Two days went by fast. I got dressed for Saturday School. Today we were taking the big test, the SAT. I didn't know if I could get back in time for Robert to pick us up. I kept watching the clock until it was finally 11:45. I thought I would never make it home in time. I asked Tim's mother if she would take me home if I paid her. She told me to jump into the car.

As soon as I closed her door, Robert pulled up. He asked me if we were ready to leave. I told him, "Yes. Let me see if Sharon is ready. The traffic is going to be bad." I didn't have time to change clothes. Sharon rushed right past me with her hair sticking up all over her head. I got my comb out of my pocketbook and started to braid her hair. The car was rocking back forth through the traffic. We found a parking spot two blocks away.

We got the tickets straight while Jean was complaining about standing in line. We finally got to our seats about the time they started to call the starting lineup. When they called Mike's name, we all started to scream. When the game started, I saw his grandmother, aunt and uncle, and I waved to them. They waved back. Every time Mike made a point, we shouted his name.

When the game was over, we wanted to stay behind and see Mike, but the crowd kept pushing us along. Robert tried to get close to the locker room, but the guard asked us to leave. Then we heard Mike calling us. We stood on the side watched a girl jump all over him. Robert ran over to talk to him but the crowd kept bunching around him, and wouldn't let him come over to us.

Sharon shouted out, "Hi Man!" Mike waved and started to push his way toward us. He hugged Jean, Sharon and me and said that he was glad that we came. His coach motioned for the team to get back on the bus. Jean said, "This is my fear, that Robert would have a lot of girls running after him and we wouldn't be a couple anymore."

The next day after seeing Mike play then watching all those girls running after him, made me take a real long look at myself. I saw how pretty all those girls were, and how well they were all dressed. They were built nicely too. I couldn't really do anything about the way I am so I decided to turn all my attention to my future.

Every now and then, my mind would drift back to those girls. The only thing they wanted was to have a handsome guy to take home as a trophy, I thought. He can dress fine, but he stills comes from the Harlem neighborhood. I thought, why wouldn't Mike desire to have another girl from a different background, but why would he wait until he goes to the Pro's to show me that he cares?

I thought, this is May and tomorrow will be my farewell day. They say May brings pretty flowers. Well, I thought, May could bring me the gift of love. All this week were half days at school so we would have time to practice for graduation. Instead of going to school, I stayed home with Mama to help her with the kids.

Mama and Mrs. Terry were friends again. They were talking up a storm until I came in the room, then they stopped talking and sat there looking at me. "So what sharp outfit are you wearing for your graduation?" asked Mrs. Terry.

"Well, we are required to wear our cap and gown. I never gave any thought to what I was going to wear under it, and I'm not planning to buy nothing because I don't plan on going anywhere."

Mama said, "Maybe you and Jean can hang out that day. Or maybe the kids in your class will have a graduation party."

"All the kids in my class are dope slingers, and I prefer not to be seen hanging out with them. All they want to do is hit on us and rub all on you."

Mrs. Terry said, "Liz, aren't there girls in your class?"

"Yes, but they either hanging out with those boys or got nasty mouths or acting all skanky. That wouldn't be a good party for me. Besides, who wants to be ducking and dodging bullets all day, Oh, that's not for me! And anyway, there's only four girls in my class besides Jean and me. And knowing Jean the way I do, she'll be with Robert."

Mama said, "I know Jean move around by herself."

"Not if Robert coming over, besides Jean been sick been off and on these couple of months."

"Umm," said Ms. Terry, as though she knew what was wrong with her.

Mama looked at Ms. Terry from the corner of her eye, and said, "There's another person that been sick these couple of months too."

"Please Tracy, Don't tell that story," Ms. Terry whispered from the side of her mouth. Then Mama and Ms. Terry started giggling like two little schoolgirls.

I looked at them and said, "I'm leaving y'all to giggle out loud." I got my things and left to go to work. As soon as I shut the door, I could hear the two of them laughing even harder.

When my first bus came, I sat beside an old lady who said that the bus before this one broke down and that it smelled like gas. She continued, "These people were hollering at the bus driver like he broke the bus." I continued to look out the window and occasionally glanced at her and acted as if I was listening. She told me, "Now child, this is the state of New York, We need a whole new state. This place has broken down buildings and dirty streets. There's trash everywhere, and there's people living anywhere. You can see a lot of problems. We definitely need someone to come and take off all these problems. This morning I got up two hours ago and leave my apartment to go downtown to my clinic. The bus broke down, I stand for fifty minutes for the next bus and now its crowded and I won't be on time for my clinic appointment. Now I got to get another appointment when

I get there. I won't even be able to see my doctor, and I know this is going to be along trip back home."

I told the lady that I was getting off at the next stop and that I enjoyed talking to her. I ran across the street to my job.

I was thinking, "Now I got to put up with Peggy rolling her eyes, now that I told Mrs. Ester about me passing the SAT Test." Inside, I stopped and spoke to everyone as they were going to their departments. Jean came up behind me and said, "Congratulations for passing the SAT."

"Thank you, Jean, for thinking about me."

"Look Liz, what are you going to wear for farewell day tomorrow?"

"I didn't buy anything to wear for that day. So Jean, what are you planning to do for farewell day?"

"Well, I'm just going to be here."

"That sounds like my plan too."

"Okay, Liz, I see you later on."

"Okay, Jean, I'm going over to my department."

Just as I turn to go to my department, I saw Peggy staring at me. I turned my back to her, but I knew she heard my conversation with Jean. I went to my department and started to work, hoping I would never see her up in this section of the store but I couldn't keep her off my mind.

Carol touched me and I jumped. She said, "Liz, are you here this evening?"

"Yes, I am, but, but my mind wasn't."

"I can see that Liz."

"Carol, you know how it is these last few days of school."

"Liz, I am excited and nervous too, but you take care of these customers or there will be some excitement here.

"Okay, Carol, I get the picture."

"Liz, you see the whole picture."

I finished and closed my register for the night. I punch out, got my sweater, and left to catch the bus. I heard Jean calling my name. She asked, "Liz, are you leaving to catch the bus?"

"Yes, like always Jean. I don't have my man picking me up."

"Well, Robert isn't picking me up tonight."

"Oh, what happened to your transportation?"

Then she had the nerve to say, "I don't know why you talking to me like that?"

"Oh, you don't remember when it was freezing outside and I asked you to wait for me?"

"Yes, but it was Robert that said he had somewhere to go."

"Okay, remember the day I introduced you to him, you didn't forget his name. So why didn't you come in to tell me that Robert had somewhere to go Jean?"

"But Liz...I was, but Robert just pulled off."

"Those tickets was given to *me* you know. I remembered the both of y'all so I give y'all two tickets to enjoy the game."

In this pitiful little voice she said, "I'm sorry Liz, if I hurt you."

"That's okay, this time. Remember that we supposed to be friends." The bus was coming so I left and got on.

The next morning was Farewell Day. It was exciting because it was my last day. I remembered that I didn't have anything to wear, so I looked in my closet and picked out my favorite dress. I hurried to the bathroom to wash but the water was freezing. I yelled to Mama, "Maaa, the water's cold!"

"Liz, just heat some water in a big pot." I went to school.

Finally, I walked into the gym to receive my cap and gown. I was seat number forty-seven in the graduation arrangement. Mrs. Jones took my hand, lead me in front of everyone and introduced me. She said, "Congratulations, Elizabeth Rosemere. You scored the highest mark on the SAT Test! This means you will receive a full scholarship to New York State College."

All of them stood up and applauded me. I was speechless. I couldn't believe that all of this was real and that I really was going to receive a scholarship to go to New York State College. The next thing I knew, everyone was congratulating me. Jean hugged me and we laughed and cried together. I told Jean, "I couldn't sleep because I was so excited about this day. A full Scholarship…"

"Yes Liz, Ms. Perfect Person."

I was a little offended at how she said that, but I just said, "Oh Jean, I'm not that perfect."

"You aren't expecting like me." She burst into tears. She said, "Why didn't I put my goals before my heart?"

I didn't want to seem insensitive, but I thought, *now look at me.* I had tears in my eyes because this day was exciting and sad. Jean was crying so hard that I had to go run and catch a cab for her. I got her in the cab and tried to calm her down.

"Look Jean why don't we go out for lunch, and we can talk all about it."

"No Liz. I want to go straight home. I need to be alone. I'm still upset about me becoming a mother."

Are you sure, Jean?"

Yes Liz. I've been to the doctor."

"What is Robert saying about it?"

"That he will take care of it. But my life is over!" She got out of the cab and walked home.

Finally, the morning came for me to graduate. The rain was coming down pretty hard. I was so excited that I jumped up out of bed and made sure I had everything in order. I felt like everything was revolving around me that day, so when I headed to the bathroom and saw that it was occupied, it felt a little strange. I demanded to know who was in there, "Who's in the bathroom?"

The door opened…and I snapped back into reality. "You could say good morning, Liz," Mama replied.

"I'm sorry, Mama, for hollering outside the door."

"Yes, I'm sorry you did that too. This is the only thing in this apartment giving me comfort and relief."

I knew what Mama was talking about and started laughing. I told her that she was funny. "Liz, are you ready for your big day?"

"Yes Ma'am! As ready as I'll ever be!"

"So what's your plans for after graduation?"

"I have no plans. No one told me about anything."

"Not even Jean?"

"Nope, not even Jean, she's not going anywhere either. This day I will spend in my apartment with y'all. Mama, is Mrs. Terry coming? Her baby is starting to show."

"Well, that is what you get when you run around with men," Mama said as though she was trying to teach me something. "Who you think she gonna blame this baby on?"

"Well Roy or Willie, but they already have older children."

"Mama, Mrs. Terry should be ashamed of herself. What is she doing?"

"Well, she's been doing this all her life. She didn't have good parents to raise her. Her older sister took care of her and was suppose to be bringing her up, but she was never home. She never took care of Mrs. Terry and she had six kids herself. She always had other women's husbands and she never got married. She was always getting drunk. Mrs. Terry was only thirteen when she went to live with her sister. She used to help her sister fight in the street with other ladies in the neighborhood about her sister messing those women's husbands. Now that Mrs. Terry is an adult and her life will never be different because she never got help. Liz, what time are you going to get dressed?"

"Mama, let me get dressed for my day."

Mama told me, "Hurry up so you can catch a cab. Do you have to work today?"

"No, this is my graduation day." When I finished washing up and getting dressed, I reminded my mother that I only had five tickets. "So remember not to invite the whole world." Then I left to look for a cab.

The cab dropped me off in front of the school. I ran into the school, and straight for the gymnasium. My English teacher, Mr. Mcholler told me to get in line so we could march down the aisle in sync. Students were scurrying all around the place trying to put on their caps and gowns and get in line. My teacher began calling the names of all 69 students that were graduating, and we all started to march to the music down the aisle. As I was coming down, I looked across to the middle of the auditorium. I saw Sharon pointing and John jumping up and down in the seats. Mama smiled with joy and waved to me as we got on the stage. We started to sing while moving towards our seats and sitting down, then the program began.

The principal talked for a few minutes, then he announced, "Elizabeth Rosemere, please stand up. This is the student that got the Class of 1977 Full Scholarship Fund to attend New York State College." I stood up, feeling proud, and accepted my award.

I went back to my seat smiling and crying. I looked up at my mother and her eyes were filled with tears. The audience was clapping uncontrollably. Mrs. Terry had her head bowed and was crying too. We sang our school song and left marching back to the gym followed by a swarm of parents.

Mama pushed through the crowd and ran to me with her arms open saying, "You are my *special* child! God could have only given me you!" Sharon and John were pushing and pulling me all over the place.

Sharon said, "So you are going to college."

"Yes, as soon as I can!"

"Now maybe we can leave Harlem for good!"

"That sounds good to me," John added.

The little children were *so* excited they couldn't be still. I only wished that my sister and brother could see this day. There was so many tears I had to put my hands over my face. Total strangers came up and congratulated me. My teacher came over and hugged me, and she was crying with joy too.

Jean came over and said, "Girl let's hang out today, neither one of us gotta work." I gave all my papers to my mother and Jean and I left to catch a cab.

"Where to, Jean?"

"To a graduation Party," she told the cab driver, "Just take us to 204 E. 24th street."

We stopped at the recreation center. As I opened the door, I asked Jean, "Whose party is this, Jean."

"Liz, just go inside."

"I opened the door, and everyone screamed "SURPRISE!" I stood there in a state of shock. I turned and looked at Jean and started hitting and hugging her.

Jean laughed, "It is your party, Liz."

I rushed over to my mother, "Oh, you threw me a surprise party!" I was so elated. I went around speaking to everyone, saying hello to my Aunt Rose and my Uncle Jerry. They grabbed me and kissed me on my cheek.

Someone grabbed me from behind and turned me around. It was Mike.

Robert yelled, "CONGRATULATIONS" all the away across the room. Jean eyes shot toward Robert. For an instant, she looked sad. I rushed over to her, took Jean's hand and gave it to Robert. They started to slow dance. Mike grabbed my hand and we started to slow dance also. He said, "Liz, Baby, you made it. And you got accepted to college. Girl, I am as proud of you as though you were my child." Then he kissed me on my cheek.

Mama came over and said, "That's enough of this slow dancing. I don't have a man to slow dance with me." Uncle Jerry said, "Tracy, let my niece and her young friend alone."

"Oh, no honey, we is going stomp and stamp all over here!"

When the Temptations record came on, Mama grabbed anyone she could find and started to dance. She and Mr. Roy danced all over the place. Soon everybody started shaking and doing the Jerk.

Mike's aunt and grandmother came in, gave me a hug and some money. I told them thanks for coming. Mrs. Terry came over to ask if Mike's grandmother wanted something to eat or drink. She said, "Yes, please give me two plates." I left them at the table.

Tim came in, immediately took my hand and we started to dance. I introduced him to everybody. Mama said, "Tim you are a hard person to find. But once we found you, boy, you are a live one." Tim took Mama's hand and they danced and Jerked all over the place. Mama's arm broke loose and she said, "Boy, you are too much for me." Tim came back and danced with Shelly, the girl in my class. They seemed to get along pretty good. She had a big smile on her face. Soon Tim came over and asked if he could get a big plate of food. Mama hollered, "No child, you just gonna get a regular plate of food. Not a plate to feed an army." Tim laughed and snapped his fingers and clapped his hands to the music.

Next thing I knew Janice was saying, "Liz you done it, you done it!" She hugged me and gave me a card.

I said, "That's right. We made it!" Jean jumped in and we were all hugging and laughing together. I noticed that some guys had come up behind Janice. I looked up and asked if they were her friends. She said, "No, they didn't come with me." So I looked at them again and saw it was Ricky, Lament and Sherman.

"Okay, girl, that's Ricky."

"Yeah, I know him. He used to go with my sister Kim." Then Janice said, "Those guys look like a bundle of drunken bums that's been in a lot of fights."

"Girl, those boys always in a fight with someone or somebody." Ricky kicked his leg out and started dancing. Janice started dancing with Lament who began throwing her around on the dance floor. Sharon started dancing with Ricky. She kept saying, "You can dance with me, but please don't break my arms."

I danced with Robert and Mama. Mike was now dancing with his aunt. Then Carol from my job came and she joined Mama, Robert and me. We all got together and started a line all around the recreation center. Mama yell, "Y'all can take that line dancing outside, 'cause its time for us to clean up!"

I got up for my last, "Go Liz, go Liz, You did it, you did it!" I was really dancing wildly. The kids came over and grabbed my leg because they wanted me to dance with them. I thanked everybody for coming and said, "This day will be with me forever."

Janice came over and softly told me that Mama had invited Peggy. She said, "But you know Mrs. Too Cute wasn't going to come."

"That's fine with me. This is MY special day."

Everybody began to leave and told me goodbye and that they had a good time. Mike came over and gave me a kiss on the mouth. He told me that he and his grandma now live in Connecticut with his aunt and her family. He gave me the address and telephone number and then he left.

Mrs. Terry took all the children home, and Aunt Rose and Uncle Jerry stayed behind to help clean up. Mama and I made sure everything was washed and put back. "Liz, this was a good jam," added Sharon.

"Yeah, Sharon, this was my day."

Sharon asked, "Is your friend Jean pregnant by that boy Robert?"

I said, "Yup, she's definitely pregnant."

Sharon continued, "Your friend is pregnant and Mama's friend is pregnant."

Mama intervened, "All right Sharon, that's not something you say to everybody." Sharon started giggling.

Mama said, "Let us go home now," as she handed the lady the keys. Mama thanked her and we began walking back to our apartment. I kept thinking about all my gifts and cards. I looked at my mother as we were walking and all I could think of was how good she felt. I knew she was proud of me. That day I really felt like my mother's Special Child.

Chapter 24

Leaving for College

It was my last day on the job, July 30, 1977, and some of my co-workers were giving me a surprise going-away party. When I went to the cafeteria, everybody on my shift was there. That made two surprise parties in a row. There was a big sheet cake on the table that said, "Goodbye Liz! College Day is here!" Lots of gifts and cards surrounded the cake. I was so surprised I could hardly manage to speak but I said, "Thanks to my coworkers and a special thanks to my supervisor for hiring me and allowing me to work here for three years. Now I'm going away knowing that y'all care about me!"

I heard someone say, "Your supervisor never did anything!" Janice, Carol, Mrs. Esther and Mrs. Elaine were standing in a group together. I knew it had to be one of them but everyone was leaving when it was said so I never really got a chance to find out who said it. Besides, I was crying too hard to see anything. My supervisor came over and told me that I could punch out early. I closed my toy department for the last time.

I got all my gifts together. Among them was a three-piece luggage set. I thought, *Oh Man, I really need this, 'cause I know my mama suitcase is old and worn out and I be ashamed to go anywhere with it.*

The set was beautiful. I looked at the attached card that read, "Your Wish Came True, Love Peggy," and there was a little heart. I was surprised she was here because she was off this weekend. I suddenly realized I had no way of getting all this stuff home. I got on the phone and called home. John picked up and I asked if Mama was home.

"Mama, my coworkers gave me a going away party! "Oh, Liz that was nice!"

'But now I need to get all these gifts home."

"Okay, let me call around to see who I can get." I went into the stationary department and bought a Thank You card. I thanked particular people for their time and patience but I start to write my thanks to Peggy first. I wrote, "Peggy, thank you for your loving gift, I definitely needed it and it will be fully used. My life took a big turn and I hope I will complete my college year. Thank you for the year we knew each other."

Someone in the cafeteria asked if I was ready. I turned around and saw Jean. "Hi Jean."

"Hey, I came with Robert to take your gifts and things home." As we got everything together I said to myself, *This was my first job, and I met so many people that helped me, but now I got to say goodbye.*

We took all my things down to Robert's car. I was crying and saying that I missed them already. Robert said, "Liz, you will be meeting more people, and when you leave them you will be crying 'cause you miss them." I bowed my head because I knew he was right. I was quiet the whole ride, I knew this was a new step in my life.

"I got three days left until I'm up and out of Harlem but my family will still be here. That will be another bundle of tears," I said.

"That's right," Jean said, "You know when you leave it's going to hurt." Robert pulled up in front of my apartment. I thanked them and gave both Jean and Robert a kiss and hug. Robert helped put everything in the apartment. Mama was standing at the door. When I got inside everybody looked at all my gifts.

Sharon said that I had a beautiful luggage set. She asked, "Who gave it to you?"

"Peggy gave it to me."

"That's nice for a person that never speaks to you. Liz, if she does speak to you two or three years after you finish college, maybe she'll buy you a house."

"Sharon, that's such a foolish thing to say."

Sharon continued, "But look at the type of gifts she's giving out." I went in my room with the baby wheeling behind me in her walker. I put all my money in a box, put the box away, then the water works started again. I knew I would miss all of my friends.

Mama came in and said, "Liz, they are really nice gifts and you need them. Well let me leave you alone." I climb in my bed and tried to go to sleep. It started to feel a little muggy so I got back up and opened a window. A drunk was trying to sing, so I put my fan on hoping to get cooler and to drown out the noise. I washed up and felt fresh, clean and relaxed. I went into a deep sleep.

The next morning I was awakened by the sounds of birds chirping at my windowsill and the warm sun beating on my face. I turned over and saw that the bird's breast was filled with bright beautiful colors. I lay there for a while, and then I got up, washed and went into the kitchen for some cold cereal. As usual, we were missing some of the essentials needed for breakfast. There was no milk, so I went to Ms. Terry's apartment.

She gave me a cup full and asked what time I was leaving on Monday. I told her that I didn't know, but I would call them when I get back upstairs. When I finished my cereal, I called the train station and asked what the tickets would cost and what time we needed to get there. The train was leaving the station Monday at 1:10 pm, he said. It would take Mama and me to the Trailway Bus Station depot. We would be leaving the bus station at 4:40

pm and arriving at our destination at 5:15 pm. From there we would take the college shuttle to New York State University.

I needed a roundtrip fare for Mama and a one-way ticket for myself. I was glad that Mama was going ride down there with me. I caught two buses downtown to the Trailway Bus Station and I purchased the two tickets. My ticket was eight dollars and Mama's was twelve dollars. I went to the bank and drew out some money. That left my account with a balance of forty-two dollars. When I got home, I went in my room, opened up all my cards and counted all the money. I added the money I withdrew from the bank and found I had a total of $592.15. I tucked it away in a safe place. Now I had only 48 hours left in Harlem.

Mama was sitting at the window in her room. I showed the tickets to her and she said, "Now we got to someone to take us and your things to the train station. Well I guess I need to get on the horn and see who I can get. Liz, do you think we need to get some chicken and fry it tonight?"

"Ok, Let me go the market." I replied. When I got on the bus, I saw Janice in the back and sat with her. Janice said, "Oh, did you like the surprise Liz?"

"Yes I did, I'm going to miss you all."

"We going to miss you too. It was a pleasure working with a nice young girl theses days."

I told her, "Well I needed a job and they hired me. That was my first job."

"Now you are going to college, you be hired at an even better job," then pushed by me with tears in her eyes. She whimpered, "That's a chance I need in my life, Liz," then she got off. I tried not to cry. I thought she was a real nice but crazy girl.

I was scared knowing that now I going to have to start all over and meet a lot of new people. I was worried that these new people might not like me. I always wondered how it would happen. This scholarship meant a full four years of free tuition but now I had to get a job all over again because I would need the proper clothes to wear and the proper food to eat. The counselor said that they would have a job waiting for me when I got there.

I was in line to pay for my food when I looked at the food in the basket. I had chicken, soda and junk food but I was not hungry I had too many butterflies in my stomach. I finished paying for my food and I was headed out the door, when someone bumped into me. I turned around but I found no one there. I rushed out of the store because I didn't want to think about Bruce and the tricks he played on me. I got on the bus and went straight home. I was looking through my pocketbook when I noticed my change purse was gone. I didn't feel anybody touching me, so where could it have gone, I wondered. I checked my pockets and all I found was some change from the Super Market. There was only enough money to get me back home.

When I got home, I put everything on the bed. I still couldn't find it. I didn't understand what happened to it. It was a good thing I left all my money at home. It was getting dark and Mama was ready to cook the chicken for tomorrow that we would take on the trip to the college. I thought back on my change purse. I said to myself, *I guess someone got $2.50 in change.* I wasn't to worried about that. All I could think about was getting to college and getting there on time. I told my mother about what happened at the market.

She said, "Its sad when you go to the market, the bums is there trying to make market wit' your money. Liz, bums is everywhere, so don't think that they won't be there in your college too. Now, we got to get ready for tomorrow. I asked Mr. Willie to take us to the train station. He'll pick us up at 11:45."

"That's real nice of him."

"Now Liz, put ten dollars in your budget for him taking us."

"Okay Mama, it is not a problem but I got to still look and see if there is a change purse around this apartment."

"Liz, just try to make sure that everything is together. The tickets, enough clothes, clean underwear, some gowns, slippers, socks, extra soap, and make sure you got your information from the school. You keep the copies and leave the original here with me in case you need it."

I called the children into the room and told them, "Aunt Liz is going away to college and I love y'all. I leave tomorrow." I saw their little faces drop. I was sad too, I told them. I put everything in my suitcases and got my bankbook. I put that in my pocketbook. Then I washed up and got ready for bed. It was already ten o'clock.

Sharon asked me, "Liz, are you going to finish college?"

"Yes! Sharon, this has been my dream ever since I was eight years old. Now this day has come." I hugged Sharon and said, "I love you," then turned over and went to sleep.

Mama called me and said, "Get up Liz, your day is here. Now its time to go." I got up slowly because I really didn't want to go.

"But I'm scared, Mama," I said as we were bringing everything into the front room.

Mama consoled me. "Liz, your life will now better your future." I heard a horn blow. Ms. Terry and Mr. Willie were waiting. Mama reminded me that, "Liz, Ms. Terry is big and pregnant now, but when you see her again the baby will be here. I went downstairs past Mrs. Mae who was looking at Bruce's apartment for the last time.

Mr. Willie put everything in the trunk of his car as I looked up at my apartment window. I could see all the children crying. Sharon was holding the baby. She was crying so hard I could hear her all the way down to the car. I waved goodbye and we left.

We got to the Station at 12:15 and the train wouldn't leave until 1:10, so we sat down on a bench and waited for the train to arrive. Mama told me that she noticed I didn't eat any breakfast this morning.

I said, "I know, it's because I got butterflies." The announcer called our train number and we rushed to get on it.

Mama said, "Make sure all your luggage stays with you." We got three hours until we get on the bus. We sat on the crowded train, hardly able to move for a while. Soon people started to leave and we got comfortable. Mama and I both fell asleep. The announcer woke us up as he announced over a loud speaker that this was the stop for the Trailway Bus station. We got up with all my luggage and got off.

The bus wasn't leaving the station for another half hour, so Mama called Katie to see how the kids were doing. The bus dispatcher called out our bus number so we hurried to get on and find a seat. The driver said that the last stop would be near New York State College. He told us that another bus would take us around to the college. He mentioned that the last bus back to the train station was at 7:25 pm, and that all our things had to be stowed under the bus.

An hour later, we got on the shuttle to take us up to the college. We passed cows, horses and farmhouses on huge plots of farmland. The only time I had ever seen things like that was on television and in magazines. Mama saw my face and knew exactly what I was thinking. She said, "I know, Liz. This is beautiful scenery."

At the college someone, I guess an attendant, asked for our names. I showed my letter and she told us to come with her. She introduced herself as my counselor, Mrs. Abanowitz. She told me that they had a job for me and asked if I could drive.

"Oh, no ma'am," I said.

"You need to get with someone that drives. As you can see, this is a lonely place without a car. Then she took Mama and me to my dorm room. She told us how the scholarship would be used and about the job, when and where to pick up my meals and personal items. Dinner was arranged for us but Mama had to go. Mama said she was pleased about all of the arrangements they had made for me.

As Mama waited for the bus I was crying. I said, "Mama what am I going to do without you." She held me and said, "Liz, I gave my love and care to you, because you are a bright loving, special child. Use all the things you've seen and heard over the years, all your experiences and your education, and you can put your life together and make yourself stronger."

Her tears fell on my face as her bus came. I watched the bus until I couldn't see it anymore. I went back to my dorm and continued crying. I was all alone now for the first time in my life.

My tears and loneliness lasted for the first six months in college. Unfortunately, my counselor had given me the impression that I was going to stay in the dorms. That's not what happened. The dorms were too full so they had me share an apartment with another girl. Her name was Zarha Kilowitz, she was Jewish and she came from a very rich and free life style. It was her apartment.

We didn't get along too well. She would make a mess and expected me to clean up after her. She thought since I wasn't paying rent I was suppose too. Even though I had a scholarship and didn't have to pay for anything, I still felt obligated to do so. I was always the one to clean up everything and go shopping for everything we needed. I planned on moving out within six months. I decided to save up some money and look for another roommate. I now worked with some lawyers outside the college are. I knew I would have to learn how to drive.

One day one of my teachers told me about a girl named Stella Brown. She suggested that I get Stella to move in with me. She said that having Stella as a roommate might be a much better arrangement. One day I met Stella in one of my coach classes and introduced myself. I asked her if she needed a roommate. I already knew the answer, but I figured it was a way to start up a conversation with her. When I first heard the name Stella, I thought she was black but to my surprise, she was a short, chubby, white girl with long wavy red hair and a lot of freckles. She had a deep country accent. Since she was from Tennessee, it fit her.

She said yes, she would like that. I told her that I was at NYU on a full scholarship and that I came from Harlem. She said, "Man, Harlem, that's not a pretty good place to live. I'm from a poor little farm in Tennessee, on a two-year scholarship."

We talked as she took me to her apartment. I told her, "I like it. Its rather small, but…"

"But its comfortable and has everything I need," Stella said, as she cut me off between words. I continued to say, "But you got to drive to get here."

She replied, "That's the whole idea, Liz. I can help you with the MVA book and teach you how to drive but you do need to get your own car."

By the time I learned how to drive, three months later, I had saved up enough money to purchase an old used car from a dealer. This resulted in me not being able to send money home for the phone bill but I did get a chance to talk to Mama a lot during the last week.

It was the summer of 1978 that I completed my first year of college. I was offered a fulltime position as a secretary at the law firm so I continued to go to school all summer long. A lot of time had passed and my love for Mike had faded. I didn't even hear from Jean or Robert. The last time I heard from them was to tell me that Jean had a baby boy and his name was Robert Linwood Jr. That was two months after I came to college.

Ms. Terry had a baby boy too. His name was William Paul Jackson. That was all the information I got from them. I also found out that Sharon was pregnant now. I didn't have the slightest idea where that poor child was going to sleep. Rolynne was four years old now. Mama sent me a picture of all the children. The rest of the kids were in school and Rolynne was in daycare. I wanted to come down to see all of them, but Mama told me to stay where I was so I wouldn't lose my job. I did as she told me to until the winter of 1978. It was my birthday. I turned twenty years old.

By that time, I thought that I had learned a lot about life from living on my own. Sharon's baby, also a boy, was born December 12, 1978. I guess things like that really do come in threes. She named him Jeffery Michael Morgan Jr. I couldn't wait to see him so I drove home for the weekend to surprise my family. Before leaving on the trip, I bought all the kids some clothes.

I sneaked into the apartment without anyone seeing me. Everyone but Sharon was in the kitchen. I came up behind them and cleared my throat. Everyone turned around to see who it was. When Mama saw me, she dropped her plate and ran towards me. Everyone else, except Rolynne, did the same. She didn't really know me because she was real young when I left. I went in the room where my new nephew was sleeping and picked him up. Sharon came out the bathroom and stopped dead in her tracks. She said, "Liz, is that you!?"

"Yes, Sharon. It's me." Then tears of joy rolled down her face. I said, "That's an ugly, beautiful baby."

"Girl, is my baby gonna be beautiful or ugly to you."

"Well it depends how you feel about the parents," and we laughed and pushed each other. I held the baby and told them how it was being in college and why it took so long for me to come back home.

"You have my number, you can call anytime you want Sharon."

"No girl, I don't have that kind of patience."

Mama said, "That's why Sharon was out there making a baby with Jeff." Sharon started giggling.

I decided to find Jean and Robert. I got in the car and drove to Jean's cousin Gracie's house. John came with me. When we got there, we ran into the old lady that lives there. She told us, "Your friend, that girl and her cousin, moved."

I described Robert to her. She said, "That boy moved to Baltimore and went to college there," so we left the apartment and went home.

I wanted to visit my old job but Mama had me driving all over the place and my visit to my friends was cut short. I saw Ms. Terry's little boy, kissed everyone goodbye and left to go back to college. It was going to take me close to four hours to drive back so I left at 11 o'clock Sunday morning. Before I left, I gave my mother some money and made sure that I played with Rolynne a little bit.

I told Mama that I still get sad when I leave. She said, "I know that Liz, because we are your family and we is all you got." So I kissed her and left.

It was the last time I ever saw Sharon. One day three months after I left, Jeff and Sharon were trying to steal a car. It skidded out of control and hit a pole. Sharon died instantly and Jeff was pinned in the car. They had to cut his legs off just to get him out.

After Sharon's funeral I was going to leave college and come home to help Mama but she told me that I had to go back to finish school. She said, "That's your real future Liz."

I tried pleading with her. "I don't need to go back, Mama. I could stay here and help you out with all the kids. I could get a job downtown."

She told me to straighten up, "No! You Will Not Elizabeth! You are the first one to graduate from high school, and you're going to be the first one to graduate from college. My God granted me one wish and it was you. If you do it right Liz, your life will be bright. Because you accomplished your goals, my grandchildren will see it and learn from it. You need to be concern about that Liz, and that only."

I had never heard her call me Elizabeth like that, I was shocked. All I could say was, "Okay Mama, is this what you really want?"

"Yes, Liz. This is what I want to see you do." Mama said, then she gave me a big hug and went in the auditorium where Sharon's funeral was being held.

My cousin Katie rubbed my back as I cried loudly, then Mama put her arms around her children and said, "God knew best how my life would turn out."

"But did God know how much it would hurt me, Mama?" I cried.

"Liz, God knows each one of us," Mama said.

"But do he know my heart and how I'm feeling now?" I wailed.

She grabbed me, "Please don't cry out! Because we need our strength in God, Liz." I laid my head down on her lap and cried. Finally, the funeral was over and we went to the grave. Kelly had Sharon's baby in her arms. As we were leaving the graveyard, Kelly put her arms around me, and crying, she said, "She was my sister too."

I kept holding on to Kelly. I tightened my hug on her. I felt as if I was having a heart attack. The tears just would not stop flowing. John rushed over to help us over the snow. When we got in our car, I looked into John's sad eyes. I hoped that he would not leave me too. Becky stayed in the funeral car, laying her head on the windowpane. I moved over to her and hugged her tight. She asked, "Is Lynne and Roland and Sharon ever coming back?"

"No Becky, they are gone forever."

She sat up. I put my arm around her to hold her back because I knew she was going to jump out and run back to the graveyard. I said, "Stop Becky, Please Stop, Becky, Don't take my hand off of you." I grabbed her and said, "because you can't bring them back!"

Mama saw all the commotion going on in the car and jumped right in. She saw the state of mind Becky was in and she held her.

Those memories stuck with me from that day on. In my second year of college, I had a new drama to deal with it. In April of 1979, Becky ran away from home. Mama called me with her heart broken. Becky was 18 years old now. No one knew where she was living, Mama said. All the problems of the past flooded my mind again.

I asked the lawyers if there was any way that they could help me out. They contacted a detective for me. He realized that my mother was financially deprived so he agreed to take the case pro bono. Mama signed some papers in order for them to start working for her but I wasn't allowed to get involved.

Eventually the detective found that Becky was living with an old man that used to live in our building. He had moved to an apartment in New Jersey. I realized this was the same guy that used to give her candy when she was little. The detectives got the police to pick her up, then they searched the apartment and found enough evidence to bring charges against him. They said there was a big chance he used to mess with her when she was a minor.

That wasn't the end of the problem with Becky because she kept running away from home. Each time, Mama cried and explained about Becky having a mental illness. I kept calling the detectives to keep track of my sister.

The last year of college was a short one with some surprises. I met Andrew in my science class and we started to date. I knew that there wouldn't be a future with him because he was going in the Navy. One thing led to another, however, and I became pregnant. It was three months before I actually believed what was happening. At the same time, Stella was leaving to go back home. I was 23 years old and realized I wasn't mature enough to be a mother.

When Mike went to the Pros and became a professional basketball player, he stopped writing to me. Now I watched as all my childhood dreams went up in smoke, all my dreams about marrying Mike and having his baby. Andrew agreed to take care of the baby, but would not agree to marry me. Stella left two months rent to help out. Andrew continued to go to college and help me pay the rent and was a friend.

One day I made a decision to go back home. Andrew had left to go home to Pittsburgh, I was left all alone with not enough money and I was having morning sickness. I worked as long as I could, then I went back home to Harlem pregnant, sick and hurt.

Mama opened her heart and arms to me.

Chapter 25

Escape from Harlem

The children were glad to see me and Ms. Terry was too. Ms. Terry laughed and said, "You're big and round with your love-hate pregnancy! You'll love the baby but you'll sure hate the pregnancy."

We all laughed then Mama asked, "When is the baby due?"

"In three months," I said. That shook me back into reality. I held my head down and sadly strolled into my room.

To my surprise, another pregnant girl was asleep in my room. Dee Dee was carrying John's baby. Her story was pretty simple. She was raised by her grandparents but they became too old to take care of themselves and moved in a Senior Citizen home. She has nowhere to go so she stays here during the week and "visits" her grandparents on the weekend. However, this weekend John would be coming home from the army.

I lay on my bed and continued to think about my problems, *How on earth is my baby supposed to have a better future now?*

Later Mama came in and reminded me that this weekend John was coming home. She told me that he would need a ride from the airport at 2:15. My back was aching and my feet were swollen but I managed to get up and got ready to take Mama to the airport. An embarrassed Dee Dee came out of the room and in a soft, humble voice asked, "Can I go too?"

Mama said, "No, someone got to be here with the children."

She looked brokenhearted and said, "Okay."

As the time to pick up John got near, Mama started telling me how John kept getting into trouble. He passed the army exam so she signed him up. He was only seventeen and a half years old. "I was a little concerned about where Dee Dee was going to live." Mama said, "I told John that I couldn't afford a house or even a bigger apartment, so she could only stay with us until she finishes school."

"Okay Mama, that's good until she gets on her feet."

"She's young, Liz. I'm not about to put her out. Besides, John wants to marry her. It's about time Liz, to go pick up John."

At the airport, as I was pulling in the parking lot, someone shouted out, "Hey, that's my sister!" We got out to greet John with hugs and kisses. Afterwards, he introduced the man standing next to him. "This is a buddy of mine. He's in the army with me. His name is Calvin M. Lukins, Jr. and he's from North Carolina."

"How do you do madam, and your name is?"

"My name's Liz."

He looked a little puzzled and said, "I see you are very much pregnant."

"Oh yes, that's a good line," I said, laughing.

At our apartment, as we were going up the stairs, I tapped John and whispered, "Where he going to sleep."

John assured me, "Don't worry Liz, he's not moving in. I know we already got someone with us."

We caught up with each other's news. Afternoon quickly turned into evening and everyone left me talking to Calvin all by myself. He asked me many questions about school and my baby's father. I told him about Andrew and that he went to college with me. I told him how he only agreed to take care of the baby and that he was not interested in marrying me, because he was going to the Navy. I said, "When they said there was a few strong men in the Navy, they never mentioned baby makers."

Calvin laughed. He said, "That's true Liz, that's what they don't ask these men. So when are you going to graduate?"

"Now that I'm going to have a baby that plan might be delayed."

He got ready for the night and slept on the couch in the front room, Dee Dee and John slept in my room with me. John and I talked all night, making arrangements to move to North Carolina where we were planning to buy Mama a house.

When the weekend was now over I drove John and Calvin back to the airport. I told John to keep in mind what we were planning to do. When we got there, John came over to my side of the car and asked me, "Do you like Calvin?

"He's okay, John. He seems to be nice."

"He likes you Liz, especially when I showed him your picture. That's why he came up here."

"Well John, he didn't come to see my big stomach."

"Oh girl, you are crazy." We laughed, hugged and kissed each other goodbye. Dee Dee was sad because John was leaving her again. We got back in the car and watched as they got on the plane. As Dee Dee and I were going back to the apartment, she started talking about how John and she were going to get married. I didn't say anything.

From the first day I met Calvin M. Lukins, we were going together but Mama never let me forget that I was going back to college. On August 1, 1980 at 2 AM, I gave birth to my precious little baby boy. I named him after his father, Calvin M. Lukins III. I never heard from Andrew again. Mama was filled with joy about the life I was making with Calvin.

Just as planned, on October 22, 1980, I went back to school. I graduated May 12 of 1981. I married Calvin on June 4 of that same year. On June 11, of that year, John and Dee Dee had a pretty baby girl. She looked just like Lynne. They named her Lynne Marie Rosemere.

On July 26, 1981 we surprised Mama with a big house in Johnson-ville North Carolina. John and I rented a van and drove up to New York to pick up Ms. Terry, Mrs. Mae, Bruce's mother, Mrs. Sue and Mr. Willie, Uncle Jerry and his daughter and grandchildren and of course, Mama. There were seventeen people in the van. It was crowded but we departed from New York City right on time and headed to 12 Glean Street, John-sonville, North Carolina.

I stopped at a Seven-Eleven to make a call. I decided to check up on things since we were getting so close. Everything was going as planned. As we all got out, we told Mama that this was where John and Dee Dee were getting married tomorrow.

I took her hand, helped her up the steps and pushed the door open. We all yelled "SURPRISE!" John and I handed her a key. Mama put her hands over her face and burst out in tears. We walked her inside and sat her down. The next thing I knew, Mama was pouring herself a drink and she and Mr. Willie began dancing.

I asked my uncle about my Aunt Rose. He said, "What? Your Mama didn't tell you? Your Aunt Rose had a stroke."

"She never mentioned it to me."

"That's probably because you were in college." Then I turned towards the kitchen and I saw the kids trying to get into Mama's cake. I put the cake in the middle of the table. The party lasted until early in the morning. It was the last time I would see most of these people.

The house had five big bedrooms but some of Mama's friends still had to go over to my father-in-law's house to sleep. The next morning we ate breakfast together, then we left to go back to New York.

Headed back to New York, we were still laughing and singing. Some were still drinking. It was wonderful being an adult, I thought. We had three different drivers. We finally got into New York, we dropped everyone off at their designated stop and gave everyone a hug and a kiss.

When we got to our old apartment, Mrs. Mae told us that she had a good time and ate a really big plate of food. We all laughed at her as we were walking up the steps. John, Dee Dee and I were left with cleaning up the apartment. I wanted to throw everything away but when it came down to it, I couldn't decide whether or not to keep Mama's clothes and the kid's toys. Ms. Terry took some of the furniture. We threw away everything except the bed we were going to sleep on that night.

That Monday when I was getting ready to throw the bed away, John decided to keep the frame. I guessed he had some good use for it. Dee Dee wanted her grandparents to see her baby. We still had some cleaning up to do in the apartment, but Ms. Terry said that she would do a little bit every week so we left the key with her.

I told her, "I saw Linda. She was all grown up."

Ms. Terry said, "And pregnant and wild too."

"She's just like her mother, huh," I said.

"Yes, Yes. Linda's company is transfering her to Delaware."

"Now we got to get back on the road." I hugged her as we were going down the steps together.

I asked her about Bruce and she said, "You thought that he would be looking all strange but just imagine how he looks. Especially with a lot of hair on his face."

"I hope Becky will find us."

"I hope so too, Liz." We got back in the van and went to see Dee Dee's grandparents.

After our visit we headed back to North Carolina. It was an 11-hour ride. When we got home, Mama was making desert for the children. We were there for only a couple of days when Mama starting complaining about having pains in her stomach and back. I still had two weeks left on my vacation when my boss got me a job with his cousin who had a law firm in Johnsonville. Luckily, I started in two weeks.

Three days after the party, I had to find a doctor for Mama. Calvin suggested that I call his parent's doctor. He told me to bring her in Friday but since that was the day I had to start my new job, my mother-in-law took her. When I got home later that day Mama told me that the doctor ran some test on her. She said, "I don't like that doctor."

"I know Mama, but they the only ones that can tell us whether you are okay or not."

I had no idea those test would show that Mama had stomach cancer. Mama and I talked about the children and who would get them. Mama decided I should have full guardianship over all of them. She let me know that whatever I decided to do with them was fine with her. I talked to Calvin and told him about our decision for the children. My lawyers said they would take my case and would take their fees out of my salary.

Calvin wanted me to wait until the doctor could give us some idea of when my mother's last days would be but then Mama took a turn for the worse. My lawyers started working on the custody case.

One day I unexpectedly got a call from Jeff's mother telling me that Kelly would take little Jeff and raise him. Kelly's doctors told her that she would never have any children. We talked about Mama's willingness to raise all the children. I told her Mama would be in court when the date came. My lawyers got responses from Lisa's mother as well. Lisa was doing fine but she still didn't have a job.

One morning I got up to change Mama and discovered she was not breathing. I dropped to my knees and shouted, "MAMA! PLEASE DON'T LEAVE ME! It was April 2, 1983. She died with a smile on her face but I knew she also had a hole in her heart.

Dee Dee came in and said, "Liz, she's gone. Now she is peaceful. She was a good mother to us."

We made the arrangements for Mama's funeral. No one could come down from New York because all the people that were at her surprise party were either dead now or had moved away and we couldn't locate them.

Ms. Terry was still alive but she wouldn't come. She said she had recently lost her big sister and now she's alone. "I couldn't bear to see her like that for the last time," she said.

Mr. Willie and Linda came to the funeral and Linda brought her children with her. She hugged me and said, "That was my mama too. I made sure that my Daddy Willie was going to be here to be with y'all."

The night of the funeral my husband and his family were there to support me. I cried day in and day out for a whole month.

I went back to New York. The custody case came up in court. Lisa's mother got her two kids. Now Devon was eight and Shevon was seven. Jeff's mother and sister got Jeff Jr., who was five years old now. I left the courthouse wondering if there would be a lot of crying. I slipped out the side door, caught a cab and caught a plane leaving New York City for what I thought was the last time. There were no goodbyes, at least I thought there would be none.

Six months later I got a call from Ms. Terry. She said that Becky came to the old apartment looking for Mama that morning. She told Becky to sit down and then told her what had happened to Mama. Becky went crazy right there and Ms. Terry had to call the police. They stayed with her until she was under control and then committed her to a hospital for 72 hours.

I talked to my lawyers and my husband and went back to New York. I picked up Ms. Terry and we were talked as we went towards the hospital. She said she was moving in with Linda up in Delaware in two months. I checked Becky out of the hospital and took her back to my home in Johnsonville.

I had to go back to New York one more time to finalize all the custody papers for the children. While I was there I made sure all of Becky's records were sent to my hometown and all the custody papers had been filed in court in New York City. The custody was finalized on April 28, 1984, one year after Mama died.

I went to visit Linda and Ms. Terry who were now living in Delaware. We talked about everything, even about Linda being Mr. Willie's child. I stayed over that night, knowing that my husband supported all my decisions. He was a loving man.

I got up early the next morning to catch my plane to New York. I had a lot of time on my hands so I decided to go to the department store where I used to work. As I was going past the lobby, I saw Mr. Carl cleaning up so I stopped and spoke.

He said, "Liz!" in surprise.

I said, "Hello." and asked about Janice.

He said, "She moved to Brooklyn and left this job."

"What about Steven?"

"Steven got fired for coming to work drunk."

"What about Mrs. Ester?"

"She died from a heart attack."

"And Mrs. Elaine?"

"She retired."

"And Peggy?"

"She got a better job and left here."

"Man, what happened to Carol?"

"She got married to Harold. The one Peggy was crazy about. They used to fight all the time on this job."

"Oh, my goodness, not perfect Peggy."

"Yes Perfect Peggy. Peggy was smart, but Carol was pretty. Peggy finished a two year college and went to work at one of those hospitals in the city."

He asked about Jean.

"I never seen Jean after I went to college."

"You know, Steven was real crazy about that young girl."

"Who need that Steven," I said. I gave him a hug and left. As I was looking around someone touched me.

I turned and faced Niecy, the one that used to go with Charles in our building. She said, "I was his fool and that son over there act just like a fool."

"Oh, that's little Charles?"

"Yes Liz, that's little Charles, and he taking the same course as his father."

I asked her what happened to Sissy. "Well Sissy, is a drunk and a dope addict."

"Where her baby at?"

"Her aunt took it, and I don't know her name."

"What happen to Wendy?"

"She got a bad disease and walk like a dead person."

"Ricky?"

"He got a life sentence in jail and Lament died two months ago in an apartment on 124 E St. Shane is living. He moved and got married."

"Well, what about Sheron?"

"She is married and traveling with her husband in the Navy."

"Leah?"

"She got a lot of children from one gang banger that used to go to school with us."

"Do you know anything about Gary?"

"Well the last time I talked to him, he told me that he knew Rolynne was his child. Is that true Liz?"

I just looked at her, and said, "I knew my sister."

"Well anyway, Gary got shot during a drive-by. Did you get married Liz?"

"Yes, I married a wonderful guy from the South."

"That's nice that you left New York City to find him. Is your mother still living?"

"No, she died one year ago."

"I'm sorry to hear that Liz."

"And what about you, Niecy?"

"Nope, never got married and I got two children. One grown and one a child."

I told her that I had to get a cab and go back to Johnsonville, North Carolina. I asked the cab driver to take me to 124 East Street. As we rode down the block where I used to live I saw the condition of the building had gotten worse. The building looked so beaten down it was a shame. There were kids all over the place. If poor Mrs. Mae could have seen this she would have died.

The driver kept saying, "Miss, this is a very bad area."

I told the driver, "I used to live here."

He continued to drive down the block slowly. I saw some streets going back downtown to First Federal Bank. I remembered the forty-two dollars I left in there before going to college the first time. I paid the cabby, went in the bank and went to the savings box that Mama and I had together. I found her life insurance policy. I had used my life insurance policy to bury her. I found another bankbook with $5,000 in it. Attached to it was a letter that said, "God blessed me with one special child and it was you, Liz." That's all it said.

I took all the cash and exchanged it for a certified check, then I caught another cab to the airport. As I was riding in the cab I wondered how Mama could have saved all that money over all those years. We passed Aunt Rose's apartment building and I remembered that she had died and that her sons were put in a mental facility.

On my way out of New York City, I thought about Mama and my life, how six children went into Harlem, six grandchildren came out of Harlem. What happened in between is my story, I thought.

I reflected on the conversation that Niecy and I had about how Mike became a professional basketball player for the Lakers. I thought, *I once had friends in Harlem. My life really began with Harlem. Now I left my heart in Harlem and my first love, Mike...made it big in Hollywood.*

The End

Special Thanks

During the creation of this book, many questions were answered and many hurdles were jumped. I owe it all to these very few but very special people.

The Clark Family: You have stood behind me in all my decisions.

Celina Lewis: You have encouraged me and contributed in a lot of ways.

Shirley Edmonson: You have worked with me in locating the perfect publishing company.

Gloria Heath: You have always lent me an ear, you have always been so kind, and you constantly encouraged me.

Leah Smith: You have assisted with the typing and also contributed in various ways.

Last but not least, Yvonne Gray: You have worked with me and have been a wonderful editor.

And for all the friends whose names were not mentioned but who were not forgotten.

I thank you—Margaret Clark, Author

Questions for Readers

1. How did you like the book?

2. What characters did you think were interesting?

3. What did you learn from reading this book?

4. What did this book tell you about the author?

5. Would you like the author to write another book?

6. How would you rate this book from 1-5?

7. Would you tell a friend about this book?

8. What comments would you like to make about the author or the book?